Secret
Shores

ALSO BY ELLA CAREY

Paris Time Capsule
The House by the Lake
From a Paris Balcony

Secret Shores

ELLA CAREY

LAKE UNION
PUBLISHING

Published by Lake Union, Seattle

www.apub.com

Amazon, the Amazon logo, and Lake Union are trademarks of Amazon.com, Inc., or its affiliates.

ISBN-13: 9781542046497
ISBN-10: 1542046491

Cover design by Shasti O'Leary Soudant

Printed in the United States of America

In memory of my mother

CHAPTER ONE

South Australia, 1946

It was a night for beginnings, not endings. For love, not death. Rebecca raised her shaking hand to her face, shielding her eyes from the artery of moonlight that glistened in a pure arc across the sea, finishing at the exact spot where she stood on the beach. It was as if the moonshine mocked her, laughing at her smashed hopes. She knew now she had been naïve. And yet, insistent questions fluttered like fireflies in her heart, each one imprinted with the things that she thought mattered in this life: love, art, strength. Kindness.

Rebecca stood ramrod straight, holding her few belongings as if she were about to climb on a bus with no idea of her destination. She didn't know where her journey began, let alone where it would end. With the determination that seemed to have kicked in during these last few hours, she heaved the wooden rowboat into the water, watching as ripples spread across the sea's glassy surface. The little vessel was only a bucket of memories now. Memories of yesterday.

She placed her things on the wooden bench in the boat—her drawing materials: charcoals, sketching paper, the small portable easel that she had brought with her from Melbourne. And her basket, which held her purse, lipstick, and a couple of changes of clothes, along with an apple and a bar of chocolate that she had grabbed before she fled.

Rebecca pushed the boat farther out, climbed in, and turned back for one last look at the darkened beach house that overlooked the bay. The place where everything was supposed to have come together. The place where everything had fallen apart.

The stone house with its wide verandas gazed back at her as if content with the turn of events, as if telling her that all was as it should have been. Even the sea was still as Rebecca rowed out to the small island in the middle of the bay. It was not as if she had not done this sort of thing before; she had rescued herself countless times in her life. But this was worse. Much worse. The beat of the oars through the water imprinted the tune in her head—much worse, pull push. Much worse . . .

She reached the island and heaved the boat up onto the rocky, silent beach. After collecting her drawing things, she tucked her wicker basket under her arm like any housewife on her way to the shops. Rebecca set off, up the small beach, making her way through the tufts of sea grass that seemed to float like delicate birds above the rocks lining the steep rise to the top of the island. Rebecca's feet in their espadrilles knew exactly where to go. She made her way, silent, along the narrow pale path of raked gravel, well kept · for the tourists, that skirted the sea on her right.

On her left, wild granite outcrops dotted the island's grassy peak. The soft thuds of the resident kangaroos were the only sounds in the darkness, until she rounded the bend to the island's wild side looking out over the Southern Ocean. Here the roaring wind whipped up Rebecca's dark hair, sending it flying in concentric circles around her face as she gazed down at the sea, which roiled like shining dragons' tails in the moonlight, making sea-swirls that smashed against the granite boulders, seaweed wafting beneath the surface.

Impenetrable.

Rebecca loved it.

She found her rock, her own boulder that hung over the ocean. There she loved to draw, sketching not what was in front of her, but what was in her mind, springing from the place that she could only access when she was alone. There she held everything at bay and drew the truth.

Rebecca sat down, tucking her thin white dress, the one dotted with tiny red flowers, around her knees. She settled her drawing paper and the backing board on her lap.

Then she reached for her pencil, which she had placed on the rock just in front of her right foot. But as she reached, the pencil rolled just beyond her grasp, just a little beyond. She could reach it, couldn't she?

Her favorite pencil slipped away from her as fast and as easily as everything else. And as Rebecca reached forward for it, in that split second of movement, she knew it was a mistake. She should have let it go . . .

But she fell—or was she flying?—down past the rocks like a tumbleweed, spiraling over the edge of the cliff that led to the darkness, to the secret depths below.

New York, 1987

No time was a good time for bad news. But a Friday seemed like the very worst time of all. While Tess's boss, Leon, would no doubt retreat to his home in the Hamptons for the weekend, Tess would be left reeling from the fact that she'd lost everything in one stunning blow. She'd spend the weekend desperate, trying to forge a solution to the glitteringly painful shock. She stared with disbelief at the remnants of the afternoon tea Leon had ordered in for their meeting—clearly, it was only an attempt to soften her reaction to his "news."

Flakes of abandoned croissant were scattered across Tess's porcelain plate. Steam still curled from her coffee. At the outset, Leon had thanked her for her considerable contribution to the publishing house. She'd guided her client, the stellar author Alec Burgess, toward three bestselling thrillers in three wonderful years. Leon acknowledged Tess's hard work, her tenacity as an editor, the sheer effort that she had put into Alec's career.

Tess had presumed Leon was going to offer her a promotion. Instead, he'd effectively sacked her.

Leon Moss gazed up at the ceiling as if something fascinating was happening above his head. Tess fought the urge to pour her coffee over his well-groomed hair. Instead, she fixed her stare on her boss's polka-dotted bow tie. His bow ties always annoyed her. Was there any hope of appealing to a man who wore such a thing? She'd always seen them as smug, and it seemed as if Leon wore them as if he were a gift to the world.

Tess slumped back in her chair. Her brain whirled with questions. Why? What had she done wrong? What was going on? How could they make such a decision?

"I've decided that James Cooper would be best suited to edit Burgess's work from now on," Leon said.

A second round of shock waves hit Tess. She sat bolt upright again and clutched her hands together in her lap.

James Cooper? James was Campbell and Black's newest hire—the literary phenomenon who edited only top-echelon books. To have James on board was magic for a writer; being associated with him made any author a guaranteed success. It was said that he had the Midas touch. James Cooper had every advantage under the sun. His literary pedigree was unmatched in New York. As the only son of Sean Cooper, the chief literary critic at the *New York Times*, and of a mother who was a well-known society beauty with twenty-seven degrees from Harvard, James would have had success stamped on his forehead from the moment he took his first breath. Apart from his literary credentials, the man was also famous for his stunning looks, perfect manners, and witty repartee.

Of course Alec Burgess wanted to take advantage of James's arrival at Campbell and Black. What on earth else could she expect?

Tess's teeth seared into her bottom lip. "I see," she said, in her best permafrost voice.

"Tess, you've done a wonderful job with Alec so far. As you know. As you know."

A piece of lead lodged itself below Tess's ribs. At the same time, the urge to run out of Leon's wood-paneled office and make a desperate call to her friend and confidante Flora was almost irresistible. Flora's finger was on every pulse in New York publishing. She would know if James Cooper's reputation extended beyond literary genius to nasty, author-stealing poacher without a second thought.

Leon went on as if nothing were amiss. "Since Alec's next book is going to be completely different from his thrillers, we're going with an editor with a different area of expertise. Alec's next novel is literary, perfectly suited to James."

Or could it possibly be that I'm not as easily able, perhaps, to garner an advantageous review?

"Tess, I've decided that you will be continuing to work on our commercial lines." Leon's voice was as calm as a summer lake.

Tess had to hold back a snarl. Had Leon rehearsed his entire speech? Probably, she thought viciously, this very morning while his wife perfected his annoying, obnoxious bow tie.

"We created a new editorial position for James, you see, as soon as we heard he was looking to move. We need to ensure that he's working with our best authors. It would be inappropriate for him to do anything else." Leon cast a glance at Tess.

Tess stayed silent. Her heart ricocheted around in her chest.

Leon's eyes remained focused on her now. Tess knew that all he wanted was for her to exit gracefully. But who did Leon think had nurtured Alec Burgess? Who did he think had brought him from an unknown midlist author to one of the nation's bestselling writers in three years? Who had spent hours of unpaid overtime slogging over his manuscripts, meeting with him in cafés, dives, real tough diners in

Midtown? Who had sat by him, drinking fetid coffee out of paper cups while he sweated over his early manuscripts in his old leather jacket, not the expensive new jacket he had now, which crinkled attractively as he lifted a hand to smooth back his fine hair when Tess met up with him in the upmarket restaurants that he paid for these days? She had sat by while he smoked endlessly, stinking up Tess's hair and clothes, and she had patiently guided his every step. If there was one thing she could do, it was spot raw talent. She'd always had an eye for that. But to be dumped right when Alec was becoming successful, right when he was on the brink of an international career? It was outrageous.

And she could do literary. That wasn't the point at all. The point was she knew Alec Burgess. Knew his every mood, his insecurities, what set him to panic. She knew when he was overloaded, how to pace him, how to encourage him. She knew not to criticize but to nurture instead. James Cooper might be a superstar editor, a wunderkind, but did that make him right for her author?

"Leon," she said. "Obviously, this decision has been made completely over my head."

Irritatingly, James Cooper's famous boyish grin flashed into Tess's head—the one that always shone out in the society pages. Now, she saw it as a triumphant leer.

When Tess's voice came out it was almost a growl. "I'm not sure how anyone could make a decision like this without proper and due discussion with all parties concerned, and that includes me. I am Alec's editor; I should have been informed and involved in decisions concerning any major changes to his career. I am sorry, but this is unprofessional. And I would not normally say this, but it smacks of nepotism. I have a master's in English lit; I believe James has the same credentials. We are the same age. We are both experienced editors. But I am the one who has worked with Alec, and you know exactly what I've done for him. How he can sit by and let this happen is beyond me. Leon, I am appalled, to be honest."

"Tess." Leon's voice was deep butterscotch.

"Yes, Leon."

He leaned forward and tented his fingers on the desk.

Tess drew in a shuddering breath. She had to speak out. "You know, if I had a dime for every time that I have been patronized in my career, I would be an incredibly rich woman." Her voice was dangerous and low. "But if I wanted to be rich, I would not be an editor; I would be an author like Alec. Instead, you see, I spend my time working hard for writers, because that is what I'm good at. And in return, I ask nothing. But there are boundaries, and my goodness, this crosses every one of them. You know how hard I've worked. You know that I haven't asked for regular raises. Because I trusted the fact that I was working in one of New York's most respected publishing houses, and I trusted that ethics would be in place." She cast her eyes over the bookshelves that lined the antique-filled office—first editions in pristine condition sat in well-dusted rows, their leather spines embossed with gold ink. Hemingway, Steinbeck, Faulkner. The firm's reputation was as solid as a boulder. Working here had been Tess's dream since she was in college.

"Tess . . ."

Tess's breathing picked up pace. Her mind flipped back to all those nights she'd worked late while her friends had gone out and met their husbands and partners. Most of them had children now. It felt as if a life force had kicked in and fought its way back into her system. Here she was, frankly, having worked herself to the bone for this author who was going to dump her the moment he saw the words "celebrity editor" and "James Cooper" appear in bright lights.

She stood, picking up her folder with the notes that she had prepared for this meeting with Leon, in good faith, when Alec had pitched his new idea to her two weeks ago.

Leon sat back in his seat and stretched out his legs. And it was then, at that moment, that Tess wanted to yell at him. James Cooper had every advantage, she wanted to say. Every stupid advantage anyone could conjure up. Why should he get her hard-cultivated author handed to him on yet another silver platter?

Being dumped was not in Tess's game plan. If she was not good enough, then good luck to them all—Leon, Alec, and the vile James Cooper.

And yet, here was the rub: James Cooper would be able to do the job. He would make Alec's book a success. So where did that leave Tess? Apparently, it didn't matter. She was fallout.

"It seems I have no choice," she said. "I suspect you have no idea what that's like, Leon. Good decision. On all your parts. Please excuse me. I'm going now."

Tess's hands shook as she pushed back her chair. She had lost her best author, and was probably at risk of losing her job as well. And yet she would simply not give in.

Leon stood up too, adjusted his suit jacket, and said nothing at all. He was not going to break his professional code, Tess knew that. Leon was not going to respond to Tess's outburst. He would play by the rules. And if a woman complained, she was hysterical.

Tess clenched her hands and dug her nails into her palms. The urge to find out the dirt on James Cooper was overwhelming. How had he done it? Tess thought again of the one person who could help. Flora. Repository for everything that was up-to-date in the publishing world. She'd have a take on it.

"Tess, take the rest of the afternoon off," Leon said. "And then I want you to meet me in my office at nine on Monday morning. We need to talk." He still sounded kind. Still patronizing.

Tess fought back everything that glittered inside her. At this moment, she had no choice but to walk away with dignity.

Once she was back in her office, Tess threw herself into her chair and dialed Flora. Flora wouldn't let this happen to her, not in her capacity as acquiring editor in one of the world's most famous romance houses.

"Flora," she gasped. "Caffè Reggio. Now."

"Okay then." Flora didn't beat around with irritating questions. "I'm with you."

Fortunately, Tess would never call her friend away from work unless something was utterly dire, and now Flora seemed more than happy to help out at the drop of a manuscript on a hard office floor.

Tess caught the subway and made a beeline to Caffè Reggio, which was below Tess's apartment and not far from Flora's office. Tess needed to go into damage control. A little cappuccino and a serving of Flora's quips could point any crisis in the right direction.

Tess felt a little calmer as she made her way back to West Third, having ridden the subway with countless people who all looked tired and worn, just like she did. The mechanics in the workshop next to her building greeted her in their usual proprietary way. Sometimes they sent her wolf whistles when she went past for her morning jog around Washington Square Park. But they always hurled abuse at any other man who tried to do the same thing.

Tess caught a glimpse of herself in the plate glass window of their small shop as she walked past: short blond bob, black suit with shoulder pads so the jacket sat just so, red coat over her arm. She might look the part of the woman who had it all, but she was fuming. She refrained from showing the mechanics her dimple today.

"Okay, honey?" the head mechanic asked. "Unusual to see you here at this time of day."

"Oh, I'm just fine," Tess said. But she noticed the way they all stood there, watching her almost warily, she thought, before turning back to their tools and their jobs.

The knots that were lodged around Tess's shoulder blades loosened just a touch as she stepped underneath the green canopy above Caffè Reggio's front door. She slipped into the familiar interior, settling at one of the round wooden tables and letting her eyes roam over the copies of old masters that lined the rich terra-cotta walls. Human drama. Italian passion. Usually she loved looking at these old prints. Whatever. She ordered a cappuccino.

When Nico, the café's longest-serving waiter, brought the coffee over for her, he paused at her table and looked at her with his deep brown eyes. "I do not like to see that look on my favorite and most beautiful customer's face, Tess Miller."

Tess let out a sigh. Nico's flattery didn't bother her one bit—she knew it was lighthearted, knew it was harmless. She had known him all the time she had lived on this street. To be honest, she was glad he was working today.

"It looks like frustration," he went on, "which means something is bothering you which you can do nothing about."

Tess took a sip of the coffee, letting the dusting of chocolate dissolve on her tongue. She shot a glance toward the door as it opened and the flurry that was Flora appeared, silhouetted against the glass.

"Tess," she said, marching toward her and dodging all the tables with the expertise of a pro. As usual, she was dressed utterly in vintage— a canary-yellow 1950s suit with a string of pearls around her pale neck. Flora's red hair sat in soft pin curls, but the expression on her face was pure grit.

Tess's friend swept into the chair opposite her, having kissed Nico on the cheek.

"Spill," she said to Tess. "Tedious board meeting in thirty minutes. Give me the damage and fast."

"I still can't believe it," Tess said. "So. Leon gave Alec Burgess's next novel to our newest hire. Guess who it is?"

"James Cooper." Flora uttered his name as if it were a stain on her coat. "Bloody hell, Tess," she went on, her British accent coming to the fore. Flora might have been working in the US for several years, but every now and then she sounded pure London, and Tess was reminded of her friend's meteoric rise up the publishing ladder on both sides of the pond. Flora inspired her, and Tess felt a new sense of energy flowing into her system.

Nico's eyes flew from Tess to Flora.

Tess stirred her coffee so fast it started to whirl. "I've worked with Alec Burgess for three years, put my entire heart into his career, made every one of his books into a bestseller. I feel as if I've worked ten times harder than everyone else. I guess it's floored me. Exhausted me, to be honest."

Nico pulled a napkin out of the belt of his apron and wiped it across his face.

Tess looked up at him, taking in his neatly brushed gray hair. His face was tinged with gray too, but his eyes still sparkled with life.

"You know what to do, Tess?" he said.

"You tell me."

"When you are overlooked, and there is nothing to be done, you must make the most of what you do have. You need to take the opportunities you have left and make them your own. That way, you will succeed. We cannot do anything about fate." He smiled.

"Sods to that, Nico," Flora announced. But she leaned across and threw an arm around the waiter, who blushed quite pink. "Tess has to fight. It's absolute rubbish. They can't just take her most successful author away from her without any discussion. What's their reasoning?"

"James is more literary than I am." The words landed with a thud and hung around for a moment while Flora's eyes rolled to the ceiling.

"James Cooper?" Flora threw her eyes to the roof. "He's a celebrity editor. His daddy probably engineered the whole thing. Probably is a member of the same darned country club as your boss, Leon . . . in fact, I could check that out for you, if you like. After a few drinks, they would have stitched up the whole thing. James is just a puppet. His father's perfect boy. He does what he's told; everyone's happy. He'll probably marry some socialite and on they go . . . It's a world I don't want to get involved in. Fun to watch, but horrible when it cuts down someone you care about. And I care about you. So, what are you going to do?"

Nico inclined his head. "No, it's fate," he said. "Everything is. You'll see."

Tess laughed. "Excellent. Thank you, both of you."

"You are showing your dimple again, which lights up the boring days of all the waiters here in Caffè Reggio," Nico said. "Make the most of what you have got. It is all we can do. And sometimes, things work out better than you might think."

"You need to take him on." Flora pulled out her Filofax, as if that held some secret answer to the whole thing. "Fight him."

Tess placed her coffee cup down on her saucer. "Brilliant. A philosopher and a warrior." She put her head in her hands and looked at them both from under her eyelashes. "The hard fact is, I'm most likely going to have to start again if they carry through with this, which it looks like they are going to do."

Nico stood up. "Fate."

"I should go," Flora announced. "Or I'll get into trouble. Tess, I want you to promise me that you won't take this lying down. You put in all the hard yards for Burgess. You should get to reap the rewards. Cooper's just a charmer, a playboy, and a spoilt upper-class rich boy dressed as a man. Fight, Tess." Flora stood up, towering over them like a golden butterfly in her batwing jacket.

Tess pushed her chair back and gave Nico a resigned smile.

"Thank you," she murmured. "But I seem to have been swept aside with a flick of Leon's well-groomed hands. I'm gutted at the moment. My brain has gone to pieces."

Flora was halfway out the door. "Call me! When you have some more news!"

"It will resolve itself," Nico insisted, placing his hand on Tess's back. "These things often seem worse than they are. Sometimes, the hardest and the best thing we can do is nothing."

Tess turned to him, stopping on the spot. "Nothing?"

"Nothing," he insisted.

"Nothing" had never been part of any of Tess's plans. As she made her way back out into the bustling street, she tugged her red coat around her body as strange nervous flutters started up in her stomach. Suddenly, she felt cold. What if this was the first in a line of steps that would lead to her being fired? What if they weren't happy with her?

Her career was all that she had.

Tess stopped at the red door that led into her apartment building, pulled her key out, then put it back in her bag. No, she'd go for a walk around the Village. She needed to think. She needed to save her job. She needed to confront Leon, and James. Fast.

And fate? As much as she adored Nico, the idea of fate seemed about as helpful as a trip to the moon.

CHAPTER TWO

Rome, 1987

Edward reached across the bed, running his hands over the spot where Edith had slept for over thirty-five years. And thought of Rebecca.

She'd whispered to him yet again in his dreams last night. *Sometimes we don't want to revisit the past, but the past wants to revisit us.* Was this some wretched new form of grief? A way of distancing his mind from Edith's death, while bewitching him in some tortuous way back to 1946?

It was as if all the years since then were melded into one tangled, insignificant whirl—Oxford, his marriage, the children, his university career. Even being in Rome, surrounded by relics from the ancient world, could not distract him from the pull of his past.

Edward sat up in bed. He ran a hand through his still-thick hair, the inevitable gray still peppered through with a few last shots of dark blond. He moved across to the shuttered French doors, throwing them open and stepping onto the small balcony, not caring about the fact he was in his pajama bottoms and his old gray T-shirt while standing above the busy street. He stared out at the familiarity below the apartment that he and Edith bought ten years ago, after Haslemere, his family estate, had finally been sold.

During the auction, neighbors and opportunists alike grappled over everything Edward's family had held dear since 1839—the monogrammed silver that graced the steamship his grandfather used for family holidays to England, his mother's exquisite ball gowns, as delicate as gossamer, the silverware that the butler counted each night in his cedar-lined pantry, where as a child Edward often perched on the bench by the window, watching while the old man decanted wine.

Now, Edward couldn't fight off his own guilt at his long-held attitude toward his family's wealth. As he moved from childhood to adulthood, he'd come to see that the famous Russell family's opulent lifestyle and the value they placed on social standing were both unnecessary and unfair. But still, he'd found it difficult, in the end, to say goodbye to his family's legacy and to those old ghosts of his ancestors that were rumored to linger in Haslemere's grand hallways. Now it seemed that one ghost from his own past did not want to say goodbye to him.

He leaned against the balcony railing, fighting with the memory of making his final way up Haslemere's forlorn gravel driveway ten years ago, passing the bell that stood sentinel by the gate that led to the stable yard. It used to be rung every morning when it was time for all the employees—the shearers, the farmers, the station managers, and the servants—to start work. In the late nineteenth century, the world-famous sheep station had employed seventy men on permanent wages. Hundreds of itinerant shearers toiled in the cathedral-sized shearing sheds when Edward's grandfather had brought Haslemere to great prominence.

When Edward sold out, there were only three employees left: a gardener, a cleaner, and one station hand. Edith had done her best, bless her, to embrace the old lifestyle with far more enthusiasm than Edward ever felt. While he'd toyed with the idea of running the paddocks as a collective, Edith had entertained none of that. She'd pushed on in the old way, relishing the idea of playing the role of the perfect country wife, putting her heart into making a gorgeous home out of the old mansion for their three children, Mary, Jonathon, and Peter, who'd roamed around the increasingly decrepit gardens, their childhoods as carefree as Edward and she could make them.

Edward spent most of his time lecturing in Melbourne, desperately trying to fund the great behemoth that he'd inherited. But his income from lecturing and writing biographies could not sustain a grand house in the middle of nowhere, and in spite of Edith's own inheritance, they were never going to be able to support the vast business that his forebears had built. Once he'd packed everything up ten years ago, he'd never returned.

But still, what he missed, were he honest, was the sense of place: the old whispering gum trees in the endless paddocks on either side of the long driveway that was lined, in turn, with oaks that his grandfather insisted on planting as a token to the old country. He missed the still, green paddocks dotted with well-tended sheep. He'd enjoyed working in the garden when he could. And he did have an affection for the great old house, with its ballroom and galleries and fourteen bedrooms and the farmhouse kitchen, where the temperamental wood-heated stove used to smoke out the whole house when it was first lit in autumn, causing everyone to flee outside. It was as if the old oven had a personality of its own—the servants named it Betty—and it had to be fed throughout the winter with logs from the gums in the paddocks, or its flame would die out.

That was the only life he had known, and yet it was based on complete inequality. He hadn't been able to resolve his feelings about that, especially after the horrors of the war, the holocaust. How could he live with such luxuries when so many had lost their lives for no reason at all?

Edward's flight to Rome was supposed to be the answer, to both remove him and distract him from his past. He'd expounded to Edith the wonders of Italy as if on a mission to convince her that the ancient world was their savior, and the new world didn't matter. He'd lectured her about the Italian passion for everything that was important—food, family. Love. And yet, now with the hopelessness of grief for everything he'd lost, he knew that coming to Rome only tied in with his yearning for that time in 1946. In this classic setting, he kept circling back to that very word he'd been so attracted to straight after the war, "modernism," the rejection of all those tenets that had held society together until the war blew apart every assumption about class and social roles—tenets that his family had stuck to for generations.

Rome hadn't helped. It had made things worse. Being among the living, breathing ruins of the ancient world made his family's 150 years at Haslemere and their adherence to parochial conformity seem as inconsequential as a single drop of rain in a storm. Edward had clung to the idea of Rome as the place where he could lose and find himself at the same time. But neither of these things had happened.

His insistent, circular thoughts of Rebecca reminded him of the routine supply flights that he was forced to take during the war, up and down the east coast of Australia, over and over the same ground, every day. Edward flew the aircraft with one hand, his eyes on whatever book he'd picked up that day from Haslemere's library: Dickens, Milton, Shakespeare, the Romantics. He'd prop them up in the cockpit in front of his nose. He'd retreated into a dreamlike world, away from reality, the war, everything, back then. Was his mind trying to do that now?

He tugged his pajama cord around his still-trim waist. He would, as usual, go out, buy the paper and his morning coffee, stand at the shining counter at Caffè Greco while sipping and people watching, then wander out into the Via Condotti, with its charming designer boutiques, before making his way up the Spanish Steps to the pure bliss of the gardens surrounding the Villa Borghese. It was easy enough to look like any other expatriate in Rome. No one knew what was going on in his head.

Edward had been playing a game of Russian roulette with himself since Edith's funeral. The way he saw it, he had two choices: he could continue like this, his mind pregnant with the past, or he could do something about it. And there was only one thing that would help. But he'd stopped writing decades ago. He had no desire to take himself back to those secret shores that he had sworn he would never revisit. That period of his life was too difficult, too frightening, and too exquisite to face. And yet it was not going to leave him in peace.

Edward moved through his bedroom to the en suite bathroom, turned on the shower, stepped in front of the mirror, and gazed at his green eyes in the bijou little room that he and Edith had renovated. He'd done his best with Edith, what he thought was the right thing. But in doing so, he'd locked himself away from the truth of his feelings throughout his marriage.

After showering, he collected his keys and enough cash for coffee and Italian bread with jam, and then stepped out of the small living room into the stairwell, but his thoughts pulled him back to Rebecca.

Had anyone known her as he had?

Edward moved out into the Roman sunshine. By the time he made it to Via Condotti, he was reminding himself that even if Rebecca's brother still lived, or her mother, or if any of those long-ago artist friends they had made together in the forties were still breathing, no one knew Rebecca Swift as he had.

It was as if, after all these years, she was talking to him, whispering in some secret language that only they had known during their brief time together, before she fell to her death in the ocean that day in 1946. As he walked he thought that perhaps it didn't matter why she was haunting him again, but one thing was clear: it would be intolerable to go one more day without doing something about it.

Edward pushed open Caffè Greco's door, took a seat on one of the leather banquettes, sipped his coffee, and ate his white roll and jam, resting his free hand on the small, round marble table. He watched people's reflections in the mirrors that lined the walls and listened to their rapid conversations, taking in a word or two sometimes.

He loved Italy with a passion, but even here, he had not been able to write. The words had dried up. He'd been given thousands of words when he was young, until they had all stopped. He would be kidding himself to think that he had written anything that mattered since Rebecca died. He'd lapsed into writing other people's biographies to avoid his own truths, which he knew would shine through if he wrote fiction.

Edward went back into the street. The crowds had picked up. He fell in step behind a boisterous family, the children's voices high with excitement, rising and lingering in the space between the crumbling old buildings, childish words becoming lost in the washing that was strung over the street. Day-to-day commonalities—Rebecca had not held truck with those. Edward felt a smile pass over his lips, and he pictured her long dark hair swinging beneath her cherry-red beret.

She would make a good story.

He could hear her teasing him, telling him to go right ahead. Some things were harder to let go of than others.

Edward stopped outside a newsdealer. But only for a moment. Then he walked inside, and for the first time in years, he bought a notebook. And strolled out again into the sunshine, relief soaring from his soul.

CHAPTER THREE

New York, 1987

Tess moved around the tiny one-room apartment that she called home. If she closed her eyes and pretended, it was easy to imagine that everything was all right. She always looked forward to going into the office in the morning. Today she'd prepared to call Alec and talk about his new book. The phone call was marked in her planner. She'd underlined the appointment in red pen. Tess had become so used to her day-to-day existence for the last few years that she'd assumed she was leading a life that would not stop. She thought she had made it, that her job and author list were both safe. Assumptions were something that she'd never rely on again.

Now she stared, helpless, around her studio in the old building on West Third. The four walls stared back at her as if nothing were amiss. Her small cream sofa sat there as usual. Tess's pale blue blanket was folded neatly on an arm, just as she'd left it this morning. The jar of basil that she had bought yesterday to make a pesto sauce still sat green and fragrant across the room on her kitchen counter. A couple of dresses hung on the front of her small wardrobe. Was it yesterday that she'd picked them up from the dry cleaners? Yesterday seemed an elusive place.

Tess sat down on her sofa with a thump.

The fact that Leon had handed Tess's best author to a man whose father was the most famous literary critic in New York was more than irksome—it was driving Tess out of her mind. She couldn't stop the pictures that formed in her head: Sean Cooper in his top-rated spot on one of the numerous talk shows he appeared on, dissecting the latest literary sensation with all the aplomb of a well-seasoned pro. Alec Burgess would be next on his agenda; Tess was sure of it. Her client, her work, and yet she could do nothing to stop the train that was leaving her far behind.

Tess was running a hand through her tousled blond bob when her phone rang. "Yes?" she answered, and exhaled the moment she heard her older sister's voice.

"Where are you?" Caroline sounded imperious. Tess's sister had a sexy catch in her voice that had been the envy of their entire high school. Caroline had always been well known for her big green eyes, dark lashes, and perfect olive skin, while Tess had always been, well, Tess. Thinner, less well developed, and stuck with the dimple she hated and which her older brother, Bobby, teased her about incessantly.

Caroline was in bossy mode. "You knew we were starting at seven. And you know that Dad can't stand it if anyone's late. Let alone . . ." Caroline's voice drifted off, as if, perhaps, even she thought she had gone too far.

Me, Tess didn't add. She stopped her thoughts from travelling down the well-worn path that they loved to take—it wouldn't matter if Caroline or Bobby were late for a family dinner. They had glamorous careers, while Tess was just bookish Tess.

Tess took in a breath and stood up. "I'm on my way."

Even though dinner at her sister's trendy apartment in that brand-new tower just off Fifth Avenue was about as appealing as lying in a cold bath, Tess grabbed her favorite red coat and her keys and rushed down the stairs of her building as fast as she possibly could.

Outside, the clouds were bilious, pregnant with what could turn into a summer downpour. Even though it was still light, there was a strange energy in the air. The streets were packed as Tess made her way down to the subway and grabbed a train to her sister's apartment.

How was she going to tell them?

Tess cursed herself for not remembering the dinner, for forgetting to change into something chic and competitive tonight. Her black shoes were mid-heeled, and that was fine for her job, but her sister would be in stilettos. Tess's suit seemed drab, and the sense of tiredness that had overwhelmed her after she walked out of Leon's office still hung over her. The situation seemed impossible, but she had to work out what to do.

She held fast to the handrail as the train wound its way underneath the city and let her gaze lose itself in the blackness of the tunnels.

That same old sense of anticipation and dread rumbled through her stomach as she made her way into the all-glass black monolith that Caroline and her trendsetting husband called home. As the elevator rose high through the building, Tess tugged at her black skirt, painfully aware that her stockings were cheap and her shoes were scuffed as well as old.

Caroline let her in, her face already flushed from a couple glasses of champagne—it was always like a party when Tess's family got together. It was as if they were all celebrating their collective new-money success, with each gathering an exercise in self-congratulation. Tess's parents had grown up in the Midwest, and her father had slaved in the sixties to set himself up as a property developer in New York. He'd made a killing and expected the next generation to carry on the tradition.

But Tess knew that her family could never hold a candle to James's family's Establishment cachet. If members of that venerable class were to bump into Tess's parents, they would probably treat them as if they were something distasteful that had stuck to their leather-soled shoe. In contrast, James's family name alone put him in the top literary and artistic echelons even before he set foot in an Ivy League university or began the career that would have been mapped out for him at birth. He would never have had to battle for anything as Tess or her family had done.

To Tess's family, books and publishing were as alien and stuffy as a dusty old library full of literary classics was to the most frivolous of fashion and gossip magazines. And Caroline's claim to fame was that she had risen to become the editor of one of New York's most famous loudmouthed glossies.

Tess hovered in the kitchen, unable to take her eyes away from her older sister sashaying about on the white marble floor, holding a flute of champagne, her blond hair cascading down her back. She was dressed casually, making Tess feel even more fusty in her suit. Caroline's stonewashed jeans showed off her long, long legs, and the flowing top that she wore revealed just enough décolletage to be sexy. Her husband, Kurt, was chopping up salad ingredients, also wearing a loose shirt over jeans that showed everything off.

They looked, as usual, like a pair of models in one of the ads that Caroline would place in *Floodlight Magazine*.

"Tessie."

Tess winced, leaning in for her father's kiss. Dale Miller's carefully clipped sandy beard touched her cheek for a brief second before Tess's older brother, Bobby, appeared and slapped him on the back.

"Dad!" he said. "You gotta come and look at this!"

As usual, the television blared the latest baseball game, throwing volleys of sound around the entire living space every few seconds when the crowds cheered a player. Dale patted Tess on the head and sloped off with Bobby to sit on one of the oversize white sofas on the endless expanse of black marble floor.

"You look all worn out!" Tess's mother squeaked, also leaning in for a quick kiss on the cheek.

"And you're not working too long hours, I hope." She framed Tess's face in her hands for a moment, searching with her deep blue eyes. "Couldn't you get a job with Caroline? There must be something we can do. I hate to see you living in that darned studio. And what about men? Have you met anyone interesting, darling?"

By "interesting" Tess knew exactly what Lucille Miller meant. Interesting meant successful, dressed like a knife-edge, someone who would fit in with this family where Tess felt like a lost old shoe. Throughout her twenties, when some popular family friend or a jock buddy of Bobby's had shown an interest in her, the whole family had pushed Tess toward whomever as if she were a meal on a plate. She'd only given in once, leading to an episode she preferred never to revisit. Work had become her escape, but now that seemed to be gone . . .

"So." Once the food was set out on the glass table in the middle of the room with its sweeping views all the way across Manhattan, it was Caroline who raised the one topic Tess dreaded to hear.

"Tess, darling," she said, in her most charming and killing tone of voice.

Tess helped herself to salad, but her stomach churned at the reality of her life. She couldn't even keep one author who now lived like her entire family did, and in doing so, seemed to have eclipsed her.

"Yup."

"You are going to thank me forever," Caroline said, her blond hair bouncing as she jiggled about in her chair.

"Go on," Lucille said.

Tess placed the salad tongs back in the bowl. "Mmm hmm," she said, taking a sip of her wine.

Perhaps she should marry a model too. Like Caroline.

"What is it?" she asked, unable to keep the resignation out of her voice.

"Go on!" Lucille said. "It's exactly what she needs."

"Well!" Caroline said. "I got Alec Burgess a two-page spread and a cover on September's issue. And you are going to be featured. We want all the gossip—from his favorite hangout spots to what he wears to bed and who his main squeeze is these days. No holds barred. Our readers will devour him. So, are you going to prostrate yourself on the floor and be my slave for life? This is big, Tess. National coverage. But I think Alec is ready to go to the next level."

Tess put down her glass.

"Excellent," she said, feeling her expression drop.

"I'm hoping it will throw you in the way of other bestselling authors, too, Tess. I'm doing this for you."

"Aren't you going to say thank you?" Lucille tossed her hair. And sniffed in that annoying way that she had.

"Great!" Tess said, picking up her glass and holding it in the air. "Fabulous. Thank you. It's just what I need."

Perfect. Timing. The conversation ricocheted around the table as it usually did. Tess stabbed her fork into her salad.

But as her family whirled on without her, Tess found renewed determination. She needed to get Alec Burgess back. End of story. She was sick of being sidelined and it was not going to happen at work.

CHAPTER FOUR

Melbourne, 1946

Cigarette smoke and the strains of Frank Sinatra drifted out into Pink Alley and disappeared into the warm summer night. Edward stood at the end of the narrow lane that ran off Melbourne's Little Collins Street, searching for an entrance to the loft above the stone stable block where the party was being held. The upstairs space at the end of the lane had clearly been converted into a makeshift studio, home to a member of Melbourne's growing coterie of artists. Here students mingled with painters, writers, and left-wing intellectuals. They rubbed shoulders and discussed what mattered in life. Together with bookshops and cafés, these lofts served as places to galvanize new ways of seeing and being. Edward had received a spontaneous invitation to tonight's party from Joy Hester, an artist whom he met at a lecture on modernism at the university. He was intrigued after talking to her and decided to at least show up.

Now, he wandered into the desolate stables, looking for a way to access the floor above. Edward guessed that the ground floor was probably used as a garage before the war, after some well-to-do person had finished with his horses and buggies. Oil stains marked the concrete floor where hay would have been piled up once.

A makeshift set of wooden steps stood at the far corner of the deserted, moody space. Edward moved toward them, then paused, one foot on the first stair and his hand resting on the chipped handrail, hoping not to get a splinter from the flaking wood.

Someone else had appeared in the stables. He sensed a presence before he heard the clack of high-heeled shoes on cracked cement. The footsteps were uneven, as if the person who was wearing the shoes was not used to walking in them.

Edward turned. The footsteps stopped.

"Well, hi there." A girl, whose voice cracked a little when she spoke, stood outlined in the hazy air. She wore a cherry-red beret atop long dark hair that Edward suspected would swing when she walked. Her dress was red, too, and it was held fast around her waist with a fabric belt. Edward admired the girl's lack of artifice as she stared up at him.

"The steps are hard to climb when you're drunk," she said, her extraordinary dark eyes lighting up as she spoke. "But once you're upstairs with them all, it's the perfect escape."

Edward sensed a smile forming on his lips. "Would you like to go up ahead of me?" he said. "It's my first time to one of these things. I'm afraid I don't know anyone much. I'll probably end up standing by myself." He had only just started at Melbourne University, studying, much to his upper-class family's chagrin, English lit.

"Don't worry, they won't let you be a wallflower," the girl said, moving toward the stairs and running her white-gloved hand over the wooden banister as if it were a polished handrail in some grand estate. "And anyway, it's the conversation everyone comes for. It doesn't matter who you are or who you know. Everyone is welcome here. As long as you have firm views on art. And politics." She started climbing the staircase, then stopped to face him.

Edward fought the urge to chuckle. "I'm Edward. Edward Russell."

The girl lit up with a gorgeous smile. "And I'm Rebecca," she said. "Rebecca Swift."

"Shall we go upstairs, Rebecca Swift?"

The studio was filled with smoke and bohemian guests. Men in rolled-up shirtsleeves and with sweaters tied over their shoulders mingled at the bar with women who were dressed like men. Empty glasses decorated tabletops and modernist art adorned the walls, the paintings looking over the party as if they, too, were bizarre guests. The scene here was about as far away from Edward's family as Antarctica was from New York.

A striking modern painting stood on an easel near the door. Two girls graced the canvas, dressed in kaleidoscopic miniskirts. Men leered at them, grabbing them from behind. It was both disturbing and strikingly honest.

"Social realism and surrealism all at once. Exactly," Edward said, half to himself.

"You've got it," Rebecca said. "That's what they're all about here."

Joy Hester appeared, a cigarette tapering from her elegant hands, her peroxided hair swept back from her attractive face.

"Hello again . . . ," Edward said.

"Joy Hester." She laughed as she spoke. "I suppose you've forgotten my name. I forget everyone's name. What do you think of Albert's work?" she went on, turning unaffectedly to the painting next to them. "Tell me."

"I hadn't forgotten your name," Edward admitted with a laugh. "And as for the paintings, they are honest and vibrant." He knew that he needed to be direct in the company here tonight. "But dark, authentic, raw at the same time. They cut to the heart of things that I think we don't wish to see."

Joy took a drag from her cigarette. "Well, we agree about that, Edward Russell," she said. "The artist, Albert Tucker, is my husband."

"Albert Tucker, of course." He was an emerging local artist. What an intriguing place Melbourne was turning out to be. After six years in the air force, during which Edward's main action was surviving a plane crash in England before being deemed only fit enough to run a supply route up and down Australia's east coast, it seemed as if life was beckoning him back. The dark years had passed.

Joy Hester chatted with Rebecca before a striking dark young man, whom Edward recognized as the modernist poet Max Harris, appeared, dragging Joy off into another conversation. Edward turned to the girl with the beguiling smile.

He didn't want her to go away.

"A drink?"

"Sounds perfect," Rebecca Swift said. She led him to the bar. "They're in a mood for a real party tonight," she laughed, taking a glass of champagne from Edward. "Often you get together with them and they are arguing about politics and art. Terribly serious. There's an inner circle. Joy Hester, Albert Tucker, Max Harris, John and Sunday Reed, Sidney Nolan, and Danila Vasilieff. Their arguments can continue on until morning . . ."

Edward leaned in close to her, not just in order to hear. He knew about Sunday and John Reed. They were infamous among his parents and their friends for having eschewed their wealthy social circles to forge a life that was regarded as bohemian. The Reeds led the modernist movement in both life and art. They'd moved out of the city and set up home in an old dairy farm at a little place called Heidelberg, where they lived in what Edward's parents decried as a "commune" famously known as Heide, growing their own vegetables and being largely self-sufficient, not to mention sharing their home with a group of modernist artists whom they'd "picked up from the gutter," according to Edward's social milieu. But the Reeds went on thumbing their noses at the Establishment. It was the class in which both John and Sunday had been raised.

What seemed to fascinate and shock people the most was that Sunday and John apparently had hearts so modern that while they loved each other deeply, they both allowed room for love that extended beyond their marriage. Sunday's long-term affair with her protégé, the younger artist Sidney Nolan, was carried on while John stood by. This state of affairs was something that repulsed Edward's parents and their upper-class sensibilities to no end. Sunday had also indulged in an affair earlier with the young artist Sam Atyeo, and John carried out a dalliance with Sam's wife, the artist Moya Dyring. It was all completely unacceptable, and yet Edward had to wonder whether it was the fact that the Reeds were honest and open about their love affairs that irked the upper classes the most. In any case, the rift between the modernists and the established upper classes was as deep as a canyon; it was political and it cut across every divide in society . . . and Edward was more than intrigued.

"Joy Hester is a bit of a role model for me," Rebecca went on. "I admire her work. She prefers drawing over painting, which I find interesting. I enjoy the same medium myself."

"Are you an artist?"

"Only an aspiring one." Rebecca tilted her head. Her beret slipped.

Edward caught it and put it back on her head.

She seemed a little self-conscious then. Edward couldn't help but think that it was as if her facade had slipped for one brief moment.

"So, why are you drawn to art?" he asked. He wanted to cut to the heart of things for some reason—to know about her properly rather than engage in small talk.

Rebecca's features softened. "I have a theory about art, and about people who feel it."

"Tell me."

"There are two worlds in this life. The first world is that of the imagination, and the second one is real life. I prefer the first world. I think it's far more important." She took a sip of her champagne and watched him from under her eyelashes. "Does that shock you?"

Edward softened his own voice. "No. In fact, I know exactly what you mean."

She looked up at him, fast, before her eyes dropped to the ground.

"People with no imaginations don't understand it," she murmured.

"That's a smart observation." Edward twirled the stem of his half-full glass around in his fingers.

Rebecca seemed to be waiting for him to talk.

He took in a breath. "I'd hate to hear that your life is difficult and you need to escape, though," he said.

She straightened, as if by instinct.

Edward didn't want to appear as if he were coming on to her, although he had to admit that was exactly what he wanted to do. He sensed that the conversation would be over faster than she could flick her dark hair if he were not careful.

"You see," he said, his voice still sounding intimate and he didn't know why, "I'm railing against the world. I would hate to think of you in a similar state."

"Why are you doing that?"

Edward gazed out over the room. And wondered if everybody in it felt as disconnected as he did. Were they all looking for some form of truth in what was becoming a more fragmented world than ever—families ripped apart by war, governments that thought they had the right to control people's thoughts and minds? People who were terrified into following them? The Second World War had blown everything apart. And yet Edward's family had not changed one bit. They clung to every tenet that they knew—the conformism of society, mixing with the right people, the tedious business of making connections—or his mother did. His father and his older brother had resorted to brandy in order to cope while everyone kept up a pretense that they were functional.

But how was an artist supposed to represent such a state of being? No wonder Albert Tucker and his circle were embracing the surreal. Was the imagination the only recourse for an artist, given all the confusion, all the tragic, appalling waste of the past six years?

"No, let's talk about you," he said to the girl in the red beret. "Tell me. When you draw, what happens?"

A frown passed across Rebecca's features. "That's easy. I feel like I'm no longer me. I can escape myself and everything around me. It's as if I'm flying."

"What's wrong with your life?" he asked. And it was right then, at that moment, that it seemed he and Rebecca began talking in a private language that he had never spoken with anyone else.

She reached in her handbag and pulled out a cigarette. Edward lit it for her, and admired the sexy way in which she held it.

"My mother is very proper," she said.

Edward nodded, willing her to go on.

"She is a dressmaker, in a boutique in the city. She's terribly fashionable. Or thinks she is. But to me, it's as if everything that she sees as important, just isn't. If that makes sense."

It made perfect sense to Edward. Why his family could not see what was important was a question whose answer had eluded him for years. The country's most elite boarding school had been a foul regime of routine and bearing up from the age of seven to seventeen, and then there had been the war with its bogus fighting over what? Land, territory, power? None of it seemed to matter at all.

"I can relate to things not being . . . important," he said.

Rebecca stood still for a moment, and he sensed that she was searching for something to say. But he didn't want to push her. He wanted to make her feel comfortable.

A safer topic, then.

"Are you studying art?" he asked.

Rebecca drew on the cigarette, then sent smoke curling out. "Gallery school. I had to fight to go there . . ." She glanced up at him.

"Go on," he said, his voice taking on another depth. Good. Perhaps she did want to talk.

"My mother was insisting I work in the shop."

"Of course she was," Edward said.

Rebecca looked up again, a razor-sharp expression cutting across her features for one split second.

Long enough.

"But in the end my uncle, my late father's younger brother, insisted that I go to art school. I was told I had some sort of 'talent' when I was young. My uncle, admirably, stood up to my mother and provided the funds for me to go. I think it's the first time I've seen her concede an argument in my life."

"Well done to him," Edward murmured. "And how is this art school?"

"The Gallery School?" Rebecca rolled her eyes. "Rows of students lined up under a tin roof. Meticulously copying sculptures. The idea of doing one's own thing is anathema to the teachers. Honestly? It's a waste of time and space."

Edward had to stop the laugh that caught in his throat. The last thing he wanted was for Rebecca to feel he was treating her as a joke. But he couldn't help himself. While he was more attracted to her than to anyone he had ever met in his entire life, he also found Rebecca's insouciance amusing. He sensed that if she were free, everything would come together and she would lead an extraordinary life.

But for now, he chose his next sentence with care. "If your father was alive, do you think things might have been easier for you? I mean, in the way of getting on with your art?"

Something passed across Rebecca's face, and he had to resist the urge to reach out and touch her cheek with his hand. It struck him again that secret depths belied the playfulness that she had shown when he first met her downstairs.

"Easier and harder in equal measures," she said.

"When did he die?" Death had become so commonplace during the war. It had become normal to talk about the end of things during the last ghastly six years.

"Eight years ago," she said. "He was an alcoholic."

Edward took in a sharp breath. "Sorry." He felt the muscles in his jaw hardening. "I'm intrigued as to what your own thing is in art . . ." And in life, he wanted to add.

Joy Hester appeared, bursting into their little circle with the handsome young poet Max Harris from earlier and Sunday and John Reed. Edward felt his senses wake up the moment he was introduced to them.

"Edward Russell," Joy said, "we are not about rules here, but I do take exception to your monopolizing our darling Rebecca all night. And besides, I want you to meet Sunday and John Reed, and this is Max. Max Harris."

"I do always say, 'Let's smash the rules and get away from them as fast as we can,'" Edward responded.

"My sort of person," Max said. His dark eyes twinkled, and he handed Edward another glass of champagne.

"Max is a poet, and he edits our magazine, *Angry Penguins*, with John," Joy said.

"We were just talking about the connection between rebellion and art," Edward said. "Internal rebellion, against everything you have ever known, in a deep sense. Not always literal."

"How serious you have become," Rebecca murmured.

Edward caught her eye and smiled.

"Do you paint, Edward, like Rebecca?" Sunday asked.

It was extraordinary how conventional Sunday looked. Her hair was pulled back in a schoolgirl headband, and yet, clearly, she was anything but traditional. Her husband, John, stood next to her, a quiet presence.

"I attempt to write," Edward said. "Poems."

"Excellent," Max said. "Even more encouraging."

Max, like Joy, seemed good fun at a party, but Edward suspected that they were deadly serious about their approach to their respective art forms—not to mention life.

"It seems so obvious to us that art and poetry are intimately connected," John Reed said. His tone was quiet and measured, but everyone in the group leaned in to hear what he had to say. "Along with music, theater, films . . . politics. Modernism can only find inspiration and expression where freedom is a way of life."

Sunday Reed cleared her throat as if she were about to speak, but then she seemed to hesitate, almost as if she were digesting the conversation.

Edward had heard that she was a little hard of hearing.

Everyone waited.

"I am proud of Max and John's work. Their focus is to uncover artistic talent. Their endeavors have been courageous so far, and certainly not without controversy. What we are trying to do is establish a uniquely Australian expression in art. Max and John publish modern Australian poetry and writing in *Angry Penguins* alongside the work of modernist artists. We are about breaking down structure and getting to the heart of what is important in life and in art, and *Angry Penguins* is the vehicle for getting our ideas out into the world. But we all know how hard it is to have our efforts ridiculed; some remain convinced that the world has not been altered by two world wars and that people do not have the right to break free from the class into which they were born." She seemed to hesitate, then looked Edward directly in the eye. After a while, she spoke clearly. "You see, I wanted to get away from my family and the strictures of my background. That was the main thing for me."

Edward's inward breath was sharp. Did Sunday know who he was? Did she know about his family? If so, he knew that she would relate to his struggles with them. Suddenly, he was overwhelmed with a sense of being at home with these people.

"The first time I met Sunday," Joy said, speaking in a more intimate tone, "I asked her if she believed in equality of the classes. She told me, 'I believe in love.'"

Yes, it was as simple as that. Why did his family have to make things so complicated? Edward stood there for a moment, quite overwhelmed by these people and their bravery.

Courage had revealed itself as one of the strongest of human qualities during the war. Now Edward sensed that had to continue in peace. His war hadn't ended. The civil war that raged inside him was a result of his intense feelings of guilt about the fact that his family's wealth and strict adherence to the rules of the upper classes repelled him. And yet, here were these two who had gotten away, who were living a life that was entirely suited to them. Regardless of their family. Was that courage, or selfishness, or being true to oneself? Edward stared across the crowded room. He didn't know the answer yet, nor did he know exactly how he would choose to live his own life.

Joy kissed another guest goodbye, then turned back to John and Sunday. Apparently, they were urgently needed by someone else. Max shot off into the crowd, joining the antics of some other louder group, but Sunday leaned toward Edward and Rebecca and touched the girl on the arm for a brief second.

"I hope we meet again," she said.

"Come on, Sun," John said. And he led her off into the crowd.

"Well," Rebecca said, "now you have met the famous Reeds. And after all that, I know absolutely nothing about you."

Edward smiled, and he leaned in a little closer. The last thing he wanted to do was talk about himself.

CHAPTER FIVE

New York, 1987

Tess marched into the elegant reception area of Campbell and Black on Monday morning and greeted the staff as if she were the most confident thing since sliced bread. Alec Burgess's interview in *Floodlight Magazine* should go ahead, and she, Tess, should be featured in that article right alongside him. Even if she was not of Caroline's world, and she knew she was not, she, not James, would be the one to transition *Floodlight Magazine* readers and Alec's fans to the literary world. Tess would be the bridge for Alec, not some new silver-spooned recruit.

Tess marched toward Leon's office, remembering all those late-night phone calls from Alec, who was frantic that one of his characters wasn't acting according to their game plan. She'd been beside him at every book launch and travelled with him on all of his book tours. The truth was, she'd done far more than any editor would normally do. And that had made Alec a success. Tess was his right-hand man. No one was dumping her.

"Leon is in the boardroom," one of the receptionists chirped as Tess stalked toward her boss's office.

"Fine," Tess said, switching around and heading back toward the boardroom.

She stopped at the entrance to the room, its walls lined with English hunting prints that hung alongside plaques celebrating Campbell and Black's many successes. If the room was meant to intimidate, it did an excellent job. She straightened her red pencil skirt. Leon looked up at her over his half-moon glasses.

"Morning, Tess."

"Leon," Tess said. The breath she took in was shuddery.

He indicated that she sit down.

"I have a proposal to make," she said once she'd settled, reining in her old feelings of inferiority amid the sophisticated surroundings. The boardroom screamed "gentleman's club," and perhaps that was what this place was proving to be. She clasped her hands together.

"I should continue working with Alec, Leon," she said.

Leon's sigh was audible.

"There are three reasons why."

"Tess . . ." Leon tented his hands on the table.

"Firstly, if Alec is going to change his style, then he could risk throwing his hard-won readers off. Having consistency with his editor is something that will ward off that risk—I know what his loyal readers respond to the best. We don't want him to have a flop, something that will turn people away. Secondly, I am willing to get right behind this, to support this change in his career. I can nurture him just as I've always done. You know how committed I am to Alec's success, and you also know that I know him."

Leon was silent.

"My qualifications are the same as James's. We both have master's degrees in English lit. I can edit a literary novel. Thirdly, and I think this is important, I've secured an interview for James in *Floodlight Magazine*." Tess went on, in spite of Leon's snobbish sneer. "A whole spread—that's national coverage in one of the biggest magazines in the country. But they want to include me in the interview. It's a focus on our long-term creative partnership. I don't think it's in Alec's best interests to change editorial direction. We need to be careful here, with all due respect to James."

Tess shot a look up at her boss. He was looking straight at her. She did her best to hold his gaze.

"Tess, while you make a compelling argument, and while coverage in your *sister's* magazine will no doubt be entertaining . . ." He adjusted his cuff links. "The decision is done. There's nothing else to say."

Tess clutched the sides of her chair.

"Leon," she said, her voice dangerous and low. "This isn't going to happen."

She took in a breath. "I've put everything I have into that writer. What's more, this has been done in the most underhand way. I wasn't consulted. I was never given a voice. I've worked here five years. For three of those I've devoted my career to Alec Burgess. I've made this publishing house a lot of money. Now, I don't want to talk about money," she said, waving her hand around at the dark paneled walls. "I know we don't do that here. But at the end of the day, you can't afford to risk this. James might be literary, but I can make books sell. And I'm literary anyway," she added. "As I said." Then felt her cheeks redden.

Darn it. She glimpsed Leon's lips twitch.

Tess leaned forward in her chair. A group of editors walked past the open door. Tess looked at them, colleagues who spent most of their time reading books. They were not confrontational people. She was the one here who had the business sense. Okay, some of them represented well-known authors. Some of them represented famous authors' estates. But in general, stability was the key to success here. Campbell and Black was all about the established order. It wasn't the sort of publishing house that rocked the boat. In some ways, Tess wished she could do so . . .

How was she supposed to appeal to Leon?

"James would hardly be a mistake," Leon said. He sounded gentle now, fatherly.

Tess heaved out a breath. "Okay," she said. "What about the personal angle? What if James and Alec don't get along? You know that I can work with Alec. You know that I can bring out his best. We are built on rock-solid foundations as a publishing house, and you know Alec and I are solid. You know that I'll deliver. I support him no matter what he writes. I'll make sure that from a business perspective this works. I'll ensure that he doesn't mess up his career. And I'll keep him focused. Alec and I are close."

"Tess, I'm sorry, but it's Alec who has requested an editor with more literary chops," Leon said. He sounded exasperated now.

"Chops?" Tess said. "And a degree from Brown doesn't give me 'chops'?" She pushed back her seat. "It appears to me that we have a problem here. Two problems, in fact."

"Listen . . ." Leon's voice was a warning.

But something had kicked in. Tess knew instinctively that this was too important a fight not to have. She could not afford to have this sort of thing happen now. What if it were to become a pattern?

"Leon, first of all, James's father is the literary critic of the *New York Times*."

"I don't think we should go down that path, Tess," Leon warned.

"Secondly, he is male." Her voice shook, but some force pushed her on. The more she thought about this, the more she knew what was happening was downright wrong. "Every last editor in this house is male, except for me."

Leon took his glasses off and ran his hand over his immaculate blond hair.

"Oh, we have women out in the copy room, women answering the phone. Women making goddamn coffee and tea! I know we pride ourselves on the fact that we have equal numbers of women and men here, but look at who holds the power in this place. In fact, we have no men, not one, precisely, in the supporting roles that the women occupy. The only woman who has a senior role here . . . is me. We need to change that. Giving women better opportunities is crucial if this publishing house is to move toward the twenty-first century. What sort of message does dumping me as soon as an author becomes successful give to the public, or to other women who might be considering applying to work here?"

"Tess, it's more a matter of giving our authors the right editors so that we can produce their best work."

"Dumped like an old Kleenex," Tess growled. "Just like that. What about loyalty, Leon?"

Leon merely raised a brow. "I think you should take some time out. Calm down. Think this through."

Time out. The words ricocheted around the room. Tess glanced up at her boss, who sat there, unmoving. She stood up, gathered herself together, and made her way to the door.

"Thank you, Leon," she said.

He nodded at her.

Tess held her head up as she made her way out of the building. She walked out onto Fifth Avenue, but the crowds of purposeful people on the street who usually invigorated her seemed irritating now. She didn't agree with Nico: fate was something you had to fight sometimes. Accepting setbacks was not her motto. It was all very well to sit back and watch life pass you by. But it wasn't what Tess did. And it certainly wasn't how she'd built up her career. But what to do when it was clear you had no choice? That was the rub, and that was the place from which she had to push on.

After an hour, Tess knew she had to go back. Her thoughts spiraled around and ended up in the same place. She marched back into the building and stood sentinel in the elevator, her shoulders rigid as a set of planks.

Leon appeared at her office door a matter of seconds after she sat down at her desk.

Tess felt her heart speed up as he came in and sat down opposite her.

"I can't do anything about Alec, Tess. He's requested James and that's all there is to it."

Tess clenched her hands into two tight balls and stared off to the side. While she was angry, while she knew it was unfair, guilty thoughts rolled one after the other like tumbleweeds. She'd done something wrong. He wasn't happy with her work. In three seconds flat, she raked her mind over their most recent meetings. Had she said something? Done something untoward? But what?

"I have a proposal to make," Leon said. "Tess?"

Tess sat on her hands and waited. Please, she thought. Just give Burgess back . . .

"I want to give you a new author."

No.

"He's experienced," Leon went on. "If you want to work on something with a little more depth, then I'd like you to try Edward Russell."

Tess searched her memory for the name. Nope, nada.

Nothing.

"I've never heard of him," Tess said. Her voice sounded strangely professional. Tough. Oddly, she felt as if she were dealing with a new person, not the old Leon, not the man who had guided her career. A man who was capable of double-crossing her. Tess wrapped her arms around her body.

"No, you probably wouldn't have heard of him, Tess."

Tess waited.

"He's written . . . poetry, years ago."

"Poetry?"

"Russell's Australian. He published three sets of poems in the 1940s which were, by all accounts, quite well received in that country."

Tess wanted to die on the spot. She thought of Alec and all his success. The glamorous launch parties. The interviews with the press . . .

"Since then, he's written biographies and had a career lecturing."

"Whose biographies?" Tess asked. But she sounded as flat as a floor.

Leon grimaced. "I think they were Australian artists. Maybe a war hero."

"Yep," Tess said.

"No." Leon laid his hands on his knees. "Tess. If you want to show that you can manage a work of depth, then Russell's manuscript should fit the bill."

"But he's not Alec."

"He's not Alec."

"I still cannot believe that this could happen."

"It does happen, Tess. It doesn't mean that you're a bad editor. It's just change."

Tess leaned her head in her hands. "I don't want to edit some washed-up Australian poet's book, Leon. I've worked too hard. I just don't know."

Leon pushed a file toward her. It slid across the surface of her desk until it stopped right at the perfect place. "Edward Russell. *Secret Shores*."

Tess heaved out a sigh. "Leon," she said darkly, "I am at a loss for words."

Leon stood up. "Don't be," he said, sounding cheerful now. "Sometimes, you have to go with the flow—things happen and they work out in the end."

Tess glared at his retreating figure.

She slid her fingers into the folder and picked up the first chapter of the book.

CHAPTER SIX

Melbourne, 1946

Rebecca let herself into her mother's house just after midnight, pulling off her shoes and slipping upstairs with the practiced silence of a thief. She ran her hand up the smooth, polished banister. There was no risk of splinters cutting into her palms here. Everything was polished in Mrs. Swift's house because Rebecca's mother insisted that Rebecca clean every room from top to toe twice a week.

Rebecca had begun to call her mother Mrs. Swift once she realized that her mother's treatment of her had never been Rebecca's fault. When Rebecca was fourteen, her mother had ripped up a drawing Rebecca had taken great care with, soon after her father's death. Rebecca had propped the little sketch up on her bedside table, setting a small jar of daisies from the garden in front of it, along with the teddy bear that her father had bought her and a photograph of him. Her mother took exception to the sketch, telling Rebecca that it was disrespectful to draw her father with a champagne bottle in his hand. But Rebecca had not understood the problem. It was simply how her father had always been. This was when Rebecca had begun to appreciate the extent of her mother's propensity for avoiding the truth.

Mrs. Swift never acknowledged that her husband was an alcoholic. She never talked about the way his bouts of drunken behavior tore at their family's heart. Rebecca ended up screaming her feelings about it in her most private pieces of art. She had hoped, valiantly, for years that Mrs. Swift might miraculously transform. Instead, Rebecca was always told to take herself away when she would burst with exuberance into the smart boutique where her mother worked, hoping beyond everything that Mrs. Swift might listen to her as other mothers did.

Rebecca moved across the landing on the top floor of the bungalow in Elwood. The sound of Mrs. Swift's radio drifted through the house. She tuned it to the same station every night. Jazz. Mrs. Swift liked to think she was modern. It was all part of her meticulous act, which only seemed to have intensified after Rebecca's father's death.

She had never known her father as a real person. He'd been a drunk version of himself, distorted by alcohol whenever he was at home. Her parents' nighttime arguments had been appalling rows during which she hid under her covers. Mrs. Swift locked Rebecca's father in the spare room when he was out of control. Then she had become meticulous about cleanliness after his death, presenting an immaculate front to the world.

When she was little, Rebecca accepted everything as if it were normal—didn't most other people live in houses where there were atrocious fights? But at the same time, her imagination developed. Drawing became a vital means of escape. She could either create her own reality straight from her imagination—drawing a better world— or allow brutal representations of the life she had to endure to emerge. Even now, her art tutor at the Gallery School was alarmed by the passionate nature of the work that appeared in Rebecca's sketchbooks.

She sat there, like all the other students. And put up with the lessons on technique. But technique didn't seem to cut to the heart of what was important in art. Life, Rebecca had come to understand, was like art—you could focus on what didn't matter, technicalities, or you could get to the point. It was the emotion of her drawings that mattered. The deepest truths were the things that were worth seeking out. The modernist movement and its correlating beliefs about both art and life excited her; new ways of living and expression seemed the right answer to the last generation's ills.

The last thing Rebecca needed after the party with her friends, people who thought as she did, was an encounter with her mother. What was more, she didn't want to think about anything other than Edward. Talking with him had felt something like the freedom she experienced when she was painting or drawing. She wanted more of his conversation—he'd also stirred something in her, there was no doubt about that.

Rebecca locked her bedroom door and picked up her pencil. She'd planned each sketch that she was going to make tonight while sitting in the tram travelling down Chapel Street and staring out the window at the darkened shops.

Rebecca selected three pieces of paper, all the same size. Smallish. When she started working, charcoal gave her the scope she needed to achieve the nuance and expression in the faces that she had to convey. She would draw over this, later, with brush and ink, but first she needed to get the essential few strokes that would bring the portraits to life.

The first two sketches were a warm-up of sorts. Max Harris with his dark eyelashes and a cigar in his hand, Joy and her peroxide hair, a knowing expression on her face. Rebecca worked fast on Joy and Max, then lingered for ages over Edward, adjusting her lamp so that it shone where she needed it as she worked into the early hours of the morning, taking great care with each stroke. Each stroke mattered. It was the way she worked. If she couldn't capture the essence of a person in a few lines, then it wasn't worth drawing someone at all. She wanted to capture their character, their true self. There was no point making drawings that didn't speak to anyone. His eyes, green, his hair, dark blond, his expression, amused, she thought, before turning again, a switch back to suddenly serious. By the early hours, she was satisfied that she had captured almost everything she needed to see in him in order to try and distill that moment, that party that had moved her in a way nothing ever had before.

Rebecca remembered that Edward had hinted at his own need to escape. Was his writing driven by the same deep forces as her desire to create? She wanted to know. She'd given him her number when he'd asked and he, in turn, had given her his.

Rebecca collapsed on her old floral-covered bed, reached out, and turned off her light. She still wore her red coat. It wouldn't matter what she had slept in when morning came.

CHAPTER SEVEN

New York, 1987

Late on Friday, Tess reread Edward Russell's first installment and placed it back on her desk, straightening the unmarked sheets of paper so that the pages sat just so. She stood up to look out her office window at the haze and the skyscrapers, avoiding gazing down at the streets below, where people bustled like busy ants and the tops of yellow taxis glimmered as the city roared on in its relentless quest for . . . what?

Now she was thinking like Edward. And yet, at the same time, she pictured the contrast between this sight and Rebecca's last view on this earth: the swirling sea beneath the rocks as she fell to her untimely death. *Her favorite pencil slipped away from her as fast and as easily as everything else. And as Rebecca reached forward for it, in that split second of movement, she knew it was a mistake. She should have let it go . . .* One decision, to pick up a pencil, for goodness' sakes. And a life was extinguished. Edward's words sent a shudder through Tess's system.

Tess ran a hand through her hair and turned away from the window, picking up her empty water glass only to place it back down on her desk. She'd been determined to hate Edward's novel on principle, but she was beguiled by Rebecca Swift. What had happened?

It was frustrating to have the manuscript arriving in small stages. Tess was used to receiving books and reading them in one gluttonous feast on a weekend. Then she would commence a second read and start editing from there, rereading over and over with a sense of the book as a whole as she worked. Edward Russell was throwing everything out of balance.

Yet, despite all the turmoil over losing Alec, she'd come to one decision she planned to stick to no matter what. It was clear that Alec Burgess was gone, so now she was going to pull out all the stops and turn Edward's novel into a bestseller.

She wandered out into the shared office space, only to stop dead at the sight of James Cooper leaning against one of the junior editor's' desks, chatting away with a group of Tess's coworkers as if he was the one who'd worked here for years, not her.

Tess hovered at the edge of the room.

"I love *The Sound of Music*!" James insisted to the group of women surrounding him.

Tess stood still and watched. Embarrassed glances had met her whenever she ventured out of her office. Word had travelled about her demotion, about the fact that she'd been cast aside for the publishing house's newest recruit. She'd shut herself away with Edward's manuscript to avoid people, had made contact with all her other clients. Tried to instill excitement in some lackluster careers. She had a firm belief in many of her writers. But now, to her surprise, she knew that it was Edward with whom she wanted to speak.

"You love *The Sound of Music*?" one of the accountants squeaked. Her eyes shone as she peered up at the deity.

Tess rolled her eyes to the roof.

"Yes," James said, dropping his voice just enough so that everyone leaned in close.

"I confess, I'm softhearted," he went on, his dark eyes twinkling and a pearly-white grin spreading across his face as he glanced around his audience. "I adore that film."

"Oh, you're a closet romantic." Leon's personal assistant faked a swoon.

Oh, for pity's sake, Tess wanted to mutter. The only romantic bone in James's body was directed toward his own ego. James represented everything that Edward abhorred in his book: social privilege, courting the right people, unquestionable wealth . . .

Tess straightened herself and moved over to the group. This was her territory. She was the social leader around here. The sooner her coworkers realized that James was a fraud, the better, in her opinion.

Everyone quieted awkwardly as Tess approached. Eyes darted to the side, to the floor, away from her. Anywhere. Tess paused halfway across the room, but only for one tiny split second, before marching on toward them. Head up. She held James's gaze. The expression on his face softened. Just a bit.

"Are we leaving soon?" Tess asked. They always went out for drinks around this time on a Friday. And Tess was always the one who organized it. "Shall we go to the White Stallion?"

Tess sensed some of her colleagues relaxing. People started moving about, collecting bags in the way they usually would.

"Sounds good, Tess," one of the young male editors said.

There was a sense of relief among them, as if Tess were back in the saddle.

Tess caught James's eye and narrowed her own eyes at him. She could do charming. She could outcharm him. "We usually go out for drinks on a Friday. But you've probably already got plans." He'd only arrived two weeks ago, and he hadn't shown any interest in drinks yet.

"No. I don't, as it turns out," James said, his voice perfectly even. "I'd love to come."

"Fabulous!" one of the assistants crooned.

"Right," Tess said. She wasn't giving away her feelings of disgust toward him here. "Well then. Let's all get going."

The walk to the bar was full of camaraderie. Everybody seemed to be looking forward to the weekend. The chat was about baseball games and kids' birthday parties, dates and all the usual routines. James walked in silence next to Tess.

"Are you okay?" he asked, his voice deadly quiet.

"Of course I am," she said, staring straight ahead.

She wanted to get away from him, her sense of fury now mingled with a need to move on. She also, annoyingly, fought with the urge to have things out, no matter where she and James were or whom they were with.

As they reached the pub, James held the door open for her. One of the team had found a table. James stuck to Tess like adhesive tape.

"What would you like to drink?" he asked.

"I can get myself a drink."

James glanced at the crowded bar and raised a brow. "No, I'll do it," he said, in a low, determined voice.

Tess looked up at him. Her voice cracked when she spoke. "Tell me, James, do you win every argument?"

But James leaned forward then, and he spoke close to her ear. "Give it a rest, Tess. It's Friday night. Don't you know how to chill?"

"Unlike some people, I don't put on an act. I have no need to brag about what I watch, for goodness' sakes," Tess said. "I prefer to play the game straight. I can get my own drink, James."

"No. I'm going to buy you a champagne." He bellied up to the bar, trying—successfully of course—to catch the eye of the bartender.

But Tess knew she was fired up. She followed him. She was not going to let him get away. A crowded bar was the perfect place. And Tess needed to get things out.

"So tell me, James, when exactly did you approach my client? Was it before you'd heard about his new book, or afterward? Perhaps you can give me some tips on how to steal other people's jobs."

James threw his head back, his handsome features breaking into a cynical grin. He was impossibly close. Tess was more than aware of, and revolted by, the fact that he was probably trying to win her over along with everyone else—his dazzling good looks must have worked all his life. He ran a tanned hand over his chin. "Look, Tess. Leon obviously thought I was the best person to edit Alec's new book. End of story. I didn't approach anyone. It's simply not what I'd do."

Tess felt her chest stiffen. "Taking on an author who's already a bestseller? Now there's a challenge. Sure you haven't just seen the opportunity to steal someone else's safe bet? Like . . . let's think . . . mine? Except, oh yes, I already took the risk with Alec years ago. I built his career. So . . . you will be doing, what exactly? Nothing? Smooth move. Is that how you've gotten all your authors?"

James handed her a glass of champagne. "Drink up. It might help you loosen that brittle facade."

Tess held up the glass and took a sip. "Cheers, James. Well done."

He leaned in close. "I had nothing to do with any collusion against you," he whispered in her ear. "I would never do that."

Tess turned to him, unable to hold back the laugh that rose in her throat.

"Unfortunately my resistance to fake charm is at an all-time . . . high. And my naïveté is at its lowest point ever. Don't lie to me, James. I'm just not in the mood."

James caught her arm.

She swung around to face him.

"This is intriguing me," he went on, his eyes latching on to hers. "Why are you so upset? It's business. I was simply given the author. He wanted to move. I had nothing to do with it."

"And you spared no second thought for the person who'd done all the background work for Alec for years. Why should I expect you to?

Due to your sense of entitlement and privilege, you think you can step all over others without a backward glance."

He seemed to jolt back a little, his dark eyes looking hurt suddenly.

Tess raised her glass to him.

But he still held her elbow.

"I don't know why you're taking this so seriously," he murmured. "It's not personal."

"Excuse me?" Tess's voice rose with the words. "The last time I checked, I was a person, James. It's just that you consider some people—people who will get you up the ladder which you worship over everything else—to be more important than others."

He let go of her elbow.

"But you know what, James?" Tess liked the galvanization of her voice. "You know something? There's no challenge in what you've done. Everyone realizes it's going to be easy to ensure Alec's book sells big, but making Edward Russell a bestselling author, that's going to be hard. If I can pull that off, then I've won this. And you know what? Nothing is going to stop me from turning Russell into a great success. In fact, I'd like to thank you. I'll rise to the occasion, you'll see."

He blew out a breath and shook his head. Glanced across at the crowd at the table. "I'm going back to meet our colleagues. All I can say is that I never wanted to harm your career."

And he turned.

"Spoiled rich boys who've never known a challenge or hardship aren't interesting in any way, James," Tess murmured loud enough so he could hear. "It's clear you fall into that category. No matter how hard you try to convince everyone here that you're something different, your veneer will never convince me."

She took a swig of her champagne and glared at his retreating back.

Round one.

Tess swooped into her office on Monday morning, picked up the phone, and dialed Rome. She'd spent the weekend working up a plan for Russell's book. And she'd come up with the perfect answer.

"Pronto," Edward Russell said.

Tess smiled at the charming Italian way he answered the phone. She'd heard Nico do the same thing in the café.

"Mr. Russell. Tess Miller from Campbell and Black." Tess swiveled her chair around to face the window. She had this in the bag.

"Please call me Edward."

"I'm looking forward to working with you, Edward. And I have to say that I'm loving your manuscript so far. It's very moving. I can't wait for the next installment. And I have so many ideas for marketing this book. But first, I have three things I want to discuss with you—deadlines, pre-release promotions, and finally, I want to make an editorial suggestion that I think is crucial at this stage."

There was a silence.

Tess twirled her gold pen around in her fingers. Visions of James Cooper kept appearing in her head. He may have won everyone over on Friday night at the pub—half the female staff had announced they had crushes the size of watermelons on him. But a few party tricks and some underhand dealings in order to get himself a job here did not mean he'd take her spot as the most successful editor at Campbell and Black. The fact was that she was intrigued by Edward Russell's book. It had beguiled her; she was fascinated by the Reeds and the world that the characters were about to enter. She wanted more and that was good . . .

Edward was still quiet.

Tess leaned forward in her seat. She loved doing this, exciting her authors, getting them enthused. Loved the way they responded to her well-tested routine. Alec had responded the best. She just had to groom Edward to replace him.

"Edward," she said. "First, I want to talk about the setting. I know that you're Australian, I know that writers like to write about their own country. But I want to suggest that we make some changes to the locations in *Secret Shores*. I'm thinking Boston. The themes will fit right in there; there are no problems with that. And as for Rebecca's death scene, there are plenty of places along the East Coast that would work well. You don't want to alienate US readers. I promise you, it will make all the difference. I'm excited about it. That's point number one."

She smiled at the gasp down the line. She'd prepared for this.

"I know you have the historical context in . . . Australia, and that's fascinating, but you can make it up and set it here. Your characters are profoundly interesting. I'm so taken with Rebecca. And Edward. Just change the setting. You know what to do."

"I'm sorry, I'm not sure that I heard you correctly. You want me to transfer the *Angry Penguins* and our modernist heritage to the US?"

"Change the names and set it in the US, Edward. You can still write about the same theme—you are onto something so strong that it will transcend setting. But it needs to be the US." Tess stared out at the tops of the skyscrapers. She'd bring him to New York. Start with some talk shows on the radio. Even his voice was charming, and so deep—it would resonate like a dream on the radio. Now that she'd . . . lost Alec, she'd accompany Edward on his book tours. She visualized the pair of them . . . He'd be a huge hit on the East Coast, and even in California, they'd like his messages. This was going to be great . . .

"No. That's not authentic," he said. "Have you realized what the book is about? It's all about a way of life that is real. It is the whole point."

"Exactly," Tess said. "The themes are fascinating. But you need to set them somewhere that readers can relate to. I'm sorry, but I'll have real trouble marketing a book set in Australia. And you're not well known in the US, Edward. It's a tough market right now."

"The setting stays as it is."

Tess startled in her seat. "Edward," she said, "you are a talented writer. But you've spent your whole career largely undiscovered. I can change all that for you. I can bring you the success that you, quite frankly, deserve. Your work is touching. I'm moved by it and I'm your most hardened reader ever. But you need to trust me. You must work with me, or the book won't sell and then I won't be able to take on anything more from you. Please, let's do this. We need to work together. I want to complement you, not drag you down. I know you haven't worked with a big publishing house before. And you see, we do things differently from the independent houses you've experienced with your poems and biographies in the past. I want to make this a huge success. Build your career. This is exciting. I'm excited. I haven't read anything like this for a long time . . ."

Tess made a face at her reflection in the window. How old was he? Sixty-five? Thanks, Leon. Darn you, James. She forced the fact that Alec Burgess was only in his late thirties right out of her mind.

Although, in any case, Edward still could build a career, even at sixty-five. He could write another ten books. Tess was certain that if they worked hard together, Edward could have a wonderful future ahead of him. It was just what they both needed. Perhaps Nico was right. Maybe this was meant to be. It wasn't what Tess had wanted, but maybe it was just what she needed right now. Edward would give Tess experience editing something more literary that would also sell. She would be able to use all those years of studying the classics to good end, sink her teeth into something with real depth and give Edward the career he had always wanted. It was a win-win.

Tess spun her seat back to her desk and reached for his file. She'd get him moving.

"Tess, what you don't understand is that my work has always been based on truthfulness." Edward spoke in a well-modulated voice. "If you haven't gathered that about me from reading the manuscript, then I suggest you're not the best editor for my work."

Tess sat bolt upright in her seat. No, no, no. She was exactly what he needed! Her plans were terrific!

She rubbed her forefinger on the top of her nose. She couldn't afford to lose him now. "Okay. All right. Let's talk about the setting later."

Strategy number two. She had to keep him in her sights. Couldn't afford to lose him . . . softly softly and all that . . .

"The setting stays in Australia, where it's meant to be," he said. "I couldn't give a darn about the money. I'm perfectly fine as I am," Edward said.

I don't think so . . . Tess did not retort. *You could be doing better . . .*

"Next, I'd like to sort out a timeline," she said. She was used to running her author meetings. Not the other way around.

"Pardon?"

"We'd like to release your book as soon as possible. So, I'd like to work out some deadlines. Here's the schedule: I'd like the whole manuscript as soon as possible. I take it you're writing it in stages, but I'd like to see the entire book in six months."

"No, no, no."

Tess placed her pen back on the desk.

"Tess. Let's get one thing straight. I don't work to deadlines."

You don't work to deadlines. *What?* The idea of a voodoo doll seemed appealing right now. Or perhaps two? One with an enormous . . . bow tie. The other one with a great toothpaste grin and dark hair made of ribbons. Lots of black ribbons. Tess's fingers itched to hold some pins.

"Tess. I'm sorry, but I suggest you go back and read my work again. Did you read it properly the first time?" His voice was soft as silk.

"I did, Edward." Tess muttered the words.

"Well. You seem to entirely miss the point. In fact, you seem to refuse, obstinately, to understand the truth about it. I don't even use a typewriter. I need an editor who understands what we were about."

Tess threw her hands up in the air. "You don't type?" She picked up the first couple of chapters of his book. Ah. Someone here had typed it up for her, knowing that she'd have a fit if she was handed a manuscript written with a pen. Tess leaned her head in her hand and propped her elbows on the desk.

"I can't tell you when each installment will arrive. I don't work that way."

Kill me now. Tess swallowed her groan.

"I write when the muse strikes—"

"Edward!" she said, gritting her teeth and staring at the wood grain patterns on her desk. Antique again, like everything else in this firm that needed shaking up. "I am sorry, but we need to sort out a timeline, or this won't work. I can't wait months for the next installment. We need to work out marketing strategies for your book. And please, would you think about the setting carefully? My editorial opinion is that we should change it, because if we don't we risk the book not selling, and that will stall your career."

"Miss Miller." Edward's voice rang into the room. "I am not happy with your complete disrespect for the nature of my work, with your disregard for the manner in which I have always carried it out, and with your blatant desire to water down the very essence of what the entire novel is about by setting it in your own bloody country!"

Tess placed her entire head on the desk.

"Are we clear?"

All her ideas for his success down the sinkhole, then.

"Fine," she said. "Fine." She'd have to pull this together somehow, but she needed to think. "Please consider my thoughts. And we will talk soon."

"I suggest you seriously consider your approach if you want to continue editing my work," Edward said. "I wasn't going to go to large publishing houses for this very reason. I'm beginning to think that I've made a dreadful mistake."

Tess stared intently at her desk, the wood grain patterns seeming to jump about and move of their own accord now. "You haven't made a mistake. I'll work with you. And together, we'll work this out." *Because I believe in your talent,* she thought. But she wasn't going to tell him that. Clearly, he already seemed to know.

Silence.

"I'll look forward to speaking with you soon," she said, and hung up.

Tess straightened herself, sitting back up in her seat.

Only to come eye to eye with James Cooper standing at her office door. He folded his arms and leaned against the frame. Tess shot him a look that would stop a firing squad.

"That didn't sound too good."

"Eavesdropping. You have the right to do that, too, do you?" Tess stood up, moved to the table under her window, and poured herself a glass of water.

"I heard you were working with Edward Russell."

Tess stared out the window at the buildings that seemed to sway in the haze.

James strolled into her office.

She saw his reflection in the window, watching in disbelief while he stopped and perched on her desk.

"I have things to do," she said. "At what point did I invite you in?" Her voice was calm enough.

James said, "I want to clear the air between us. There's nothing to be gained by us being in conflict."

Tess stifled a laugh. Her career was everything to her. Alec had been everything to her career.

"At least this way the author is staying with Campbell and Black," he said.

"Don't you dare suggest he was going to leave. He wasn't." She felt anger coil in her like some dark serpent. She wanted to kick him out of her office. But she wouldn't do that.

James was watching her.

She stood perfectly straight, arms wrapped around her body, tight as clamps.

James didn't move. And then, slowly, he placed something on her desk. He must have had it in his hand the whole time.

"I thought you might like this," he said, his voice suddenly soft. "It's from my father's collection."

Tess felt her eyes narrowing into slits.

James simply nodded at her before walking out.

After a while, Tess glanced down. It was a book. She picked it up, in spite of her fury. A first-edition, leather-bound copy of Edward Russell's poems. His name and the date were embossed on the front in gold.

1946.

CHAPTER EIGHT

Melbourne, 1946

Edward picked up the notes he'd taken during the first lecture the morning after the party and wandered out of the lecture hall into the bright Melbourne sun. It still startled him sometimes, the clear Australian light, even though he had been back in the country for well over eighteen months. Edward chose not to dwell on the fact that if his accident had not sent him home, he would probably have been killed in the D-day landings.

He stopped in the shade of a Moreton Bay fig tree on the path that led away from the university's oldest college, pulling out the slip of paper on which he had written Rebecca Swift's phone number. He was still surprised he had managed to ask her for it before leaving the party last night. He had never seen himself as a smooth talker. He felt that he lacked the skill that so many of his war compatriots had with girls. His air force mates effortlessly chatted up women when they had been stationed in Tasmania, training as pilots just out of Launceston in the early years of the war. Taking advantage of the local girls had seemed wrong to him. Now, at twenty-four, he smiled at the serious-ness of his youth.

Trips to Cataract Gorge at midnight with female company had become de rigueur for his friends, but Edward chose to stay back at camp and write. He laughed alongside the others about their antics. He would never judge them, but he knew he wanted something differ-ent for himself, something with more depth and honest feeling than a fumble in a park. It had always been that way.

His next lecture started in ten minutes. He wanted to call Rebecca now.

But Edward needed a telephone. And the only place in the univer-sity that had a students' phone was the office in the union building. This was furnished with a cedar desk where a woman in a soft butter-yellow cardigan sat reading the paper. She peered at Edward over her glasses as if he were interrupting her from some important task.

"Could I use the telephone to make a call?" he asked, then cursed his own stupidity. As his sister, Vicky, would point out, why else was he going to use the telephone?

"Two pence," the woman said. "A two-minute time limit for all calls."

Edward handed the money over and felt his cheeks reddening as he walked to the small wooden cubicle that afforded only a small vestige of privacy.

What he was going to do if Rebecca did not answer, he had no idea. But she had said that her classes started at eleven on a Wednesday—it was her late morning. So all he could do was hope.

When she answered, she sounded confident, the Rebecca whom he had spotted first. The fact that he now thought of two Rebeccas made him smile a little as he held the phone to his mouth.

"Hello?"

"Rebecca." He swallowed. "It's Edward Russell, from last night . . . how are you?"

Her laugh lilted down the line. "I'm just fine, thank you, Edward. Where are you?"

Edward smiled. The confident Rebecca for certain. "University," he said. He would have liked to elaborate, but he was acutely aware of butter-yellow cardigan. "Listen, Rebecca." A breath. "I wanted to get in touch to see if you might be free . . . tonight."

"I'm supposed to be studying!" She rushed out the words.

Even her voice was delicious.

"What are you doing now?" she asked, after a brief silence.

Now? He grinned. A lecture on Milton . . .

"Nothing," he said.

"Perfect." She gave him her address—Elwood, not far from the beach. As Edward hung up and slipped out into the hot day, his head was full of plans. Where could he take her?

His step was light as he strolled to Grattan Street. Until he stopped dead on the sidewalk. His Aston Martin sparkled in the sun. He hadn't even thought about that little problem until he encountered it now, sitting there as if nothing were amiss. Edward hesitated, his hand raking over his chin. Normally its gleaming pale blue trim and the chrome grille polished to a high sheen—by the chauffeur whom his mother insisted that they still employ—would not even register with him before he climbed inside and wove his way back to Toorak. But now it was almost painful to look at the little car.

What would Rebecca think?

The two-seater convertible was a knockout, something he knew most girls would jump into at the snap of a finger. But how would Rebecca react to his wealth? There was no doubt that his background was about as far from hers in Elwood as a fairy-tale castle was from a Nissen hut. He'd put off troublesome thoughts about how he'd explain his background to a modernist after the party last night, preferring instead to remain in the dreamy haze that meeting Rebecca had induced. But there was nothing for it. He was going to have to raise the topic of his family at some point and just see how she would react.

He proceeded to the car.

Once he'd made his way through the city and down toward the bay-side suburb where she lived, any doubts Edward had felt about his family's status, not to mention their political stance—opposed to everyone's at the party last night—were overtaken by excitement at the prospect of seeing Rebecca again. He pulled up outside her house, a bungalow on Dawson Avenue, which ran directly to the beach. Perhaps they would stroll along the sand today. Avoid the car entirely. He jumped over the door, landing on the sidewalk with its trimmed trees.

Rebecca's garden was also seriously maintained. The front fence, which was whitewashed and low, was freshly painted and the front lawn was edged with clipped hedges and flower beds that stood sentinel in the heat. Not even the searing summer had caused them to droop. He wondered if Rebecca was expected to stand at attention in the same way. She had mentioned her mother . . .

Edward stood on the long veranda, running his hands through his honey-gold hair. The front door was black, with a brass knocker in the shape of a fist. Even outside, the stink of caustic cleaning products was potent in the afternoon heat.

Before he had a chance to raise his hand and knock, Rebecca opened the door. She wore a white cotton dress studded with tiny red flowers. Her dark hair waved underneath a wide-brimmed hat, cascading down her shoulders in the most charming fashion. She wore red lipstick, something that Edward knew his mother and sister would detest, and red-heeled sandals.

He grinned. "You look delicious," he said, reaching forward instinctively and kissing her on the cheek.

Rebecca linked her arm through his. "Let's get out of here," she said. "I'd invite you inside, but Mrs. Swift's seats are no good for anything but perching. She's got them covered in shining plastic in case any visitors leave a stain."

Edward felt his forehead crinkle into a frown. Her tone was light, but he suspected that was deliberate, and he hated to hear about her home life being in any way constrained. He led her around the front lawn, taking care to remain on the immaculate path that circled the green space. "I'm glad of one thing about your mother."

"What's that?"

"I'm glad she works in a boutique," he said. "Your outfits are charming. You obviously have flair."

"Oh! Do you like my hat?" Rebecca performed a little twirl by the front gate before leaning down and opening it, then standing aside for Edward to go out.

"Yes, I do like your hat."

But Rebecca had spotted the car. She looked up at him, her brown eyes widening in the most adorable of ways.

Edward laughed then. "You are funny," he said. "I'm afraid it's mine, but I thought we'd walk along the beach. If you like."

Rebecca smiled at him from under her hat. "I'm not going to tell you that I'm impressed by your car. I would never do that. Follow me."

He laughed again and held out his arm. She took it. He wanted to take her hand in his other hand and hold that too. He glanced down at its softness where it rested in the crook of his elbow.

Edward stopped for a moment once they reached the end of the street, taking in the expanse of white, unspoiled sand. During the war the only trips he had made to the seaside had been quick visits to one of the family beach houses when on leave, where the landscape was wild and windswept, with waves from the Southern Ocean crashing treacherously on the rocks.

But here, there was none of that. Several children played in the shallow, clear water. The beach's gentle beauty was perfect for a first date, and that was what he hoped this would turn out to be.

Edward held Rebecca's hand while they walked. The feel of it was exactly as he had imagined, and the closeness of her was almost impossible to resist as she walked with him, her hand swinging in his as if it were the most natural thing in the world.

"I talked your head off last night," she said. "I want to know all about you. For a start, you must be terribly dashing."

Edward sighed. Where was he supposed to begin? "I hope that doesn't put you off."

"Do you?" she asked, her tone razor sharp.

"Yes," he said, keeping his voice firm. "Well, Rebecca, the thing is, you see, my family own property. Actually, quite a lot."

Rebecca was quiet beside him, but she nodded.

Edward focused on the old broken jetty ahead and went on. "I may as well tell it to you straight. We own three sheep stations in South Australia. My great-great-grandfather started up the first Merino station in the country—it's now the largest and has been since late last century. My great-great-grandfather literally stepped off the boat from England and agreed to drive three hundred sheep across the country to the new colony in South Australia, on foot all the way from New South Wales in 1841. In return, he was given a land grant. He kept a portion of those sheep, and throughout his lifetime, expanded his holdings, ending up with most of the land we own now. The main property, where we live most of the time, is called Haslemere. My grandfather, his only heir, then turned the house and garden into something quite . . . beautiful. He caused the sheep stations to thrive and bought another one in the west of the state, and, I guess, started up this sort of idea that the family would live like English aristocracy here in Australia. Due to my grandfather's efforts, the family ended up with . . . well, a steamship on which they travelled to England, apartments in London, a house here in Melbourne, and two beach houses in South Australia as well. I know it's all rather grandiose. I struggle with it and I do understand how it conflicts with . . . modernist views."

He stopped. Rebecca was staring straight ahead, her expression intent. Edward shuffled his shoes in the sand. Had he killed their budding friendship before it had a chance to take off?

She picked up a stone from the foreshore and threw it out into the sparkling water, then watched its ripple effect.

"I felt more at home with the people at that party last night than I ever have with my family's wealth. The war changed everything for me, and I guess deep down I've never believed that people should be judged on their social standing, or that others should be exploited for my family's sake. I'm not sure whether my feelings are justified, given my immense privilege, but at the same time, meeting Sunday and John was riveting—I'm not the only one who feels constricted by my background, no matter how much I care about my family."

"The thing is, with all the wealth comes . . ." He hesitated. Was he boring her? Sounding like a wealthy upper-class fool?

But she faced him, her expression serious. "Keep telling me. I want to know."

He swallowed, but she stood there, her brown eyes clear.

His voice was shaky, but at the same time, some strange urgency propelled him to speak. Had he ever told anyone how he truly felt about his life before?

"I don't want to sound unappreciative. But the thing is, I was sent away to boarding school when I was seven. My mother, bored with life in the country, spent most of my childhood years travelling in Europe. It was important to her to be presented at court. That sort of thing . . ."

"Did she come home for your school holidays?" Her question was so to the point that Edward smiled.

"No." It became easier to talk. "There were a few desperate Christmases when I did write to her and beg her to come home. But she didn't seem to see the point of being here. Didn't seem to think it mattered. So, no, I didn't go home on the holidays, unless my older brother and father came to pick me up, which happened . . . once over the years."

Rebecca looked out over the water. "You hear of artists and actors and writers having these darned unstable lives," she said. "It's as if we are blamed for that. But I often wonder whether it's the other way around. I think people become artists and writers as a result of the situations that are forced upon them."

Edward took a step toward her, reaching out a hand to stroke her face. Her skin was soft and tanned and flawless. The sense of intimacy between them hit him with such acuteness that Edward never wanted it to go away.

"You're spot-on, Rebecca. And I think you're right about the things we can't see being the things that matter in this world of ours. I'm glad I met you."

"Tell me what happened after boarding school," she whispered. "Tell me the story."

He wanted to lean down and kiss her. But he daren't. Not yet.

"I trained in the air force," he said, his voice still shaking a little, but perhaps it was only nervousness. "I was sent to France as a pilot. I wasn't a bomber pilot, but I dropped parachutists who were helping with the resistance, until my plane crashed in the south of England. At which point I was sent home with injuries and assigned to shuttle runs up and down the Australian coast."

"Thank goodness," she said, and looked up at him, a gentle expression on her face.

He marveled a little at what he knew was her genuine warmth. The world seemed so brash at times. And people seemed brash too. Edward had never quite fit in with any of it, he knew that. As for the war, the whole thing seemed to be the most monumental cock-up of all.

"Rebecca," he said, still adoring the sound of her name on his lips. "Can you promise me something?"

She turned to look up at him. "I can."

"Don't tell anyone what I've told you about my family," he said. "I have never confessed how I feel about their—our—way of life to anyone."

She held a finger up to his lips. "I'm good at keeping secrets," she whispered.

And he reached out a hand, ran it down the side of her cheek, leaned forward, and kissed her softly, a whisper on her lips.

CHAPTER NINE

New York, 1987

Tess opened the small leather-bound book of poetry, stopping to read the title. *Still Life, A Collection of Poems.* The pages were made of thin paper. Tess was careful when she turned them, as they were delicate, and each one was edged with gold. Gilt. It was something Edward had known all his life. The little book seemed somehow representative of a time when people took care with the production of things, a past when Edward's family must have lived surrounded by unimaginable luxuries such as this beautiful little book.

The poems were testaments to a kaleidoscope of emotions—the flare of love, pain, cries for the devastation of war—while his sense of the landscape around his home wound itself into each piece like a silken ribbon. He wrote about its lingering beauty in spite of cold, hard human catastrophe during the war years, while love whispered too, remaining the one strength that could redeem humans in the aftermath of all the destruction.

The book was published in 1946 with a preface written by John Reed.

Tess placed the book in her briefcase, settling it in its own compartment. She gathered her coat, her mind still drifting toward the soft gum trees and paddocks where flocks of wild birds would take flight into the vast Australian sky. Practical matters seemed of less importance somehow, and she wanted to linger in the atmosphere he'd created. She didn't want to think about anything else, not for a while. It was a long time since she'd read work that moved her in this way—years, perhaps?

She moved out of the office, her head down.

And froze in her tracks when she reached reception.

James and Alec Burgess stood together by the elevators. As the doors opened, Tess felt her insides coil as James rested a hand on Alec's back, motioning for him to go in first.

Suddenly, Tess felt an urge to confront them both with their betrayal. It was so strong that she found herself marching toward them as they stood in the elevator, placing her hands between the doors as they tried to slide closed, prizing them open and placing one red-heeled shoe between them.

"Tess?" James reached forward and slid the doors fully open for her.

Ever charming. Tess muttered her thanks. She forced herself to push any lingering ideas about beauty, about Edward's belief in things that mattered, right out of her head. Instead she eyed James, her gaze beady and dark.

James looked away. In the uncomfortable silence that was only punctuated by the soft sounds of the elevator descending, Tess turned to Alec, who had the grace to stare down at the floor, as if there were something fascinating happening around his feet.

"Going out for a drink?" she said, sounding as nonchalant as a schoolgirl making plans for a milkshake.

Something wicked slipped in. Why should she be a victim, standing by and taking all of this rotten behavior? Well and good, she would do her best to work with Edward Russell, no matter how difficult he seemed to be. But at the same time, her sense of being betrayed was not going to disappear fast.

James squared his shoulders and coughed slightly, before placing his hands in his pockets and leaning against the side of the elevator. Tess sensed his eyes on her, and his posture, his relaxed, avant-garde approach, fanned further flames. How dare he? How dare he be so casual about taking her hard-won, coveted author out for drinks, or for dinner, or perhaps to some club, Tess thought irritably. A men's club. That would be it.

"How is your new . . . partnership going?" she asked, her voice dripping with the allure that she knew James possessed.

Both men looked at the elevator buttons. Alec shuffled up and down on his heels.

"I never had the chance to hand things over. It's funny, how you can cut someone off, someone who has worked hard and been loyal to you, without a backward glance. It's something I could never do." She sounded bright now, as if her words were laced with some new flavor. She swept her glance from one of them to the other.

Alec ran a hand through his hair, which was just starting to thin a little on top. He'd admitted such a thing to Tess only last week, when they'd had lunch together.

"Look, Tess . . ." Alec's voice cracked a little when he pronounced her name. "It's nothing personal."

The elevator came to a standstill. They were on the ground floor. The time between the thud of the landing and the doors opening seemed interminable.

Tess was not going to be in the business of making things easier for either of these men.

There was an awkwardness while both James and Alec waited for Tess to leave the elevator first. James held the door open.

"After you, Tess," he said.

A cynical smile appeared on her face as she swished past him out to the lobby. They all stopped by the fountain, the most ill-at-ease group in the world. Tess arched her brow and folded her arms hard against her chest.

"You know," Alec said. He reached a hand toward her, only to draw it back. "Thank you for all you've done for me. You've been great."

The breath Tess let out was audible.

James glanced around the lobby. Was he hoping someone would come to relieve him from this awkward conversation?

Tess stayed put. "I won't pretend I wasn't stunned," she said. "Forgive me for thinking that I put in all the hard work and have been sidelined now that you are famous and successful, Alec. It's just not something I thought you'd do."

"Perhaps we should all go out for a drink," James said. He sounded firm. Confident. Tess wanted to kick him.

"I don't think that we should have any bad blood between us over this," he went on.

"I wish you all the success in the world for your future novels, Alec." Tess cut James off, even forced herself to smile at them both. "But I don't want to come out for a drink with you, because that would be insincere. Not authentic, you see." She winced at the way she'd adopted Edward's language.

"Tess." James, unbelievably, spoke her name as if it were a warning.

But Tess cut him off. Her voice cracked a little now. "Truly, I wish you all the best for the remainder of your career, Alec. I'm sure James is a fine editor and I'm sure you will continue on with great success." She held her head up.

Alec took a step closer to her, then back again.

"Goodbye, Alec. Goodbye, James," Tess said, and strode toward the door to Fifth Avenue.

While her insides churned, and in spite of the fact that she had no idea how she was going to convince Edward Russell to see sense, she knew that she'd found something in Edward's work that was more genuine and honest than anything she'd seen in that elevator today. And she was going to stick with Edward now. She was going to make her new author into a success, no matter how difficult he was turning out to be. She could do it. Alec was testament to the fact that she'd done it before . . . only this time, she would not be overthrown by James Cooper. In fact, she swore she would never be bulldozed again.

CHAPTER TEN

Melbourne, 1946

It was still light as Edward's car purred past the late nineteenth-century mansions of Toorak—each immaculate property a remnant of the wealth that had flooded into Melbourne during the booming gold rush days that started in the 1850s, when one of the world's richest shallow goldfields caused Victoria to be described as California all over again. In the following decades, the city became known as "marvelous Melbourne," one of the world's biggest cosmopolitan cities. And yet now there was almost an atmosphere of hush in the tree-lined streets of the most prestigious suburb. The green lushness of it all seemed to offer protection from life's ills.

And yet a happy family was something that had eluded both him and Rebecca. Wealth was no cure for difficult relationships.

Edward pulled into the driveway, parking his car behind his father's Rolls-Royce. The family butler appeared at the front door the moment Edward climbed out. Edward slammed the car door shut with a more ferocious snap than he meant and grimaced at the familiar facade of the redbrick mansion that his grandfather had built at the turn of the century.

It was hard to say when this feeling of unease at his family's wealth had begun; it had crept up on him over the years. Being stuck in a Nissen hut crowded with men sleeping in rows on camp beds had opened Edward's eyes to the way that he'd taken his privileged position for granted. He'd formed some of the most genuine friendships of his life during the war years. But he'd never confessed his wealth to the friends he'd made during that time. Instead, he'd enjoyed the freedom that came with being out of Australia and not, for all purposes, a member of the famous Russell pastoral family.

Now he moved past the ivy-covered facade of the house, three stories high with twenty windows looking onto the street. The exterior was imposing—Georgian with four tall chimneys standing sentinel on the roof. Edward greeted the butler and went into the grand entrance hall, wondering if he could make an escape upstairs to his room.

But his mother called out to him from her post in the living room that overlooked the back garden. The clink of her glass on a table resonated into the entrance hall. It was drinks time. Rituals governed the Russell household and the family stuck to them as if they were a pillar of support in themselves. Edward placed his car keys on the walnut hall table and strode past the formal rooms to the living room, with its French doors overlooking the Mediterranean garden out the back. His parents still employed three gardeners here full-time.

"How was university?" Celia Russell was arranged on a silk sofa by the fireplace, her strawberry blond hair falling in waves around her gamine face. Birdsong fluted in through the open doors. A glass bowl of pale roses sat on the mantelpiece. Celia had a room dedicated to arranging flowers. The flower-arranging room was the only room that the female members of the family entered apart from their bedrooms and the living rooms in the house. It had been this way for generations.

The women in Edward's family never went into the kitchens or to any of the practical areas of the house, nor would they dare intrude on the study or the gentlemen's parlors that were the domain of men.

When a maid appeared with canapés, Edward's father, Angus, arrived as if on cue from the garden. He removed his white panama hat, laying it on the polished mahogany table by the door, then stood framed in the doorway, his feet wide apart. Edward had inherited his father's green eyes and blond hair, his tall height. As far as personality traits, Edward hoped that he had inherited very little at all.

"Ah," Angus said. "I see you've returned from the fray, Edward."

Edward moved over to the drinks cabinet, poured himself a sherry, and helped himself to a slice of cucumber topped with a sliver of radish and a swirl of cream cheese. Angus always behaved as if Edward had returned from battle, whether he had been at school, out with friends, or to the library to escape and read a book.

When Vicky appeared, a petite version of her mother, she sashayed across the room, helping herself to a delicate serving from a plate of yet more cucumber arrangements. The vegetables had been delivered straight from the hothouse at Haslemere, just one of the many alluring features of the property north of the wine country in South Australia where the family's fortunes had originated in the 1840s.

"Edward's been naughty," Vicky said, ignoring the drinks and settling herself down next to her mother, who patted the sofa with her manicured hand. "You were spotted heading toward Little Collins Street, Edward. Last night. Not those infamous bohemians, surely? There are wild rumors about them!"

Angus poured himself his first glass of brandy. Once he had finished, he reached for his own particular wine glass, filling it to the brim with claret and making his way back to the French doors to stand there again. Master of the house; Edward couldn't hold back the thought. And what a sham that idea was, a voice inside his head mocked.

But Edward sat down, too, and sipped at his sherry. "How has everyone's day been?" Vicky was clearly bored. And onto him. He would have to divert her.

"More to the point," said Angus, "how did your day go? I hope that university course is teaching you something useful. How long did you say it lasts? Three years, was it? Couldn't you study commerce? Something useful like Robert is going to do now that the war is over?" Angus's words hung in the beautifully decorated room.

Edward put his sherry glass down on a table. The drink tasted acrid. He'd had the same conversation with his father over and over again.

Edward needed to slip out of delightful Rebecca Swift mode into family combat mode, and fast. "We are studying the classics at the moment, Milton and Chaucer." Would he ever give up hoping that someday they might understand?

"Oh, I adore the fact that you are clever, Ed." Vicky examined her nails. "But do tell us where you were last night. Was it somewhere deliciously naughty?" She sat forward, an eager expression on her face. "Have you met someone interesting? Are you going to become an *artiste*?" She threw off the last word with a flourish.

Edward chuckled and crossed his legs. What a funny girl she was. "I wish I had the talent to do so, but sadly, darling Vicky, I cannot paint."

"But who did you meet?"

Vicky was going to persist.

Edward shrugged. "People," he said. "Sunday and John Reed, Max Harris, Joy Hester." The noise of the party flashed into his head. Intelligent conversation. Conversation that made sense and that would leave his family perplexed.

"But what did you think of them?" Vicky went on.

Edward frowned. If there was one thing about Vicky that was anathema to the way she had been raised—to be polite and unquestioning according to the strictures of their class—it was that she was persistent. Unlike everyone else, Edward liked to encourage her to be herself.

He leaned forward in his seat. "Well," he said, "I find them interesting, Vicky. To be honest, I'm intrigued by their modern views. I met Joy Hester first at the university, and one thing led to another. What they all have to say makes sense to me."

His mother raised her eyes to the ceiling. She didn't approve of women who worked. *Career girls,* she would sniff, if the topic was raised.

Vicky leaned forward in her seat. "You know that Sunday Reed has been excluded by her brothers from bringing those friends of hers to their house at Sorrento? Their belief in sexual freedom and a new 'modern' way of life is all so distasteful and odd." Vicky's voice resonated through the large room. "Sunday and her husband, John, had to rent a property farther along the coast for the summer. They are outcasts. The question is, do you really want to get to know them, Edward? Do you want to be associated with them and risk social rejection?"

Edward felt his jaw stiffen. "Vicky, your choice of language doesn't shock me, but . . ." He glanced across to his mother. Celia stared fixedly out the window.

But Vicky wasn't going to let up. "And what's more, you must know about their political views. John Reed is nothing but a communist. And yet, he and Sunday are wealthy members of our class. Nothing but rich people pretending to be poor. What do you say to that?"

Edward forced himself to take a breath. He had never felt the urge to be nasty to Vicky. He adored her, and the way she spoke her mind was encouraging. He did not want to break that in her.

When they were young, Robert, Vicky, and he had been close until Edward went to boarding school at Geelong and Robert, as the eldest son, was sent to England for his education. Clearly, the young Robert had not coped. He was such a different person now as to be hardly recognizable. It was as if boarding school had knocked something vital and alive and kicking out of him. Six years in the war had done the rest. His worrisome dependence on alcohol was exactly like Angus's, and yet Celia ignored it in them both. For Edward, Angus and Robert were like a dark undercurrent, running deep below the surface of all the family's gentility. It was one of the reasons he hadn't found his own house during the last year and a half. In some way, he wanted to try and fix the awkward situation in which his family had landed.

Celia had found her own ways of coping with her husband's fondness for drinking. Edward knew his mother's travel was an escape. He knew she wanted to get away, that she was a woman who hated being isolated out at Haslemere, stuck with a husband who resorted to alcohol in order to get through each day. Then the war had hit. And now, every member of his family seemed to have come out of it as if they were each from a different planet.

"Well," Edward said, "yes, they are privileged. Yes, they are rich, as am I, but from what I've seen in the war, our class looks down on people like the Reeds. They are true modernists, true believers in freedom of the spirit who have the courage to live as they feel. They are formally of our class and yet they are despised. But, you see, they are living in a manner that adheres to everything we fought for during the war—the freedom to make one's own choices in life. What could possibly be wrong about that?"

"Oh, for heaven's sakes." Celia brought her hand to her forehead and drooped back in her seat.

"And the fact that everyone says John Reed studies communist rhetoric—is that adhering to what we fought for in the war?" Vicky leaned back on the sofa, looking as sweet as a girl at a garden party, her eagle eyes stuck on Edward.

Edward picked up his drink from the delicate table by his side. "But they believe in the *liberal* spirit, Vicky. They believe in freedom of expression in the individual, in art, and in life. That is the true definition of modernism. Without freedom, how can we express who we truly are? Surely that is the antithesis of communism, which is the reduction of individuals to an anonymous mass. Freedom of the spirit is why we fought against Fascism, and one thing is for certain: we did not fight that war in order to go backwards to the old ways."

But Celia's brow furrowed. "I can't see how they are possibly the right people," she said. "You need to be careful, Edward. The Reeds' way of life, living off the fruits of the land, seems very communist to me, no matter what excuses you give them. And isn't Sunday having an affair with that artist Sidney Nolan while her husband just accepts it? The son of a train driver?"

Edward held her gaze. Why did the upper classes feel so entitled to judge?

Vicky continued in an intimate tone, as if she were not revealing something that all Melbourne knew. "The point is Sunday Reed has rejected her family. It's far more than growing vegetables out on a farm and having affairs. I have to admit it scares me, you spending time with them. Are you going to reject us, Edward?" Her large eyes were two iridescent pools.

Angus coughed. "More to the point, we can hardly entertain the thought of their having anything to do with us," he said. "Think of the scandal, Edward. What hope would Vicky have of making a decent marriage if we are all tainted by your association with the Reeds? We employ loyal workers who look up to us, at every property we own. We will lose their respect if you associate with these people. We will become repositories for gossip. And as for these people's . . . proclivities, if you are linked with them, you are linked with that as well. You have to stop it before it takes off."

"Come on, Father . . ."

But Vicky interrupted. "Haven't you heard about their friend Max Harris? You know he went to court over the indecent nature of the poems he published in that magazine of theirs. He was set up by two local poets, who wrote a whole lot of trashy poems and sent them to Max, calling them 'modern.' Apparently the two poets simply acquired random words from dictionaries and thesauruses, threw them together on the page, and called the results modernist poetry. Max fell for the hoax and published the poems in his wretched magazine. Honestly, Edward, do you want to associate with all that? The poems were declared indecent. These people seem intent on breaking everything up—families, society, traditions. Everything that is civilized about the world." Vicky's eyes glittered.

"Your civilized structures are merely a way of keeping the lower classes under control." Edward turned to stare out at the garden. What had he done? Betrayed state secrets? The irony of their attitude confused him. They criticized communism because it was fundamentally not about the individual. But wasn't he trying to be a true individual rather than a sheep who followed the family rules?

Angus growled his words. "Someone at the club told me that one of their cohort, Albert Tucker, found some painting in a bicycle shop window and that painting went into *Angry Penguins* too! These people are the laughingstock of Melbourne, Edward. They're never going to get anywhere in the real world. They're living in a utopia. They might have wonderful theories, but those theories are never going to work. Human nature will get in the way of their pseudo-communism, their anti-structure, their nihilist views. Greed, ambition, power, these things are as inherent to man as breathing itself. Communism will break down. It won't work because it, too, is open to exploitation. None of this is practical, Edward. No matter what your political system is, some will rise to the top while others suffer. Let's face the facts; without society—marriage, religion, class, and so forth—we will go backwards, not forwards. We need rules in order to survive as a society, or ultimately we don't know who we are or what rights and obligations we have to each other." Angus lifted his glass and finished his claret in one swig. As if he was raising a toast to himself.

Edward stood up. He moved to the fireplace. "The fact that an artist could only afford to show his work in a bicycle shop window makes him unworthy of attention? Because of his class?"

"If you want to be taken seriously, Edward, if you say you want to write . . . then these people are not the people with whom you should associate. They are not regarded well in the top literary and artistic circles by any means," Celia murmured.

Edward managed to control his voice. "You mean they are not well respected among the Establishment art and literary circles. But Sunday and John Reed are supporting artists who otherwise could not support themselves in order to pursue their talents—there is surely nothing more admirable than that. Yes, modern art with its absence of form and the Reeds' 'modern' way of life break down structures, but isn't that a positive result of what we've just seen in the war? Isn't there something wonderful in ultimate freedom, the ability to love, to paint, to live as we choose? I'm sorry if such ideas are challenging to your perceptions of what society should be, Father. But can't you see you are becoming threatened, and rightfully so?"

Angus coughed again. "The point is, Edward, these people, who are ultimately members of our own class, are actively attacking our sort of people. We have become their scapegoats. Do you want to become a party to that? They are attempting to turn us into something unfashionable, distasteful, and laughable, while the entire time they are living off the fruits of their own ancestors' labors!"

There was a grim silence. Edward shook his head and stared at the polished wooden floor. Celia stood up, went to the gramophone, and played some Schubert. Polite salon music.

Edward marched over to the French doors and gazed outside.

"Our family heritage was not built on left-wing radicalism." Angus's voice boomed through the room. "And my goodness, Edward, you've benefited from your forefathers' hard work."

Edward felt his jaw tighten.

"Your friends can go and live in the USSR if they want to carry on like they are, quite frankly," Angus said. "We need stability after the war, not all this free-living stuff. These people will not be successful in the end, Edward. None of them will. They are an anomaly. Don't waste this family's time."

Edward closed his eyes.

When Vicky spoke, her voice broke a little, almost as if she were about to burst into tears. "Apparently, if you've been invited out to the Reeds' farm at Heide, then you're in the inner circle. Have you had an invitation yet? You'd be quite the target for them. Getting you would be a real coup for the Reeds and their friends. Don't you see? You'd be their next project, Ed. They are simply trying to make a point. You're exactly what they want!" Her voice rose.

Edward winced.

Celia stood up and moved toward the bellpull. "I can't talk about this anymore."

Coldness seemed to lodge itself in the air, spreading itself around the room, turning everything that was familiar—the antique bowls and the mirrors and the elegant books—into something new and strange. It was as if the conversation had touched on something right now. Was the firm ground they thought they all stood upon only a precipice? And if Edward jumped off, would he take his whole family too?

But the idea of loving whom one wanted to love rather than marrying to please the people in this room, the idea of living simply in order to support others doing the same, the idea of treating people as equals—were these really such radical thoughts?

Edward stared at his face in the mirror above the fireplace. But instead of seeing himself, he saw the quiet way in which John Reed stood by Sunday, the intelligent manner in which the man listened to Edward and understood where he was coming from. It was as if, for the first time in his life, Edward had found people of a similar background who felt the way he did, people who felt that there was a deeper truth than money, ambition, connections, power. Why should he have to give up his feelings? A simpler way of life was a sensible approach after the horrors of war.

"It's a different world now, and we all must change." He chose each word with care, almost biting the words out, one by one. He was not going to let them see how rattled he was. "Politics aside, we can't hold people back because of their class. As for these 'bohemians' as you call them, if they are experimenting with a gentler, kinder way of life, then why should we judge them? We must be open to other ways of living. There are other ways."

Celia tugged on the bellpull, clutching it so hard that it swung to and fro.

"Where is Dennison?" she croaked. "You are hungry, Edward. Clearly not thinking straight."

Dennison appeared, adjusting his formal suit jacket and standing to attention.

"Dinner, please," Celia said, as if his very appearance was a reprieve from the gods.

The servant nodded, unquestioning, no expression on his face, and turned back around. Edward held his hand to his mouth. How long were servants going to accept being nothing but trained monkeys, when they had just returned from saving the entire darned nation from Hitler?

"It's not going to last, Mother," Edward said. "We have to show more compassion. And we have to change things at Haslemere. We've got to move with the times."

"I said, enough, Edward." Angus strode out to the formal dining room.

Even Vicky was silenced.

Edward stepped out into the cavernous entrance hall, glaring through the doorway at the sight of the polished dining table with its setting at one end for four.

"We will change the topic of conversation," Angus announced. And the slur in his words from the several clarets he had knocked back already was ignored, as usual, by all of them, while the thought of

Robert, out at some godforsaken pub, lurched into Edward's heart. Goodness knew what was going to become of them all.

Edward went out into the garden after dinner, which was a strained meal. Polite conversation, seen as a balm by the upper classes, didn't seem to work anymore. Robert appeared during pudding and started a rattling conversation about horse racing with his father.

Celia and Vicky seemed relieved at the sight of their inebriated son and brother—did they regard him as a protector of their way of life? The idea was a joke.

Cigar smoke drifted out to the garden while the sound of balls hitting each other from the billiards room resounded in the evening air. This was punctuated with the clink of brandy glasses. Avoidance. It never worked, not at all. If there was one thing Edward had learned during the war, it was that one could not stick one's head below water and ignore the forces of change that constantly swept through the world.

Edward made his way up and down the raked-gravel pathways, trying to focus on the crunch of his feet on the path. His grandmother's fastidiously researched Mediterranean plantings twinkled in the glow from the lights in the living room. She'd brought back exotic species from Italy, Greece, and Spain during the nineteenth century. The twentieth century had smashed his grandparents' carefully cultivated world apart, and yet the visual reminders were still here. It was people who had changed. And politics. Edward lit a cigarette and paced. When the phone rang, its peal caused him to jump.

Vicky called out in her shrill tones. "It's some girl on the phone, Edward. Someone called Rebecca." Her last sentence was muttered. But Edward sensed that even Vicky had had enough. The conversation had teetered dangerously close to collapse this evening, and it seemed as if everyone wanted to take a step back. He stamped out his cigarette and went inside.

"Rebecca?" Edward picked up the phone from the mahogany table in the hallway. It was odd how Edward had grown up surrounded by such things, never questioning them, never realizing or appreciating that some poor soul had probably been paid a pittance to create them. A vase of flowers sat next to the phone as if bright and determined. Edward realized that his voice had come out harsher than he intended. He closed his eyes. Rebecca. He couldn't express how relieved he was that she'd called.

"Edward," she said. "I'm sorry—"

"Don't apologize." He growled the words.

There was a silence, then a shuffling sound.

Edward felt his senses prick up.

"I'm going to hide under the house in the cellar," she said. Urgent. Desperate.

"What?"

Her voice dropped. "It's Mrs. Swift," Rebecca said. "She ripped up my drawings. I could only save three. I'm sorry, I just . . . need to get away right now, and I wasn't sure who to call, and . . ."

"Don't move." Edward felt his chest thump. He reached for his car keys. "I'm coming now. Sit tight."

"You don't have to do this." But her voice was almost too small to hear.

"I'll be there in twenty minutes."

"I'll come out as soon as I hear your car. Thank you."

"Good," he said, and hung up. He strode toward the front door without telling anyone he was going out.

CHAPTER ELEVEN

New York, 1987

Tess laid the notepaper down on the table next to her empty coffee cup. The thin pages were covered with Edward's slanting handwriting, his words flowing with hardly a correction, barely a letter crossed out. Since receiving Edward's first installment, Tess hadn't wanted to read typed-up copies. She didn't want mere transcripts of Edward's real work. She'd requested that the originals be sent straight to her when they arrived from Rome. She rested her chin in her hand and looked out the window of Caffè Reggio to the street outside.

Nico moved across to sit down next to her. Tess sensed that he'd been waiting for her to finish reading. She smiled at her friend.

"How are things, Tess?" he asked, tucking a cloth into the pocket of his white apron.

"Well," she said, "I have a new author who is based in Rome."

She swiped a look at Nico under her eyelashes, noticing the way his eyes crinkled into a smile.

"Roma? I told you it was all meant to be."

Tess tilted her head to one side.

"Fate," Nico pronounced. "Or Italy. Whichever way you want to put it."

"Your faith is stronger than mine, Nico."

"I saw the expression on your face while you were reading this work." He rested an olive-skinned finger on the page. "You were absorbed. So."

Tess let out a small laugh. "He seems a very difficult writer."

Nico watched her, his eyes steady. And waited.

"He won't stick to deadlines, and he insists on sending me handwritten work." Tess tidied up Edward's papers.

Nico chuckled. "That's good."

"No, it's not."

"He's Italian!" Nico threw his hands in the air. "No Italian would stick to deadlines or rules. They are not important!"

Tess leaned back in her seat. "Nico . . ." but she was smiling. She waited a beat. "Not Italian. Australian."

"Next best thing. Laid back."

Tess grinned. "He lives in Rome. He's moved there."

"People move to Italy for only one reason, Tess."

Tess raised a brow.

"And that is to connect with life, to set their priorities straight. We all do it at some stage in our lives, but Italy is the best place for it. I would bet that's what your author friend is doing in Rome."

"Well, Nico, I concede you could be right there."

Nico moved to stand up. "I'll get in trouble if I sit here with you." He grinned, his face still boyish in spite of all the years.

Tess reached for Edward's manuscript, but still a sense of doubt prickled at her mind.

"Is there anything else bothering you?" Nico asked.

Tess tucked the pages in the folder where she kept Edward's notes and placed it in her briefcase. Her fingers alighted on the cool leather cover of Edward's book of poetry.

"I need to get this book to sell. I suggested we change the setting of the book to the US rather than Australia."

Nico shook his head and tutted.

"Nico, I know what I'm doing. But the writer refused. And that got me wondering about why he was so defensive about the setting."

"It is only natural. He is proud of his country . . ."

"No, that's not it." She had to come clean with the thought that had been burning in her mind since she'd started reading the book. "I'm convinced his work is autobiographical. I think that's why he's so protective of the book."

Nico stayed quiet.

"Which leads me to another idea. The author needs to raise his profile. I want to market the book as a true story."

"What makes you think it's based on the truth?"

Tess shrugged. "Everything in it. But you know what?"

He shook his head at the same time she did.

"I'm going to find out. And when I do—"

"Treat him with respect," Nico said.

Tess stood up. "I'll treat him with respect," she said. "I always do. I'm very loyal, Nico, but you know that. The true-story angle could make all the difference. I think I might just have hit on a way to make this thing sell."

"But will he like it?"

"I'll convince him. Watch me."

Tess walked out of the café. There was still time to catch the library, if she was fast. She'd needed space from the office this afternoon, so after a meeting in which James had been extolled for his work with Alec Burgess, Tess had decided to read Edward's manuscript in the café.

But now she needed some answers and fast. It was clear, Tess thought, as she strode to the subway, making her way through the teeming crowds to the escalators, that Edward was based on Edward

Russell. But one question bothered her. Had he really been in love with a Rebecca Swift?

Tess was used to the vagaries of writers and the varying levels of autobiographical material in their work. She knew that when it came to some of her clients, writing about their pasts was subconscious, veiled in an assortment of cloaks. But this book, she suspected, was different. She suspected that Edward wanted to revisit his past. And he felt compelled to write about it. But why?

She was going to have to confront Edward with her thoughts soon. There was nothing wrong with nurturing her authors, but she was also a businesswoman. She needed to sell copies, and she needed to have Edward on the same page.

An hour later, Tess sat in the Rose Reading Room with a selection of books on Australian art on the table in front of her. In here, she always had to force herself not to become distracted by the still beauty of her surroundings. The frescoed ceiling and rows of tall arched windows lent an air of timelessness to the quiet space. She'd taken to coming here sometimes for a sense of peace, and now, the fact that it was going to be the place where she might find the answers she needed about Edward seemed fitting, somehow.

She reached for the book that she had found on 1940s art in Australia. Its cardboard cover showed a black-and-white photograph of a striking woman lying on a beach. As she turned the pages, her eyes drank in the photographs. There was a Sidney Nolan painting of Ned Kelly, the great Australian bushranger's yellow eyes angled off to one side. And a picture of Joy Hester, painted by her husband, Albert Tucker. Joy's blond hair was curled, and she had a troubled expression on her face. Tess drank in image after image, the distorted, modernist human shapes all making sense to her—surreal representations of people, reminiscent of Picasso's, all odd angles with images of bleak cities in the backgrounds, dark industrial landscapes.

But no matter how hard she looked and no matter how intrigued she was by the postwar art, there was no mention anywhere of a Rebecca Swift.

Tess picked up the next book, a pictorial history of Heide, John and Sunday Reed's home. The vast vegetable garden; the mist hanging over the Yarra River at the bottom of the garden; the library, lined with dark wooden shelves that were stacked with books; Sunday Reed, John Reed, Sidney Nolan, and Joy Hester sitting around the fireplace having afternoon tea—all the images were completely absorbing. Tess didn't notice that the shadows were lengthening across the vaulted room as the afternoon drifted toward evening.

Instead, Tess read on, fascinated with Sunday and John Reed. Indeed they had supported artists and they had lived in a communal way with their circle of friends. As Edward wrote, invitations to visit them at Heide were a big deal—so there was still some sense of underlying formality in their approach. They refused to be called patrons, and their relationships with the artists they supported were fascinating and complex, as was their relationship with each other. Tess drank in photos of the Yarra River in summer, where Sunday and Sidney used to go and bathe beyond the willows when they were lovers. She was moved by the photos of Sunday and John, together, looking into each other's eyes. It was clear that John was Sunday's true love, the man whom she adored in the end, even after her passionate, turbulent affair with Sidney Nolan ended. The human dramas intrigued Tess as much as the art.

Sunday's love affair with Sidney ended abruptly when he left her in the summer of 1947, seeming to realize that she'd never leave John. Sunday, devastated, took Sidney's Ned Kelly paintings to Europe in an attempt to win back her lover, but it was not successful—they never reconciled. Sunday wrote that she felt that the blood was draining from her life when Sidney married John Reed's younger sister, Cynthia, in

1948. Sunday then remained faithful to John until his death, which was followed by hers at Heide in 1981.

Tess placed that book to the side, her thoughts and feelings aswirl with the complexity of it all. Even among the most bohemian spirits a sense of betrayal could still run deep. Was it truly possible to live freely as they had supposedly done? Or did humanity and passion and possessiveness get in the way?

Tess picked up the last book in her stack. She pushed on, intent to find Rebecca, sure that there must have at least been someone who inspired her character, if nothing else. The way Edward wrote about her was too real, too vivid. And if she were honest, Tess wanted Rebecca to have existed. She, too, had fallen under the spell of the girl with the swinging dark hair.

This book was smaller, a paperback. It dealt with Melbourne artists in the 1940s, in particular. If there was nothing here, she'd have to trawl through newspapers next.

But as she scanned the pages of the little book, taking in the now familiar images, Tess forced herself not to get waylaid by peripheral stories, but to home in on Rebecca Swift. At the beginning of chapter three, she halted. Read the opening three times. Glanced at the clock. Ten minutes until closing time.

Tess stood up and made her way as swiftly as possible to the nearest library desk, resisting the urge to run.

"Do you mind if I photocopy this page?" she asked the woman in front of her, memories of Edward's encounter with the phone operator with the butter-yellow cardigan reeling into her head. Except the woman she stared at wore putrid pea green.

Five minutes. A warning bell rang through the library, loud enough to stir anyone from the deepest concentration.

"I'm sorry," the woman explained to Tess, "but the photocopiers are closed now."

Tess clutched the little book. She couldn't borrow it. It was a reserve book. She mulled over the problem as the woman walked away. And looked at the paragraph again. Just one paragraph. In a book about postwar art in Melbourne, Rebecca Swift was acknowledged as an unrecognized, talented artist who died tragically when she slipped from a rock on an island off the South Australian coast. There had only been one showing of her work in the winter of 1946 with the Contemporary Art Society in Melbourne, whose members were seen as an avant-garde, anti-establishment, and renegade lot. Their exhibitions were even described as degenerate by newspapers at the time—their work was too confronting, too honest, too raw, a shock to the Establishment artists and their circles at the time. Rebecca's paintings and drawings remained in the collection of Sunday and John Reed at Heide.

Rebecca's work, the author claimed, was also very likely overlooked in the 1940s after her death because she was a woman. Rebecca's relationship with the biographer and lecturer Edward Russell and her connection with his famous family was acknowledged in the book. Rebecca's death was viewed as a tragedy, a mysterious tragedy. But that was it. Nothing more. There were no photos of the girl in the red beret. Tess made her way toward the exit and placed the book on the counter in front of the librarian with great care. She thanked the woman and did not stare at her green cardigan. She walked out into the bustle that was New York City.

Tess needed to have Edward acknowledge Rebecca as a fact.

As she stood on the sidewalk on Forty-Second Street, Tess was hit all of a sudden with the sounds of the city. The noise and the constant movement were almost overwhelming after the hush in the library, too much after she'd been picturing another time, another place, where there was a cottage and a quiet riverbank set among gum trees, where every emotion had sweltered while the embers of Sunday and John's love for each other had remained strong. The great love affair between a woman who loved art and the young artist she'd supported from the start of his career until he left her hit Tess . . . and she thought that Sunday had lived her life to the fullest.

Tess made her way down to the subway. She would contact Edward and be straight with him, or she would regret it. She would call him now, while the Heide story grabbed at her heart. Tess told herself sternly that it was not a case of getting in too deep. It was business and she was a businesswoman. That was all. She simply had to convince Edward to view his work as a business proposition too.

Should be an easy task . . .

CHAPTER TWELVE

Melbourne, 1946

Rebecca appeared on the footpath as soon as Edward pulled up in front of her house. He frowned in worry at the sight of her. Her face was alabaster in the glare of his headlights. One hand was up at her left cheek. Edward reached across to open the passenger door of the Aston Martin. Rebecca climbed in as if each movement were a delicate operation. And faced straight ahead.

Edward reached out, his hand barely brushing hers as it rested on the seat between them.

"Darling . . ." The word fell from his lips as naturally as anything in the world.

She started at his word, but her gaze remained fixed straight ahead.

He wanted to take her in his arms and hold her. But outside her mother's house? He had to keep himself in check. Edward turned the car in a circle, away from the beach, past rows of bungalows, their windows lit up in the inky darkness.

"Thank you," she said, but her tone was half-dead.

He drove down the street and onto the next one, a mirror image of the last. Every one of these avenues in endless stretches of suburbs seemed to go on and on. How many dramas were being enacted in these benign settings? He pulled the car over. Shut the engine off. And turned to face her.

"Rebecca," he said, steeling himself against what he knew he was about to see.

She looked back at him, holding her head up. The deep bruise across her left cheek was slashed with a jagged cut that glimmered red in the glow of the dashboard. Edward forced himself not to swear. Instead, he reached forward and rested his hand on her arm.

"You have to promise me that you're not going back." He was surprised by the growl in his voice.

The soft sounds of her breathing lingered in the space between them. He sensed that she fought emotions that brimmed so close to the surface that she would break down if she talked.

Edward turned back to the steering wheel, his face set. He started the car and drove on, grimly, toward the city, plans forming in his head as he wove his way up the Paris End of Collins Street, past Georges department store with its magnificent window displays—stilted mannequins showcasing imported fashions with plastic smiles planted on their fake plastic faces. He thought of his mother and his sister on their endless shopping expeditions in these places—it was how they filled their days.

What if he were to show up with Rebecca in this state at their house in Toorak?

The idea was a joke.

"My mother works in that shop there," Rebecca said suddenly, her voice still heavy, looking out the window for a second before facing the front again.

Edward nodded. Rebecca's listlessness sent chills through Edward's heart.

Edward glanced out the window at the shop opposite Georges department store, taking in the small boutique's pale pink facade, its black front door and elegant potted plants on either side. More mannequins stood staring out at him through dead eyes. Just so. He knew that boutique well enough. Vicky and his mother frequented it too. It was one of the acceptable places to shop. There were a few. Edward scowled and drove on.

He approached Little Collins Street. If his plan didn't work, he would come up with something else. Once he'd stopped outside No. 166, he turned to Rebecca and took her in his arms, achingly aware of her cut and bruised cheek, which rested so close to his own.

It was as if he could feel the gash burning his own skin.

When he looked up, one hand stroking her hair, a light came on in Gino Nibbi's Leonardo bookstore, and the bookseller whom Edward had known since he was a teenager appeared in the yellow light behind the window. Gino had provided Edward with a haven during the trips he'd been forced to take with his mother and sister to town. Edward had wandered into his shop one day in his youth. It was Gino who encouraged Edward to follow his deep desire to write. Now, the light from the old man's bookshop illuminated Rebecca's face. Edward gazed at Gino's distinct profile, his aquiline nose, his still-black hair that stood straight up. When the older man looked toward Edward, Edward raised a hand.

Gino moved toward the door of his shop.

"Rebecca?"

She stirred. Beauty, Edward thought, scarred by the brutal reality of life.

"Darling, we can trust Gino. He is a friend," he said. "I have an idea that might work, but we need him to help us."

She nodded and a little sigh escaped from her as if she were weary of this world and everything in it.

Edward, hating this, climbed out of the car, shutting the Aston Martin's door with a quiet clip that resonated up and down the narrow street with its shops and studios. Rebecca would find comfort here. She'd fit in with the artists who crowded the studios. Café Petrushka and Ristie's Coffee Shop were places she'd enjoy. And a block away, the Eastern Market would inspire her, with its mix of hatters and cobblers, cheap clothes and food stalls. She'd be amid life. Not stuck out in the suburbs with her mother. Things would seem less overwhelming with so many people about. Cities created distractions. Edward knew that. Even now, people strolled down the vibrant, well-lit street, past signs flashing and blinking in the night. He opened Rebecca's door, waiting while she climbed out.

Silently, at the shop door, Gino took in Rebecca's injuries and led them through his charming bookshop, past his beautifully arranged collection of art books, his finest-quality prints of the Impressionists and Gauguin. Just being here, surrounded by art, Edward felt a sense of comfort. But then anger bit at him. If people like Sunday Reed wanted to garden and support artists, if people like Gino wanted to surround himself with books, then these were their own forms of beauty. What right did people like his parents have to criticize such benign choices?

Gino pushed open the white-paneled door that led to the back of the shop. In silence, a timeless silence between humans that was complicit and that said more than any words ever could, Gino indicated that Rebecca go into the bathroom, handed her a washcloth and some antiseptic cream that he retrieved from a cupboard. Then he placed his hand on Edward's shoulder and led him back out to the bookstore, closing the kitchen door behind him.

"It was her mother," Edward said.

Gino listened while Edward talked.

"I am more than happy to lend her the studio upstairs," the older man said after a while. "My wife used it occasionally to teach Italian to singing students, but she has a job at the Conservatorium now. The studio is empty. It's basic, but there is a bed that Rebecca can use." Gino's Italian accent rippled through his words.

Edward almost sagged with relief. "I am more grateful than you know. I'll go home and get her some supplies from the kitchens. She is an art student, by the way. It might help if I give her some art supplies while she's here. I have some things at home . . ."

His mother had dabbled in sketching years ago. Celia had engaged an expensive art tutor one summer. Her work had been striking—the tutor had encouraged her. But then Edward's father had started to drink even more heavily as the Second World War became inevitable. He hadn't dealt well with the Great War and the thought of another one overwhelmed him. He would rant about the state of humanity until the family could bear it no more. Celia never sketched again.

Gino nodded. "Yes. She'll want to draw." He ran a hand over the stubble on his chin. "I should be able to get her a job when she is ready. Not yet, but when she is. A job at a restaurant down the street. I know the family there. They are a nice family. It will only be waiting tables, but it is better than doing nothing. There is nothing worse than that."

"Thank you." Edward looked at Gino, this man who had been decorated for bravery during the First World War, only to become a pacifist at the end of it, and saw two simple things: strength of character and kindness.

Rebecca appeared through the door that led out back. She reached a hand up to her face, still patterned with flecks of crusted blood. Edward moved toward her and held her. The older man rested a hand on Edward's shoulder.

Rebecca woke early the following morning. She lay on the narrow bed a few moments and gazed around the studio. Everything seemed to shine in the bright morning light. Apart from the bed, there was a kitchen sink, a rudimentary oven, and a small wooden table set with two wooden chairs up against the window, which looked straight out at the other buildings in the narrow street. The floorboards were bare but clean and the bed was covered with a quilt that was pale blue and white.

The easel that Edward had brought last night sat ready with a fresh piece of sketching paper pinned to its front. Charcoals and pencils were lined up on the horizontal board underneath, along with a brush and ink. Morning city sounds peppered the studio: trams, the odd shout, trucks delivering their wares to the shops.

Rebecca reached a hand up to her swollen cheek. She sat up, swinging her legs slowly over the side of the bed. They ached too. Every part of her body seemed to ache with tiredness and sadness and lack of hope.

But on the small cabinet near the sink, either Gino or Edward had placed a bottle of antiseptic for her face, along with a ream of cotton wool that reminded Rebecca of her days working as an assistant nurse on an air force training station during the war. Mostly, she'd dealt with small accidents that occurred during exercises. But twice there had been plane crashes. Now, she felt as if she had returned from battle herself.

Tenderly, she washed the good parts of her face, the water like a cool stream running over hot rocks. Then she tore off some of the bread that Edward had left for her, buttered it, and spread it with honey. She sliced and ate the apple that sat on a blue-and-white plate, and after she had dressed and used the bathroom downstairs, went to the little easel.

Two hours later, the beginnings of several sketches laid out on the table, she heard the unmistakable sounds of Gino opening the shop downstairs. She listened while his solid footsteps made their way around the bookshop. When she heard the click of the door that led from the shop up the narrow staircase to the studio, she moved toward the door and opened it.

"Rebecca," he said. "Are you all right this morning?"

"I am, thank you." She felt her sore cheek burn red.

The older man simply nodded. His tone was calm and kind. "Rest today, Rebecca. I'll be in the shop if you need me. Edward is coming in to bring you lunch. I've already spoken with him this morning on the phone." He looked thoughtful for a moment. "He and I will help you," he said. "Please don't worry."

Rebecca nodded and sent her own silent thanks toward him. Last night, she had hit a new low. Before she rang Edward, once her mother had finally stalked out of her bedroom—the effects of destruction lying around as if Mrs. Swift had laid waste to Rebecca's entire life—she had lain on the bed shaking and crying, curled in the fetal position. She had never found herself in such a desperate state before, and now she shuddered to think about it. Sometimes it seemed that life was like one great brick wall that wanted to stop her from having the love in her life that she wanted, from doing what she loved—creating art. Were those things too much to ask for in this world?

Was the world so cruel that it would deny her, a young woman, the simple kindness that seemed to arrive effortlessly into other people's lives? She knew it existed. Look at Sunday and John Reed. Her mother's torturous cruelty seemed like a full stop that overruled everything.

But this morning, as she listened to the steady tread of Gino's steps retreating down the staircase, Rebecca realized that if one human could take away all your dignity, there were others who were there to give it back. She knew what had begun to stir in her. Edward and Gino had given her back hope.

Three weeks later, if someone had asked Rebecca about the last tumultuous month of her life, she would have told them that after the worst that could have happened had happened, it seemed that everything had started to turn around. Edward and Gino had been to visit Mrs. Swift on the day Rebecca moved into the studio, and her mother had apparently caved at the sight of the two distinguished men who had arrived at her doorstep to advocate for her daughter.

Rebecca's determined protectors returned with her clothes packed in a brown suitcase that had belonged to her father once, along with her drawing supplies and, touchingly, several small ornaments from her dressing table. Gino's idea, Edward told her. Edward brought her enough books to keep her occupied—several biographies of artists— and Gino hung three Impressionist prints on the walls of her funny little studio, a Monet, a Gauguin, and a Manet. He laid a Turkish rug on the floorboards that he said was a gift from his wife.

Once the bruising on her face had become less repugnant, and when Rebecca became confident enough to step out into the world, she accompanied Gino to an interview at the Italian restaurant at the end of the street. She was struck by the warmth and the seemingly unsinkable happiness of the large, boisterous family that owned the little trattoria. The simplicity of their life seemed to prove that when things worked well, life could be weightless.

But even so, Rebecca's easel became the repository for all her tumultuous thoughts. She found inspiration for her work on solitary walks on the streets of industrial South Melbourne. Somehow, making sketches of the people who worked there, people who spent their whole lives toiling in factories, spurred Rebecca to express how she felt about this new life after the war. She was compelled to reflect the relentless repression of the human spirit that had started during all those harsh years of world conflict.

She allowed her imagination to roam free while she took in the faces of people whom she studied, day after day, in the street. The gray, lifeless realm of the factories was a metaphor for her own troubles.

When Edward arrived as usual one Sunday, Rebecca was sitting in her small studio surrounded by brush and ink sketches. No longer did she have to hide her work from her mother. And for the first time in her life she could express properly what she wanted to say outside the confines of the Gallery School, where such dark themes expressed in the modernist style would be denounced as oppressive, as unsuitable. She still attended classes, but she questioned whether she should continue next term.

Edward leaned down and examined them all. "Darling," he said, "these are seriously good."

He picked up a drawing of a woman, a factory worker. Rebecca had distorted her features, overblowing her body, while her head was small. She'd used crosshatching to emphasize the perspective of the stark building behind her that loomed larger than the woman, overwhelming her, while the large, sweeping brushstrokes that she'd employed for the woman were inspired by the other modern artists who believed that true essence could be found in only a few lines.

"You capture people's inner selves in the most extraordinary way," he said. "I'm taken with how you use distorted shapes and break away from structure to convey meaning in your subjects. I'm so glad you can work freely here."

Rebecca knew that Edward understood and accepted her without reservation. The closer she became to him the more she could open up and draw. And at the same time, she seemed to be on some sort of determined mission—every new sketch had to outdo the last.

She looked forward to her late-night discussions with Edward and Gino over a bottle of wine, in which they all agreed Australian artists needed to become more confident in expressing their own idioms on the canvas, rather than following the European traditions.

Rebecca moved over to stand behind Edward, wrapping her arms around his waist. She leaned her head on his shoulder.

He turned to her, murmuring in that intimate way that was his own. "If a writer has to find his own voice, then an artist needs to find her own style. It doesn't matter if it changes over time," he said, "because that doesn't change the truth of it. But there's something here that is and will always be uniquely yours. It's what matters most. And that is the very thing that will move people when they encounter your work." He took her face in his hands. "No one can take that away from you. No one. Remember that." His eyes darkened, and she reached up, kissing him and closing her eyes for one delicious moment.

"You know that Sunday and John Reed have people to Heide only by invitation?"

Rebecca nodded. "I know. No matter how modern their ideas are on art and life, they are not people who encourage uninvited company."

"Well. We have an invitation, darling. They invited us there today when I saw them last night. Would you like to come out to Heide for lunch with me? Sidney Nolan will be there; other than that, it will be you, me, Sunday, and John."

He tilted his head to one side, and for a moment, Rebecca sensed that he was slightly nervous in asking her. And that struck her as sweet. The Reeds' world seemed perfect, and Rebecca dared to hope that their way of life was something that Edward might consider replicating with her.

"What better way could there be to spend my Sunday afternoon?" She smiled. "Thank you." Her hand lingered in his.

These days, she was almost able to smile at the fact that her mother used to criticize her for her passionate nature. Edward seemed to revel in it. The overwhelming sense of living life to the fullest that she felt around him was as addictive as drawing itself. The only worry that coiled inside her was the fact that he had not introduced her to his family as yet.

Edward took the road out to Bulleen, winding his way through the Yarra Valley, the same countryside that had inspired those earlier Australian artists in the Heidelberg School. There was something mesmerizing and dreamy about the green paddocks, the old market gardens, and dairy farms that meandered along the riverbanks. The air was scented with the tall eucalyptus trees that lined the water's edge.

As they approached the long wooden fence that protected John and Sunday Reed's home from Templestowe Road, Rebecca thought how accepting and different her new friends were. There were no judgments being made about where any of them came from. And they all lived and expressed themselves in their own ways—there was no one way of expression, and yet they shared such common ideas about what art should mean.

Edward drove up the pale gravel driveway that circled a lawn planted with fruit trees. Rebecca didn't know where to look first. Sunday and John's wooden house sat to the left of the immaculately raked driveway. Sunday would sometimes get down on her hands and knees and smooth the gravel out herself, Rebecca knew. In front of the painted house, neat box hedges surrounded a small front garden, and beyond this was a high old brick wall. The wall's green door was open, showing glimpses of Sunday's famous vegetable garden.

Rebecca knew that Sunday was a beautiful cook. She was renowned among her circle of friends for her gorgeous, simple lunches, and Rebecca was comforted at the thought of being nurtured by Sunday, even if only for a few hours.

Bees danced around the lavender and roses that were directly in front of the house. Sunday might be a proponent of modernism in art, but her garden was a blend of formal French box hedging, well-tended fruit trees, lawn, and a wild English flower garden. The whole space was a beautiful palette. Sunday, Rebecca thought as she climbed out of the car, may not be an artist who painted on canvas, but her Heide garden was clearly her way of expressing herself.

Smoke curled out of the chimney in the white wooden cottage. Sidney Nolan sat on the small front porch, sketching in the sun. His brow was furrowed in concentration and his handsome dark features were enhanced in the sunlight. Rebecca found herself desperate to pull out her own materials and sketch him in turn.

Sidney laid down his pencil and rolled up his sleeves when Edward pulled up outside the front door. His shirt hung loose over his khaki shorts and his face lit up in a genuine smile. He shook Edward's hand and kissed Rebecca, avoiding her newly healed cheek.

Footsteps sounded through the green painted door under the archway in the brick wall. Sunday appeared, holding a basket full of salad leaves in one hand, while in the other she held a straw hat. She wore a soft cashmere sweater and corduroy trousers. And it struck Rebecca again that Sunday was so outwardly conservative, and yet here she was, behind modernist artists and a publishing enterprise that was seriously avant-garde.

Sunday's light-colored hair was held away from her eyes with a headband again. She moved toward Rebecca, hugging and then releasing her and running her eyes over Rebecca's face. Rebecca looked down at the ground. She would always be self-conscious about what her mother had done.

"I'm so pleased you could make it," Sunday said, her voice quiet and soft. "I can't wait to talk to you. You must be starving! Our lunch is straight from the garden."

Rebecca was grateful to the older woman for talking about ordinary matters while she led them into the cool interior of the house and down a long hallway, its high ceilings providing more wall space for art. Rebecca had to watch that she didn't trip over the artwork that was stacked down each side of the hallway. What she would give to sit down, lay them all out on the floor, and take them all in, in one glorious afternoon.

She had a glimpse of the famous Heide library through the first door on her right, its walls lined with dark wooden bookshelves. Comfortable chairs and a soft sofa sat opposite the fireplace. A desk was set in the bow window, overlooking the fruit trees and roses in the garden outside.

Sunday led them farther into the house. On their left, John and Sunday's bedroom door was open. A baby grand piano sat against open French doors that led to the side garden. In the long, narrow kitchen, with its old farmhouse range at the back of the house, Sunday put the kettle on, and Rebecca leaned against the wooden dresser that was filled with charming blue-and-white crockery.

So perfect, and yet it was all such a rebellion against Sunday's privileged background. Rebecca knew that Sunday had dispensed with servants and such trappings of her class, preferring to do her own cooking and spending hours working in the garden herself. Rebecca watched while Sunday prepared their simple lunch. Sidney helped, and Edward offered to slice salad onions.

Sunday placed a huge loaf of whole wheat bread on a wooden platter.

"We churn our own butter." She smiled, pulling two perfect butter pats with her own seal decorating them out of a cool safe.

It was hard not to marvel at this enterprising woman. She had grown up as the daughter of one of Melbourne's wealthiest real estate families, coveted, indulged—and here she was showing how love and good companions provided more sustenance than all the comforts money could buy.

When they filed into the dining room, Rebecca clasped her hands tight. Tins of paint were stacked at one end of the long dining table along with sticks of charcoal and tins of linseed oil. Against the wall, paintings that were immediately recognizable as Sidney Nolan's were lined up. The imagery in the artist's work was stark—Ned Kelly, the legendary bushranger who fought hard against corruption among the late nineteenth-century wealthy squatters and the police force, his helmet looking like a vast black cage on his head. Rebecca turned to Sidney, who hovered behind them, his eyes running over his own pieces, frowning.

"Sid has been up all night," Sunday said, moving over to one of the striking pictures, running a hand along its top edge. Almost in a proprietary manner.

"Sidney and Max Harris returned yesterday from a trip up north to Kelly country," Sunday went on.

"I grew up with stories about the old folk hero from my grandfather," Sidney said. "My grandfather was one of the police officers who were involved in the manhunt for Kelly in Victoria in the late 1870s. But regardless of this personal connection, I'm fascinated by the way myths such as Ned Kelly's famous rebellion against colonialism become associated with our country. Kelly and his battles have become ingrained in our psyche. You know, I see the Kelly story in some ways as representative of us, here at Heide, of what we are trying to do. We're questioning the Establishment in the same way Kelly did, albeit in a less dramatic manner."

He looked at Rebecca then, as if he were studying her face. To her horror, she felt a red flush stain her cheeks. Did he, too, know of her shameful secret, of her difficulties establishing any sort of independence from her own mother? He had avoided kissing that cheek . . .

But as he went on, his storyteller's lush voice sending them all quiet, Rebecca forgot herself. Ned Kelly had fought against the odds, Sidney reminded them, and was hanged. He'd lost. Or had he? The legend was one that every Australian knew. It was part of the country, part of who they were. Kelly's defiant stand against the Felons Apprehension Act, a draconian law allowing any citizen to shoot a declared outlaw on sight, and his pleas to end discrimination against poor Irish settlers opened up people's eyes in the end. Was it possible, in time, that modernism, too, would one day be recognized as something worthwhile by society if the Heide circle persisted with their quiet protests?

"Max and I went to Glenrowan," Sidney said. "We wandered around where members of the Kelly gang were killed by police during Kelly's last stand in 1880. And it was as if the old vigilante was still there. His ghost lingered, you know, around the Glenrowan Hotel. You can feel him where he took his stand, but let the townsfolk go, only to be shot and wounded himself before they hanged him in Melbourne Gaol for murder. Kelly was protesting against everything. The antihero. The outlaw. You know he wanted Australia to be a republic?"

Rebecca's eyes widened.

"He was modern," Sidney said, his voice soft in the silent room. "Just like us. Looking for a deeper truth, a better altar at which to worship than keeping the status quo and following the old rules of society. They shouldn't mean anything here. We are all humans. None of us are any better than anyone else."

Rebecca cast her eyes over Sidney's thoroughly modern sketches. Ned Kelly had suffered for questioning everything. And the fact that he was an everyday man made him the Australian epitome of a hero. Rebecca sensed again that something important was happening at Heide. She hoped that one day this small revolution would bear fruit. And she wanted, more than anything else, to be a part of it. She reached a hand up to the place where her mother had hit her.

"I don't know what I'd do without Sun," Sidney said, turning to Sunday.

Sunday moved over and took her lover's hand, and they stood there. And Rebecca was struck again by Sunday's sensitivity toward everything, by her affectionate nature and her very open heart.

"She stayed up with me all night," Sidney said, running his free, paint-stained hand over his chin. "Feeding me coffee while I worked. I've almost done the whole bloody series overnight."

After lunch, Rebecca curled up on the floor in front of the fire in the library, sketching, surrounded by the high walls lined with books. Edward went for a walk with Sidney and John. Sunday sat on one of the sofas. The crackle of the fire was a comforting companion while Sunday watched Rebecca work in silence. It was as if the older woman were attuned to the process. It was as if she had some rare gift for understanding not only art, but the artist herself. Sunday was a nurturer, in every sense of the word.

When Sunday finally spoke, Rebecca continued to draw, and the woman's voice became a counterpoint to her work.

"You know, people criticize John and me for being rich people look-ing for a creative outlet. But I only invite people here who pursue truth in life and art. Watching you work, Rebecca, seeing the expression, the concentration on your face, only serves to reinforce my beliefs."

Rebecca stopped drawing for a second and stared into the gleaming red coals in the fireplace. Something stirred inside her; perhaps it was the woman's mesmerizing voice.

"I see much of myself in you, twenty years ago," Sunday said softly. Rebecca looked at her.

"I know that our backgrounds are different," Sunday went on, her voice a murmur against the open window. "But you see, in many ways, they were the same. Great expectations were placed on my generation too. We were taught to obey, just as your mother has tried, and failed, to teach you, Rebecca. We were taught not to be the center of our own world, but rather to curtail our ambitions. You see, speaking out or having an opinion was not done in our circle. We were expected to marry our socially engineered matches. Our educations were not rigor-ous. Girls of my class were never taught to think. Rules, regulations— our lives were governed by those at the all-girls' school I attended in Toorak. We were warned, you know, to avoid undue displays of emo-tion. We were told never to ask probing or impertinent questions in any conversation; touchy subjects were to be avoided at all costs. It was unthinkable to disagree with any man, let alone our fathers. Expressing ourselves and using our brains was discouraged. If we wanted to gradu-ate to our careers, which were marriages to hand-picked husbands, then we needed to obey all the rules. If you didn't . . . well, you became an outcast. It was brutal."

Rebecca curled her legs underneath her body and stayed quiet.

"Those rules were taken for granted back then, Rebecca. No one considered questioning them, not in my class. Wealth and a successful husband were too alluring an attraction to risk being oneself."

Sunday stood up, moving across to stand closer to Rebecca by the fire. "But, you see, I hated school. And I was starting to question the patriarchal nature of my well-to-do Melbourne family. I married young, to my family's great concern, a man called Leonard Quinn. He left me, in Paris, alone and very ill. I thought I would die." Her voice cracked.

Rebecca stayed still.

But then Sunday frowned. Determination appeared to come back into play. "You see, the point is, things can get better, Rebecca. You must always remember that. You trust someone, whether it is your mother, or a lover—your husband, the man whom you have been told you must trust with every ounce of your heart. But then you reach a lowest point, after that person has let you down, abandoned you, when you must decide whether to move forward, to stay put, or to go backwards. You always have a choice."

Rebecca laid her pad of paper aside, tracing her fingers over the intricate patterns on the Turkish hearth rug. Her heart pulsed in her chest. Sunday was hitting every note that mattered now.

"I would like to think," Sunday went on, "that I've managed to move forward rather than stay in one spot. Moving forward involves risk. You have to trust again, but, believe me, you can. The only way to trust is to trust."

Rebecca felt her jaw tighten.

"One day you might thank your mother for a difficult childhood. It probably inspired you to become an artist."

Rebecca looked up sharply. Was that what she was?

"And, Rebecca, don't be afraid of loving Edward, because no matter what you have been through, love is something that is always worth it in this life. Love and art are what I believe in, because they both spring from a place of truth."

Rebecca waited for a moment before she spoke. "I still worry that I am wrong for him," she said. And glanced up toward the window. If he were to be out there, to hear her voice her fears . . . "He hasn't introduced me to his family, you see, Sunday. And we are getting so . . . close to each other." There, she admitted it. She hated to think of what Edward's family would think of her—of where she came from.

Was Sunday right about forging ahead no matter what, or was she just a lucky aberration, a woman who found an extraordinary man in John Reed, who felt the same as she? And the fact was that they had both been confident enough to stand up for their beliefs not only within their families, but in society, where they were reviled by both the established art world and the upper echelons of Melbourne. Sunday and John's views on equality were too threatening. They were seen as communists, which was the very worst insult people could give them.

Would Edward have enough conviction to live as he felt?

Sunday moved back over to the nearest sofa, sat down, and reached out and stroked Rebecca's head. "Lose the script that's been placed in your head, Rebecca. I did. We women have to do that or we are simply absorbed. I see a relationship between you and Edward that has the potential to become as wonderful as what I have with John. When it happens, take the opportunity with both hands. Run with it. Otherwise, you will only regret what could have been."

Rebecca reached up and took Sunday Reed's hand. She felt at home here and if there was any chance that she could find such a place for herself—such a life for herself as this, a Heide of her own—then she was not going to leave any stone unturned.

Sunday stood up. "Let's go for a walk down to the river. Then it will be time for my famous arvo tea!"

Rebecca stood up, too, laying her sketches aside. Perhaps she would leave them here, as a parting gift for this extraordinary woman.

"They have challenged everything," Edward said, as they drove home in the twilight, replete with Sunday's delicious apple cake, which they had enjoyed by the fire in the library as afternoon tea. The gum trees on either side of the road took on ghostly, asymmetrical shapes. "And they have won," he said, his words seeming to sift out into the still paddocks.

They drove in companionable quiet through the countryside and all the way back to Little Collins Street. Gino had left lights on in the shop so that Rebecca could see her way upstairs.

She pulled out her key, leaned across the car, and kissed Edward. "Thank you," she said. And then, not wanting to hold it back, Sunday's words deep in her heart where she knew she would always keep them, "I love you."

He leaned forward, his forehead touching hers. "I'm in love with you," he whispered. "Darling, come to Haslemere for Easter. Come and meet my family."

Rebecca ran a hand over his cheek and he took it from her and caressed it with tiny kisses, like stars scattering on a fresh canvas. Surely, if Sunday could love freely, so could she. If Sunday could make a marriage and a love affair work, surely a love affair between two people of like minds but different social backgrounds could work too.

Warmth radiated through Rebecca's entire body while Edward kissed her. And she thought she had never been luckier, or happier.

All she asked was that it would last.

CHAPTER THIRTEEN

New York, 1987

Every meeting at the office was filled with Leon's congratulations toward James. Tess started avoiding working there; she slipped out whenever she could. She'd chosen to spend her lunchtime at a small diner near the office. The cappuccino here was so strong a spoon could stand up in it, and the chocolate powder that was scattered on top of the milky coffee was thick and lustrous.

Tess pulled out a notebook and made a list, an action plan.

Here was the sum of the situation. Negatives: First, Edward insisted on setting the book in Australia. Changing that was clearly a deal-breaker for him. But it would not enhance sales in the US. Second, Edward wasn't going to accept any deadlines. So she had no idea when the book was going to be released.

Tess took a sip of the too-hot coffee and winced.

Positives: Edward was sending in regular chapters, so he seemed to be in the swing of writing. And Tess now knew that the book was autobiographical. But she still had to convince Edward to let the world know that Rebecca had existed.

Tess picked up Edward's old book of poems, settled back, and read on.

The poetry was filled with strong, simple lines. The language was economical, and the meaning was as clear as a bell. It was such a shame he had stopped writing for so many decades, such a shame he hadn't developed further, as he had the beginnings of a remarkable voice. Something had stifled it.

Tess sighed, then jumped as the sound of footsteps in the otherwise quiet restaurant stopped right at her table.

"Tess?"

She looked up.

The scent of sophisticated aftershave eclipsed the greasy fried-food smells that lingered in the diner. James Cooper stood over her. Tess cursed herself for choosing a table in the window, where she could be spotted so easily from the street. She tried to slide Edward's poems back into her bag.

"How are you finding them?" James asked.

"Fine," Tess said. And put the book away.

"Can I join you for a moment?" He shot a glance around the diner while tugging at his navy blue tie.

Tess shrugged, indicating with a flick of her hand that he sit opposite her. She stirred her coffee, blending the chocolate with the foam into a whirl.

A waitress appeared.

"I'm not ordering," James said. "Thanks."

The waitress didn't budge. Tess's lips curled upward. Tough, old-school New York style.

"Surely you could enjoy a cappuccino, James?" Tess murmured. "Or an espresso? It's smaller. Which means you can leave sooner."

She didn't miss the twitch of James's lips.

"A cappuccino," he said, holding eye contact with Tess.

"Are you sure about that?" the waitress asked. So, she was going to join in on the banter.

Tess liked the woman even more than before.

"Yes." Still staring straight at Tess.

The waitress pulled the top page off her notebook and stuck it on the table before walking away.

Tess placed her spoon back on her saucer. Sat back and waited.

"There's something I want to say." He glanced around the diner.

"Are you being followed, James?" Tess couldn't resist it.

"Don't be stupid."

She raised her cup to her lips.

His coffee arrived. He gulped it in one swig before putting the cup back down, then tapped his finger on the red Formica tabletop. "I'm going to cut to the chase."

"It's what you do best, after all. Strike at the heart. Take what's not yours."

"No."

She raised a brow.

"I don't know how many times I have to tell you that I had nothing to do with taking your author. He was handed to me. I also didn't know that you would be so . . . upset."

"How about we agree to cut the word 'upset' from our dialogue? It implies a sort of petulance that I don't think equates to the seriousness of the problem we have at hand."

James pushed his coffee cup away and leaned forward, talking in a quiet voice. "The fact is I didn't steal him. End of story. I'm sorry for the effect it's had on you. But the thing is, I came here to . . ." He shook his head.

Tess placed her hands in her lap. Her heart had started, annoyingly, to flutter in her chest.

"My father," James said, his voice sounding low and deep and close, all of a sudden, "is intrigued by the sound of Edward Russell's new book."

"Oh, is he." Tess blew out a breath. Well, that was excellent. It would be just the thing to have Sean Cooper, the most senior *New York Times* literary critic, pulling Edward's book to shreds. Sean was famous for doing that. And it would be a complete coup for James. She'd known that he'd have his father favorably review Alec Burgess's book. She just hadn't gone so far as to think he'd mess around with Edward. Clearly, James was nastier than she'd thought. She sat back, folding her arms and frowning at the table.

"Leon told me that Edward Russell's book is a love story," James went on.

There was a silence. Why was Leon discussing her author with James? Tess frowned. Whatever. She would never let what had happened with Alec occur again.

James tented his hands on the table.

"The thing is, Tess, he was wondering, my father, that is, if you would like to come for a drink with him, with us, that is, after work tonight." James glanced off to the side now and stared out the window at the gray street.

Tess's flutters swelled into thumps. What did he think she'd do? Fall over and swoon, grateful for the crumbs he was handing out, gasping at his feet? She pressed her lips closed and waited a moment.

"Because he's interested in *Edward Russell?*" Why would such a powerful figure in the literary world want to waste his time on some unknown Australian novelist who had gone nowhere for the last forty years? Had Sean Cooper really given James that book of poetry? What if James had found it in some old secondhand shop and handed it to Tess as a joke? Her thoughts may be irrational, but for good reason, she told herself.

"My father offered to have us over to my parents' apartment for a chat . . ." James's voice trailed off.

Ha! Even James was having trouble doing this—being so underhanded that he could not, or would not, simply admit the truth. He was going to make darned sure that she did not turn Edward into a success, because if that happened, then the wunderkind Alec Burgess might just want her back! And where would that leave James? Looking like a fool, looking exactly like Tess had a couple of weeks back? Tess glared at her utterly unappealing coffee.

"A chat?" She raised her hands in the air and reminded herself of Nico. "I find this a little disingenuous."

James stared out the window. "You might think that. But you know what, Tess, it's not. It's an offer to meet my father. He, as it happens, is also genuine. He's the real deal, Tess, I promise you that."

Tess shot a look at him. Authentic? Someone associated with the man sitting opposite her was authentic? She fought to stifle a laugh.

"What's more," James went on, "he's a fan of Edward's. My father loves postwar art. And writing. He finds the era fascinating. And he's not going to destroy Edward's book or his reputation." He turned back to face her. "Or your career."

Tess rubbed the back of her neck.

James pulled out his wallet and slid a couple of dollars for the coffee across the table to her. "I don't know exactly what your problem is, but you have one. And it's stopping you from getting where you want to be."

Tess reeled at his words. "How dare you." She leaned forward. Silently, she slid his money right back. "How dare you make personal comments that are based on nothing. Haven't you done enough already? And you know what? What you've done to me is never, ever going to happen again. You've crossed every professional boundary that anyone could ever cross. But I'll tell you this. You will not cross personal barriers. We work in the same office, so cut the games. I know your type, and I don't like it. You can't come in here and ask me out for a drink after what you've done. I play things straight. I've worked hard. And you came along and took it all away in one swoop. I hope, James, that you're proud of yourself. Frankly, I don't know how you can live like you do. And now, I'm going. I came here for some peace, if you must know. Because I'm utterly sick of you carrying on about my lost author in every meeting we attend. It sickens me."

"Tess."

She grabbed her bag. What more damage could he possibly want to do?

He leaned forward and rested his hand on hers for one slight, tiny second. Then drew it away.

Tess started.

"Tess," he said, "I promise you that my father thinks highly of Edward Russell. Dad's not trying to rip you off, or hurt your career in any way. He just wants to meet you. He's intrigued by the book. I know how much you want to make this book a bestseller. And I agree. It could well get there. But talking to a literary critic, building anticipation—what harm can come of that? Dad could well decide to mention it before he reviews the book. His reach is huge. Surely for Edward Russell's sake, you can put aside this thing between us and talk to my father?"

Tess's resolve hardened. She would not let him get to her any further. She gathered her things up with more dignity this time.

But she also realized that if she declined Sean Cooper's offer, she'd be risking getting on the wrong side of one of the most influential people in the industry. So what was she supposed to do?

James waited, his eyes unwavering, staring straight at her.

"You know what," she said, enunciating her words with perfect clarity. "The thing is, I can see that your father could have an . . . influence on Edward's book. I know that if I turn down your 'offer' I risk losing Edward the publicity that could escalate his reputation and his sales in the most influential spheres in the country. But I swear, James, I want your word that you are telling the truth about your father's motives. Presumably, you have some sense of moral dignity. If you have, you can at least attest to that."

She glanced at him, but remained strong in the face of the naked hurt in his eyes. He'd effectively destroyed her career, whether intentionally or not. She would not give in to any charm whatsoever.

He lowered his voice. "All I can say is that I never wanted to hurt you. And I promise you that I'm telling you the truth. My father knows about Edward and his friends. He's intrigued by their art, by their views, by the battles they had. Nothing puts my father off more than blatant commercialism."

Tess opened her mouth and then closed it. Sean Cooper had probably never had to worry about where the next cent was coming from in his life.

"Can I get you both anything else?" The waitress's accent cut into the air.

"No, thanks," James said. "Just the check."

The waitress wrote out a bill on her notepad and placed it on the table. "You have a great day now," she said.

Tess slid cash for her coffee onto the check, just as James did exactly the same thing.

"I know it would benefit Edward for you to talk with my dad."

Tess slung her bag over her shoulder. She eased her way out of the banquette, her hands feeling clammy against the slick material as she moved. And stood up.

James stood up too.

She stopped a moment right next to him. "Against my better instincts, I'll talk with your father. But I swear, James, if there is anything disingenuous about this . . ."

James's gaze was fixed on her. "I'm not saying it again. I'll see you at five at reception." And he stood aside so that she could leave first.

Tess buried herself in nonsense for the rest of the day, focusing on administrative things that needed to be done. At five o'clock, she made her way to the bathroom, glaring at herself in the full-length mirror that hung at the marble entrance. She reminded herself that she'd be stupid to turn her nose up at Sean Cooper, but trusting James seemed about as smart as stepping into an alligator-infested swamp.

If she were honest, the thing that complicated matters was that she'd admired Sean Cooper from afar for a long time. She found him interesting and stimulating. Having the chance to meet the famous critic was awe-inspiring and nerve-racking at the same time. Tess pulled out her compact, did a quick emergency touch-up, squirted a little Chanel, and redid her lips. Her blue suit was professional, and at least she was wearing a pencil skirt that suited her frame. The killer heels would give a no-nonsense message to James if she had anything to do with it. She marched out to reception.

James turned when she swung quickly into the lobby. She found herself frowning again at that slight expression of hurt on his face.

"Hello," she said, her voice brusque. She was all snappy efficiency, but what did he expect?

"We'll go straight to meet him at home, if that's okay," James spoke softly.

"Fair enough," Tess said.

James stood aside for Tess to make her way to the elevator. He hailed a cab outside the building, and they rode in relative quiet up past Central Park, although Tess's nerves were on a shoestring. She felt ready to pounce should he say one word. When they stopped at a grand apartment building overlooking Central Park, Tess stared up at the tall, all-glass apartment block and then tried not to frown as they moved through the understated lobby. Tried not to think about Alec Burgess, fitting right into this refined, literary-elite world now that he was successful too. Was that why he'd moved across to James? To fit in with the literary Establishment? There was no doubt James had more cachet than Tess could ever muster when it came to the right connections. But when had the "right people" become more important to Alec than doing the right thing by others? Tess was reminded of Edward's confusion about his own family. She glanced around the lobby. Edward's book must be getting to her. She would have to stay focused, and wary.

An elevator operator pressed the button for James to allow them access to his parents' apartment. As if James could not do that for himself. Tess forced herself not to roll her eyes.

James chatted easily with the elevator operator, calling him Ernie and introducing Tess as if they were old chums. As they stepped into his parents' apartment, Tess found her eyes feasting on the delightful sight in front of her. Turkish rugs and worn leather sofas decorated a room that was lined with bookshelves. The tall windows that ran down one entire wall almost seemed to bring Central Park inside. Sean Cooper, who looked even more elegant and urbane in person than he did on television, came over to greet them, holding out a hand. He looked ten times friendlier than in the media.

"Tess. So great to meet you." His dark eyes were the image of James's. "James admires you, I know that. So that makes this doubly nice."

James admired her? The only thing she had to say about that was that James clearly had inherited his charm from his father.

"Coffee?" James made his way across to the kitchen, which was vast and to the side of the inviting space.

"Yes, thanks," Tess managed to utter. What had she expected? Of course Sean Cooper was going to be exactly like this around his one and only son.

"Come and sit down, Tess."

The rattle of the coffee grinder enveloped the room, too loud to allow for any conversation. When James sat down on the sofa next to Tess, handing out mugs, he cut straight to the chase.

"Dad, Tess would love to know why you're intrigued by Russell's book."

Sean leaned forward, cleared some space on the coffee table, and placed his cup on a round coaster made of soft wood. "I can assure you that I am genuinely interested, Tess. I would never invite you here for any other reason."

Tess took a sip of her coffee. What had James told his father about her? But then she shook away that thought. She had to stop letting her annoyance at James get in the way of progress. Edward. She was here for Edward. End of story.

Sean's voice was almost mesmerizing—deep, soft, and clear. "I hear the book is a love story." He paused a moment and looked toward the window. When he spoke again, it was as if his voice were coming from some far-off place.

"Is the girl in it called Rebecca Swift?" he asked, his voice sifting into the quiet room.

Tess placed her coffee cup down.

"Why do you ask?"

Sean sat back in his seat, crossing his legs.

Tess had to associate the word elegant with this sophisticated, intelligent man.

"I'm asking you because I suspect that she's exactly what Russell needs to write about. It had to happen sometime. And if he is writing about that period of his life, then it's going to make a massive difference not only to his career, but also to yours," Sean went on, in his honey-smooth voice.

The room seemed silent now. Tess was suddenly aware that not a pin-drop of noise came in from outside. Their little circle of three had become intense.

Tess waited. She either worked with Sean, or against him. And she reminded herself he was Sean Cooper. Were she honest about it, she had no choice.

She let out a breath. "The girl in the book is called Rebecca. And, well, I admit that I had the same sense as you. I looked her up. Rebecca Swift. The authorities reported that she fell off a rock on the Australian coast. It was tragic."

Sean was quiet for a while. Tess was acutely aware of James moving right next to her, bringing one leg up to cross it over his knee. She stared at the coffee table.

When Sean spoke, he seemed to be choosing his words with care. "Does Edward know that you are aware he had a love affair with the young artist?"

Tess shook her head.

Sean raised a hand to his chin. "Before we talk about that, I've been thinking about Edward. You see this with writers, with artists. If they lose inspiration the effects can be dramatic. When Edward lost Rebecca, it was as if he lost his muse. His early poems, which he wrote during their relationship, showed such promise, such anger and passion and challenge—in terms of challenging existing structures, forms, and meaning—that had he continued down that path he would have ended up being an important writer of his generation. His ideas were radical. Once Rebecca died, he lapsed. Had a stable, to be honest, boring career. He took up a safer option. Other people's lives. Biography. Edited literary magazines, lectured on English lit. He never made a living out of his writing.

"He hid behind a facade and never, ever wrote his own truth. Not after she died. The question is, did he also fail to live in a manner that was true to himself after he lost Rebecca? I suspect so. Which is what the modernists were all about—authenticity in both life and art. Edward lost both. Now we have a chance for a remarkable talent to rediscover his potential, at least in his work. It's too late for him with Rebecca— but the idea of a searing love story between a young writer and an artist will resonate with people. You have a role in nurturing his writing. I look forward to the results of your collaboration with him, Tess."

Sean leaned forward, resting his hands between his knees. "As for the circumstances surrounding Rebecca's death, she was not the first to be drowned and lost on that stretch of coastline. And the sea there is notorious for shark attacks."

Sean's voice cut into Tess's thoughts. She couldn't stop herself from picturing Rebecca's awful death. Tess's stomach plunged. How Rebecca would have suffered, would have known she was going to die . . .

"Rebecca was only twenty-four. But it was at Edward's family's beach house. The guilt he must have felt from that alone could have stopped him from feeling he had any justification to write anymore."

Tess turned to the tall windows. The idea of sharks and Rebecca seemed even more unbearable.

"There's more." Sean's voice was soft.

Tess wrapped her arms around her body.

"The other thing that I think you should know is that when an exhibition of art was held posthumously by Sunday Reed and the Contemporary Art Society, Rebecca had several works displayed. She was hailed as a real talent. Rebecca was thought of by critics as someone who could have had a flourishing career in modern art. Sunday's talent was for finding and nurturing artists. Sunday has been recognized, in the end, as one of the most significant figures in modern art in that country. However, all of Rebecca's artworks are in Sunday's collection. They are effectively hidden from the world, you see. Sunday didn't sell them after Rebecca's awful death. Rebecca's work was ahead of her time. There is no doubt there would be considerable interest in her drawings were they to be released to the world along with the book."

Tess nodded.

"The Heide circle were young moderns, trying to forge a new life out of the shatters of war. It was all-encompassing, you know, what they did, their rejection of the Establishment. From the way they lived, to the way they loved, freely, to the way they approached marriage, modernism went to the very core of themselves—especially in terms of the way they viewed art."

Tess picked up her coffee. "I don't think Edward will want to publicize his personal life. I think that even if I let him know that I've learned the book is autobiographical, he will not want any publicity. In fact, after the last couple of discussions I've had with him, I'm concerned that he could even back off writing the book because he's so opposed to commercialism in any sense. But I do think in some ways, like any story, Edward's story is not entirely his own."

She stopped.

James adjusted his position on the sofa.

"If he were to release the autobiographical nature of the book, even without Rebecca's work, then the sales for him would be—"

Sean raised a hand. "Tess, confront Edward. Ask him about Rebecca Swift. You and I both know that if he goes public about the relationship with Swift, the book will sell exponentially better. But more to the point, tell him his story will resonate with people because it's human, a love story, a story about a man who has closed up for forty years, because, quite frankly, I think that's what he's done. Without Rebecca he hasn't been able to write. It's the idea of a muse that intrigues me, of losing that one person who inspires everything. That's the angle you need to take."

Tess looked at him sharply.

But Sean went on. "So, yes. I support the idea of encouraging him to go public about the truth. After all, he believes in authenticity, so not telling the truth to the world smacks of hypocrisy. The truth is multilayered. There are so many intertwined factors, not to mention different points of view, but at its heart, it usually boils down to one thing—honesty toward oneself and others. And I hate to say it, Tess, but Edward's book is going to be much better than those thrillers that you've built your career on so far. I could never have reviewed those." He looked at her over his glasses and a smile played on his lips.

Suddenly, James stretched his arm along the sofa behind Tess's back. "If Tess pushes Edward too hard, I'm worried she could lose his trust. She could risk losing him."

"What I'd suggest," Sean went on, "is that you get Edward to confess that it's a true story, first up. Then take it step-by-step from there."

"I don't think he'll do it," James said.

Tess looked at him, steel setting into her thoughts.

"You don't know that, James," Sean said. He went on, smooth as ever. "I'll review the book once it comes out, but you have a lot of work to do, Tess. And focusing on Rebecca's death, her story, and the political and artistic postwar background is exactly what needs to be done."

Tess nodded. She knew that.

James stood up and looked at his watch. "I have to go. Out for dinner."

Tess swung around, suddenly alert. Who was he going out to dinner with? She shook that train of thought out of her head.

Sean stood up.

"Good luck working with Edward. He's a fine writer. And you know," he said, as they hovered by the elevator door, "I've always had this sense that he needed to, well, for want of a better word, explode into the world. And you are going to have to be the one to get him to do so."

Tess pressed her bag to her chest.

"Thank you, Dad." James leaned forward, patted Sean on the back.

"Thank you," Tess said, taking Sean's hand when he held it out to her.

After the elevator doors opened, James waited for Tess to step inside while Ernie held the door open for them. Inside the elevator, Tess stared straight ahead, acutely aware of James next to her.

"You know what I think," he said. "I just don't think he'll react well, but you can try."

"Yes," Tess said, looking him squarely in the eye as the elevator slipped to a gentle stop. "I will definitely try, James."

She saw that almost hurt look pass across his face again and suddenly felt overheated as she stepped out of the elevator into the charming lobby.

Tess reached for the dress that hung on the front of her white-painted wardrobe the following evening. Its black velvet bodice sat luxuriantly above the golden flounced skirt with its dipped-at-the-back hem. She stepped into the glamorous frock, reaching back and zipping it up before moving across her studio and checking her reflection in the full-length mirror on the back of the bathroom door. Her hair swung; her makeup was perfect. And yet, she felt nothing but worn out; all day, doubts had plagued her about the best way to approach Edward.

Somehow, she needed to marry Edward's modernist outlook with the commercialism that would cause his work to shine. While Tess understood that the modernists had been trying to redefine themselves after the war, commercialism, business, and opulence were the buzz-words now, in publishing as well as every other business. It was the eighties. Surely Edward would not insist on living in the postwar auster-ity bubble that existed in 1946?

Fair enough, he didn't agree with the way his family operated, but he must have felt attachment to his childhood home, to the land that his forebears had worked, to the garden, to the beauty of the place. And now, was he honestly willing to give up the possibility of turning his book into a real success? People loved true stories. Rebecca herself should not be ignored, and what was more, the love between Edward and Rebecca was timeless. It would appeal to romantics all over the world.

Tess slipped out of her apartment and indulged in a taxi. She stared out of the window and took in Manhattan's glittering lights as they cruised toward the Plaza for the gala evening in celebration of the publishing industry and authors.

Once inside the Terrace Room, Tess mingled with her overwhelmingly male counterparts before sitting down at the editing team's assigned table. James was next to her, facing away. He chatted with another colleague while Tess talked idly with Martin Haymes, one of Campbell and Black's most senior editors, who regaled her with stories of his weekend fishing trips, while repeatedly mentioning that he didn't enjoy these functions in the least. Tess found her mind drifting.

She placed her cut-crystal glass back down on the white tablecloth and gazed at the elaborate gilt decorations, the glistening chandeliers, the white- and gold-painted arches that framed the trompe l'oeil decorations on the walls. It was a monument to wealth, to what, in fact, the eighties represented. Luxe. Grandeur. Was there anything wrong with such things?

Tess's own grandparents had lived simply after the war. Neither side of her family had been wealthy during the fifties and sixties, and Tess's parents lived a far more opulent lifestyle now than they had when they were young. Surely for Edward it was time to move on, to take advantage of the new world that had emerged after the war. It had been proven that communism didn't work, that Fascism was a failure. But

Tess knew she was dealing with deeply held beliefs when it came to Edward. She adjusted her shining skirt.

When Martin told her he was off to mingle, Tess took a sip of her champagne. Relief at the end of his repetitive conversation blended with the realization that James's neighbor had stood up too.

James turned to her.

"So," James said, shooting a glance toward the dance floor, where several couples drifted about. "Don't you hate these things?" His voice was soft and smooth.

Tess smiled, surprised at that opening to the conversation. "Oh, come on, James. This is the sort of event you were born to attend. You're not fooling me by denying it."

James looked at her momentarily, his expression hard to fathom, then picked up his glass of champagne, taking a sip. He placed the fluted glass back down and leaned in closer to her. "I hate these events more than I hate every damned charity event that I have to go to with my family, every dinner party for whoever is the latest celeb in New York that my mother hosts, and every tea party that she has for all her friends who do nothing but flit between fundraisers. You have no idea."

Tess caught her breath. "But you're in the social pages constantly."

"Yup. You think I enjoy that?" He sat back in his seat, throwing his arms behind his head.

Alpha pose, Tess thought, narrowing her eyes. But she couldn't help but admire those well-chiseled features . . .

She leaned forward. "Hang on. You're the life of the party at work. You're charming all the staff, and don't interrupt me," she went on as he brought his chair forward and sat closer to her. "When you're in the society pages, you look happy enough—it's as if you're related to the Kennedys, for goodness' sakes. And you always have some charming woman on your arm."

She did not want to sound as if that bothered her, but for the moment, she felt like challenging him, and that intrigued her.

"You know," he said, "in spite of the fact that you're an editor, you seem unable to read subtext, Ms. Miller. Do you wonder, then, that you're struggling with an author who wants authenticity in his work?"

Tess picked up her champagne and knocked back a swig.

"What I do wonder, Mr. Cooper," she said, leaning forward herself, surprised at the sense that she and James were in their own little bubble now; it brought to mind Edward and Rebecca's sense of feeling in their own circle, but she pushed the thought away. "What I wonder is why you put on such a facade. If you really hate all this so much"—she glanced around the room—"then why do you put on an act? Why don't you live your life the way you want to live it? What's holding you back?"

A rueful smile passed across James's face. He sat back in his seat again, and watched her. "You have no idea, Tess. I think if anyone's putting on a facade, it's you."

Tess pushed her seat back and stood up. And nearly bumped straight into Leon, who had appeared behind Tess's chair. His wife, Tania, stood beside him, glowing as she held her husband's hand. Her blond hair was pushed back from her face in two wings, and she wore pale pink taffeta with a flounced skirt that was fit for a palace.

"Hello!" Tess said, as if they were a life raft for her sinking ship.

"Tess, James." Leon patted James on the shoulder. "Great to see you two bonding. Aren't these things terrific? Such a wonderful evening put on for us all!"

Tess smiled at Tania.

"Tania and I are going to dance. James, why don't you ask Tess? Join us. Both of you. I'm looking forward to you both moving forward with great success in the coming months!"

James reached up and whispered in Leon's ear. "That would be incredibly generous on my part. Can I say no?"

Tess focused hard on Tania's shining face. The other woman's expression remained fixed: pink lipstick, pink cheeks, a permanent smile that never died. Tess knew that Leon's wife would never enter into anything remotely controversial. Tess had long ago realized that Tania only dealt in politeness and euphemisms. Was that how she survived in her role as an executive wife?

Tess stood up.

"Excuse me. I must catch up with some . . . friends." She looked James straight in the eye and moved away.

But annoyance pinched her insides as she moved through the room. She forced herself to focus on the crowd, catching hints of conversations that drifted out from the endless round white tables, festooned with voluminous blooms. Deals were being struck as Tess made her way past every group. No one was hiding the fact that tonight was all about work.

Usually, Tess loved losing herself in business. It didn't matter whether it was Sunday morning for brunch or a dawn breakfast at some swanky Manhattan café, Tess was always available when there was an opportunity to progress. The harder she worked, the longer hours she put in, the more successful her career. It was simply how things worked.

But when she lost Alec Burgess, she tasted the tang of failure for the first time in her working life. She'd been forced to confront the fact that her career might not always be the one iron-safe thing she could rely on, and at the same time, while she hated to admit it, Edward's book had affected her. She was starting to see her own surroundings in a different light. And yet, if Edward wasn't going to fit into the way things were done at Campbell and Black, then Tess was risking losing everything she'd worked so hard to build up. It would be as if she'd lost herself.

Tess stopped at the edge of the room, glancing about the chattering groups. She was looking for one specific person. It took her a few moments to see the safe haven she sought.

Flora was at a table across the room. Her red hair swung around her face. She wore, as usual, vintage: a bright green 1950s dress, flared at the skirt, tight at the bodice. Tess loved that Flora didn't care about what anyone thought. Confidence, that was what Flora had. But how she did it, Tess had no idea. Flora's rise to acquiring editor with the top romance publishing house in the world, bringing a stable of successful authors with her, remained legendary in the industry.

Tess slid into the empty seat next to her friend.

"You look like you've just had an encounter with a moaning specter," Flora laughed. "What's up? Tell me!" Flora poured her a glass of champagne.

More champagne . . . Tess took a sip and gave Flora a rundown of recent events.

"It's completely obvious what's going on here," Flora murmured. "In standing up to James, which you had to do, you've obviously gotten to him," she said. "Or he wouldn't have felt the need to get right back at you in return tonight when Leon suggested you dance together."

Tess groaned. "Do not put me in one of your novels! Just think outside the world of romantic fiction here. Because this is real life. And the two do not merge. Zero chance. We both know that."

She would never say anything to disparage Flora's disastrous love life. Her friend had a trail of nasty ex-boyfriends, and yet she seemed to forge on with this idea that if you fought for what you wanted, everything would turn out for the best. Flora never gave up hope. Perhaps her views were more similar to Nico's than Tess had first thought. It was just that they both approached things in such different ways. Flora, in turn, accused Tess of being a cynic.

"You should let go of that carefully guarded exterior," Flora went on. "You know I think that. Just go for it. See what happens. James is intriguing. From what you've just told me, there's something cooking up between you. Something's brewing here." She tilted her head. "Actually, I think what's happening is that he's your equal. He's challenging you and you don't like it. So you're sparking off each other. And of course you're challenging him up front. Nobody's probably done that before. He's so set in his life, always gets what he wants . . ."

Tess put her glass down and fumbled about for her evening bag, clutching it like a life raft on her lap. "Hang on. Stop. James stole my client, end of story. Now he's feeling guilty and trying to make amends by introducing me to his powerful father. While telling me a whole lot of stuff about how he 'doesn't really enjoy mingling in the top social circles in New York, because it's not who he is.' I'm not stupid, Flora. He's trying to charm me, like he does everyone else. Because it doesn't suit him to have a colleague upset with him. That's it. End of story. Tonight he showed his true colors. He's a fake, a fraud. Says one thing, does the other. I'm not going to bore you with clichés . . ."

But Flora leaned a little closer. She traced a pattern on Tess's glass with her lustrous pink fingernail. "He's upset you. Doesn't that tell you something in turn?"

"Don't be ridiculous." Tess looked at the swirling couples on the dance floor. Leon and Tania were in the middle of the crowd. The song was slow. George Michael. Tess watched while Tania wound her arms around her husband's neck.

"For goodness' sakes, look at that," Tess muttered.

"So beautiful," Flora said.

Tess rolled her eyes.

"He's coming over," Flora announced. "Ten o'clock, making a beeline for you."

Tess started to stand up.

But James arrived before she could get up and flee.

"Tess," he said. "Flora."

"Hello, James!" Flora trilled. "I heard about your new job."

James held Flora's eye. "Yes." His tone was short.

Tess sometimes wondered if Flora lived more in her own imagination than in the real world that was unfolding at her feet. Tess saw through James, well and good. Flora was intelligent. Why was she constantly duped by charming men?

James narrowed his eyes. And looked, Tess thought suddenly, a little like James Dean. But that was very stupid thinking. She tapped her fingers on the table. If he wanted an argument, then she was right here and ready.

"Tess," he said, "would you like to dance?"

There was a silence.

Flora almost leaped out of her seat but Tess shook her head.

"Thank you," she said, pushing her chair the rest of the way back, "but I have things to . . . do." And she walked away. She was furious that her breathing was shaky, and also furious at how violently she wanted to get away.

CHAPTER FOURTEEN

Haslemere, 1946

Rebecca's heart hammered as she and Edward approached Haslemere. Her glance swooped over the honey-colored house, taking in every detail: pale roses that traced delicate patterns across the Victorian facade, a fountain in the middle of a manicured lawn, a clipped green hedge. A peacock's call broke the otherwise quiet afternoon. On the veranda, two blond women, clearly Edward's mother and sister, lounged on wicker chairs.

Rebecca transferred her sweaty hands to her lap, smoothing out the printed dress that she had worn on the day that she and Edward went to the beach. Now she worried that it was all the wrong color. Both the women on the veranda wore pale blue. Red would seem callous, sharp. Dare she say it, cheap?

Edward pulled up on the sweep of gravel outside the veranda, moving around the car to open Rebecca's door. Rebecca did not know where to look. And it was as if all the old insecurities that had been drummed into her by her mother were back again. How could she possibly expect to fit in here? These were the women whom her mother served in the boutique, not people with whom the likes of Rebecca could expect to associate.

Edward stood by the car a moment. "Come and meet Vicky and Mother." He sounded fine, but his eyes darted to the two women who watched.

Rebecca swallowed the lump that had formed in her throat. As if on automatic pilot, she placed her hand in Edward's and climbed out of the car.

She stood up straight, held on to her hat, and made her way up the wide slate staircase to the veranda. As she and Edward approached, a thin smile appeared on Edward's mother's face. Her daughter nodded, but Rebecca saw in an instant that the girl's blue eyes were narrowed into slits. And yet, did she detect a little amusement on Vicky's face?

"Mother, Vicky, this is Rebecca Swift," Edward said, his voice sounding well-modulated, perfectly cultured. A little different from her Edward.

Rebecca winced at the sound of her surname. It sounded cheap, too, in the midst of all this quiet assurance. She held out her bare hand, then cursed herself for not wearing gloves for travelling. But it was hot, and she hadn't thought about such things.

Celia rested her own soft hand in Rebecca's for a moment. "Delighted to meet you, my dear," she murmured.

Edward's younger sister's eyes were definitely dancing.

Rebecca sat down, each movement that she made seeming heightened, somehow. Edward poured lemonade. Rebecca, thirsty after the long drive, avoided grabbing the cool, delicious drink and gulping it down in one go. She hoped that the fact that her hands were shaking was not obvious to anyone except herself . . .

"Did you get lost, Ed?" Vicky asked, turning her attention to Edward and widening those blue eyes into two round orbs. It struck

Rebecca how innocent the girl—who had to be around twenty-two or so—looked, but how filled with insouciance and almost sarcasm her voice was. "We were expecting you for lunch."

Rebecca put the glass down, the sugary drink having restored her strength a little. She placed her hands in her lap and laced her fingers together.

"We came up the old road. Wound our way through the paddocks. I wanted to show Rebecca that route," Edward said.

"How tedious. Everything looks the same out here. They're only trees, for goodness' sakes." Vicky turned her attention to the garden, as if there were something fascinating going on in the fountain. "But Edward sees things that I swear no one else bothers to look at."

Edward chuckled next to Rebecca. He handed her a plate of sweet cookies while his gaze still lingered on his mother and sister. Rebecca would never admit she was starving. She took a piece of shortbread and raised it to her lips, but suddenly, the thought of swallowing it was impossible. She placed the delicate cookie back on her plate.

Edward's mother observed this debacle and Rebecca felt her cheeks flush.

"You see, Rebecca, Vicky and I spent much of her childhood travelling on the continent," Celia said. "Australia is dull for her at times, no matter how attractive our landscape is."

"I imagine it would be," Rebecca said. "Dull. After the excitement of Europe."

It was as if she were playing a game of tennis in which she was not sure how to hit the ball. This was Edward's sister and his mother, she reminded herself. His kin. There had to be some thread, some connection she could forge. The two women seemed relaxed. They didn't appear to be worried by her.

Rebecca forced herself to take a deep breath. "You are so very fortunate to have travelled on the Continent," she said.

Celia inclined her head. "Indeed. I know. Have you been to Europe, Rebecca?"

"I'm afraid I haven't, no."

"Haslemere does have its own beauty," Celia said. "And Vicky, there is something in the landscape out here. It helps if you have grown up with it." The older woman smiled at nothing in particular.

Vicky gazed into the distance again.

"Edward tells us you are an artist," Celia went on. She sounded a little warmer now, but Rebecca sensed that the older woman was probably trying to be polite. It was an act, she suspected. How could Celia Russell be pleased that her son had brought home a girl who was clearly not the right sort of person? Rebecca had seen enough of the women who frequented the shop in Collins Street to know that she must seem strange and overly sensitive to them.

"I draw in charcoal and brush and ink, yes," she said. "But I wouldn't go so far as to describe myself as an artist."

"But you are studying art," Celia said.

"Yes, at the Gallery School. It's not . . . well. It's not quite what I had hoped it to be," she murmured. "But I do appreciate the opportunity to be there."

"I once took some art lessons," Celia said.

"You were good at drawing, Mother." Vicky's voice rang in the still air.

Rebecca caught Edward's eye. He winked at her.

"I would have liked to continue," Celia went on. "But I haven't had the time."

"Perhaps you could draw with Rebecca," Edward said.

"I think my opportunities are lost now."

"What will you do with your art course, Rebecca?" Vicky said.

Rebecca smiled at the younger woman. "Well, I don't know," she said. "I haven't thought."

"One step at a time," Edward murmured.

Rebecca reached for her lemonade. The journey had been long, and she felt grubby next to Edward's pristine sister and mother.

Edward picked up on her mood. "Would you like someone to show you to your room, Rebecca? Perhaps a little while later, I could show you the garden. I want you to feel at home here."

Vicky sat up taller in her wicker seat.

Edward rang a small bell on the table. The sound of footsteps tapped along the wooden veranda. It was a bucolic setting, Rebecca thought, dreamy and perfect for lazy afternoons in breezy outfits. A maid appeared, a young woman of around eighteen.

"Clare, would you show Rebecca to her room, please?" Edward said.

The girl nodded.

Rebecca stood up. "Thank you," she said. "It was lovely to meet you."

Celia smiled. "It was, my dear."

"It was fun to meet you, too, Rebecca," Vicky said.

But it seemed impossible to know what to think, or what Edward's mother and sister honestly thought of her. Rebecca followed the maid along the cool veranda and through a screen door into the interior of the house. They went through a conservatory, resplendent with vast potted palms and more wicker seats, into a long gallery, bordered on one side with leadlight windows.

The maid walked in silence past several closed doors before entering a room that overlooked a sort of wild garden. Rebecca's eyes roamed to the window. Outside, a cedar tree threw shadows over dark, untamed plantings. But the room was decorated in light colors—perhaps to make up for the rich, verdant garden outside—with light green-and-white striped wallpaper, a pale green carpet, a chair, and a four-poster bed. A painting of two children hung above the fireplace. When Rebecca looked at them, it was as if their eyes followed her.

Rebecca turned to the maid, who appeared to hover.

"There is a guest bathroom next door," the maid said. "Is there anything I can do for you, Ma'am?"

"I really don't need you to look after me." Rebecca took in the girl's pale eyes. What would it be like, being stuck out here working for Celia Russell?

"Mrs. Russell insists that we look after each and every one of her guests," the girl said.

Rebecca smiled gently at the maid. "But you see, I am not Mrs. Russell's guest," she said. "I am Edward's."

The girl looked down at the carpet. "There is a guest bathroom for your use next door. You are welcome to have a bath. Please, make yourself at home here."

Rebecca dropped her voice. "Thank you." She was slightly taken aback by the girl's acquiescence. Her good manners.

The maid nodded and went back to whatever task she was meant to be doing now. Rebecca closed her bedroom door and leaned her back against the white-painted wood. Then spotted something. She went over to the small desk below the window, where, like a salvation, her drawing things were laid out.

After an hour of blissful sketching, she went into the bathroom next door and soaked in the warm tub. When she was back in her room and dressed, the maid appeared. "Excuse me, miss, but Master Edward is waiting for you in the library."

As Rebecca followed the maid along the gallery, she was able to take in the beauty of this old mansion with more of a sense of calm than she had felt earlier. When the girl led her into a vast room decorated with William Morris–covered sofas, where bookshelves lined the room from floor to ceiling, Rebecca gazed around and smiled. Heide's smaller library came to mind, filled with Australian novels and books on art. Rebecca had to wonder who took the time to read the wonderful collection in front of her.

She hoped it wasn't only Edward.

Edward stood by the mantelpiece, looking like the lord of the manor. Seeing him there was a little unsettling. He had changed into a pair of white moleskin trousers, and his light blue shirt brought out the color of his eyes.

"I'm seeing you differently here," she had to say. "You look like the perfect country gentleman dressed like that."

And suddenly she had to ask herself, which was the real Edward? The man who had seemed so at home with the modernists in Melbourne, or this one, who seemed equally comfortable out here on this grand old station? Did he know which he truly was himself?

"I know all this is overwhelming at first," he said, his voice soft and close. "But it's really just . . . home," he said. "I'd like to show you around."

"I'd love that. And it's beautiful here." She sensed that he needed reassurance.

He moved toward the paneled door that led directly to the driveway. She followed him into the late-afternoon light. English trees threw shadows on the drive. Edward made his way around the house to the back garden, moving across the lawn, then waiting for her to go first through an arch in the thick hedge. This led to a myriad of gravel pathways overhung with rose arbors and old frames lush with exotic species that Edward explained his grandmother had brought back from Spain. It was as if she and Edward were wandering in some ancient, long-held sanctuary, a testament to the creativity of generations past.

It was different, of course, from what Rebecca understood of Sunday's relationship with the land and her garden at Heide—or was it the same? Did the fact that whoever planted this wonderland did not have the same ideals as Sunday matter? If they had both wanted to make something beautiful, was it relevant where they stood on the political divide?

Rebecca found herself questioning again as she wandered by Edward's side. It was so hard not to become entranced by this, by this wealth, by the beauty that went with it. And yet . . . she held the same ideals as the Reeds and hoped that Edward did too.

"I love to garden," Edward said suddenly, his words coming out urgent, as if, perhaps, he were making an explanation for everything out here. Explaining that he contributed to this. That he was not some lazy bystander, the entitled younger son. "Of course it's not what I'm supposed to do."

Rebecca looked up at him.

He stopped at the peacock aviary.

Rebecca's eyes drank in the birds' jewel tones, her gaze shifting while the peacocks moved, their feathers luminous as they passed from the shade to the sunlight.

"I have ideas but my parents don't approve," Edward said. "I think we should allow other farmers to grow crops on our land. In fact, I think we should convert the paddocks to a collective, sharing profits with other local sheep graziers, who would, in turn, contribute stock. As for the garden, I would make that more productive, more sustainable, to supply food for us and even for our neighbors. We have so much land to take care of. As it is, Haslemere is losing money. Badly. That needs to change. Before it's too late."

Edward walked as if with a new purpose, his arm around her. Rebecca felt a smile dance on her lips as she walked next to him, following him through the glass conservatory, its vivid orchids hailing from the Far East. When they came back out into the garden, he led her to a green wooden door set into a high brick wall. Edward took her hand and led her through to the stable courtyard with a clock tower. At least forty horse stalls overlooked the ghostlike space. But only a cat lazed now, alone in the center of the silent square. Once the courtyard would have rung with the shouts of hundreds of men. It was impossible not to feel their echoes lingering in the empty space.

Edward moved over to lean on a fence at the far end that overlooked the paddocks as the sun dipped and pinkness cast itself over the land. Curlews and magpies called to their mates.

"What a beautiful place to grow up," Rebecca murmured, staring at the still beauty of the paddocks under the vast Australian sky.

"It was," Edward said, his words drifting between them. "Vicky and I spent hours in the garden, dreaming up games when we were young. Robert was gone to boarding school by the time I was five. We did have a strict nanny, but we were blessed with a kind governess, and we had plenty of time out here to ourselves. And then . . ." His words trailed off. "Then. We were separated, so young, and everything changed."

"Sunday talks of rules for people of your class," Rebecca murmured. "I'm beginning to see what she means."

"That's it," Edward said. "That's exactly it."

"Do you have a choice now, Edward?" she asked.

That was the question that hung between them—the choice between his family's way of life or a new way of living. A sheep bleated somewhere out in the green expanse.

"I think I do."

Rebecca's gaze darted around the serene stillness in front of them, while her thoughts tumbled along of their own accord. "But Sunday and John have had to lose everything that they knew in order to create that new life. Would you really want to do that?"

Edward turned to her then, tucking a loose strand behind her ear. "I know," he whispered. "I know."

And he drew her close.

She felt her heartbeat race when his lips touched her forehead.

"I love Haslemere," he said, murmuring into her hair. "My connection with the land out here is not measurable in any terms. But at the same time, I can see what it is to have freedom from it all. Sunday and John may look like people from their class, but they feel differently.

Their way of life is bold and experimental, revolutionary, in a quiet sort of way. But it's a leap, and it's a leap I just . . ." His voice trailed off.

Rebecca reached up and placed her fingers over his lips. He leaned down and kissed her. Until the sound of footsteps on the courtyard cobblestones clipped into the evening air. Edward pulled away with a start.

"Edward!"

Vicky stood in the middle of the stable courtyard, her arms folded. "Mother wants you back in for drinks at eight," she said. "Father has arrived home, along with Robert."

Something cold sliced through Rebecca's system.

"We won't be long, Vicky." Edward's tone was calm.

"You'll get in trouble, that's all I'm saying."

"Don't let her get to you," Edward murmured, as his younger sister marched back to the house. Her figure looked slight now, her blond hair hanging in loose waves, as if it had been curled for some event or other to which she was not going to go.

"I understand where she is coming from. She seems astute though, Edward. I think she sees beneath the surface of things too," Rebecca said. "Perhaps it's a good thing that I've met your family out here, away from the city."

Edward threw an arm over her shoulder. "Yes, although things can seem heightened out here without the distractions of Melbourne."

Rebecca leaned into his shoulder as they wandered back through the courtyard to the house.

Edward held the heavy front door of the house open for her, standing aside.

"The dinner ritual starts at eight. I'm afraid they are sticklers for time," he whispered. "It's seen to be rude to arrive even a few moments late. You'll hear the butler ringing the gong; just come to the library then."

He held her hand a moment, lingering, before turning and moving to the left, to another wing of the old, echoing house. Rebecca stood for a moment in the long gallery, wondering about the ghosts of past generations—the ancestors who had worked so hard to build Haslemere up. What would they think of the modernists and Edward's attraction to their new way of life? Rather than moving toward her bedroom, Rebecca turned, suddenly wanting to spend even a few precious minutes alone out in the fresh air before meeting the rest of Edward's family for dinner.

CHAPTER FIFTEEN

New York, 1987

The next morning, seedy from lack of sleep, Tess crossed Fifth Avenue and entered her building. The smell of coffee permeated the reception area. Several of her colleagues stood around, chatting about the ball. While caffeine was gorgeously tempting, Tess needed her own space. She'd determinedly pushed thoughts of the evening out of her head ever since leaving the Plaza. Instead, she'd forced herself to focus on Edward. Once in her office, Tess picked up the phone. This was it. She was going to confront him with her plans. There was no point putting it off for another moment.

Leon stood at her door.

"Morning, Tess," he said, his voice perfectly bright, eyes bright, tie just so.

Darn the tie.

"Morning, Leon." Tess smiled her brightest smile right back.

"I'm calling a meeting about next week. Could you come over now? Does that work for you? Apologies for the short notice."

Tess placed her phone receiver back in the cradle. "As a matter of fact, that's just fine," she said, almost falling out of her chair with real relief that she could put off her phone call to Edward for another hour.

Leon moved to go out. "I'm so glad you had a good time last night. And Tess?" he went on.

The smile she gave him was so tight it hurt.

"Thank you for being such a good sport about Alec and James. I appreciate it. You've done well. Don't let anyone tell you anything different. See you in the boardroom in five minutes."

Tess turned to her water jug and poured herself a big glass.

A few moments later, she sat surrounded by the usual array of suits.

"So," Leon said, "I want to confirm plans for next week."

Tess picked up her pen. She'd decided to hit Edward with it straight. Tell him how it was. There seemed to be no other way forward with him. If he wanted authenticity, then he needed to get in the real world . . .

"James and I, as many of you know, will be in Rome for the week."

Tess's head shot up like a bullet. She grabbed the side of her leather chair. Rome. She racked her brain. Of course. The Festival Internazionale di Letteratura.

James and Leon going to Italy now?

Edward lived in Rome.

A meeting here in the boardroom. Good place for an announcement. No chance of a tantrum from poor old Tess. Excellent. She fought the urge to yell at them both.

Ten minutes later, the meeting was done, Leon having successfully engineered people to take over where necessary when he was away for the week. All the plans were in place. Tess wasn't even on the page. Again.

She stood up, dragged herself to her office, closed her glass door, sat down in her swiveling chair, turned a spin in it, and leaned heavily on her desk. She was going to think this one through. Not give them the reaction they expected. Not this time.

So, James could hardly not have known he was going to Rome, say, two days ago when he took her to his father's apartment. And last night, when he spoke with her at the ball? He just hadn't seen fit to mention it. His tactics were astounding.

Tess buttoned up her suit jacket and made her way down the corridor to Leon's office. Leon was at his desk. On the phone. Tess waited outside the glass wall, her head filled with plans.

"Come in, Tess." Leon stood up once he was finished and opened his door.

"Leon," she said, "can we talk for a few moments?"

Leon stepped aside.

Tess bumped into the chair in front of his desk, righting it a split second before it toppled to the ground.

"What can I do for you?"

Tess winced at her clumsiness. "You see," she said. There was no other way. She had to do it. "I need to tell you something about Edward's novel."

Leon picked up a pen, started shuffling papers.

"It's autobiographical."

Leon looked up and put the pen down.

She had him.

"Go on," he said, his voice dropping a few decibels.

"The love story in the book is based on a young man who is also called Edward—an unusual setup in itself. I'd been reading, wondering myself what was going on and why he'd done that, but then it turns out that the love interest in the book is based on a real artist called Rebecca Swift. I've found out that Rebecca Swift was a talented art student who drowned in 1946. Rebecca's death was something of a loss to the art world in her country. But Edward has mentioned nothing to me about his novel being based on a true story."

Leon stayed quiet.

"The famous Australian art patron, Sunday Reed—although she's more than an art patron, she supported artists all her life—organized an exhibition of Rebecca's work soon after Rebecca died. Apart from that, Rebecca's story has been lost. Her work is hidden away at Heide, the Reeds' famous home. Leon, I want to talk to Edward about the possibility of his releasing the true story behind the novel to the world to coincide with the release of the book. Talk shows, you know the drill. But he's very into, well, avoiding anything commercial."

Leon slid his chair closer to the desk. "You want to approach him with care."

"Absolutely. Which is why I haven't rushed in yet. But the thing is, I think it would be better to approach him in person."

"You want to go to Rome. Tess—"

"Yes. I do. I need to come too. I'd like to be at the Festival; that's one thing. But I have to talk to Edward in person. It's not going to work on the phone. He has these ideas that are so stringent, and if I can just spend some time with him, have a chance to explain the benefits of publicity . . . then that's in all our best interests, including his."

Leon began shuffling through a pile of papers on his desk.

Come on, Tess thought. *This will benefit you, Leon.*

Leon looked up. "What sort of chance do you think you have? Can you convince him?"

"Yes," Tess said, lifting up her chin. "I'm extremely determined to do so. But I have to give it the best chance I can. And I can't do that from New York."

Leon peered at his notes. "How would you feel about James approaching Edward on your behalf? I want him to go, because the Festival is right up his alley. It's what he does."

Tess forced herself not to state the obvious. Instead she said, "Leon, if we send James, what sort of message is that giving to Edward?"

Leon tapped a few numbers into a calculator with his pristine white fingertips.

He doesn't do any housework, Tess thought. Fingers were immaculate. No gardening. Doubt he liked getting his hands into the soil like Edward did. Why was she surprised?

"Leon," she said. "You wanted me to have the opportunity to work with Edward. You and I both know what I did for Alec's career. You have to trust me to deal with Edward Russell on my own and have faith that I can and will make his novel a bestseller. It's what I do."

Leon inspected the mess of papers on his desk. "Well." He let out a sigh. "I don't need a trip to Rome right now, to be perfectly honest. I'm snowed under, and I'm just not wanting to be . . . away from things . . . for a week."

Tess waited.

Leon shook his head. "Look, Tess, if you were to take my place and go instead, then the deal is that you have to convince Russell to work with us, not against us. I heard he was messing around with deadlines from the marketing department. If he doesn't want to be professional, I don't know that we'll be able to publish him after all. Do you see what I'm saying?"

"Crystal clear." But a stone fell into Tess's stomach. If Edward were dropped, then where would that leave her? She pushed away her annoyance toward James. "I'm determined to convince him, to alter his stance," she said. "Ideals are all very well, but you have to know where to draw the line with them."

When Leon spoke, his voice was a little shaky with relief. "I have to tell you I was going to be in great trouble with my son if I went away next week. He's performing in a play . . ."

"You won't want to miss that." Tess smiled at her boss.

"No. I hadn't told him I was going away. I hadn't told Tania either . . ."

Maybe she had things a little wrong about Leon. Maybe Tania was not so . . . perfect after all.

Leon's phone rang. "I'll have Alice see to the changes. There'll be a cost involved, but to be honest, Tess, it sounds like the company is better off absorbing that than risking Edward's book not reaching its full potential. I look forward to hearing how you get on."

He picked up the phone.

"Thank you," Tess mouthed.

He waved at her, frowning at the next problem he had to face.

Tess moved out of the room, turned into the corridor, and refrained, but only just, from punching the air. The moment she had confirmation that her tickets were sorted, she picked up her phone and dialed Rome.

"Edward," she said, "I'm sorry that we got off to a bad start. I was wondering if we could meet next week? I will be in Rome for the Literature Festival. I'm sorry if I came across as a little abrupt during our last phone call."

"No." He sounded implacable.

Tess drooped down in her seat.

"It's me who needs to apologize."

She brought her hand up to her mouth.

"Let's have dinner while you're here. And Tess?"

"I'm here."

"The answer's simple. We need to meet each other halfway."

Tess blew out a breath. "I agree. I think your book is going to be wonderful. I'm loving it. In fact, I know it's going to be great."

There was a silence down the phone. "We'll organize where to meet when you get here. Have a safe flight."

"Thank you." Tess felt the itch of her conscience once she'd hung up. She needed him to exploit himself, his family, and Rebecca in public, with the media.

Did that make her any better than James?

CHAPTER SIXTEEN

Haslemere, 1946

The horizon beyond the endless paddocks was stained a deep pink. Rebecca leaned against the fence at the edge of the old stable yard. She could not help but imagine the whispers and rustles that would fill the landscape overnight; snakes, possums, and mopokes would take over the paddocks while everyone in the grand old house slept.

It was the landscape that had drawn her in out here, so uniquely Australian, vast and beautiful and wild all at once. As darkness fell across Haslemere, she should have been seated at her dressing table and looking at her three-tiered mirror, being attended to by the maid. Instead, she'd found herself drawn not only to the ancient landscape but to the garden with its secret paths and the vast old mansion, where she sensed ghosts of generations past, of the women who'd married into the Russell family, living in such opulence as to have a steamship of their own. The endless, grand rooms fascinated her. She'd poked her head into the vast farmhouse kitchen, then gone in, as it was empty. Glancing into the servants' small living room that led to their bedrooms and the laundry, she thought of all the lives spent here in service, while the family lived in splendid grandeur.

Rebecca turned back from gazing at the endless sky. She wandered through the quiet stable yard, opening the chipped green wooden door set in the old stone wall that she and Edward had taken when they left the garden, wandering back toward the roses that glistened in the dim light. She passed the aviary, big enough to house tall trees, and the conservatory with its tropical plants.

Rebecca made her way past the tennis court, its sagging net sitting as if waiting for someone, anyone, to play a game again. Beyond the tennis court, there was a folly, a tower that apparently Edward's grandfather used to sit in while watching games of tennis in the station's heyday when the house had been full of guests. So, where to with all this? How would Edward's legacy marry with his modernist views?

And that begged the next question—unless someone with a slew of both determination and money took these old places on, what was going to become of these wonderful reminders of the past? How was all the hard work of previous generations and the lifestyle that these mansions demanded supposed to ring true with the generation who had just been through the war? No one wanted to work in service any more. Clare seemed an aberration to Rebecca.

Rebecca stopped by a wall that crumbled, the old sandstone tumbling to the earth in places. What Edward wanted was not going to be simple. She only hoped his dreams—which by now were intertwined with her own—were not going to be impossible in the end. She turned back to the house, wandering through darkness now.

She went into the front door, passing through the long gallery, past the library, greeting Clare and entering her bedroom. She still had an hour or so before dinner, so she sat down, pulled out the cartridge paper that she had brought from her tiny studio in Melbourne, and began to sketch.

Rebecca stood at the doorway to the library precisely at eight p.m. The family was grouped around the fireplace and a waiter in black tie handed around drinks on a silver tray. But that was not what caused Rebecca to come to a standstill. It was the unexpected guest. A sense of panic rose; her outfit was all wrong. The black dress she'd chosen was a castoff from the store where her mother worked. It had a slight defect in the bodice, but no one would know except Mrs. Swift. Rebecca ran her hands over the flared skirt, wishing now that it fell to her feet in elegant cascades like the dress that the stranger wore as she stood laughing with Edward's mother in the center of the family circle.

And it was at that instant, at that moment, that the girl turned around, along with Celia, whose face was flushed with delight. Their laughter stopped as their eyes landed on Rebecca, who felt acutely the way in which the other girl eyed her simple black dress up and down. But then the beautiful girl, and she was undeniably beautiful, made her way across the room, a smile lighting up her elegant features—wide smile, warm green eyes, blond hair swept back from her tanned complexion as if it were the most effortless hairdo in the world. Her long pale gold dress swished on the carpet and she wore black gloves.

Where was she off to? A ball?

She held out her hand to take Rebecca's, clasping it, smiling into Rebecca's eyes.

"I'm Edith," she said. "Any friend of Edward's is always a friend of mine. Charming to meet you. Johnson?" she went on, to the butler who hovered with drinks. "Come and bring Rebecca a drink."

Rebecca felt her eyes widen at the way the girl seemed to be running the party.

Edward extracted himself from a conversation with a young man who was an older version of himself—clearly his brother, Robert—and made his way across the room.

"Rebecca," he said. "Sorry. I was just about to introduce you. This is Edith. An old family friend."

Celia wafted over in oyster silk. "An old family friend?" Celia chided Edward. "Well. That's a funny way of saying she's very important to us all."

An odd expression passed across Edward's face.

"Edward and Edith have known each other since they were very young," Celia said. "Edith's family owns another station, a little way up the road. Her mother, Elspeth, is my oldest, dearest friend."

"We're a-hundred-miles-away neighbors." Edith laughed.

Edward chuckled.

"Well put." An older man appeared next to Rebecca. He dangled a cigarette from one hand and held a glass of red wine in the other, but Rebecca started at the smell of whiskey that emanated from him. "What are we all standing around the door for?" he asked.

"Good point, Angus!" Edith laughed. "Let's move back to the fireplace."

Rebecca's chest started to thump, but what was she supposed to do? She had little choice but to follow the other girl's lead. Little choice but to be entranced by her along with every other member of Edward's family, it seemed. And Edward? What did he think of the beautiful girl in their midst? Edith seemed to have a glow around her, a certain something that was hard to define.

Although, if she were honest with herself, Rebecca knew what it was. It was class. Upper-class confidence. There had been several girls with this effortless panache at the small private girls' school that Rebecca had attended in Melbourne. Her mother had insisted on sacrificing other things to pay the fees so that Rebecca would meet the right sort of people. But she knew that at some of the more famous girls' schools, Edith's behavior was de rigueur. Ironically, her mother would approve of her relationship with Edward . . .

Rebecca clutched her champagne glass. The thought of swallowing the acidic drink turned her stomach into a swirl.

"Father, Robert, this is my friend Rebecca Swift," Edward announced. He'd adopted his stance by the fireplace again. Rebecca smiled at the two men who flanked Celia. On closer inspection, she noticed the telltale bloodshot red of Robert's eyes and the way his hand shook slightly rather than resting calmly by his side as Edward's did.

"Good to meet you, Rebecca." Angus's voice was liquid, murky with alcohol. "Welcome to Haslemere."

Rebecca saw the way Edward's father's eyes darted to Celia. Was it panic that she noticed in his glance?

"Thank you." She couldn't find any other words to say.

"I've always loved this room," Edith said. "It's my favorite at dear Haslemere."

"Edith comes here to ride regularly," Celia said to Rebecca, as if she were explaining how things worked to a young child. "We hold the hunts here. Edith's a terrific horsewoman. Do you ride, Rebecca?" she asked.

The only horse experience Rebecca had ever endured was with a pony when she was eight years old. It was on a farm where her family had gone for a holiday, a rare event, which was painful for them all. The pony had chased Rebecca around the paddock, determined to bite her. Rebecca had been the smallest one there and the pony had taken exception to her. She had avoided anything equine ever since.

"I confess I don't ride," she said.

"Vicky and Edith will be going out in the morning. You should join them. They are both excellent horsewomen and could teach you in no time at all."

"That is, if you're interested," Edith said, her eyes sparkling.

The warmth in the girl's expression seemed genuine, that was the strange thing. If Rebecca's instincts were right, Edith wasn't making fun of Rebecca or looking down at her in any way at all.

"We'll see," Edward said. "Rebecca's a talented artist. She loves to draw. In the morning she and I might go for a walk."

Rebecca shot at look at Edith, and saw a flame of embarrassment rise on the other girl's cheeks. And suddenly, Rebecca fought with empathy for this girl. Was she in love with Edward? Rebecca hardly knew what to think.

Dinner was announced.

As they all proceeded to the dining room, Rebecca took the opportunity to gather her thoughts. To adjust to the newcomer. Had Celia invited Edith as competition for Rebecca?

When she sat down at the cedar dining table, Rebecca felt as if she had landed in some grand old English estate. The room's deep red wallpaper was imposing, but at the same time, it closed in on the room. The polished table gleamed with silver cutlery and porcelain plates that were monogrammed with the family crest. Edward's father, oddly, had a packet of Bournville dark chocolate open on the table beside him. Rebecca wondered if he ate this to hide the smell of whiskey on his breath. And was reminded of her own father, who used to keep peppermint chocolates for exactly that reason himself. Oddly, now, in spite of the grand surroundings, she felt strangely at home with his behavior.

But Edith stumped her. Because it didn't take much to see Celia's plan.

"So, once you and Rebecca have gone sketching in the morning, or tramping around the paddocks with the sheep, what will you do after that, Edward?" Vicky piped up. She wore a simple blue dress, with a wide cowl neck and lace over the collar. "Please, darling, don't work in the garden. You mustn't be a complete bore. At least, out here, you're away from those darned bohemians. You know they were all described in the papers recently as 'degenerates.' Sorry, Rebecca." She smiled. "But you can't behave as if you are one of them while you are here with us."

Rebecca instinctively leaned toward Vicky and smiled back at her. She was becoming more and more drawn to the way Edward's sister spoke her mind.

"Your idea of boredom and mine are clearly quite different, Vicky," Edward said. "I might help Stewart in the garden. Or I might take Rebecca for a drive to show her some of the more beautiful spots around the area. We'll see."

"I think it's sweet that you enjoy the garden, Edward," Edith said. "But surely, you can leave the work to the gardeners who are paid to labor there?"

Rebecca chewed on her lip. Stopped herself from wincing.

"Well said!" Angus piped up, before taking a swig from his claret glass. "Darned right, Edith."

"You know how much I enjoy working the soil," Edward murmured. "But it's dinner time. Let's not get into an argument about the Heide circle. They are not here to defend themselves, after all."

Rebecca took in a shaky breath. Maybe she was being melodramatic, maybe she had it wrong, but as she watched the interactions, as dinner progressed to a rare indulgent dessert—no one had such luxuries after the war, so where did they get such things?—Rebecca knew with certainty that she and the modernists were seen as a real threat.

Even if there were only a few veiled references to the modernist artists, subtle criticisms made it more than clear that Edward's family wanted to keep Edward in his place at home. They would tolerate Rebecca for now, but clearly they saw her as having little significance. Ultimately, she was sure they would sweep her under the rug as a short diversion in Edward's life just as they seemed to be sweeping aside the fact that Angus and Robert consumed three bottles of wine between them during a two-hour meal.

"Well," Celia said, once they were done eating, "I think we'll repair to the sitting room."

She led them all past two rooms, Angus swaying at the back, while Robert wandered off by himself. Celia moved into the room opposite the library with a circular window that overlooked the garden. It was the perfect size for a soiree. A grand piano sat in the window alcove.

Rebecca's eyes shot over the priceless porcelain that was arranged on white shelves around the room, and the curtains that looked to be spun with gold thread.

"The curtains were installed for the Prince of Wales's visit, Rebecca," Celia said. "He was scheduled to come here back before the Great War, but he never did come to Haslemere. It was a shame, as the family built a ballroom for the visit, upstairs. It's my bedroom now."

Rebecca turned to the older woman. Had she just admitted that she and Angus slept in separate beds? And what about the girl who'd settled herself on the delicate sofa opposite? Was she after Haslemere and a life with Edward that involved separate rooms?

Couldn't these women see that this was only living in a gilded cage? Rebecca loved Edward, but were they to stay together, she knew that everything would have to be different. And extremely so.

The next morning, Vicky and Edith appeared in the dining room, dressed identically in wide-legged jodhpurs, with long boots that showed off their equally elegant legs. Their hair was swept back in hair nets and they wore identical white shirts with ties.

"We'll just have a small breakfast," Vicky announced, when they stood as if looking for appreciation. "Then we're off. Jester and Horace are saddled up. We've already been out to see Finn."

"Finn is our groomsman," Edward said, leaning toward Rebecca as she sat eating a boiled egg.

Celia clapped her hands at the sight of the two beautiful girls. "How marvelous," she said. "And the weather is perfect. I do like the fact that you get out in the fresh air from time to time. Are you sure you won't join them, Rebecca?"

Rebecca looked down at her pale green dress. "No, thank you, I won't." She felt something kick in—perhaps it was the spirit of Sunday urging her on? "I'm going to draw."

"The tower is the best place for that," Edward said. "I'll write while you draw. We'll spend the morning that way." He looked straight at his mother.

Celia brought her white napkin up to her face. "Edward, are you sure you wouldn't rather join the girls?"

"Quite sure," Edward said, and reached out his hand to cover Rebecca's.

Rebecca shot a look at Edith. And felt her stomach plunge as Edith's face fell.

Had the girl panicked and secured an invitation to Haslemere to stake her own claim? The thought that there might be more to Edith Harding than Rebecca had given her credit for last night seemed more threatening, and in some ways more upsetting, than what Rebecca had imagined Celia was scheming. Rebecca could understand that Edith may be determined to marry into a family of her own class, and she could also see why Celia would want Edith as a daughter-in-law. Edward was also a far more appealing catch than poor Robert, anyone could see that. But if Edith did love Edward, that was more complicated than just a marriage of convenience.

Half an hour later, Edward led her into the old stone tower that overlooked the forlorn tennis court, unlocking a black wooden door. Inside, his grandfather's folly was furnished simply, with an upright piano sitting alone in one corner. An old book of Schumann sonatas sat on the stand. The keyboard cover was up and the rich grained wood of the instrument was highly polished.

"I love it in here," Edward said, turning to her and using that intimate voice that she had come to adore.

"Do you play?" she asked. And thought of his expensive boarding school education. Was there nothing these people couldn't do?

Edward leaned on the staircase that wound its way up to the top floor. "I used to play, yes," he said. "Writing and playing music weren't brilliant accomplishments to have at a boys' boarding school. Luckily, I could kick a ball around as well . . ."

"I can only imagine . . ." Rebecca lifted her eyes upward. "Another staircase," she said. "Like when we first met . . ."

He took a step closer to her then, and Rebecca moved toward him at the bottom of the narrow staircase. His arms were around her waist, gathering her toward him, while she reached up, as if it were the most natural thing in the world, wrapping her arms around his neck. He leaned down and kissed her, and she was lost in that tender place.

After a while, he pulled back and took her hand. "Let's work together, darling." He started making his way up the winding staircase, his footfalls sounding solid, almost reassuring in the quiet.

When they reached the top floor, she faced him. "This is perfect," she whispered. By a set of charming French doors that overlooked a small balcony and the tennis court, an easel had been placed. On it were Rebecca's favorite tools—charcoal and ink—along with a new set of brushes.

"Thank you," she murmured.

Edward leaned against the small desk that sat against the back wall. Placed his folder of poems on it. Rebecca swept her eyes over the comfortable chair, its footstool covered in navy blue, and a small Turkish rug. A bookshelf was filled with books on writing.

"My mother bought those. She does believe in my writing," he said. "As long as none of it interferes with her view of how my life should be lived, then there is nothing wrong with a hobby," he said. "Sometimes I think she thinks that I will grow out of this writing and poetry phase if she indulges it. But what she doesn't realize is that none of this is a phase with me. None of it, Rebecca."

Rebecca turned around, filled with the magic that seemed to have wound itself around them again. She burned with questions about Edith and the hostility she'd sensed toward the Reeds last night, but she knew that if she pushed Edward to talk about that topic now, it could break the spell.

Once she'd settled down to draw, all her energy came out fast, in a fury. The light that drifted in, filtered by the balcony that was framed with ivy, sent speckled patterns onto her paper. Edward wrote behind her. She reveled in the sound of the scratch of his pen, the way he put his pages to one side as he worked, stopping every now and then, clearly to read what he had written. She was aware of him, but at the same time, she was in her own world, just as he was in his. And this, each of them having a passion of their own, she thought, was the perfect basis for their relationship. It was exactly the way things should work.

When the sun was high in the sky and the morning light that had shone with such pleasant contours onto her easel had dissipated into harsher midday light, Rebecca put down her charcoal. Edward leaned back in his wooden chair, his hands clasped behind his head.

He swiveled around to face her.

"That was perfect. Working alongside you . . ." His voice trailed off. "I love this . . ."

She took a step toward him, then hesitated.

He stood up, made his way to the deep blue chair, sat on it. He held eye contact with her and reached out a hand. She moved across to him and took it, and he gently pulled her down onto his lap.

"Edward," she said. "Edith . . . ?" Her voice trailed off, her fingers tracing delicate patterns on the palm of his hand.

"My mother," he said, his eyes on Rebecca's fingers, "wants me to marry Edith, darling. And Edith's mother wants precisely the same thing. We grew up together. Edith doesn't know me at all, though; you have to know that. She has no idea who I really am anymore. She's a lovely girl, but, darling . . . she's not in any way, anything like . . . you . . ."

Rebecca sighed. "But she's of your class. She's perfect as far as your family is concerned. Your family has clearly decided that the Reeds and their circle are degenerates. How will they cope if you deepen your association with them, which is, if I am not mistaken, what you want to do?"

He took in a breath. "I definitely don't want the life that my parents have. I want something better. I want something real. Coming home, I can see how false all this is. How the Establishment is like a breeding ground for horses. It is as if members of each generation are like colts placed in the ring to make a suitable marriage. We're sent to the right boarding school before we can think, before we are old enough to truly know ourselves. I suppose it's important to get us locked in with the system when we are young, before we start thinking for ourselves. But the war changed me. It's changed the way I want to live my life. I've seen how fragile life is. I've seen my friends die. Gone forever. Everyone's lives matter, not just those who come from a particular class or a certain country—one side of some border and not the other. The Reeds and their circle not only accept people for who they are, but they keep moving forward—which is the true sense of modernism. They do not go back. They keep pushing further. Sunday's remained determined to strike her own path, and I think it's those individuals we will remember in the end, not the followers. I want to determine my own future," he said.

"Rebecca." His eyes darkened and he reached up, gently pulling her down toward him, and she closed her eyes. It was heaven.

He was her heaven.

How could Celia and Edith possibly be any threat?

CHAPTER SEVENTEEN

Rome, 1987

Tess opened the shutters in her hotel room, looking out over the narrow cobblestone lane that ran off Piazza Barberini. Pale blue sky shimmered like a silk ribbon between the old buildings above her head, while conversation drifted up from below, echoing around the street. If Tess closed her eyes, it wasn't hard to imagine she was in the distant past.

She wandered barefoot across the cool terra-cotta tiles, past the double bed with its pristine white cover. While it was tempting to sink into the armchair near the window and read, avoiding the heat of the afternoon, Tess wanted to walk around the ancient city. She'd never been to Rome before.

She slipped on her ballet flats, picked up her handbag, and made her way out onto the landing.

James appeared from the room next door.

"Tess," he said. "You've settled in okay?"

"I have," she said, keeping her tone light. The flight had been awkward. James was the last person on this earth Tess wanted to sit next to for hours. She'd watched the film that was shown at the front of the plane and then pulled out some work.

While she was not going to dwell on his rudeness toward her at the ball, she was also not going to allow herself to be caught up by his charm or be tempted by any offers of kindness. Their relationship had to be professional. That was all.

She moved toward the stairs.

But James rested his hand on the iron balustrade of the staircase that wound its way to the ground floor.

"I was just going out," Tess said.

"Would you like some company?" He sounded tentative.

Tess stopped.

"Are you familiar with Rome?" he asked. "Because it's better if you know your way around."

"Really? I thought I'd drift and play things by ear. Wouldn't that be a better way to discover Italy?" Tess had to suppress a smile. All those chats with Nico must have resonated somehow.

But James stayed put. "We both know that we need to talk, Tess. We can't work together like this."

"I was just going for a walk. End of story, James."

"What are you doing tonight?"

"I have plans." The words came out in a rush, but it seemed important to make it clear that she was busy.

"Oh." The word lingered between them. "Okay."

She'd asked at reception about restaurants near the hotel. And they were going to reserve her a table at a local family-run trattoria on the next street. Tess found herself staring at his hand on the railing. His nails were squared off and neat.

"Can I come too?" he asked.

Tess took the opportunity to slide past him. She started to trot down the stairs. She wanted to forget about New York—couldn't he read the signs?

James followed her.

"Tess," he said, his voice echoing through the stairwell as he followed her down, "we both know if we're going to work in the same office we need to get along. What else can I do to prove I didn't take Alec from you? Leon assigned him to me."

Tess reached the first floor and made her way past the intimate reception desk to the heavy door that led into the street; pushing it open, she went out into the heat. "I'm going now, James," she said.

He pulled on a pair of Wayfarers.

Tess glanced to the side. She couldn't stop the smile that spread across her face. How ridiculously handsome he looked wearing those! He was just the sort of man she'd avoided all her life. Too good-looking, too successful. Too intelligent. He was probably exactly what her silly family would choose for her if they could. Socially, he would be a massive step up for them, and they would never stop reminding her of that if they knew she'd even met James Cooper on the subway, let alone that she was working with him, even if on the very worst of terms. She folded her arms.

"Look, Tess. I'm sorry about the thing at the ball. I clearly didn't . . . handle myself very well. I was just a bit frustrated after our conversation."

Tess tapped her foot on the cobblestones.

"I want you to give me a chance. We should get to know each other, try to work together, you know. I think we need to bury the Alec Burgess thing, once and for all."

"Of course you think that. Why wouldn't you? It suits your sort to have everyone at your disposal." Tess turned down the street.

"Tess." He was right there next to her.

She stopped at the first intersection she came to. The street that ran across the lane was sunlit, but Tess remained in the shade. Then, suddenly, she went left, only glancing at the smart little shops that lined one side of the street. People sat under white market umbrellas on the other side, sipping coffee. Tess moved on toward the end of the street and hurtled right past a clutch of Vespas. A group of impossibly good-looking young Italians lounged around in a small square outside a church. The afternoon was still and lazy and warm. It wasn't the place for fighting. All she wanted to do was blend into the old enchanted place. But James kept pace beside her.

"I think we should talk," he said, his voice low.

They came to a wide street. Tess stopped. She would like to see the Pantheon. Drifting was not going to work with James sauntering along beside her. She charged ahead, past a supermarket, down another side street. Graffiti spattered the solid grilles that were pulled down over shop windows. A group of tourists wandered along in shorts, backpacks hanging from their shoulders.

Tess hesitated a second at yet another intersection.

James took her arm and turned her to face him. "You're going in circles. Why don't we walk toward the Pantheon?"

Tess's smile was tight. Of course. What did he have now? ES annoying P?

"It's a ten-minute walk down Via del Lavatore, and we'll pass the Trevi Fountain on the way," he said. "Come on. I'll show you."

So, James knew his way around Rome. Of course he did. He probably had visited here every year since he could walk. Was there anything else he'd like to prove that he could do better than her? But she did want to see the Pantheon.

As they made their way down Via del Lavatore, passing shops laden with tourist wares, the atmosphere became gritty. Restaurants flashed cheap bright signs, while shops sold postcards and plastic suitcases tied together with strings on the street.

Restaurant hawkers called out to them, hassling Tess to come and sit in one of their plastic chairs, to linger at tables laden with plastic tablecloths where customers sat with greasy pizza in the golden afternoon light. This wasn't the Rome she wanted to see. Tess felt her shoulders hunch as she walked alongside James.

But suddenly the road opened up into a piazza and a beautiful old church overlooked groups of tourists and the Vespas parked around the square's edge.

And there it was. Tess gasped. The Fontana di Trevi. James pulled off his sunglasses, his eyes searching her face.

"There we go," Tess murmured, her eyes drawn to Oceanus's muscular body, his abundant beard.

James moved closer to her. "The fountain's placed where an ancient Roman aqueduct ends," he said. "According to legend, this aqueduct takes its name from a woman whom the Roman soldiers met when they were thirsty and tired. She led them to the source of water that feeds this aqueduct and restored them back to health."

Tess kept her focus straight ahead. In spite of the crowds of tourists snapping pictures, their loud voices echoing through the heat, the sense of his standing close behind her, his voice like toffee, was starting to get to her.

"Let's go to the Pantheon," she said. Anything to move on.

"Okay," James murmured.

Tess made her way through the throng. She walked next to him as he wound his way down the Via delle Muratte to the Via del Seminario. Deliberately, she forced herself to focus on her surroundings, tall office buildings. Wrought iron lamps hung from the old facades, lending a nineteenth-century feel. Tess felt her insides curl as they passed quiet alleyways.

James walked confidently, as if he knew the streets of Rome as well as he did those of New York. Tess hugged her arms around her body. And then she stopped dead still as they reached the piazza at the end of the street.

There it stood, right in front of them. Nearly two thousand years of wear and tear sat graciously on its proud facade. She moved out to the center of the Piazza della Rotonda to stare at the classic perfection that rested before her eyes.

"Hey," James said.

She turned to him.

"Why don't you go inside on your own? I have a few things to take care of." He smiled down at her.

She started a little, not sure how she felt about his decision not to come with her.

But he took a step away from her then. "Thank you for letting me join you," he said.

"That's fine!" Her voice was far too bright. "But . . ." she trailed off.

He stood there for a moment, waiting. "Enjoy it," he said.

James disappeared into the crowds on the cobblestones, while Tess stood there in front of two thousand years of history, feeling more confused and less significant than she'd ever felt in her life. But there were two things that stood out in her jumbled thoughts: one, during that darned walk, she had felt undeniable stirs of attraction for James, and two, she was starting to wonder if he was right. Had he had nothing to do with Alec's defection? Had he simply been told he was Alec's editor, and had Leon and Alec engineered the move?

Tess glanced around the ancient square as if it might hold the answers before moving toward the entrance of the magnificent old building in front of her. She wandered inside, her head tilted, as every other person's was in the vast space, toward the tiny pinhole of clear, unadulterated light that shone in through the ingenious open circle in the dome.

The next morning, Tess had to force herself to focus on Edward Russell. He was enough to deal with without her having become foolishly attracted to James Cooper. Both men were trouble; each was born into a different type of privilege, and yet in many ways the two of them were so alike that Tess hardly knew what to think. And they'd both crashed into Tess's life. She had to deal with them. The problem was, she had to work out how. As she wandered through the Basilica of Maxentius, which was all set up for the festival, the wondrous old curved space with its vaulted roof started to work its Roman magic and calm her circling thoughts.

She sat down a little early in one of the chairs that had been set up for the first reading, fanning herself with her program, glad to be out of the searing heat that enveloped the city. And spent the day being fascinated by the young poets whom she heard reading and inspired by the authors who spoke so well about their work. She spotted James a few times, but last night she'd deliberately suggested they go to separate events so that they could swap notes after the festival. And so that Tess could get a grip. She had to focus on her work.

By six o'clock, the sun still beat hard on the Forum. Tess lingered in the temporary bookstore that was in a marquee outside the Basilica of Maxentius, entranced by the books for sale. She eyed James making his way to her through all the festival guests.

"I took your studied lack of eye contact with me as a message that you wanted to be completely left alone."

"You could hardly blame me," she murmured, picking up a book of poetry.

He picked up another volume, by one of the most charming poets who had spoken at the festival so far, and flipped it over, not looking at Tess as his next question popped out with more insouciance than anything else. "Have you worked out what you're going to say to Edward Russell?"

Tess already held several slim volumes under her arm.

"I'll get there. I'm still thinking about it."

She felt James's eyes run over her face. "You're meeting him at eight?"

Tess nodded, her arms full now.

"I think we'd better stop buying books." James held as many volumes as she did. "So . . . what are your thoughts about him?"

Tess moved across to the counter.

"I've decided the best approach with Edward is to be honest," she said.

James nodded. "I'm of the firm belief that if in doubt, tell the truth."

Tess swiped a glance at him, standing right next to her in the line. She half wanted to believe him here in the lazy heat; if she were honest, a niggling part of her wanted him to be the person he said he was. But, she admonished herself, he'd taken her author, not told her he was coming to Rome, been utterly obnoxious at the ball. He was a work colleague, nothing more. She forced herself not to smile at the way he'd opened one of the books of poetry he'd chosen, his eyes running across the page, clearly concentrating on the words.

He kept up a steady banter on the way back to the hotel, and Tess found herself laughing with him a few times. Lightening up and avoiding controversial topics seemed to work well. But when they arrived at the hotel, he stopped at the bottom of the stairs, leaning on the balustrade. He seemed to have something he wanted to say.

"Tess," he started, finally. "I hate to do this, and I didn't know how to tell you, but Leon called me this morning. He insists that I come along with you to meet Edward tonight. I told him there was no need, but he wouldn't take no for an answer, I'm afraid . . ."

Tess took an involuntary step back. "What?" Dread sat in the pit of her stomach.

James raked a hand over his dark hair. "Leon's worried about breach of contract given what you're about to approach Edward with—the fact that we're about to ask him to reveal his novel is based on his past, not to mention that we want him to talk about Rebecca in public. Leon's also concerned about Edward's ad hoc approach to his work. We need to get him working with us, Tess, not against us. Leon just thinks I've had experience with . . . more literary types and their vagaries."

Tess could not hold back her retort. "So, who do you think I've been working with throughout my career? Dinosaurs? Apes?"

A grin passed across James's handsome face, but then he shook his head. "This isn't a directive from me. Leon just thinks having two of us there lessens the risk of any breakdown in the contract. What you're about to do is hardly conventional."

Tess put her bag of books down on the floor in front of her and regarded James. Her last conversation with Edward had been better than the first. She'd thought she'd made some progress.

"Remember, it's also only one meeting," James said, his voice soft.

"The implication is that I can't handle even one meeting myself. I don't like this."

James appeared to consider this. "I'm worried that if you refuse to have me along, Leon will say you're being unreasonable. Edward clearly wants to work on his own terms, and you're about to throw a massive wrench in his gears. He's not going to be happy. And Leon knows how annoyed you were at having to work with him in the first place. I hate to say it, but I think he just doesn't want any sparks to fly. He thinks having a third person present could tone things down. That's all. I'm sorry it has to be me, Tess."

Tess let out a groan. "It was hardly surprising that I felt some resistance toward the idea of editing Edward at first."

"I know."

"But, you know what? Now that's not the case." Tess looked down instinctively at her handbag, where Edward's little book of poems sat, and tried not to think about the fact that James had been the one who lent it to her. "It's different now. I want to work with him. And I need to develop my working relationship with him, James."

"Yes." He stood there.

Tess ran her free hand through her hair, her hand slick from the heat. "James."

"Mmm hmm?"

She looked straight up at him. Met his eyes. Saw the expression in them soften, and hardened her own resolve. "I hate to say this, and I don't want to be suspicious, but if you were in any way interested in soliciting yet another one of my authors . . . if this is some scheme . . ."

"No," he murmured. "It wasn't me who made the decision about Burgess. I don't know how many times I've got to reassure you of that. And this isn't me, either."

Tess took in a shaky breath.

He propped his arm against the banister, leaned a little closer to Tess.

She didn't move but just looked at the floor, her lips set.

"I promise you that I will never, ever solicit Edward," he said, sounding as if he held all the secrets locked in one special place. "You have my word."

Tess wrapped her arms around her own waist. This was insane. The magnet, the full force of attraction that she was feeling toward James was the last thing she needed. She was already completely off course with her career; now she wanted the man who'd caused all her problems? Utterly irrational. Tess wanted nothing of the sort.

"I think that Edward could be a career breakout for you," he went on in his honey voice. "And I have no doubt that you'll make him a success. But I promise you, I am completely supportive of your career . . . and of you." He paused. Reached out with his hand, then drew it back in. "Are we all clear now?"

Tess looked up.

A slight frown creased his forehead. "See you back here in an hour? I promise, I'll just be there to keep Leon happy." He picked up her book bag from the floor and handed it to her.

She reached out and took it, but as she did so, it seemed as if everything moved in slow motion. And she turned away from him, not wanting to look into his eyes. This was crazy.

It had to be Rome.

Back in her room, Tess collapsed on her bed, kicking her shoes onto the floor. But then, in a panic, she went into the bathroom, one idea fixed in her head. If James could look stunning, and effortlessly so, then she was not going to let herself down either. What was more, if she was going to convince Edward to agree to her plan, then she needed all her armor intact. One hour later, she checked her appearance in the mirror. Her eyes sparkled. And her insides danced. But in spite of all that, she admonished herself: do not do anything nonsensical with James.

But as she made her way down the stairs, Tess sent silent thanks that she had brought her favorite strappy red dress. It flowed from the bodice to just above her knees, and its color gave her confidence. That was all. Nothing else.

James stood in the lobby, wearing a white shirt that was open at the collar and a black jacket and trousers. There was something about the way he stood there, so upright, right on time . . . Tess shook her comparisons with the men she'd dated right away. This was not a date.

"You look beautiful," he murmured.

Tess stopped and clasped her hands together. She must focus on Edward. But when she walked past James as he held the door open for her, she noticed he smelled like heaven. His hair was still slightly damp from the shower. *Stop it. Idiocy,* she reprimanded herself.

Be professional, Tess. She couldn't afford to make a serious mistake.

James made his way to the restaurant, chatting, keeping his gaze straight ahead, dodging the crowds as if he were a born Italian, taking Tess's arm a couple times when they almost bumped into people, letting it go as soon as they'd passed. He told her stories about the writers he'd seen that day and encouraged her to do the same. By the time they reached the lane where the restaurant was, she was smiling and at least feeling a little more relaxed about the task ahead.

Tess spotted Edward Russell as soon as she stepped inside the restaurant. He looked so gentlemanly in his white shirt and light trousers, with his hair neatly combed, that Tess, for an absurd moment, pictured the little boy who had been sent off to boarding school, while Celia swanned off to Europe. Then an image of him as a young man walking along the beach with Rebecca ricocheted into her head. She turned to James.

"That's him," she said. "I'm sure of it."

"I know it is." James slipped a hand into the small of Tess's back.

She loved the feel of his hand on her back, but told herself off for thinking that, and then moved toward Edward. James stood aside, allowing Tess to shake the older man's hand first. Edward's skin was slightly tanned. His face was lined in a handsome, rugged way. Once they were seated, Edward asked about the festival, and by the time they picked up their menus, Tess was laughing at both her companions' easy talk.

James sat back once they had ordered and were sipping Chianti. There was a moment of quiet, and Tess knew that the time was right.

"Edward," she said. "Something has come to light, and I want to talk to you about it. It would be remiss of me not to, in fact."

Edward turned to her, his expression so relaxed she almost doubted her motives again.

"It's about Rebecca," she said. There was no point beating around the bush.

Edward placed his glass of wine down on the table.

Tess kept her eyes steady on the older man. She was ludicrously aware of James next to her, ludicrously annoyed that she wanted to move closer to him, but she forged ahead.

"I'm afraid that I found out she was real," she whispered.

Edward shot a glance down to his lap. "I see," he said. When he looked up again, the expression on his face reminded Tess of that hurt look she'd seen pass across James's features a couple times. She was starting to link these two men together.

There was a silence.

"How did you find out?"

"The library," Tess said. "I felt there was so little separation between you and the book."

Both men seemed to lean in closer to her, and now thoughts of the circle that Edward wrote about between him and Rebecca came to mind. Circles . . . the Heide circle, the upper-class one that so intimidated Rebecca . . . and the one that seemed to be forming now. She was glad James had come along. He seemed entirely in tune with Edward, and, she had to add, with her as well . . .

Tess took in a breath. "Most fiction is autobiographical," she said. "But what I want to know, what I want to ask, with all respectfulness toward you, is whether you would be willing to reveal that Rebecca is based on a real person. I understand it's sensitive. Enormously so."

Tess held Edward's gaze and sensed that she was starting to move forward from losing Alec. Decisions had been made for her that were beyond her control, but here was a chance to take the things she had left and shape them into something new, with a different approach, one she had not used before in her life or in her work. If Tess were honest, she was starting to feel a swell of new promise for the first time in a while.

"The thing is, Edward," she went on, "if you revealed the truth, you could generate incredible interest in the book. The true story will resonate with people. If you were willing to share it, then I think you'd do extremely well."

Edward sat quite still. He picked up his glass of water, placed it back down on the table again. "Tess, I've never, ever written for commercial purposes. It's not what I'm about. Surely you know that."

The food arrived. The waiter asked several questions. Pasta. Would they like Parmesan cheese? Yes? He came back with it. Would they like cracked pepper? And returned with a giant grinder.

Tess caught James's eye and he raised his brow at her. She felt herself blush in return. Would they like more wine? They had to try a local Italian variety. Would they like the waiter to tell them all a joke? They all looked so serious and this was Roma!

"We are fine. Thank you," James said.

Edward added something in Italian. Clearly, he charmed the waiter. Definitely did the trick. The waiter went away bowing.

"How theatrical," James murmured.

"I'm never more reminded that we are all players on a stage than when in Rome," Edward said. "How does that look, Tess?"

"Delicious." Tess smiled. She adored pasta, she had to admit.

James and Edward chatted about the wine for a few moments. Then James stopped and Edward was quiet too.

"Edward," Tess said, "it runs deeper than simple commercialism. Were you to speak honestly about your past, to open up about it, I think readers would empathize with you in the most rewarding way." She took in a breath. "You would open yourself up as human, as someone who has loved and lost and survived. That is something to which we can all relate."

She sensed James's eyes on her. Had she gone too far? But the problem was, she meant it. She hated to think what her family would make of the words she'd just spoken. For a ghastly moment, she pictured her sister, Caroline, throwing back her head and mocking her, her beautiful green eyes alight with mirth. *It's to do with being human? What are you talking about, Tess? Just focus on the prize!* And Tess's whole family would laugh and laugh at what they would see as a gauche attempt to speak some truth she thought she'd found.

But Edward's expression was serious. Of course it was. He was Edward.

James was watching him and staying quiet.

"Tess," Edward said, finally. "Let's forget the commercial side of things for one moment. Because, to me, there is a difference between writing how I feel about life and making sense of it in a certain way, as opposed to telling the world about my experiences and thoughts in base terms, in some sort of television interview, which I think is what you have in mind. It seems too naked to me—unsavory. Does that make sense?"

James glanced at Tess before he spoke. "With all respect, your story and the ideals of your friends would resonate with people were you to talk about them openly. And then there is Rebecca. What you young moderns did, what you felt, was real. You were searching for the truth. And I have to say that in this day and age, the modernist philosophy seems more important and more relevant than ever. We live in an era of greed, but you and your friends questioned everything, and goodness knows, we need more of that right now. It's more important than ever not to sit back and believe all that we are fed these days about wealth and money building and greed. To me, we move in circles. Our prosperity means that we are rotating back to valuing exactly the things that you modernists fought against. And where will that take us in twenty, thirty years' time?"

Tess could only agree. While she'd originally thought that Edward needed to move with the times and take a more commercial approach to his work, perhaps it was equally important to look to the past, to not replicate the mistakes that people such as Edward's family and their class had made, because the bubble would burst in the end. And now, with the prevailing attitude toward power at all costs—power suits, power meetings, power lunches, even power naps had become catchphrases of the decade—maybe it was time for Edward to write about the long-term costs of such attitudes.

Tess leaned forward in her seat. "If you opened up about Rebecca, imagine. You'd be bringing her to life again. All her drawings, all her paintings hidden away there at Heide. What if they were released? Wouldn't you like that for her? Doesn't she deserve to be remembered properly? If you let it get out there that your novel is based on a true story, it would also be your opportunity to get the story right, rather than waiting for some hack, some smarmy journalist, to find that it is a true story and sensationalize it. You wouldn't want that for Rebecca, and quite frankly, I've grown fond of her. So neither would I."

She sensed James smiling next to her.

But Edward looked despondent. "I don't want to put a brake on your plans, Tess. But I don't want to go public with my past. Some things are too . . ."

Personal, Tess thought, *close to the bone,* as Edward's voice drifted off. She saw a smile flicker across James's face as he looked at her. As if he were sharing something private with her, an unspoken truth. But she could only feel that if Edward had really wanted to protect his past secrets, he would have changed the names of the characters in his book. So why had he not altered them if, deep down, he didn't want anyone to find out the truth?

CHAPTER EIGHTEEN

Haslemere, 1946

Celia Russell announced that they were repairing to one of the family beach houses for a few days just as Edith tried to convince Edward to come out riding with her for the afternoon.

"We are going out to the far paddocks. Do come with us, Edward! I always get lost out there. I know my way around my own property, just not yours especially well, I am ashamed to admit."

Celia's eyes glistened as she glanced from Edward to Edith and back. Rebecca hated to think cruel thoughts, but she couldn't stop imagining dollar signs running through Celia's head as she planned a union between the two. Their lands would be joined. It would cement the Russells' and Hardings' vast wealth if the two families became one, even if Edward was the second son. Plus, if Edward were married to Edith, he'd have little time for those bohemians. Edith would take over and charm him away.

Rebecca shuddered at the thought.

Edward instantly turned to place his hand over her free hand on the table. He shot a glance toward her. Rebecca felt her cheeks going pink.

Now Celia was looking at her too. She mustn't let this get to her. She and Edward were real. They were what mattered among all the things that didn't count. Their love for each other was it. She just had to calm down about Edith. But the problem was, the girl was actually . . . nice.

"I'm going to do some gardening this afternoon," Edward said, his voice matter of fact, his hand warm and strong on Rebecca's. "I want to mulch some of the more delicate beds before the weather turns and the nights become cooler. I have some seedlings growing in the glasshouse that I want to plant out before we leave."

Edith started as if he'd slapped her in the face.

"Edward." Celia was firm. "We employ five gardeners. Don't be ridiculous. Go out and keep Edith and Vicky company. I've told you time and again, dear, that this is not your role, nor do you need to concern yourself with such matters as the garden. Can you imagine someone of your consequence in England digging potatoes, when they have two young women offering an afternoon of riding? Honestly, Edward. I do hope that you get over this tiresome phase. Once we are at the beach house, at least you will not be able to persist with this notion of dirtying your hands!"

Rebecca sat back in her seat and felt her eyebrows rise to the decorative ceiling.

Edward firmed his grip on her hand. "I assure you, Mother, it's not a passing phase." Edward's voice was firm. "And I do remind you that were I to go out riding with Vicky and Edith, then Rebecca would be left alone."

"Rebecca and I can take tea in the sitting room. I would never have left her on her own," Celia said. "I was going to spend some time with her, Edward. Rebecca and I need to get to know one another a little better."

Rebecca saw Edward's eyes narrow. He waited a beat before replying. "Very well. Rebecca, darling, would you be happy to spend the afternoon with my mother, while I garden? I'm so sorry, I can't go out riding today," he said, softening his tone as he addressed Vicky and Edith.

Rebecca didn't look at either of the other girls. But she felt indignation emanating from Edith as if it were fire.

"Of course," Rebecca said, meaning it. If she were honest, her feelings for Celia were confusing. She understood the older woman's desire to see Edward married to a girl of whom she approved. Rebecca also had to admire the way Celia ran things. Her husband was clearly unable to cope, and she must be worried about her oldest son. The burden of the family's responsibilities would rest on Edward's shoulders since Robert didn't appear to be able to manage their holdings without him. Rebecca could see that Celia needed Edward to stay in line, to support the family and not to stray.

But she hated the fact that all her time with Edward had to be fought for. Celia seemed determined to interject, to try to run things her way, whether it was by introducing Edith to the house party, or in myriad other ways. One thing was clear: Rebecca was up against a singular opponent.

It had gotten to the point where the Tower was the only place that they could be themselves.

Breeding and good manners seemed as important to Celia Russell as false appearances were to Mrs. Swift. It was clear that to Celia, Edith wasn't just the perfect match for Edward, she was the only one.

But then, what else could anyone expect of a woman of Celia's background? Had Rebecca honestly entertained any idea that Edward's mother would somehow share her and Edward's modernist views? She had to stop wishing Celia would change. She had to stop wishing that Celia would become a Sunday, a kindred spirit, someone who would have more concern for the things that mattered.

No matter how much Rebecca wished Celia was different, or had a deeper, more sympathetic attitude toward life, Celia was not going to change. Rebecca knew she had to accept Edward's mother as she was, just as countless women before her had done, no doubt. She had to try to see things from Celia's point of view and do her best to get to know her. There was no point trying to glean from Celia something that clearly was beyond both her way of thinking and the set of beliefs that governed her entire existence. None of this was really her fault.

Rebecca gazed out the window at the garden. The fountain sent lazy spirals of water into the heat. She'd fallen gradually under Haslemere's spell. Over the past few days she had forged a real connection to the land out here and had taken to walking up the long oak-lined driveway in the mornings before everyone was awake—well before Edith or Vicky made an appearance at breakfast after being attended to by their maids. Rebecca ventured alone into the paddocks early in the mornings, reveling in the fact that her shoes were muddied on the grass. She understood and could see why Edward loved this place so much, and why he must feel such conflict at the fact that none of it married with his views on building a new life after the war.

Now, the maid, Clare, appeared. She stopped right by Rebecca's chair and held out a small silver platter. An envelope addressed to Rebecca sat on it, along with a letter opener. Rebecca sensed the other women's glances, along with their raised eyebrows. She turned the envelope over. The letter was postmarked Heide. Sunday's handwriting looped across its back.

"Do you mind if I excuse myself?" Rebecca asked. A sense of delicious anticipation arose in her heart.

Lunch was almost finished. Fine porcelain plates held the last of the cucumber sandwiches, cut in precise squares, and everyone was too polite to take what was left. Rebecca felt more and more like some sort of mess in such tightly controlled surroundings. A silver teapot sat pristine on the tablecloth and next to it was a plate of elegant cookies. Rebecca hated to think how hard the servants worked to support the extravagance of the Russells' lifestyle.

"Go ahead, Rebecca," Celia said. "I'll be in the green sitting room when you are finished with your letter."

Edward let go of her hand.

Rebecca didn't like to admit even to herself the enormous relief she felt at seeing Sunday's handwriting.

"Enjoy your afternoon, everyone," she said, and slipped out to the gallery, then along to her bedroom, where she threw herself down on her bed.

Heide

Darling Rebecca,
I hope you don't mind. I have taken some time to peruse your work. (I always take my time to consider art. I think it's important to do so. I don't hold truck with hasty decisions anymore in life. Once bitten and all that, I'm afraid!) Well. The point is, I have shown some samples of your work to the other members of the CAS (The Contemporary Art Society in Melbourne)—the sketches that you did while you were here for lunch with Edward. We are intrigued by your style, especially the rendering of faces so finely done in brush and ink, the way you capture a person's nature in barely a few strokes. We also love the landscapes of Heide that you "threw off" while you sat on the floor by the fireplace.

Thank you for leaving them here for me. I feel that if an artist has talent, then I will do all that I can to lend my support. The thing is, the CAS would like to see you expand your work so that it can be exhibited as part of our next exhibition here in Melbourne. What do you think?

You have real talent. What worries me is that we don't want you to be seen as "Edward Russell's girlfriend," the girlfriend of a member of one of Australia's foremost families. You need to establish yourself as Rebecca Swift. It's been a horrid problem for Joy Hester. She's always viewed as Albert Tucker's wife.

Anyway, can we exhibit a few of your pieces here in Melbourne? Let me know what you want to do.

Sun.

Rebecca read the letter twice, then lay back on her bed, staring at the white ceiling. Rebecca glanced back at Sunday's correspondence in her hand. She was right. Referring to women artists as somebody's wife or girlfriend was something that had to stop. Rebecca stood up, opened her wardrobe, and placed the letter in the pocket of one of her light summer coats. She then made her way out to the gallery and down toward the small ladies' sitting room, where she knew Celia would be waiting.

With an instinct that seemed to kick in all too often of late, Rebecca ran a hand up to her cheek as she sat down on the sofa opposite Edward's mother. Pale pink sofas rested on soft cream carpet and the whole room was framed by a picture window that gave a splendid view of the well-tended garden. A peacock called in the distance.

"Tea, Rebecca?" Celia asked, reaching for her bellpull.

Rebecca refrained from pointing out that she was already awash with tea. Hadn't they just had lunch? Still, if tea was going to improve relations with Edward's mother, then tea she was going to have. Rebecca loved Edward and found herself determined to make things work with his mother.

"Thank you," she said, arranging her legs just so on the delicate sofa.

"How are you finding Haslemere, Rebecca?"

"I love the landscape around here. The light on the paddocks is different every time I go out. I've been trying to blend the right color in my room, to capture the green in different states. And the scent of it is heavenly." She stopped. What was she doing? Celia would think she was mad.

"Yes." Celia waved in the maid with a tray of tea. Ran her hand over her chignon. "I'm glad you like the . . . paddocks." She pouted while the tray was set down on a small polished table between them, set with a glass bowl of pink roses. Visibly took in another breath. "It can be rather quiet out here though. Not ideal for a city girl like you."

Rebecca watched while the older woman poured tea. There was something calming about the timeless ritual. Perhaps it was because it crossed barriers. In any case, Rebecca's heartbeat steadied a little as Celia handed her a porcelain cup.

"Thank you," she said. "You know, I'm happiest when I'm drawing or sketching. I do love the excitement of the city, I admit that. I love meeting people. Melbourne is full of such interesting folk." Folk. Woops. That wasn't part of the language of the Edith Hardings of this world. Rebecca felt her cheeks tingle. She started over. "What I mean to say is that I find the countryside inspirational, for my work, but it also soothes the mind."

Celia stopped with her teacup halfway to her mouth. "Oh, I see," she murmured.

Rebecca winced. "It is clear that Edward adores Haslemere," she said. But she was floundering, panicking about her use of the right word. Was *love* too strong a word for people of Celia's background? Was it a word they used in their circles? Rebecca shot her gaze around the rosebud-wallpapered room as if it held all the answers.

"Edward is intimately connected with this place," Celia murmured. "It is his home."

The woman stared out the window a moment and something passed across her face, a shadow. But her voice was firm when she spoke.

"I'm afraid that . . . well. I would hate to appear indelicate, but . . . there is something you should know. Our wills are clear in that nothing goes to any spouse of Robert's, Edward's, or Vicky's. Everything goes directly to their children."

Rebecca gasped. "Please," she said, "I'm not—"

But Celia held up a hand. "I'm not saying you are," she said. "But I like to make things clear to people. I don't like to beat around the bush. You see, under the circumstances, we need to be careful about such things . . ."

Rebecca stared at the luxuriant carpet. It was almost as if it, too, were rejecting her. As if she'd ever think anything of Edward's inheritance. If only Celia knew her true feelings about what was important.

Which of course was the problem. Celia simply did not think that way at all. And not only did she not think that way, the older woman would have difficulty understanding that anyone else would. But Rebecca was going to try to understand Edward's mother, even if it killed her.

"I can assure you that my motives are genuine," Celia went on. "The boys have had every gold digger you can imagine setting her cap for them. I'm afraid I've become a little cynical. You see, the Russell family is quite unique."

Yes. Rebecca stayed quiet. She was beginning to see, indeed.

"You see, dear, Edward's position is unusual."

Rebecca smiled at Celia. And for some reason, started to feel sorry for her. This life of hers had to be on the way out. Was this some attempt to stop the inevitable? Did she have no regard for the fact that Edward had a will of his own?

"Edith's mother and I hope to see Edward and Edith married. And, while, dear, I know he finds you sweet, I just can't sit here and allow you to build your hopes that he is in any way available or not already spoken for, if you see what I mean. I do know this is awkward, but I hope you understand. And I'm genuinely sorry because I can see that there is real affection between you and dear Edward."

"Yes, it is real," Rebecca said. "It's based on truth."

She suddenly felt an overwhelming urge to push her own point. "Don't you think, Mrs. Russell, that affection, that the things that run deep are more important than a match made for social reasons? Because, you see, I love Edward. And I can promise you, I always will. I know I could never hurt him or leave him. He is so very dear to me. Don't you think that is important? I just . . ." her voice trailed off. All her senses were heightened. She had to advocate for herself, even if she was shooting herself in the foot.

Celia turned to her. "Well, of course, yes. But surely affection between a couple will grow after marriage. I do find you quite lovely, my dear, and I'm sure Edward does too. It's just that, well, Rebecca, if we are being honest, the heart of the matter is that the people with whom you are friendly, the Reeds, those artists, could pull Edward away from his family. Angus and I are most concerned about it. And I'm sure you don't want that."

Rebecca bit her lip. She placed her teacup back down on the table in front of her. "I can see that," she said quietly. Because she did understand. To lose one's child to people who thought your entire lifestyle was abhorrent would be unimaginable.

But what was the answer to all this? To expect Edward to give up his beliefs, beliefs that had been formed in the fields of a long and bloody war, beliefs that reflected the need for change, the need to rebuild a better world, how could that possibly be something any mother could ask? It was asking him to be a false version of himself. It was asking him to go backward and it was as difficult as asking Celia to change her own views on the way life should be lived.

The situation was impossible.

Rebecca stood up, clenched and unclenched her hands. Any pretense of sitting politely seemed to have escaped her now. "Mrs. Russell," she said to the woman, who was clearly in distress. "I do see how you feel, but to be honest, as a woman, all I can tell you is that my feelings for Edward run so deep that it would be impossible for me to walk away from him. He is not only the man I love, but a true and trusted friend who has been there for me. All I want is for him to be happy."

Celia's expression was set. "His happiness and the happiness of my family are the key, Rebecca. Think about it. Were he to marry you, could you promise me that he would not go off and do something similar to Sunday and John Reed? Can you not see how detrimental that would be to everything this family has worked so hard to achieve, to our reputation, our standing? It would be a scandal that would be unfair to his sister, to myself, to his brother and his father. The modernists have been implicated as deviants. In court, no less. Oh, maybe he would live that way for a while, but can't you see, eventually he would want to return to the life he's always known. I wouldn't want to take a man away from his family if it were me. I'm not sure how you could even consider it, to be honest."

"But I don't care about the things that matter to you." Rebecca's words were low and raw. "You see, what I believe in is love, Mrs. Russell, because, in the end, isn't that all that matters?"

Celia started fumbling, as if she were reaching for a pocket or a handkerchief or some such thing.

Rebecca could not stop the wave of sympathy that tore through her heart. "Mrs. Russell . . ." she said.

But the older woman held up a hand. "Love," she said, "dies when certain things kick in. But family, tradition, hard work, being a woman who, if she has any intelligence at all, can stand behind a man and keep a family going through . . . all sorts of ills, that is what constitutes strength. Character. Edith has it. Please, will you just understand."

And with that, Celia stood up.

Rebecca moved aside as the woman almost ran out of the room, her face reddened and blotched. Rebecca realized, stunned, that Celia was about to burst into tears.

A week later, Rebecca sat in her room at the Russells' beach house on South Australia's coast. She'd made a phone call to the restaurant in Melbourne to arrange a little more leave and her classes did not resume for another week at the Gallery School. She'd kept attending them, even while she lived at Gino's, because her uncle had given her the opportunity, but she found herself enjoying her own creative explorations more and more now that she was away from Mrs. Swift.

Celia's decision to move the family to the beach for a period had given Edward's mother the distraction, Rebecca thought, that the older woman clearly needed. Things had been tense between them since their discussion about Edward. Conversations had been brief and unsure. Rebecca fought the whirl of her own emotions—love for Edward, bewildering confusion toward his mother, and if she were honest, a sort of primal need to impress Celia, mixed with a real abhorrence for her cynical approach to marriage.

The beach house was at least a change of scene. Rebecca was beginning to see how hothoused one could become when stuck out in the country with only family in attendance.

She had to ask herself: could she stand such a life?

The beach house was long and low and built of thick, white-painted local stone. It was surrounded with wide verandas and a sloping lawn that looked over the beach. A wild island sat out in the bay opposite the house with great granite boulders on one side. Rebecca was drawn toward the untamed beauty of the island and often found herself gazing at it from the beach, watching the sea crash against the windswept cliffs on the island's rocky shores.

There had been parties on the beach with other young people, while Celia and the older generation sat about on deck chairs sipping champagne and watching, with beady eyes. Rebecca felt that her every move was being scrutinized, and she knew she was the subject of the older generation's gossip.

Escape became, once again, her preferred option. Escape, of course, had been how Rebecca had always dealt with Mrs. Swift. Rebecca was hardly unused to taking such a path in her life, so it seemed natural to run away and paint. It was just what she did.

If Edward went out fishing with his father, Rebecca would ensure she was away from the other women in the house. She'd take the opportunity to pick up her sketching materials and pull the family's wooden rowboat from the beach, rowing out to draw on the island in the bay. She favored sitting on a granite boulder on the island's wild side, one that overlooked the treacherous, roiling sea that thundered on the jagged rocks below. Rebecca was thrilled by the waves that crashed and exploded into a million tiny white shards before becoming foam flecks on the rocks, rocks that were remnants of the ancient volcano that existed thousands of years earlier on the far edge of the bay. Sometimes Edward came with her to her sacred spot with his notebook. He would sit on one of the benches that lined the treacherous path around the island's edge and write while she worked.

But today, Edward had gone fishing with a group of young men, having taken the family's little yacht out, hoping to catch the succulent King George whiting that was the local catch around here. He had kissed her on the cheek before flying off to the beach.

Rebecca could see why Celia had brought him here.

Rebecca had her sketching materials ready in a leather pouch that Edward had bought for her in Melbourne. As Rebecca stepped down to the garden, she stopped. Someone was on the veranda behind her. She turned, having to shade her eyes to focus on the older woman standing at the screen door.

"One of my friends here had a daughter who was keen on art when she was younger," Celia said. Her voice was a little shaky. It was the first time they'd been alone since that day of tea and candor.

Celia stared out, still, at the bay that shone like a pane of polished glass. "She gave it up. Entirely. She could not keep it up and be the mother her children needed her to be."

Rebecca drew in a breath.

"Wouldn't you rather spend time with Vicky and the other girls? There is a group of them coming over today. They are going to sew in the sitting room."

Rebecca pressed her lips together. Sitting in a room bending over needlework? Rebecca's mind filled with the wilds of the sea.

"Edith is . . . going tomorrow," Celia said.

Rebecca looked up, sharp. Was Edith giving up? Edward was being hopelessly attentive to Rebecca. If Rebecca were Edith, she would have left days ago . . .

"Thank you, but I will stick to my plans," Rebecca said. And at that moment, she decided one thing. There was no point being in conflict with Edward's mother. Rebecca would operate this way: she would make her own decisions and would not allow herself to be pushed around or made to feel guilty for loving Edward so much.

But Celia, clearly, wasn't done. "Rebecca . . ." Celia fidgeted now, still not looking at Rebecca, but gazing out to the sea as if she were talking to some distant person out there. "People are saying you live more in a world of your own than in the real world. I'm just warning you. You don't want to become an outcast."

Rebecca jolted a little at the word. Was there real concern in her voice? She stood, holding the satchel that contained her sketching things.

"I do need to go and work, Mrs. Russell," she said. "I have to send some pictures to . . . the Contemporary Art Society in Melbourne." Mentioning Sunday would be a disaster. "I thank you for your concern."

But as she made her way down the veranda steps, the garden seemed to sway and spin about as if it danced to its own strange tune.

And then she turned back to the woman who still stood there. A woman, Rebecca thought, who looked a little helpless.

"Don't worry," Rebecca said. "I'm not strange. I simply like to draw."

A frown spread across Celia's features. She patted at something imaginary on her dress. "Oh my dear," she said.

Rebecca smiled slightly before feeling instinctively for Sunday's latest letter, snug in her pocket.

Heide

Dearest Rebecca,

I have shown your work to other members of the CAS and we all agree (please do not get a big head, my darling) that you show a remarkable talent, that your career could be strong. Please keep sending me work while you are at Victor Harbor with the Russells, and we will organize this exhibition. It is exciting, is it not?

And what I find wonderful is that you, like me, have found such solace, such a partner in Edward as I have in John. I cannot tell you how much John has altered my life. I know you have had trials in your past, my dear. But what I believe in, Rebecca, is love.

You know, a while back, I saw a group of men in a black car driving through Melbourne. They looked so severe and serious and wealthy. And I thought, what a horrible group of men they looked to be! Well, you see, they were my uncles.

We cannot choose our families, and equally we cannot blame ourselves if they blame us for wanting to strike out; it is our prerogative to be true to ourselves. Don't get caught up by things that you do not value, Rebecca, because, in many ways, I sense in you a younger version of myself, sensitive, wanting some sort of faith in people— I wonder if you have always put on a hard, frightfully bright act. The one solace I have, even though our backgrounds are so vastly different, is that you won't make an unfortunate marriage, as I did with my first. I married a charlatan, a man who was all pretense. You will never do that.

You have what you need within you to succeed. It's all there. And you have Edward, someone who believes in you.

You have everything, Rebecca.

Keep painting!!

À bientôt, *my darling girl,*

Sun.

Rebecca knew things were changing and she sensed a change in herself. Even a few weeks ago, would she have stood up to Celia as she had done lately? No, she would have put on an act as she always used to with her mother, would have pretended everything was fine when it was not. Edward was giving her renewed strength, she knew that, but she was also finding it on her own.

Rebecca made her way along the path that wound through the bracken and bushes to the beach. The sea was pearled and clear. Rebecca moved down to the rowboat, slipping her leather sandals off and closing her eyes at the first sting of cold sea water against her sand-tickled feet.

She pushed the boat out until it floated in the shallows, then climbed in, picking up her oars and placing the paper bag that she had filled with apples and chocolate and ham sandwiches on the seat next to her.

The work that she was doing here was the antithesis of the controlled, tedious sketches that she was required to undertake at the Gallery School. Apart from the fact that she was in love, meeting Edward had come at exactly the right time for her art.

Perhaps she did need to have faith that things would work out.

CHAPTER NINETEEN

Rome, 1987

Tess glared at the endless, aqua spirals of water that glistened into the Trevi Fountain. James was the last person she wanted to be with right now. He'd walked her out of the restaurant after they'd said goodbye to Edward, staying quiet beside her until, finally, she'd come to a standstill right here. The fact was, her career was going backward. And she saw James as the cause of the whole disastrous landslide.

She slumped down on one of the stone benches overlooking the fountain. The piazza was quiet. Only a few tourists lingered. Mostly young lovers, Tess thought irritably. It wasn't fair. She'd worked so hard for years. She was thirty-four. Being the daughter of a property developer who spent nine months of the year in Florida hardly gave her anything like the society connections that James enjoyed.

So, had she been doomed from the start? Was it inevitable that when someone like James came along Tess's career would be pushed aside so he could move in and take over? Tess always ended up with the inevitability of the glass ceiling, no matter how many other excuses she searched out. Because the glass ceiling was a certainty. The glass ceiling was a sure bet—and it seemed that social privilege and being male still held sway, no matter how hard people tried to stand up to those powers.

James stood next to her, one foot resting on the bench.

"Talk to me, Tess," he said.

Tess felt a wave of tingles on the back of her neck. "I'll just watch the fountain."

He sat down next to her.

Instinctively, Tess moved a little farther away from him along the bench.

"I have no doubt you can still make a success of this. You have a fantastic reputation."

Tess rolled her eyes. "Yes, as the dumped editor of Alec Burgess."

James folded his arms.

"I'm going to talk to Edward again," she said, turning back to the lit-up buildings that surrounded the square. "I'm going to try, once more, to see if he'll go public."

James shook his head. "I don't think that's a good idea."

"What?"

"You spoke well in there, but he's not going to budge. And the book will be fine without his going public, Tess. Just fine."

"Yes, but that's the point, James. I don't want it to be just fine. I can't afford to be just fine, James. Too many women settle for that in their careers. Don't you see how hard it is?"

When James spoke, his voice was low. "But why does it have to be the fast track with Edward? In my experience working with literary authors, with authors who write authentically, you've got to be in it for the long haul. I have no doubt you'll get him to where he needs to be, but one step at a time."

Tess stared at the water.

"You're on some sort of mission here. And I don't know why."

"James."

"Leon has given you an amazing opportunity. To work with Edward. Most editors would jump at that chance because he's unique and real. He tells an intriguing, original story. But you want to haul in publicity. It's a bit . . ." He looked up at the sky.

"What?" Tess barked the word.

"Tacky."

"Tacky?"

"I think so."

"How so? How is wanting to promote an author tacky?" And pictures of his parents' charming, understated apartment flew into her head . . . along with images of her own parents' home in Florida. All white. Marble everywhere. Leather, new shining leather, tons of it. New money. No contacts in the Establishment. Was that how he viewed her? Tacky?

"Tess," he said, leaning forward and speaking close in her ear. "What is it that you're competing against?"

Tess's words were low and firm. "What you don't quite understand, given your privileged, bookish background . . ." She looked up at him, but he was waiting, even nodded her on.

"What you fail to understand is what it's like growing up not fitting in with your family at all. Try the stunning older sister, the one who now edits a gossip magazine, and my brother, who earns a six-figure salary as a Realtor, selling houses to folks just like your parents, not that he'd ever fit into your world on his own terms. And I certainly don't fit in with it . . ." Her words trailed off and she pressed her lips together.

James fought with a smile and failed. "Well, thank goodness. What a breath of fresh air you are. I just don't know why you worry about it."

Tess couldn't hold back the cynical laugh that escaped from her lips.

"No, I'm serious," he said. His voice was low.

"Are you?" Tess asked. "Let's see. I have . . ." She started counting with her fingers, as if ticking off a list of things to do, "a tiny studio in the Village, which is not big enough to swing a parakeet in. I've lost my one stellar author, the person my parents always mentioned whenever they introduced me to someone they were trying to impress. Quite frankly, I don't fit in. Anywhere. So you see, James, I am possibly . . . screwed. No matter how hard I try, it's family or the glass ceiling that stops me. It's hopeless."

"Oh." James's tone was light. He trailed his hand into the fountain.

"That's disgusting," Tess said. She was up for a fight, and he was messing with the water fountain? "You'll get typhoid."

He laughed, flicked a bit of water at her. "Nope. It's Roman. The water of life. It's all you need."

Tess rolled her eyes at him.

"Okay," he said. "But you've got an interesting job. And you like to read books. I'm sorry, Tess, but I just don't see the problem. Because, to me, that sounds pretty great, to be honest. Why are you trying to be something different from yourself?"

Tess stared at him a moment.

He tilted his head to one side.

"You don't know what you're talking about," she muttered. "Couldn't possibly understand."

He leaned forward. He looked so earnest that Tess cracked a smile. "It's very simple, you see." He reached out, his hand trailing over her cheek. "You're perfect as you are. You'll sort Edward out, I know it. But just give him some time. And do it the way you want to do it, not the way you think you should do it."

He was close, but Tess couldn't move. Didn't want to move . . .

"Tell me," he murmured. "When was the last time you read a book like Edward's?"

"What a strange thing to ask in the middle of a deadly serious conversation." But her voice was low now and a delicious sense of the allurement that she'd felt around James since their arrival in Rome seemed to enfold her like the softest cashmere glove.

James took her hand.

"I used to love books with more depth," she said. He was still close. "When I was a teenager, I devoured Tolstoy, Austen, the Brontës . . . but once I started working, then I guess I started reading thrillers, books that were faster paced. My own choices seemed sort of odd in a world where bestsellers reigned supreme, I suppose . . ."

"You don't need to impress everyone else. Because that isn't what matters." His lips were touching the top of her head.

She closed her eyes; she hardly knew or cared who else was around. He leaned closer.

"What's wrong with us? It must be Rome," she whispered. There was no point denying what was going on.

"You know, back in New York, your family would be . . . completely unacceptable to mine, Tess." His lips were so close to hers that she almost felt them.

She let out a giggle.

"My mother planned a wife for me," he murmured.

She pulled back and held his face in her hands.

"I, in my early twenties, was so eager not to upset the boat, you see—"

"Oh, really?"

"I went out with the girl from a suitable family. We even got to the point where we discussed marriage."

"Oh." But she could not laugh at that.

James rested his forehead on hers. "But I wanted something different."

"What's that?" Tess barely whispered the words.

"Someone real." His eyes darkened.

And he leaned closer, brushing his lips onto hers.

CHAPTER TWENTY

Victor Harbor, 1946

Edward appeared at the French doors that led to Rebecca's bedroom. She turned from where she lay on her bed, tidying up the work she had done out on the island today. Her plan was to have at least twenty pieces ready to send off to Sunday well in time for the CAS exhibition. Rebecca was loving the diligence of working toward an exhibition. Not to mention the fact that it gave her something on which to focus other than her worries about fitting in with the Russell family. Work seemed to be her best distraction, a salvation, in fact. Thank goodness she had it. Imagine having nothing for herself at all. Edward opened the screen door, stepping into the coolness of her room.

Rebecca laughed, shrieking as he approached her, holding up a fish, teasing her with the glass-eyed dead thing. She giggled and sprang off the bed.

"A plump mullet, the best catch of the day, apart from you," Edward said, catching her around the waist with his free hand and showering kisses onto her cheek, her neck, everywhere.

She leaned into him, loving the warmth of his old fishing sweater and the feel of the rough hairs on his legs entwined with her own smooth, bare calves underneath her dress.

"I thought we'd row out to West Island and make a fire," he said, his voice lingering, muffled in her hair. "I want to cook this fish for you on the beach, then watch the sun go down with a good bottle of wine."

"Sounds like heaven." Rebecca smiled. "Promise you won't tip up the boat."

He tickled her ribs and she nudged him.

"I'm going to take a shower," he said. "But once I'm done, let's go."

Rebecca ran her hand down his arm.

Once they were in the boat, with the sea lapping against its wooden sides and gulls swooping in the endless blue sky, Rebecca felt as if nature were embracing them. It was part of them, and they it. After Edward pulled up on the second little island out in the bay, a steeper, wilder affair than Rebecca's Granite Island, they scurried about together in the short, knotted bushes that lay above the rocks, reaching with their bare hands to collect sticks and larger pieces of wood to make a fire. Rebecca rolled up the sleeves of the sweater that she had borrowed from Edward, reveling in his smell and in the thought that while his clothes were close to her body she felt part of him, and he of her.

He cooked the fish, crisping it on the flames and serving it on old tin plates with potato chips that he had cooked to perfection in an old saucepan on the fire. Then they sat, wrapped in a blanket together, watching the flames flicker—peaking and dying down in a timeless dance. Every now and then, Edward would lean across to the pile of firewood they had amassed and throw another log onto the blaze.

Rebecca sipped at the wine in her tin cup. Edward's billycan hung on a tripod above the flames, and once they had finished the last of their wine, he poured billy tea for them, strong and smoky out of the tin bucket that his family had used for generations here on the beach. And he brought out seed cake, cutting them each a good wedge and putting these on one plate to share. He reached forward idly, placing soft, melting morsels of cake in Rebecca's mouth, sometimes in his own. Rebecca sipped at the strong, hot tea and leaned her head back against his shoulder.

"I want to ask you something," he said, murmuring into her hair and then moving down, his lips caressing the side of her neck. "Tell me this. Have you ever been in love before? We've never talked about that."

Rebecca sighed. Had she been in love? She reached up, entwining her arm around his neck, her eyes still fixed on the flames, each dancing to its own tune . . . just as she wanted to do, just as Edward wanted to do.

"I've never had feelings for anyone in the way that I do for you." She smiled as he dropped a soft kiss on the top of her head. And leaned in closer to the contours of his body that were becoming as familiar and as dear to her as her own life itself.

"What I want to do," Edward said, his words soft and almost unbearably close, "is to be with you and to write. If only it could be so simple." His voice held an urgency.

Rebecca stroked the back of his hand with her fingers, and he caught them up, pulling her hand up to his lips.

Lightness seemed to envelope her body. It was perfect. Surely nothing could stand in their way now.

CHAPTER
TWENTY-ONE

Rome, 1987

Tess lay awake for hours. While it did not seem a good idea to be developing feelings for James, one relentless question beat the same tune in her head, a question that she would never have contemplated having to consider a few days ago. What was going to happen once she and James were back in New York?

Had their interlude in Rome been just a couple of whispered conversations, a kiss in one of the world's most romantic cities? James had walked her back to the hotel, his hand brushing hers as they went to their hotel rooms.

Tess sat up in the moonlight that filtered through the gauzy curtains onto her bed. Perhaps it had just been an entr'acte. She groaned and lay back down on her pillows with a thump.

When morning came she showered and dressed, half-joyful with anticipation about the day ahead but half in a panic that perhaps last night was only a dalliance for James, nothing more. He might never see her fitting into his world. And yet, Tess couldn't believe she was thinking like that. She stared at herself in the mirror. Her eyes glowed as she thought about him. He was handsome and intelligent, he made her laugh, he was well read, he liked to travel, and he'd gone out of his way to be kind to her. And yet, she had serious reservations.

She made her way down to the lobby, but when she went to open the hotel door, it was pushed toward her instead.

She stepped back. Edward almost fell into her.

The buttons on his pale blue shirt were not done up evenly, and he held a straw hat close to his chest. Droplets of perspiration rested on his forehead.

Tess opened her mouth to speak, only to find James right behind her, holding the door open above Tess's head. She only just managed to stop herself from closing her eyes and inhaling the deliciousness of his aftershave.

Edward. She must focus on him.

Edward fanned his face with his hat. "Forgive me for arriving unannounced. But you see, I have hardly slept."

That makes two of us, Tess thought wryly.

Edward's glance bounced from Tess back to James. "I've been thinking. I was remiss last night. I . . . you caught me by surprise. Writing is such a strange thing. I guess I just never thought that you'd be so quick to find out about . . . Rebecca. I don't know what I thought when I started writing about my own past. Perhaps that I'd get away with it, because it was so distant. Another time and place, to me only existing in my memories now." He stopped, let out a sigh. "Tess, James. Is there any chance we could go and have a coffee somewhere nearby? I'd like to talk with you."

"Of course we can, Edward," Tess said.

But it was all she could do to focus on the older man as the three of them strolled down the street. Her eyes wanted to dart toward James the whole time as he walked along beside them. She made a point of striking up a conversation with Edward about the literature festival instead. Distraction seemed to be the only solution right now. So Tess chattered the whole time, knowing her voice sounded as tinny as a plastic whistle. At least Edward seemed as keen as she was to talk about anything and nothing as well. Deliberately, she walked next to Edward, keeping her distance from James in case she gave something away—a smile, a look.

Edward wasn't stupid. James stayed quiet.

Edward stopped outside a café on the corner of the Piazza Barberini. Its windows overlooked the square and tables were set for breakfast.

"Is this all right?" he asked.

All Tess could do was nod her head. If someone had told her even a few weeks ago she'd be kissing James Cooper in Rome and then having breakfast with an Australian poet whose sales, well, could have done with a bit of a boost, and whom she was fast coming to adore as well, she would have told them they were mad. And yet, here she was. James held the café door open, and Tess motioned for Edward to go in first. Once Edward was inside, James caught her arm.

"Tess . . ."

But she scuttled past him, shaking her head, only to be horridly aware of him walking behind her.

Edward organized a table for them, speaking in fluent Italian to the waitress. Tess collected her thoughts. But as Edward lifted the leather bag he'd carried over his shoulder onto the table, his gnarled fingers taking great care unbuckling the straps, Tess felt her stomach take another dive. Slowly, with reverence, Edward laid three sketches on the table in front of them.

The moment Tess's eyes alighted on the first sketch, a wave of flutters passed through her belly. No one had to tell her what it was. She leaned forward, her eyes darting from one sketch to the next. The urge to pick the pictures up was so strong that she had to place her hands on her seat.

Edward and James continued chatting but she couldn't concentrate on the words that they said. The sketches made no sense. While she knew what they were, knew exactly when Rebecca had done them, and was strikingly touched by the fact Edward had brought them today, she was having the most distinct trouble reconciling them with something else—something that bothered her and did not seem right. It couldn't be. And yet, it was as if she'd seen a face in a crowd and recognized the person's features while being unable to assign the face a name.

Edward chuckled at something James said. Then they both went quiet.

"Tess?" James asked. "Aren't they terrific? She manages to capture a person in a few brushstrokes, doesn't she? The essence of a person," he added, his voice dropping down.

But Tess's thoughts darted in circles, only to keep returning to the same spot.

"They are lovely," she managed. And reached out for her glass of water, gulping from it.

She sensed James's eyebrow go up next to her, but stayed rigid in her seat.

"Well," Edward said, sounding expansive, generous. "I'm glad you like them, Tess."

Both men were clearly waiting for her to expand. James had hit the nail on the head as far as Rebecca's work went—her ability to capture the essence of a person. Tess, horridly aware of the silence as the two men sat there, conducted an internal debate about what on earth to do. Should she tell them she had seen pieces in New York very much like the ones she was now looking at? She'd sound mad. Insane. She stared at the sketches hard.

After more silence and polite waiting on Edward and James's part, Edward picked up the thread of conversation. "This one is of Joy Hester. She was an artist too. But she died in 1960, of Hodgkin's disease."

Tess could not tear her eyes away from the strong, beautiful face that stared back at them. But it wasn't the face that had thrown her.

It was the essence of it.

"Max Harris," Edward went on. "Such a lively chap—a poet and editor of the *Angry Penguins* magazine. Great fun at parties." Tess had seen a photo of Max Harris in one of the books she'd read in the Rose Reading Room and even though her thoughts were awhirl, she still marveled at the way Rebecca had picked up the sparkle in the young poet's eye. His wiry black hair, oval face, and soft, deep eyes were the image of the romantic poet. He held a cigar, and a scarf was slung over his neck.

"What happened to him?" Tess asked.

"Max is a bookseller." Edward smiled. "He also founded the *Australian Book Review*. The Ern Malley hoax, in which he was set up by two young poets, marked him deeply. The worst of it was that he was successfully prosecuted in a trial for publishing indecent material, content in those fake Ern Malley poems. Max was fined five pounds. In many ways, he kept his distance from the world after that. He continued to write but also admitted that in his poetry he was vulnerable, and he wanted to keep those who didn't wish him well at bay. So he went into the commercial side of the book industry and became a respected critic."

"I've heard of the Ern Malley literary hoax," James said. "It was an international affair for a brief period."

Tess fought a blinding urge to run out of the café, find a phone, and make a call. Get on a plane back to New York? She'd have to book a flight soon, or she'd drive herself mad.

"It was internationally reported," Edward said.

"Yes," James murmured. "Such a shame."

"It goes to show what mass media can do to an artist." Edward caught Tess's eye.

She picked up her coffee cup, only to have it almost slip between her thumb and forefinger. Tess managed to catch it right before it crashed to the table.

James reached across, took it from her hand, and placed it back down.

"Max was on the cusp of a promising career as a young poet when the scandal started," Edward went on, his eyes travelling from Tess to James and back.

Oh, he was a pro at awkward situations, Tess thought. And sent up thanks for the older man's presence at the table and perhaps, ironically, to Celia for raising him with such perfect manners.

She pushed her soft roll around on her plate. There was no way she could stomach anything now. Several possibilities rose into her head. She wasn't back in New York until tomorrow.

"Tess," James said, "are you sure you're okay?"

Edward paused for a moment, lifting his head up from the third sketch.

"Oh, Edward," Tess managed to say, when she finally gave her full attention to the portrait of Edward in front of her. But the words were a whisper.

"Yes . . ." Edward said.

Tess stared at the sketch. Edward's handsome young features were a little clouded. Again, just those few brushstrokes and she'd captured him. Tess bit hard on her bottom lip.

"She'd only met you once," Tess said, in spite of the turmoil in her mind. "But it seems that one meeting was enough to really see a person. And one meeting was enough to fall in love."

She sensed James starting at her words.

"Those were days that will always remain with me, and those people, well, they touched my heart," Edward said.

"I know they did," Tess said, her voice soft. She had been trying to convince Edward to exploit his love affair with Rebecca. Now, looking at Rebecca's work, she was repulsed at her own behavior.

"Edward," she said. She took in a breath. "Would you mind if I took a couple of photos of Rebecca's work? The . . . editorial team would be fascinated to see Rebecca's sketches."

"I don't mind," Edward said. "Go ahead."

"Thank you," Tess said, avoiding James's eye, which was trained on her like a loaded gun. As soon as they were out of here he'd be peppering her with questions. But as she snapped a few photographs and looked even more closely at the sketches, she became convinced that the strong instinct she had was spot-on and her panic turned to thoughtfulness—how could it be? How could that have worked? But slowly, she started to add things up.

"I'm sure the girl in question wouldn't have minded you taking photographs," Edward said. "As long as you aren't going to reproduce anything for commercial purposes . . ."

"We would never, ever do that, Edward," James said.

"Well." Edward shifted himself in his chair a little. "I just wanted to show you these. And Tess?"

Tess nodded dumbly at him.

"I'm sorry that I can't be of more help with your publicity. I'm afraid it's not a thing I deal with very well."

No, but publicity, Edward, could be about to find you . . .

"You'll be wanting to get to the festival." Edward eased himself out of his chair. "And I'm aware that I need to get my work back to you, pronto."

Tess looked up at him, catching the way his green eyes twinkled. And thought that the last thing she wanted to do was see his heart broken a second time.

But what choice did she have, in the end?

Tess sat bolt upright for the entire flight back to New York. She kept her seat upright, too, pretending to focus on the film that was showing on the hazy screen at the front of the airplane, even though it held no interest for her. At least she could pretend to be fascinated by it and avoid James's questions.

"I wish you'd talk to me," he said, for about the thousandth time, once the credits were rolling. Tess couldn't even recall the title of the film. She pulled out her eye mask. Nearly everyone around them was sleeping.

"It's nothing," she said. "Just work-related stuff."

Which was true—to a point.

James tipped his seat backward a bit. He looked at her, clearly sleepy—and sexy. Stubble shadowed his chin.

He reached out to her, tracing his hand down the side of her face. "Well. If you want to talk about it, you know I'm here."

Tess leaned toward him, but her stomach fluttered with doubt. So far, for the record, she'd lost her best client, kissed the man who stole him, then become hopelessly involved in a decades-old love story. If that wasn't enough, now she faced a situation that she suspected could push not only Edward's book but his life into the stratosphere. Excellent progress so far for a person who prided herself on her dedication to her career. She could see good reasons now for having avoided getting involved for so long.

CHAPTER TWENTY-TWO

Victor Harbor, 1946

The sun made its final, graceful way down to the horizon before settling in a glorious explosion of fire against the horizon as Edward rowed them back from the island. As they neared the shore, the moon rose to replace the sun, sending an arc of light across the bay.

Edward pulled the oars through the silent, still water. Evanescent drops fell from the polished timber of the oars into the secret depths below. He maneuvered the dinghy onto the shore and climbed out, his bare feet sinking into the soft sand while the water stung his calves. Rebecca helped him lug the wooden boat up the beach.

He leaned down and kissed her on the forehead while she stood next to him, her feet bare in the sand. She looked more beautiful than ever tonight.

"That was heaven," Rebecca said.

"It's only the beginning," Edward whispered, taking her slim frame in his arms and wrapping her in an embrace. Over the top of her tousled, salt-sprayed hair, he gazed up at the house.

It was lit up as if for a party.

He smiled and took Rebecca's hand. "I think," he said, as they wandered toward the path, "we should carve out a life like Sunday and John have." He stopped, taking her shoulders in his hands. "Can I tell my family that's what we want to do?"

She leaned into him. "I adore you," she whispered. "It's exactly what I want . . ."

They came out of the bracken-lined track and crossed the expanse of well-tended lawn on their way toward the house.

His mother stood on the veranda, a lone figure.

Edward waved to her. And felt a pang of regret for her, for her life. He hated to see her watching out for his and Rebecca's return. If only, he thought for the millionth time, his father and brother were stronger, if only his mother could have the life that she deserved. He hated that everything had been such a disappointment for her. Brushing Angus and Robert's alcoholism under the table was not the answer to their family's problems. Edward knew he should do something, insist they get help, ensure that Robert could take over the role he was born to play. He'd be much better at running the family businesses than Edward; Robert had no qualms about fitting into their class. No. This hiding behind a pretense that the family was as it had always been for generations—strong, successful, and stable—had gone on long enough.

Celia did not wave back. Instead, she seemed to melt into a wicker chair, her head throwing itself back as if of its own accord. Edward let go of Rebecca's hand. He flew up the veranda steps to his mother, his footsteps punctuating the silence, and leaned over his mother's frame. It struck him how small she was and how vulnerable she seemed. Her eyes were closed and her chest rose and fell, but only in small flurries.

"Mother?"

Suddenly, guilt engulfed him. Celia had too much responsibility. He should have stepped in before this. His mother had never signed up for marriage to an alcoholic.

Edward shouted for his father, running a hand over his mother's still face.

"I'll get someone," Rebecca said.

"No. I will. Wait here."

Everything was deadly still in the house as Edward dashed through the rooms. The old farmhouse kitchen was quiet. A leg of lamb sat abandoned on the wooden table. The stove was lit, and an odd assortment of vegetables littered the table. An onion was chopped in half, its pungent smell blending with wood smoke. Edward almost retched as he stared at it for one horrible second.

He called for Marie, the cook. Silence.

Edward ran to his father's bedroom, annoyed suddenly that his father had always slept separately from his mother. Had Angus ever tried to treat his mother as anything other than the breeding mare that the family so obviously required? Everything was in its place because the maids kept the room just so, but there was no sign of his father.

Edward tore down the hallway to Vicky's room.

As he ran and called out, the house seemed to pulsate and blur around him.

He would check on Celia, then call for an ambulance or drive her to the local hospital himself if she was awake. But should he move her? Probably not. He raked his hands over his head and pushed open the screen door that led from the living room back out to the veranda.

She was awake. Her eyes darted from Rebecca to Edward and back.

"You are here."

He hated that it was resignation, not relief, that clouded her voice. Edward crouched down next to her.

She looked helpless. Her life had been directed at first by her father, whose business interests had taken a dive during the Great War, when bad management of the family's assets had been confounded by the loss of Celia's only brother in the Somme. Celia's marriage to Angus Russell was viewed as salvation by her family. She had sacrificed herself while Angus's father had paid off her father's debts and taken over her family's steel production interests.

When he was young, Angus had been besotted with the beautiful Celia. His father had bought him his bride. She'd been treated by her own father as if she were a commodity.

A small moan escaped from Celia's lips. Her body was racked with tremors and her teeth chattered.

Edward turned to Rebecca. "Could you get something to wrap her in, Rebecca?"

He'd seen this in the war. Shock. Probably not a heart attack. What had she witnessed?

He cast about for something to cover her with. His instinct to protect her was fierce. He had memories of her walking him around the gardens at Haslemere when he was a child. When she had started travelling with Vicky, she'd placed him far away from the troubles—in boarding school so that he could get the education he needed away from his father's drinking and outbursts, which would only become worse. As he stared at her, helpless, he had to confront thoughts that had bothered him in the past. What if in sending him away, she'd protected Edward, rather than abandoned him as he'd always thought? What else could his mother have done? She had no training, no way to support herself if she left his father.

Silently, Rebecca appeared with a blanket. Edward tucked it over his mother. Celia still trembled and her breathing was quick.

"Rebecca. Brandy," he said. "In the butler's pantry. The glass-fronted cabinet."

Rebecca nodded, returning with a large spoon and the bottle.

Edward cradled his mother's head in his arms while spooning the rich amber liquid down her throat and tipping her head back like a baby's. "Everything will be all right," he murmured. Dull, useless words.

Celia sat up, her eyes flickering as if in surprise at his presence. But then she darted a look at Rebecca, before her eyes lit up with panic again. In one ghastly movement, she thumped her hand on top of Edward's, which held the spoon, causing it to crash and clatter onto the wooden slats of the veranda.

"I'll take you to the hospital. It's going to be faster than calling an ambulance out here."

But Celia placed both hands on the arms of her chair as if to stand up, only to fall back again, hard. "It's not me," she whispered.

The back of Edward's throat thickened. He'd pushed suspicions away since the moment he laid eyes on her, and now he prepared himself.

When she spoke, his mother's voice was as faint as the faraway call of a bird. "Edward," she whispered. "Oh, heaven help us, Edward."

CHAPTER
TWENTY-THREE

New York, 1987

At last morning came after an interminable night spent alone with jet lag. The moment the sun was up, Tess was too.

"Mom?" she said, the second her mother answered. Glimpses of light were just appearing around the edges of Tess's curtains. Her mother was an early riser. She would not mind a call at this hour.

"Tess!"

"How are you, Mom?" she asked.

"Fine. I'm fine. Honey, Dad's playing golf later this morning, but would you like to—"

"Could I come over for breakfast?" Tess cut over her mother's voice.

"We'd love that."

Tess winced at the relief in her mother's voice.

"I'll come over right now." She hung up her phone and grabbed her house keys.

Once she was inside the apartment, the "New York pad," as her father called it, with its white tiles and columns, black leather sofas, and sleek minimalist decor, it was clear that her father was itching to go play golf. Dale Miller's golf cap was ready for him by the front door, along with a sports bag, which no doubt Tess's mother had packed for him first thing this morning. In some ways, Tess's father reminded her of Leon. His life was measured out, run meticulously. Tess's mother was his social secretary. It worked for some, Tess thought, as she felt her shoulders tighten.

She wished she knew how life was going to work for her. The last thing she wanted was to end up as the support person for someone else's career. At thirty-four, she'd come to love her independence. If she were going to consider a relationship, things would have to be equal.

James was attractive and charming; that was true. But Tess knew now that underneath it all, he was also funny, kind, and loyal. That kiss had loomed large in her jumbled thoughts last night. She still worried that if things developed further between them she could end up being left in James's wake.

"So, what's up, Tess?" Her father finished his bowl of muesli—one of his latest dietary fads. Dale Miller had the figure of a young man.

Tess had one question to ask her father. There was no point putting it off.

"Dad," she said. "You know those sketches you have in your study? The ones by Rumer Banks?"

Dale Miller nodded. "Always buy art with an eye to future growth, Tess. Don't think much of them, but I got a tip from someone in the know about art that Rumer was on the rise. I'll hang on to them until she's dead. Then I'll auction them off."

Tess swallowed the bile that rose in her throat. No matter how much her father's attitude repelled her, she knew she herself would not have questioned it a few weeks ago. But for now, she had to keep on his good side if he was going to agree to what she wanted to do.

"So, where did you get them?" That was a neutral-enough question.

"Picked them up at auction, from a private owner back in the sixties. Damned good price."

"But they're ghastly!" Lucille started clearing up plates.

Tess swiveled her head around to face her mother.

"That's why they've never seen the light of day beyond your father's study, Tess. Just a few brushstrokes on a piece of canvas. Stupid stuff. Honestly, Dale, Tess could have done them when she was in grade school!"

Just a few brushstrokes. Tess steadied her breathing, which had suddenly begun to rush.

"Mind if I take a look at them, Dad?" Tess asked the question easily. Her father's study was his sanctuary.

Lucille surveyed her husband from the kitchen. "Dale, you make some weird investments, but those, surely, have to take the cake. I'm not into that modernist stuff. I prefer something more realistic and traditional myself. At least I could have a Thomas Kinkade painting in my house without grimacing every time I looked at it."

Tess smiled at her mother. "Just interested, though—they're from the 1950s, right?"

"Nineteen fifty-eight and nineteen fifty-nine," Dale said, looking at Tess with a little more respect. "The old Rumers ended up doing damn well. Despite your mother's reservations, the point is, no matter what sort of art you're talking about, I know what's a good buy and what's not. All art is a commodity, Tess. Don't you ever forget that."

"Dale, you'll be late for golf! I'm going to my Jazzercise class this morning. It'll be a gossip catch-up as well. They're all having grandchildren." Lucille shot Tess a pointed look. "Suppose you can't tell me that you've met someone since we caught up last?"

Tess reeled with the memory. She stared at her parents and could barely mumble a word.

"Do you mind if I go take a look at the sketches?" she asked.

"Oh, go on, if you must, Tess." Lucille dismissed her with a wave of her manicured hand.

Tess stumbled her way down the staircase, her chest thumping out its own hard beat.

The office seemed to loom in front of her, expansive and modern and well-kept. The two Rumer Banks sketches hung precisely one above the other on the wall to the side of his black desk.

Tess moved across to the sketches, her stomach somersaulting as she reached for the glossy photos of Rebecca's work that she had in her bag.

Her eyes flew to the one that had catapulted into her thoughts the moment Edward had pulled Rebecca's sketches out of his satchel in Rome. Two arched eyebrows, an elongated nose, an older man wearing a suit and tie, his head distorted against his body. Rumer Banks had drawn triangular shapes around his eyes, and long lines ran from the sides of his nose to his chin. Tess held her photos of the sketches close to the frames on the walls.

The second sketch was of the out-of-shape woman Tess remembered so well from long ago, her eyes sagging, her nose bulbous. The woman's dark eyes stared somewhere out into the distance, and her lips were drawn downward in a grimace.

Tess swung around when her mother appeared at the door, hiding the photographs behind her back.

"Darling, we're both heading off now. Happy to see yourself out?"

Tess nodded, almost dumb with relief that her mother hadn't seen her photos. Tess moved over to the door, leaning in for Lucille's kiss on her cheek, flush with her favorite perfume—Arpege by Lanvin.

Tess winced and turned back.

"I'll let myself out, Mom."

"Okay!" Lucille trilled, glancing at Rumer's sketches on the wall. "I have no idea what your father sees in those, but never mind. It's all in the name of progress, I suppose." She adjusted her velour tracksuit.

"Yes, progress . . ." Tess murmured.

Once Lucille had tripped off, Tess reached for the phone on her father's desk.

It seemed Rebecca was the key. To everything.

Before any doubts could stop her, Tess picked up the phone and dialed Flora at home.

"Flora," she said, with a sense of relief when Flora picked up.

"Tess! Good to hear from you! More to the point, have you done anything about your delectable Mr. Darcy character? I loved the way he was marching around after you at the ball! I am one hundred percent certain that you're viewing him in the wrong light."

Typical Flora.

"Well," Tess said, sitting down in her father's leather swivel chair, leaning back in it, and giving it a twirl. "I may have kissed him in Rome." She waited a beat.

It only took two seconds.

"Tess! Fabulous! He's gorgeous! So what's happening now?"

"I'm not sure. Not rushing into anything, obviously, but he has kind of . . . gotten under my skin. He worked hard to prove that he didn't take Alec from me on purpose. And, well, I think I believe him now."

"I'm thrilled!"

Tess chewed on her lip and gazed around her father's all-black office. "Yes . . ." she murmured. "So. I'm sitting in my father's office, staring at two early sketches by Rumer Banks from the 1950s. Dad bought them as an investment years ago. Since I'm editing a book on modernists, do you know anything about the elusive Rumer Banks?"

"Elusive's the word, honey. Nobody knows anything about Rumer Banks."

Tess scrutinized the pictures in front of her.

"The story goes like this: only her dealer is aware of her real identity. I think the art world and buyers have come to respect that about her. She doesn't want fame, doesn't court any of that. But she's viewed as one of the most talented artists of her generation. Her works sell for millions these days."

Tess sighed. "She hates publicity, I know that. Does anyone have any idea why?"

"Nope."

Tess's mind was working in more logical circles now. "Do you happen to know how old she might be, Flora?"

"She'd be at least in her sixties now."

So, in her twenties in 1946.

"Does anyone know where she might live?"

"There have been rumors about Carmel-by-the-Sea. Journalists have tried, believe me, but it's kind of a taboo thing. You know, people respect her privacy in some ways, which is odd in this day and age."

Tess sat up. "Carmel?"

"Now about that gorgeous man . . ."

"Flora, I have to go. We'll talk soon. Ciao!"

Tess was in the office first thing on Monday morning with all her information set out on her desk. After spending hours in the library on the weekend, she'd confirmed the one lead that Flora had suggested—Carmel-by-the-Sea.

Tess knew if she slowed down and thought about what she was doing, she might find reason to pause, but she also knew that if she didn't find Rumer, it would bother her for the rest of her life. What came over her like a wave crashing on her own solitary rock was that selling copies didn't matter one bit anymore. It was Edward. Edward and Rebecca and the fact that they had to see each other again before they died. If they could. Now that she'd met Edward, Tess wanted him to have the chance he'd clearly never had, for whatever reason, to find happiness with the woman he'd loved all his life.

Rumer was an artist who didn't want fame. Rebecca would never have sought fame. Rebecca had disappeared. Rumer had kept her identity secret. Rebecca had made an art form of running away. She'd run from her mother to ensure her survival. Had she run again? Had she destroyed all evidence of the girl who had existed before Rumer Banks?

She'd only left a handful of drawings and paintings back in Australia, and Sunday Reed had looked after those. They'd been hidden away at Heide. There had only been one exhibition forty years ago. While Rumer's work had become easily recognizable now, Rebecca Swift's work had been left for dead.

Switching back to her research on Rebecca's death over the weekend, Tess had also discovered that Rebecca's body had never been found. So. Edward had never had closure. And that was why Rebecca Swift lingered on in his soul, gone, but not buried. The fact that she'd haunted him since Edith died made sense.

But at this point, even though Tess still didn't know what had gone wrong between Edward and Rebecca, one thing was clear: the past may well be some strange, secret shore, but if it was haunting Edward enough to make him want to write a book for the first time in forty years, enough to make him want to revisit it as soon as his wife had died and he was free, then Tess had an obligation to tell him that Rebecca might not have died that night in 1946.

One lead, one chance to find her. Carmel-by-the-Sea was mentioned in three articles by three separate journalists as Rumer Banks's home. Tess looked at the photocopies of those articles that she'd laid out on her desk and studied them alongside her photos. She had to make sense of this quickly.

Tess leaned forward and picked up the phone.

"Pronto?" Edward said.

"Edward? It's Tess." Tess winced at the high-pitched tone of her voice.

This was not her story to keep secret.

"Edward," she said. "There's something you should know."

There was a silence.

"Have you heard of an artist called Rumer Banks?"

"Vaguely," he said. "She is US-based, a mystery, isn't that right? I'm not any more familiar with her than that, I'm afraid."

Tess took in a breath. "As soon as I saw Rebecca's sketches—this is going to sound odd, Edward, but bear with me—I noticed that Rebecca's work bore more than a resemblance to Rumer Banks's sketches."

Edward stayed quiet.

"You see, my father also . . . well, you could say, in his own way, he admires Rumer Banks and owns two of her early sketches from the 1950s. She is famously prolific, so it's not so unusual for smart investors to have bought her work years ago. All Rumer does is create art. Apparently, she's hidden herself away from the rest of the world, and from what I've read, she's leading an almost hermetic existence, it seems . . . Edward."

"Hang on—"

"Please hear me out, Edward. When I saw Rebecca's sketches, your sketches, I noticed not only that Rebecca's work was strikingly like Rumer's. I wondered if they were by the same artist."

She waited a few moments. Her heart pounded out a triple tattoo. Either she was about to be ditched again, or . . .

"I know it sounds crazy," she murmured, wishing, so intently, that she was there with him, sitting in some café in Rome surrounded by Italian art. "But Edward, the work is so similar, I have to ask whether Rebecca may still be alive. I have to ask whether she may not have drowned at sea, but instead reinvented herself as the mysterious Rumer Banks. I think she ran away again."

Silence.

Tess's stomach turned on itself.

"I don't think," Edward said finally, "that you could possibly understand the loss that I went through. I want you to forget we had this conversation. Rebecca is dead. I've been living with that fact for forty years, believe me. She's gone. If you think that somehow finding out whether Rebecca reinvented herself under a pseudonym could be another publicity stunt for your career, then I will seek another publisher."

Tess felt her shoulders droop. Silently, she cursed the way she'd approached him when they'd begun working together.

"If you want to continue with this project, would you please keep things professional," he said. "I have no interest in any more tactics that are clearly directed toward publicity on your part. It's becoming obscene."

And he hung up.

Rome, 1987

Edward placed the receiver onto its cradle, his heart hammering in mismatched beats. He gazed at the intricate patterns that decorated the Turkish rug he'd saved from Haslemere. Then he went over to the kitchen.

Edward's hands shook as he lifted the electric kettle. As if in a trance, he moved across the small kitchen to the sink and turned on the tap, forcing himself to focus on the water as it ran from the faucet into the kettle's white lip. He had to stop before he could fill it enough even for one cup of tea, furious with his old vibrating hands, age spots tenanting the places that once, Rebecca had stroked . . .

He leaned against the Formica bench, closing his eyes against the tears that stung the backs of his eyelids, old half-formed things that had never fallen years ago, when they should have.

He had never been able to let them out.

Guilt returned like a wasp. Stinging in repeated patterns, again and again, in the same tortured spot. He'd been so wracked with everything at the time it all happened that he'd been unable to see past his own nose. If the past was another country, he'd left it far behind. For years that had worked.

Until now.

So what should he do? Gaining control of his feelings was his first quick instinct, like capturing a bad spirit in its den. No matter how much his life might want to move in circular patterns, Edward wanted to stick to a straight line. Writing about the past was one thing. Taking a step back and risking living it again was simply not something he was prepared to do.

CHAPTER
TWENTY-FOUR

Victor Harbor, 1946

Rebecca rushed down the lawn, her dress flapping behind her, down the path through the bushes onto the beach. It was as if a spool of black ribbon had wound itself around the entire Russell family since the horrifying facts surrounding Robert's death had come to light. Edward was in an abominable place that was impossible to reach. The house was filled with hushed discussions about the importance of covering up the amount of alcohol that had been in Robert's bloodstream when he stumbled into Edward's car and drove like a madman until he finally, in some death wish, wrapped both the Aston Martin and himself around a tree.

Rebecca sat by in stunned silence as the press figured more in family conversations than Robert ever had. It was impossible to tell what was going on with Celia, but she constantly diverted the family from any talk about the boy they had lost, the person he was, and the tragedy of his drinking. Rebecca could only watch helplessly as Edward tried to convince his mother that they needed to talk about the drinking, to acknowledge that it had caused Robert's death, and to help Angus. In the face of Celia's stony resistance, finally, he appeared to have given up.

It was too late, after all. The deed was done. The worst had happened.

Robert was dead. So what was the point in going over it? Edward withdrew from everyone. He'd told Rebecca he wanted to think his own thoughts, make his own decisions. He'd shut her out. Had become a pale and muted version of himself. It seemed he was afraid that Celia would collapse if he raised anything controversial.

Vicky's face, when she appeared, was the color of a frozen lake, blue undertones rendering her soft features almost ghoulish. But she wasn't going to let up either; she was not going to acknowledge the truth about the family's problems.

Rebecca saw mirror images of the time after her own father's death. Rebecca had to tell her friends that her father had died of a heart attack. Not the truth. Never the truth.

Robert's tragic death brought back searing feelings about her father. She lay wide awake at night, stuck with memories of her own loss. Grief seemed to be a complex circle that spun itself into patterns; it was hardly a linear process. Did time have any bearing on it? Rebecca thought she'd gotten over her father's death years ago. And yet, more than anything else, right now it seemed that she and Edward were both locked in torturous worlds that were heartbreakingly separate, and yet intrinsically the same.

Rebecca now saw with startling clarity the way her mother swept everything under the carpet in order to forge on. Celia's attitude highlighted it until the realization cut into Rebecca's heart. Rebecca could see so clearly what was happening, how this failure to face up to the truth wouldn't work in a year, or ten years, or twenty, but she could only stand by and watch, helpless.

Cry, for heaven's sakes, she wanted to say to them all. Don't sit in this stony cold state! But stoicism was supposed to be a sign of strength, and she knew better than to confront them in their grief.

Rebecca sat through the funeral in the local church in the pew behind the family, staring at the back of Edward's rigid head. Robert's body was to be transported to the family graveyard at Haslemere, where he would rest on a hillside overlooking the paddocks that his forebears had turned into a sprawling estate.

The evening after the funeral, Rebecca stood on the beach staring out at the sea.

She knew with deadening certainty that her relationship with Edward was breaking down. Celia could not have been less subtle about Edward's responsibilities had she wielded a sledgehammer. The older woman told Rebecca repeatedly that Edward's role was fundamental to the family's future now. And suggested that Rebecca should go home.

Rebecca dipped her toes into the warm shallows that puddled in and out, gentle, tiny wavelets.

But how could she abandon Edward? She would not walk out on him, ever. He'd been there for her when she needed him. She, in turn, would be here as long as he needed her. But did he need her? Did he want her here?

Rebecca painted furiously. Her work was her only balm. She mailed sketches and paintings that she made while keeping well out of the way in order to calm her circular yearning to be with Edward. She missed him. But this was not the time to tell him that. Instead, she spent hours sitting on the beach or on the island, where the wild gray sea seemed to marry perfectly with the turbulence in her soul.

Beneath all the swirling, broiling mess, she had moments of pure clarity, just as sometimes the foamy water parted enough to show the ocean's depths. She loved Edward. She would do so until the day he died, so she would stay here. Sunday was right. Love was all we had. Love was all that mattered. She had to believe in it, or she would be lost.

And so she would wait for him to get through this. She would give him the space he needed and let him grieve. No matter how long it took. Rebecca knew that he loved her. He would come back to her once things were done.

Sunday, as always, understood.

Heide

Darling Rebecca,
I think you are right in giving Edward some space. I think you are also right in that this time is for you to paint from your heart. Go to your island, don't hold it back. The CAS is delighted with your work and your sketches will hang alongside Sidney Nolan's and Albert Tucker's in their next exhibition in Melbourne. Grief is uncontrollable sometimes. Out of it will come your best work. Things will resolve themselves. Just hold out.
Edward will come through. Your love is too strong for anything else.
Take life one day at a time. It is the only way we can control our lives at times of indomitable grief.
My love,
Sun.

The delight she should have felt at the fact that her work was being hung alongside Sidney Nolan's and Albert Tucker's seemed irrelevant, washed aside by worry about Edward, about their future. For the first time in her life, her art was only a distraction, not a refuge. Rebecca tugged at Sunday's letter in her pocket. She had no idea where this crazy, wild sea storm was taking her next.

CHAPTER TWENTY-FIVE

New York, 1987

Tess waited on a black leather sofa in the lobby of her office building, her hands clasped in her lap. Her suitcase was lined up, with her cherry-red scarf tied to its handle. She'd grabbed it at the last minute, not only so that she could identify her suitcase, but it seemed appropriate for this journey. It was a wave of hope, somehow, to Rebecca Swift.

Tess focused on the tall windows that looked out over the busy street. It might not sound rational to anyone else, but to Tess, Rebecca being Rumer made perfect sense. She'd run away from her life, and she'd hidden herself away for decades. And she'd painted. Tess was sure of it.

The elevator doors slid open. James walked into the lobby and marched straight toward her.

Tess folded her hands tighter in her lap.

He stood, blocking her view of the streetscape. James's voice was low and deep. "Tell me what you're doing."

Tess tightened her lips into a bow.

"Okay then. Here's the thing." He sat down beside her. "I think I know."

Tess felt her heartbeat go double time. Where was the taxi?

He wouldn't understand. She couldn't tell him. He'd think she was crazy. And tacky. His use of the word still caused her to wince.

"Leon said you were going to Carmel-by-the-Sea," he murmured. "I presume he knows why."

Tess smoothed her hands down her outfit.

James crouched down in front of her, sending a glance around the room. "I went to the Rose Reading Room, Tess. I admire Rumer Banks, you see. But I thought it was too far-fetched to say anything to you about my suspicions before I'd checked it out back home, and I wasn't sure whether you'd made the same connection. You could have talked to me, Tess. But Rebecca's work has been locked away at Heide, and Edward has kept those sketches to himself. I doubt he even showed them to his wife. We have to appreciate how much it must have cost him to show them to us."

Her favorite spot in the library. The Rose Reading Room. She'd underestimated his knowledge of art.

Tess clasped her hands and stared straight ahead.

"Hey," he said, as she watched the constant movement out in the street. "Are you sure you want to do this?"

"You haven't read Edward's book," she said. "You don't know how much he loved her. If I don't do this I'll regret it for the rest of my life. It's nothing to do with my career."

James ran a hand through his tousled hair.

Tess focused straight ahead. If she thought about this too much, she'd tell herself to stop—to put her career first. The room seemed a blur now, people came and went as usual on a busy Friday morning. But somehow, beneath all this day-to-day bustle in the world, truth and honesty and getting to the heart of things were all that mattered now.

Edward and Rebecca had been right. And what was more, Tess had known it all her life. She'd toed the line for far too long now. She had to start making her own decisions. She had to start standing on her own two feet. And if that meant striking out on her own, then so be it. She knew how she felt about James. No one, not ever, had treated her with such respect as he had. No one affected her as he did. But she still knew that she had to follow her heart where it was leading her right now.

And if she had a chance to find Rebecca Swift, then she was going to take it.

"Tess," James said, "if Edward finds out you're doing this, he's going to be furious. Your job, your career . . . you can't afford to lose everything."

Tess gritted her teeth.

James reached out, touching her hand for a brief second before pulling it back. "You're getting too involved, taking everything too seriously," he said, his voice achingly close.

Tightness clamped her chest. Everything? As in him, James, as well? She glared at the window, determined not to let him rattle her.

A yellow cab stopped outside the glass-fronted building.

She stood up. Looked him straight in the eye. Fought an urge, almost as strong as her own heartbeat, to reach out and trace her fingers over his face, his lips. He had that hurt look in his eyes again. She knew he was worried about her. But still, she held his gaze. "If Rumer is Rebecca, which I think she has to be, I want to know why she did it. I need to know why she left. I want to know why she hid herself away from the man she loved, and I want to see if there is any chance that they can find happiness again."

James's look seared into her. For a moment, something twinkled in his eyes. He leaned forward, his lips brushing the top of her head. "Let me come with you," he murmured into her hair.

But she shook her head, even though her hands wanted to reach out and hold him as he held her. "No. I have to find her myself," she said.

"Be careful," he muttered, as the taxi driver took her suitcase.

James walked with her out the front door and hugged her roughly again before she climbed into the cab. "Call me if you get stuck. I'm here. You know that."

Tess nodded. "I'll be fine. I just want to find her."

James stood on the pavement while Tess rested her head on the vinyl seat. It was as if she were unpeeling layers of a bound onion—she had to get to the core of the thing. Everything was interlinked: the way she'd been carrying on at work these past few years, the way in which she'd handled herself around her family for a long time, perhaps even the deep-felt fear she knew that she still held about trusting that James held her best interests at heart. Tess didn't know what the answers were yet. But she suspected that Rebecca had also run away. She didn't know why, but she wanted to know if the older woman was still alive and if she would consider taking the risk to live the authentic life that she had left behind. Tess wanted to know the measure of Rebecca's courage, and while the stakes were high—her job, Edward's trust, and her relationship with James—she wanted to know the measure of her own courage too.

Carmel-by-the-Sea, 1987

Tess gazed out of the taxi window at the couples who wandered through the seaside town's pretty streets in the midafternoon sun, window-shopping, relaxing, enjoying life. But as the taxi moved deeper into the town, Tess felt a sense of unease. How many art galleries were there in these streets? Over one hundred, apparently. She had two days to find Rumer Banks. And Rebecca Swift had made an art form of running away.

The taxi stopped on the corner of Dolores and Fourth. Once Tess paid the driver, she stood in the shade of a large tree, its leaves vivid green in the California sun. Tess carried her suitcase through the inn's courtyard, with its bright bougainvillea cascading over the boundary fence, and settled on the best of three hundred plans that she'd brainstormed on the flight over.

First, she checked in. In her room, she vaguely took in the promised glimpse of the mid-blue ocean from the window. Tess glanced quickly over the double brass bed with its white comforter and the elegant bathroom with French bath products, but she wasted no time in going back downstairs to reception.

Tess listened while the receptionist told her that drinks were served in the library. She turned, taking in the grand piano in front of picture windows overlooking another courtyard with an explosion of blooms, as if she were interested in such things. Politely, she made appreciative noises about the cozy fireplace, the bookshelves replete with classic novels that lined the warm room.

"It all looks gorgeous," Tess said. "Complete heaven." She took in a breath. "Can I ask you a question? You see, the thing is, I'm a real admirer of . . . Rumer Banks."

The girl nodded as if this were no surprise.

"I was wondering if any galleries sold her work around here?"

The receptionist's smile did not falter for a second. She turned to the row of neat pamphlets that were displayed behind her desk, pulled out one, clicked her red pen, and showed Tess a map.

"Modern Beauty deals with Rumer Banks's work." The girl drew a line straight down Dolores Street and then traced her pen along Sixth Avenue, drawing a large star halfway up the street. "You won't miss it. It's a green wooden building with a big picture window and red geraniums in the window boxes."

It was more than tempting to ask a tiny probing question about Rumer, but the last thing Tess needed was to put anyone off.

Yet.

This was a small town. Some of the residents must know who Rumer was, if she did indeed live hereabouts. Tess took the map with her on the short walk under the canopy of trees, passing immaculate houses and chocolate shops, then turned onto Sixth Avenue. The sun still beat down in the gaps between the shade, throwing speckled patterns onto Tess's dress.

The gallery was exactly as the girl described. Its picture windows and flowers fit like a silk glove with this town, as did most of the boutique shops and galleries. Tess pushed the door open. The airy room was empty apart from the woman who sat behind the desk. Tess glanced at her, sizing her up.

So, was this Rumer's agent? The woman who had exclusive knowledge of who she really was? The woman wore heavy-framed glasses, her hair was cut razor short, and she sipped from a large mug of coffee with a slogan: "Speaking one's mind is a pleasure."

Tess felt a flutter of nerves. She turned away from the formidable-looking owner, if that was who she was, and gathered herself for a moment. Then stopped. Because on the wall in front of her hung two paintings by Rumer Banks.

The first one was of a girl, braids flying behind her head. She was running beside an older woman who wore a pinafore. They were on a deserted street. Neither of them looked toward the foreground of the painting. Tess took a step closer. Eucalyptus lined the bare, dust-ridden road along which they went. It could be California, but to Tess, the setting screamed Australian outback as brazenly as if Rebecca had shouted the words out herself. Tess was reminded of Sidney Nolan's work. In the distance, a derelict old cottage sat, its tin roof sparkling in the sun.

Tearing her gaze away, Tess moved to the next painting, her shirt prickling against her skin even though the space was cooled with air conditioning. And found herself staring at a painting of an old woman sitting on a bench. Rumer had rendered the back of the woman's head—again, the woman's face was hidden away—in exquisite detail: the hasty nature of her bun, the way her shoes were worn, dusty, red slip-ons, and again, a red dirt street.

"Rumer painted these a while ago. She has only just decided to release them. They are unique in that sense."

Tess faced the woman who sat at the desk.

"Are you familiar with her work?" the woman asked.

"A little," Tess said. "I'm intrigued by the mystique that surrounds her."

The woman seemed to contemplate Tess. "The fact that Rumer Banks hides her identity seems anathema to us in this day and age. She prefers to share herself in perhaps the most intimate way, through her art. But she doesn't have any interest in publicity."

Tess turned back to the painting of the woman and child. She couldn't stop the feeling that this was a rendering of Rebecca and her mother, alone in a cruel landscape. And yet, there was something of a conundrum here.

Edward had picked up that Rebecca only presented a cheerful version of herself to the world after their first conversation; he'd seen how she carefully hid her real self from most people, except Edward and Sunday, it seemed. And yet now she was doing the opposite, showing her deepest self through her art, while Rebecca, if Rumer was Rebecca, was hidden away from view.

Tess was going to have to start asking questions before someone else walked into the gallery. The woman flipped through a brochure and reached for her phone.

Tess straightened herself and took her chance.

"I was wondering," she said quickly, "does anyone know who Rumer Banks really is? I mean, someone must?" *You, if you have rights to sell her work.*

The woman was firm. "Rumer's desire for privacy is something that is well established. Everyone respects it, to the extent that I think if anyone revealed who she was, they'd be tainted by reputation. It's as if Rumer is protected by her admirers. At some level, people would worry that she'd stop painting altogether. No one's going to find out who Rumer is any time soon." The woman looked at Tess, her eyebrow slightly raised as if challenging her to ask another question.

Tess knew she was at a crossroads—she could give up and walk away, ask more probing, useless questions, or share something with the woman herself. Option three seemed the only solution. She sat down in the chair opposite the woman's desk and reached inside her handbag, her fingers alighting on the photos of Edward's sketches.

She raised her head and held the woman's gaze. "I have something that will interest you."

The older woman folded her arms.

"The thing is," Tess said, "a . . . friend of mine owns some of Rumer's early work."

Her hands shook as she handed over the photographs of the sketches Edward had showed her in Rome.

The woman was silent, but she took the photographs, turning them over to examine their backs first. Then, frowning, she studied the sketch of Joy for what seemed like an age. She did exactly the same thing with the drawings of Edward and Max Harris. Then laid them down on the table in front of her. But she didn't offer them back to Tess. The expression on her face was impossible to decipher.

"Can you tell me where you got these?"

Tess kept her voice quiet and firm. "The sketches were done in the 1940s. They belong to . . . someone I know." She watched the woman's eyebrows knit together. "They were done in Australia."

The woman looked up sharply. "What makes you think that?"

Tess watched the woman. "The person who owns them brought them from there. I have reason to believe that . . . Rumer . . . gave them to him as a gift."

The woman picked up the sketch of Max Harris again, holding his cigar at that distant party in Pink Alley. She held it at arm's length, then pulled it back closer to her face.

"My friend is Australian," Tess said.

"What is the person's name?"

"I'm sorry. The owner is my client. We haven't yet introduced our-selves. I'm Tess Miller."

"Janet," the woman said, speaking slowly now. "Janet Burke. So, are they wanting to sell them?"

"No. They aren't for sale."

"It's just a matter of authenticating them, then." Janet placed the pictures on her desk.

"Yes," Tess said. "Do you . . . would you say that they are likely to have been done by Rumer?"

"I can't confirm anything until I have seen the originals."

Tess waited a beat. "I understand. Tell me, do you have exclusive rights to sell Rumer's work or do other galleries in Carmel-by-the-Sea also sell her work?"

The woman sat back in her seat. She looked as if she were thinking about whether to answer the question. "I have exclusive rights. As I said, unless I see the originals, I can't comment. If your contact thinks he or she has some original sketches of Rumer's, then you should bring them here to me. I couldn't attest to their authenticity without a proper examination. And I would have to do that according to all the proto-cols. Obviously I can't decide on the spot."

And who could, Tess wondered?

Rumer Banks, of course . . .

"Would you consider showing the sketches to Rumer?" she asked.

"They are photographs, Miss Miller. If you want them authenti-cated, we must sight the originals."

Tess decided to try one last tactic: standing up, as if she were about to leave.

"Look," Janet said.

Tess stood still. It was clear that Rumer lived in Carmel-by-the-Sea. No one here had questioned that supposition. Tess just had to find her.

"I can't tell you whether or not Rumer was in Australia at some point," Janet said. "Surely you understand that I would never reveal any information that might compromise my client's well-respected privacy to anyone who walks in here off the street."

Tess waited. Yes, she understood, just as she felt the same way about her author, Edward, no matter how frustrating he was at times. The fact was she found him endearing. And if Janet were working with Rebecca, if there was an inkling of that old Rebecca left, then Tess was more than understanding as to why Janet, in turn, would feel a deep sense of loyalty too.

So, a deadlock then, each of them entranced by Edward and Rebecca, if she were right.

Janet pulled her glasses off, not losing eye contact with Tess for a second. "If you want to do so, bring me the originals. I can't offer you anything more."

"I understand. Thank you," Tess said. But the idea of even asking Edward to show his original sketches to a gallery owner who specialized in Rumer Banks? She may as well shoot that proposition down.

Tess said goodbye and made her way out into the street. Late-afternoon shadows cast long shapes onto the sidewalk, and she felt as if the trees were closing in on her. She stopped a little farther down the street, tiredness kicking in. She was starting to run out of plans. It seemed a hopeless business. If she had come straight to the point of contact for Rumer and hit a dead end, then what hope did she have of finding Rebecca now?

The pristine street with its well-to-do, gleaming cars parked along the curb seemed cold and distant now, as if it were a place where Tess didn't belong. The old Rebecca would hardly fit in here, either.

A café beckoned, its windows framed with cheery checked curtains. Coffee seemed like an excellent idea. People sat at wooden tables near the window, and tubs of roses decorated the front entrance. Tess stepped inside and ordered an espresso. She needed to kick-start her mind.

Not far from the counter, a brochure stand was propped up, popu-
lated by glossy advertisements for local galleries. Tess wandered over to
have a look. In center position, a yellow piece of paper was printed with
black ink. The beelike colors drew Tess; she picked up the brochure and
studied it. A lecture, tonight, on local artists from Carmel-by-the-Sea,
in a gallery.

At 7:30 p.m.

Tess looked at her watch. It started in three hours.

Plan B.

Three hours later, Tess took in the panel on the stage. They looked
formidable enough—an art critic from San Francisco, the owner of the
large gallery where the talk was being held tonight, and two local artists,
both looking to be well into their fifties. They all wore half-moon glasses
that were balanced on their noses, and when anyone put up a hand to
ask a question, all the panelists frowned. Tess hardly knew how she was
going to approach them with her far-fetched questions.

It became clear after she had sat in the audience for ten minutes
that the community here was tight-knit. The conversations that buzzed
around her were testament to the fact that everyone knew everyone else.
Breaking into their circle and getting them to reveal a treasured secret
was going to be like cutting hard rock open with a penknife.

The longer the evening wore on, the more Tess became convinced
that getting any information was going to be impossible. Nevertheless,
once the panel opened officially for questions, Tess raised her hand.
Holding the roving microphone in hands that were slick with sweat, she
spoke in a voice that sounded as high-pitched as a small bird's.

"I wanted to ask about one of the local artists. Rumer Banks."

There was a general turning of heads. The people in the row in
front of Tess looked about as friendly as hunters about to shoot their
prey. Janet was right. People were protective of Rumer. Tess probably
couldn't have chosen a worse place to start than among a group of art

aficionados. But she stood a little taller. And reminded herself that she was as protective of Rebecca Swift as they were of Rumer Banks.

"What makes you think Rumer Banks is a local artist?" the gallery owner snapped.

"Name?" the art critic shot out at the same time.

Tess paced her words. "Tess Miller," she said. "I . . . have a special interest in Rumer's work."

The gallery owner lowered his glasses farther down his nose.

Tess kept eye contact with him, in spite of the fact she felt a deep pit forming inside her stomach. "I am here because I have seen, lately, some sketches that I think might be hers. I would like to verify them, and I was wondering if someone here might be able to help."

"Who owns them?" The art critic leaned forward in his seat, tapping his fingers on the table as if he were preparing for a fight.

"A private . . . collector. The sketches are strikingly similar to Rumer's early work. I want to know whether they might be hers."

The audience began to murmur. Suddenly, the room felt hot.

"When were they done?"

Tess took a breath. "1946."

The art critic leaned forward, speaking as if he were making a general announcement to the whole room. "Rumer Banks did not start working until the 1950s. There is no evidence of anything in the entire country that was painted by her before 1950. It's highly unlikely that this person has a Banks in their collection. However, should you wish to follow up, the best thing to do is to go talk to Janet Burke at Modern Beauty. She will point you in the right direction. Now. Do we have any further questions?"

Several hands went up. Tess hovered a moment, gripping the mic. But the person who was running around with it was at the end of her row. The man next to her held up his hand to take it, looking at her as if willing her to just sit down already. Tess sat down in her seat and stared straight ahead, hearing nothing more that the panel said as the microphone went to someone else.

"We'll have a short break," the gallery owner announced several minutes later. "Tea and coffee in the gallery. And afterward we'll discuss a major exhibition that we are planning to host here in the fall."

One person moved in Tess's row, then another, until everyone followed each other, sheep-like, out of the room. People shuffled past Tess out in the main gallery, making a beeline for their friends and acquaintances. Tess scanned the crowd. Trying to talk to people here was a complete waste of time—the collective view was clearly that Rumer's privacy was sacrosanct. She went toward the exit, stepping out into the warm evening. Lamps lit up the sidewalks on George Street. The street was deserted.

Tess stood in the pool of light cast by the gallery windows, gazing back at the people milling inside. The front door of the gallery slammed shut just as Tess started to make her way along the street. Footsteps clattered behind her on the pavement. Tess stepped out of the way to avoid being bowled over.

"Who are you and what do you want?" A woman's voice jolted into the darkness.

Tess turned, fast, to find herself face-to-face with a young woman. Tess took in the thin red dress that the woman, who looked about Tess's age, wore. One spaghetti strap had fallen from her shoulder. Her dark hair was tousled, and her eyes burned into Tess's own.

The stranger crossed her arms around her slim frame. "What is it that you want? What sketches do you have?"

A couple came out of the gallery. Tess's companion looked toward them; the expression on her face, if Tess was right, was one of fear. The young woman stared at them until the distant sound of their shoes tapping against the pavement was the only thing left.

Tess took the opportunity to have a good look at her companion. She kept her voice low and quiet so as not to upset the woman further.

"The sketches belong to someone I know. Someone . . . someone who used to know . . . Rumer," she said.

The young woman squared her shoulders.

"I think the sketches were done when she was in Australia. In the 1940s. When Rumer was young." Tess almost whispered the words.

The woman's eyes darted about the empty street.

"I'm an editor in a publishing house in New York," Tess went on, keeping her voice deliberately calm although she had to clasp her hands together to stop them from shaking visibly. "The sketches I have belong to someone who I think used to know her when she was young . . ." she said. "In Australia. There is something else."

"Go on." But the girl still didn't make eye contact.

"The owner of the sketches is writing a novel about his love affair with the girl who did those sketches, sketches that look exactly like Rumer's work. The girl had dark, swinging hair. She liked to wear red."

The girl's chest heaved in her dress.

"She favored red berets and red dresses," Tess whispered. "Her mother worked as a seamstress in a boutique in Melbourne."

The girl's glance tore from side to side as if she was scouting the street for eavesdroppers.

"Listen," Tess said. "There are several problems. If the novel is released, and if Rumer is indeed . . . Rebecca Swift . . ."

The girl clenched and unclenched her delicate fists.

"Then," Tess went on, "Rumer is going to hear about the book. I know how hard Rumer has worked to keep her life private from the world. I know what happened to Rebecca Swift in Australia. She fell from a rock into the sea and drowned. But if Rumer's two lives are about to collide, then the explosion is going to be huge unless she takes things in hand. I sense that you know what I'm talking about," she said.

The girl glanced up the street.

"Can I ask what your name is?" Tess went on. She felt like a snake charmer. It was not something she was proud of, but she had come so far now . . .

Her companion hesitated. Her gaze was still off in the distance when she spoke. "Sunday," she said, almost as if challenging Tess. "It's Sunday."

Of course it was.

Tess understood the walls that Rebecca's daughter—because that was who she undoubtedly was—must have lived with all her life. And Tess understood that those walls were going to be as tough as stone to break down. She had to convince Sunday that she, Tess, was not a threat, that she was on their side. That she understood something of what Rebecca had done and that she even knew about hiding, whether it was from yourself, or the world, or your family when you were not comfortable being who you were. She understood about putting up walls now, but if she'd come to realize one thing, it was that walls did not fix any problem. Eventually things had to be dealt with; eventually things would always come to a head.

"Does the name Edward Russell mean anything to you?" Tess asked, her words seeming to linger in the lamplit street.

Sunday remained stock-still.

"He is writing the most searing, poignant love story about Rebecca—a novel," Tess said. "I think she will want to know about it because it's set for international release."

Sunday's mouth worked. "Nobody knows about this. No one. It's the only way she's survived."

Tess resisted the overwhelming temptation to reach out and touch Sunday on the arm. "I'm the only person who has read the manuscript. So far. As Edward Russell's editor, it's just my job. I haven't done anything or said anything, and I won't until we've spoken to Rebecca."

Sunday wrapped her arms around her waist. "You have to promise that you won't try anything ever again like you did tonight in front of all those people."

"I'm sorry. I had to find her or it would have haunted me, just as your mother is haunting Edward. It seems we can't let go of some things, no matter how hard we might try to push them out of our lives."

Slowly, Sunday opened her bag and pulled out car keys on a leather key ring. "You're going to have to talk to her. I'm just . . . you've stunned me. But you'll need to come with me now."

Sunday turned and clipped down the street, her head up.

She stopped at a station wagon. Opened the passenger door. Tess climbed into Sunday's car, pushing aside doubts about safety, trusting her instincts that this was okay. They both had to trust each other.

So she trusted the girl who drove her out of town, first toward the beach, then along the road north that snaked past the pitch-black sea.

Rebecca stood on the balcony that overlooked the ocean. The sadness that sat inside her these days was even more poignant than her own tragedy—something that she had painted out of herself for forty years. But now, what seemed insurmountable in the inky darkness was this question: was Sunday, too, destined never to love and be loved?

Rebecca knew that it was her fault. If there was one thing that she had wanted to do in this life, it was to provide a stable home for her daughter. The shades of her own childhood haunted her, and she had been so determined that her daughter would have the support she'd lacked when young. But marrying Sunday's father had only been some vain attempt to stamp the past out.

What hope had she had when she'd only ever loved one person all her life? No one was going to measure up to him. She was better off on her own than inflicting her shipwrecked heart on any other man. Her past wasn't fair to anyone else.

At least she could put on a facade. And that was what it was, her life, the life that she had supposed to be ingrained in truth. All those ideas they had shared together only existed on some distant shore. At least there was still her art. At least there was kindness. She could live by that. And there was love, love between herself and her daughter. It was enough. She knew she was still lucky.

Rebecca knew that.

When the flare of Sunday's headlights shone into Rebecca's eyes, she stood taller in surprise. This was unlike Sunday, but she could tell by the sound of the approaching engine that the car was her daughter's. A visit, now, when she'd been worrying about her? The yellow head-lights obliterated Sunday's face as she made her way past the eucalyptus that bordered the driveway. Rebecca was struck with the thought that something was wrong.

She gathered her cardigan around herself and made her way down the wooden steps from the balcony as Sunday pulled up in the driveway. And brought her hand up to her mouth. As Sunday opened the door, light flashed onto another face. Someone unexpected was in the passenger seat. This was not something they did. Sunday and she had held a tacit understanding for years and years. Bringing strangers home was not part of it. Rebecca tried to make eye contact with Sunday, but her daughter looked at the ground.

The girl in the passenger seat climbed out and moved toward the house, as if in slow motion now. Her eyes were almond shaped. She wore blue jeans, a pale blue T-shirt. Rebecca tried to calm her racing thoughts.

Tess held out her hand. Rebecca's face was exactly as Edward had described it, and her hair still hung loose around her shoulders as it had in the book. She wore a pair of cream trousers and her white shirt looked to be made of silk, with buttons wrought of delicate pearls. Over it she wore a cream cardigan of cashmere or angora wool. Tess smiled at the thought that Celia would be somewhat miffed at Rebecca's material success.

Rebecca was silent as Sunday talked to her mother in low, fervent tones. But Tess's heart skipped about in double time. Her eyes darted up to the luxurious, modern, understated house.

Finally, Rebecca turned to Tess, brought her hand to her mouth, let out a sob, and ran back up the stairs to the house.

Sunday inclined her head to indicate that Tess should come inside. Tess followed Sunday up the stone steps, her eyes appreciating the fruits of Rebecca's obvious success when she stepped over the threshold. Such tasteful furnishings—simple, pale sofas almost floating on polished floorboards, rugs decorating the space with its view out at the black ocean—where else would Rebecca Swift live? During the daytime, she suspected the whole room would appear to drift high above the sea.

"Mom," Sunday said, but Rebecca was halfway across the living room toward the kitchen. Finally, she faced them, standing behind the kitchen counter. As if it were protection. Rebecca remained perfectly still. Tess couldn't tear her eyes from Rebecca's still-beautiful face.

"Rebecca." Tess stumbled on the word.

Rebecca slid down onto a bar stool.

"Mom. I'm sorry, I had to bring Tess to you. You need to talk to her." Sunday moved toward her mother and ran a hand over Rebecca's back, her fingertips drawing circling patterns as if to soothe her in some old time-honored way.

But when she spoke, Rebecca's voice was steel. "Who are you?" she asked, glaring at Tess. "What is it that you want?"

Sunday made a small, protesting noise. "Mom."

Rebecca turned to her daughter. "Sun, I think it would be better if Tess and I talked alone."

Silence.

A few moments later, Sunday leaned down and kissed her mother on the cheek; the two dark heads, one still dramatically beautiful, one slightly more delicate, were close for a moment.

Sunday looked to Tess. "I'm going to let Mom hear you out alone. I think it's best. And, please, Mom, just let Tess talk to you."

When Sunday clicked the glass front door shut, Rebecca stood up. But her hands shook as she reached up to her cheek. It was an instinctive movement, clearly, but Tess couldn't hold back the shudder that formed in her chest. That cheek. Mrs. Swift. Her heart went out to Rebecca.

"I am going to make coffee." Rebecca's tone was ice.

Tess took in a shuddering breath. What if Rebecca had changed over the years? What were the chances she'd want anything to do with Edward's story? What if she tried to stop it from being published? Rebecca began moving around the kitchen, pulling out mugs, grinding coffee beans. The noise shattered the otherwise silent space.

Finally it was quiet again, and Rebecca handed Tess a steaming mug. She tipped a jar of chocolate cookies onto a solid earthenware plate, letting them scatter like a pack of cards. Then Rebecca made her way across to one of the large sofas by the fireplace.

Tess hovered. Her eyes darted out to the blackness.

Rebecca waited, watching her. "Who sent you here?" she asked, seeming a little more in control now. "You can sit down, if you like." She waved at the sofa opposite her, but the motion was vague.

"No one. I came of my own accord." Tess placed her coffee mug on Rebecca's glass coffee table. A handful of select art books sat on it, along with several ceramic works. Tess perched on the edge of the sofa.

Rebecca waited in silence.

"Edward Russell . . ." she managed to say. This was ten million times harder than she'd anticipated. Tess's throat was constricted and her breathing was too fast, no matter how hard she tried to slow it.

Rebecca stood up in a sudden movement, sweeping across to the fireplace and standing there, reminding Tess of Edward standing at the fireplace in the library in Haslemere, dressed as a country gentleman. It seemed Rebecca was the one running everything now. Their situations had been reversed, and yet was either of them happy?

Tess found her eyes darting around the room in order to avoid staring at Rebecca, and she was struck suddenly with the fact that everything in this house was undeniably modern; nothing was old or time-worn. Rebecca's gorgeous home must only be a few years old too. The way Rebecca dressed was entirely up-to-date. Nothing harked back to the past.

Rebecca was still a modernist then. But the fact that there was no hint of nostalgia here gave Tess a sense of unease. She shuddered at the thought that Rebecca might have ended up anything like her Mrs. Swift or Celia, who had both been pros at pushing everything that mattered aside. Tess felt more determined than ever to get through to the woman who she knew was deep inside.

"Edward's wife died recently," Tess said. "He found himself haunted by the past. He's writing a book about you, about your love affair with him. I am his editor, from New York. The only way he can deal with his memories of you—of your tragic love affair—is to write about them. I've found his work incredibly moving, and to be honest, that is quite something for me. I usually edit . . . thrillers, you see."

Rebecca stared out at the darkness.

Tess gathered herself. She had to keep this succinct. "Rebecca, the fact is, he showed me some of your sketches. My father owns two early Rumer Bankses. They were too similar. So. Here I am. I'm sorry. I just had to find you. The way he writes about you, the love you shared. The stories of Heide and the modernists. You were onto something so strong. I can't stop thinking about it. Rebecca, he knows you so well that he's writing you back to life."

Rebecca stiffened.

"His novel is beautiful," Tess whispered. "I am completely struck by the love he clearly had . . . for you. For the love he still has, Rebecca."

Rebecca turned then, and for one split second it was as if her face softened back into the face of that girl whom Edward had described with such clarity in his book. The one Tess felt she knew so well. But Rebecca's eyes looked more alone and lonely and haunted than ever.

"No one knows who I am," she said. "No one. The fact that you do is the only reason I am listening to what you have to say."

Tess leaned forward in her seat. "Yes, but your choice not to seek publicity is in line with the modernists. Entirely. It didn't take me long to place the strands together."

Tess hesitated, but then she opened her bag. Slowly, as if coaxing a timid animal, she pulled out her photographs of the sketches and held them out to Rebecca.

Rebecca flew back to the sofa. She reached out her hand, which shook violently as she took the images, grabbing them as if she were starved. She flicked through them, her eyes running over the images as if satisfying some long-lost thirst, darting sylphlike as she took in her own brushstrokes.

"He kept them, still, after all these years?" Her hand shot up to her mouth, as if the notion were impossible.

Tess leaned forward. "Do you think he could ever part with them?" She could not contain the break in her voice. "You and I both know that Edward would never view art as a commodity. We both know that for Edward art is something to keep, to treasure for generations to come. And the fact that you created these pieces . . ." She thought of her father and his "we'll enjoy it for a while then sell it" attitude to everything, found herself repulsed, then felt her jaw set tight. If Edward embodied authenticity, then how did she, Tess, appear to him?

"Edward is living in Rome," Tess managed to say.

Rebecca's dark head shot up but she clutched the photos to her chest. "Rome?" she said.

Tess nodded.

"But what made you come here?"

"You. Edward." Tess felt a glimmer of hope that this might just work out . . .

"So, why not just publish the news that I am Rebecca? You are a businesswoman. Why bother to warn me?"

Tess's fingers were cold when she laced them together.

"Rebecca," she whispered. "You know the answer to that. I came because Edward thinks you are dead."

Rebecca stood up suddenly, moving across the room to the picture window, her back to Tess. A breeze blew in from the sea, throwing the trees outside into strange shapes. "You see, Sunday Reed once reminded me that when catastrophic things happen in life, we have three choices: to go forward, involving risk and reinvention; to go backward; or to stay stuck in one spot. To remain in Australia would have been unbearable. I like to think that I moved on, you see. I took a risk. I came here."

"Except Edward clearly still loves you."

"I don't want to see him." Rebecca changed tack, cut her off. "I don't want you to tell him that you have found me. Let him write his book. Let it go out there. I would never stop him from writing from the heart, if that is what he is doing. But I want you to promise me that you will never tell him I'm alive. You will keep this secret, or I swear, Tess, I will take you to every court in the country. You have to promise. Everyone thinks I am dead. My mother died thinking I was drowned. I ran away, and in doing so, I hurt people—Sunday Reed, family, friends, Edward. If you reveal this, then my entire life, and Rumer's, becomes a sham."

Tess took in a sharp breath. "But what if you could reunite with Edward and make amends with your past? What if Rumer the artist and Rebecca the person could be one and the same instead of two separate people, one of them only a distant memory, and one of them running from everything that you, Rebecca, believed to be true? After all, you've been forced into a hermetic existence because you don't want to reveal your true identity. Isn't this the perfect chance to come full circle and unite your past with your present for good? You are successful now; in no way are you anyone's inferior. You can be entirely yourself. Edward would never expect you to give anything up for him—he never treated you that way. He always treated you with the utmost respect."

But Rebecca's voice, when she spoke, was edged with flint and steel. "It was Edward who had a choice," she said. "No matter what he's written in his book, the fact is, he did not choose me. And the only way I could deal with that was to write my own ending. Which I've done quite well, it seems."

She laughed, uncertainly, and waved her hand around at the trappings of her success.

"What about Sunday Reed? Couldn't she have helped if you'd stayed?"

"I was ashamed that I had lost Edward. I would never have been able to live the life Sunday had."

"Did she stage her exhibition of your work?"

Rebecca brought her hand up to her throat before nodding, a slow, steady movement. "That was why I was so surprised that Edward has my sketches. I would have thought that he would have given them to Sunday after I was gone, for her exhibition. Gotten rid of them as he got rid of me."

"We both know he'd never do that."

Rebecca cut her off. "But he did."

"Was it his family?" Tess whispered.

Rebecca let out a heavy sigh. "Life got in the way. And ultimately, he made his choice—I was simply a choice for him."

"And the fact that he still loves you?"

"I believe in love," Rebecca said, "because I felt it. So I know that it exists. I still feel it. But Tess . . . I never want to see him again. Because he turned me away. And as I said, if you tell him who I am—"

"I wish you would see him." Tess was surprised at the passion in her voice.

But Rebecca stood up. "It's been . . . a revelation to meet you. It really has. But now I'm tired. This was all . . . another time, another place. I'll drive you back into town. And I ask you this. Keep everything to yourself. Don't tell anyone, not a soul. Promise me?"

"Rebecca, please."

"No," Rebecca said. "It won't happen. Because you will keep quiet."

"Of course I will," Tess said.

Rebecca moved toward the front door and collected her car keys from a small dish on a side table. Next to the keys was a collection of shells. "So," she said, "I'm able to cut and run; I always was."

Tess rose from the sofa. "Forgive me, Rebecca, but you can be kind to yourself. There is no rule that says you must deny your heart what it wants."

Rebecca turned to face her, narrowing her eyes. "That's interesting, coming from a hardened New York businesswoman."

Tess pressed her lips together. Was that how she came across? How little we seemed to know ourselves and how intimately we thought we knew other people.

"Well," Rebecca went on. "Let me tell you a couple of hard truths of my own. I'm not going backward. It would be fatal. The past is some far-off place that only exists in our memories. In any case, I've come to think over the years that I read more into it than was ever really there."

She opened the front door, holding it wide for Tess. The sea's strange whispering sounds came through in the night.

"I can't give you a happy ending, Tess," Rebecca said. "This is not some story; this is not art—it's real life."

Tess followed the older woman out onto the balcony. A sea breeze whipped up Rebecca's hair, sending it flying around her face.

Tess climbed into Rebecca's car and then watched the older woman's beautiful brown artist's hands turning the steering wheel back toward the sea.

Tess stared out at the fathomless sea.

And asked herself one question.

Why?

Once she was back in her room, Tess knew what she wanted to do. She wanted to talk with someone as soon as she could, and if there was one person with whom she felt like discussing Rebecca, she was completely certain it was James.

CHAPTER
TWENTY-SIX

Victor Harbor, 1946

The gunshot cracked, ricocheting into Rebecca's dream. She opened her eyes, unsure for a moment whether she was asleep or awake. She lay still for a moment, the silent darkness eerie in the old beach house around her. Soon the sound of footsteps thumped in the hallway. There were hysterical voices—Celia's and Vicky's, and then Edward's quieter response. A scream. A door closed. Rebecca brought her hand up to her mouth. Then, half shaking her head, fumbling for her dressing gown, she climbed out of bed and moved toward her doorway. She stood there a moment, suddenly unsure whether she should join them or not.

Silence loomed now, and the passage swirled around her. Pictures, side tables, tennis rackets against the walls, everything seemed to move. Rebecca's footsteps echoed like heartbeats when she finally started to move.

Only one person owned a gun in this house. As she made her way down the hallway, Rebecca remembered how Edward had told her that

Angus had shot a bullet through Celia's bedroom window at Haslemere once. Celia had locked him in the billiard room because he was drunk, but he'd escaped through a window into the garden in the dead of night. Rebecca took in a shuddering breath and turned the handle of the sitting room door.

Celia lay on a chaise longue, one hand resting against her pallid face. Her cheeks were the texture and color of white silk and her pale dressing gown was wrapped tight around her body. Rebecca raked her eyes over Edward's mother for bullet wounds. But there was nothing. Angus had not shot his wife . . .

Vicky knelt next to Celia, her pale hand stroking her mother's head. Edward leaned against one of the French doors that led to the veranda outside, facing downward, his mouth drawn into a tight grimace. His body heaved as if every breath were a labor.

"Mother . . ." he murmured, but the word was wretched, the antipathy of its own meaning. "My brain has gone to pieces."

Rebecca clutched the brass door handle, but her fingers were stiff.

"What was he *thinking*?" Vicky wailed.

"Edward." Celia's voice was deep, primal. *"Edward,"* she moaned.

Edward moved across the room toward her, only to turn halfway as if instinctively, as the wail of a siren rent the night air, the night that was only supposed to be punctuated by the sounds of the sea lapping in and out from the beach.

When the ambulance stopped outside the house, red light sent circular patterns over every piece of Celia's carefully placed furniture, highlighting her comfortable sofas, the roses that had been brought in especially, as if making a mockery of it all before sweeping its red dart toward Celia, then Vicky, then back again over the ceiling, highlighting all the cracks on its surface.

Rebecca, suddenly desperate, only just resisted the urge to run to Celia and comfort her. In the grim seconds while the door of the emergency vehicle swung open and voices sounded in the velvet-soft darkness outside, it was as if the room drew in closer to cloak them all.

Edward moved through the open French doors to the veranda, parting the gauzy white curtains, flooding the room with red. Rebecca watched him, torn, wanting to run to him, too, to hold him in her arms.

Men's voices filtered in from the night, stilted, practical voices.

Rebecca felt her breath coming in great shudders as they carried the stretcher up the veranda steps, wheeling in solemn procession past the sitting room toward Angus's bedroom. The sound of it rattled through the room.

A few minutes later—or was it seconds?—not long, a body passed by under a white sheet, and the sheer curtains flapped in the light sea breeze. They lifted Edward's dead father down the steps to the garden.

Rebecca swallowed hard.

One of the ambulance workers reappeared, parting the curtains as if he were an actor on the stage.

These doors were designed to welcome guests, not herald the dead.

"Mrs. Russell," he said. The man moved toward Celia and leaned over her, lifting her wrist and checking her pulse as she lay there not moving while her husband was carted away.

The man disappeared again, returning with something in a small paper cup. As he raised the older woman's head and helped her to sip the liquid, she looked so much less intimidating, Rebecca thought, than the coiffed perfection that Rebecca had first seen at Haslemere. Here was a woman who had lost her son and now, in some gruesome turn of events, her husband. Death, it seemed, was a leveler for everyone. Celia was, after all, human when she was stripped of all the pretenses that great wealth tended to provide.

Rebecca felt her own eyes soften as she gazed at Edward's mother. Just then, Vicky turned to face Rebecca, a flash of annoyance in her eyes. Edward appeared at the French doors again, and it was as if all the life force had gone out of him. His eyes were deadened.

Rebecca moved toward him, one hand stretched out. "Darling, Edward . . ." she said.

"Edward." Celia moaned the word.

In one swift movement, Edward made his way past Rebecca to his mother and the ambulance officer who tended her. He knelt beside Celia and took her hand.

"What can I do?" Rebecca hovered in the background.

"Nothing, not now, Rebecca," he murmured, as she stood there, helpless.

She brought her hand up to her mouth, catching Vicky's gaze as it shifted toward her, but only for a second before Vicky, too, ran to her mother, and the three of them, all that were left of the once-great dynasty, huddled together like lost children on a rock.

Rebecca swayed, her heart thumping as if someone were pelting it like a drum.

"Best if we bring Mrs. Russell with us, sir. She'll need observation." The ambulance officer spoke in measured tones.

Edward reached out, resting his hand on the emergency worker's shoulder. "Thank you," he said. And the ambulance officer ran out to bring in another stretcher.

Both parents then, one dead, one collapsed. A brother lost.

"I'll go with them." Edward spoke to Vicky. "Try and get some sleep, Rebecca."

As Rebecca turned, she clutched at her stomach, her body wanting to bend double with both pain and guilt at her own circuitous, relentless thoughts. Edward had not wanted her. She was not part of the family. Could she ever really be part of his world?

The family's manager arrived from Haslemere the next morning. Edward spent hours locked away with him in what was supposed to be Angus's study. Another awful funeral. Doctors came and went once Celia was brought home, but she remained in bed. Vicky did not talk to Rebecca, except about the most rudimentary of things. Rebecca decided to talk to Edward when he came out of the hush that was Celia's bedroom, closing the door silently behind himself.

"She is sleeping?" Rebecca asked, looking up from the book that she'd been pretending to read all afternoon.

Edward nodded, but he moved toward the front of the veranda, standing square and facing the lawn. Silently, Rebecca placed the book that she had lifted off the long wicker seat beside her, in the hope that Edward might come and sit with her, back down on the seat.

"I hate to see you like this," she murmured.

"There's nothing you can do," he said, his words thick and hard.

Rebecca stared out at the gray sea. Thin layers of foam lined the island. She wrapped her arms around her waist. "I wish there was, darling," she said.

She sensed his mouth set at her choice of words, even though she could not see his face. It was as if some silent, unspoken boundary had raised itself up between them. Would they ever be able to break it down? Did he want to?

"There isn't anything to be done," he said.

"Would it be easier if I left you alone with Celia and Vicky?" she asked, hating the question, hating the thought of the answer that she might receive back.

Edward still gazed out at everything and nothing. "We'll talk soon," he said. "Don't go just yet."

His final words wrapped around her like fog drawing in from the sea.

Rebecca fled to the beach. She spent hours out on the island, drawing. Then sent them all off to Sunday, hardly knowing what she'd sketched. Deep shadows came out from inside her. She drew faces, then went over them in brush and ink. They were distorted, both women and men, figurative, representative of something—she hardly knew what. Strange shapes emerged. Lost men, the soldiers she'd tended in the makeshift hospital, images from what she'd read and seen about the concentration camps. Then renditions that only she knew were Angus and Robert. The war was supposed to have ended when victory was announced, but it lingered long after all the dancing in the streets. And she wondered how little control they had over the way they dealt with their pasts, how they dealt with trauma.

Rebecca dealt with her own uncertainty and her own grief the only way she knew how—working at a furious pace, the turbulent sea a perfect companion for the storm in her soul. No side was the winner. All of them, all those young men and her father and Angus and Robert, had been sent off to both world wars at the very cusp of their young lives, at the very time when they should have been finding out who they were, not what they could cope with. Not what they could endure in the face of bullets and violence and pure hatred and greed over land and politics and control.

And yet women were supposed to rely on them, for food, shelter, everything. It was the way society was supposed to work.

The whole construct was tumbling down like a house of cards. And men were still expected to shoulder their grief alone. What worried her to the depths of her soul was that Edward seemed determined to do just that.

Edward sat on the veranda a few days after his father's death, his ears picking up the night whispers in the garden but his mind locked in chaos. He walked around during the day as if on automatic pilot, tending to Celia and Vicky while his thoughts tore at him, thoughts that utterly flooded his mind during the long, still nights. And only one thing was clear—change was going to happen, within the very heart of everything he knew. And the only person who could make those changes was him.

But how was he going to pull his family back together and run all their interests, and how was Rebecca supposed to continue with her art, have the career she deserved, while being chained to the Russell empire, chained to a husband who now owned half the darned state? The last thing he wanted was for her to be viewed simply as his wife. Marrying him would stifle any chance of her living in the way they'd both dreamed about, now that he had no chance of living away from his family. And yet his family in turn would lose every ounce of their legacy with no one to run it. His plans with Rebecca seemed to have drifted away.

And yet he returned to one thing. An authentic life lived without him would be far better for Rebecca in the long run. No matter how much he loved her, more than life itself, he had to let her go. To do anything else would be selfish on his part. He'd seen enough of what marriage to a man who was weighed down with his inheritance could do to a woman. Rebecca would die a slow death, were she expected to be a lady of the upper classes. He flicked a gaze back to the closed screen door that led to his mother's room.

At least one of them deserved to be happy. And that person was going to be Rebecca. Angus's death was the last nail in the coffin that was his relationship with Rebecca. He and Rebecca were not meant to be. What would become of Celia and Vicky if he abandoned them now? He was all they had. If he walked away from his family and pursued his dreams of writing and living with Rebecca in the manner that Sunday and John Reed lived, it would be abdicating all his responsibilities. It would be cruel. He could never live with himself if he did such a thing.

And Rebecca needed to see where her art would take her, because Edward was sure it would carry her a long way if he didn't hold her back.

As he stood up and made his way out into the garden under the vast Australian sky and the Southern Cross, Edward raked his hands through his hair. What was more important? Love or family?

How could anyone possibly choose between the two? Perhaps the only choice was Rebecca herself. Perhaps the only choice was to give her the freedom that she so rightly deserved. He loved her. No matter how tormented he was, no matter how much uncertainty broiled in his head, he knew that the only kind thing to do was to let her go.

A wallaby emerged from the bushes, grazing on the lawn and looking up at him before pricking its ears and hopping away again. All he felt now was guilt for bringing Rebecca here. His chest hurt with the knowledge that he should have known better.

Edward walked back to the chair on the veranda, slumping down in it and staring out at the blackness again. He reached for the coffee that had become his constant companion during these lonely, sleepless nights. It was cold.

He thought about the sum of what he'd inherited—Haslemere, two beach houses, the house in Melbourne, not to mention the two stations in South Australia, vast tracts of sheep country, all employing managers, household staff, and farm workers with families, for goodness' sakes. What was he supposed to do? Sack all the employees? Men who'd returned from the war to the only safe haven they knew, their jobs with the Russell family. If he gave Rebecca the life she needed, what was he supposed to do? Tell everyone else he was selling out? His family was responsible for so many livelihoods.

He couldn't afford to be selfish, not for anyone's sake.

There was no turning back to last week, or a few days ago. He was here. This was now. Everything had gone wrong.

Edith was born to the role of a station owner's wife. Edward set his jaw as he marched into the house, pausing a moment outside Rebecca's bedroom. Light sent a thin golden ribbon under the door.

The temptation to go to her was so overwhelming for a moment that he had to drag himself away from the door.

He had to let her go.

As he made his way to his bedroom, he knew what the grim answer was. Edith. He'd make arrangements to marry her, soon.

Rebecca was sitting out on the veranda the following evening rather than going to bed. She'd seen Edward sitting out here at night. She couldn't bear him being alone, couldn't bear another night of lying awake in her room while she heard him pacing around outside, as she had done the night before and the nights before that. The lemon glow of the lights from the sitting room highlighted the novel she was not reading. Enough was enough. She would keep him company.

Surely enough, he appeared through the sitting room doors, a worn, gray version of himself. His green eyes were streaked with red, and his forehead was crinkled with new lines.

"Rebecca."

She looked up at him.

His gaze was averted. His mouth was drawn downward, reminding her of the expression on his face when Angus had been wheeled away. She placed her book on the side table next to her chair.

"It's not going to work out," he said, looking at the floorboards, shifting his feet. "You and I."

Rebecca's gut dive-bombed as if a flock of birds inside her plunged down, down. White shock clamped over her. She reeled backward in the chair as if she'd been pushed. Or hit. No matter how much she'd been expecting it, the shock was relentless and hard. Rebecca clutched at the armrests of the old wicker chair and thought suddenly that she would never come here again. Would not see Haslemere again. His life would go on without her; she'd never know what happened to him next.

"You don't mean that," she whispered. He couldn't mean it. Their love was stronger than this, stronger than battle lines or practicalities, or anything that anyone could throw at them. He was the one person on this earth whom she loved above all others. He was her family.

She brought her hand up to her forehead, while slumping back in the chair.

"I've booked you on a train back to Melbourne tomorrow." His voice, disembodied from everything, went on.

Rebecca had no words.

"I'm sorry," he said. "This is no place for you. I can't do what I wanted to do now." Final. If she knew Edward, she knew that every word he uttered was well thought.

Cold, brutal, truth.

He didn't love her enough back. So, she'd been mistaken. Had been under an illusion, was that it? Was she, then, some distraction, before he settled down with someone, God forbid, like Edith?

Her teeth started to chatter in shock.

And then anger swept through her. She wanted to throw her book in his face. After all his talk, after all their dreaming, he was going to regress? Duty, family, society, expectations. He hadn't meant any of what he'd told her. And what did he expect she would do? Ask him to abandon his mother and sister? She would never do such a thing.

"You don't mean this," she said. "I'm here. I'm not going anywhere."

"Rebecca," he said. "We cannot continue on. And I have thought about it. Everything has changed. I cannot commit to you. I'm sorry."

She jerked herself out of the chair, moved toward him. "Tell you don't mean it," she whispered.

"I mean it," he said. "No more. It won't work."

"Edward, I love you," she said, and her voice cracked. "I want to get through this with you. I want to help."

"You don't understand. My responsibilities, the stations. All those people—employees who rely on my family. I can't walk away. And Edith . . ."

Rebecca couldn't stop a laugh that rose, bitter, in her throat. "Edith?" she whispered hoarsely. The word spun a hole in her thoughts about supporting him, about helping his family. He would prefer Edith did that? "You are joking, Edward."

She looked up at him, and he looked straight at her.

And she knew.

It was at that moment that she saw the seriousness in his expression. He meant it.

She drooped back down in her seat. "Edith?" she said, as if repeating some line in a play. "Edith?"

"She knows how to run things. You deserve a career."

"And what of love? And what of the fact that I will support you? I'm committed to that."

"I think we both know that the world doesn't take kindly to love, Rebecca. Not in war, not in peace. It's a poet's dream."

"And yet you are a poet," she whispered back. "Your dream was to be one. Why can't we," she measured out her words, "why can't we do as John and Sunday have done? What is stopping us? We can still be there for your family—it doesn't have to be a complete break. If we could talk to your mother. Vicky is intelligent . . . we can still support them both and help them get things organized until they are on their feet."

"I'm no John Reed. I can't do what he and Sunday have done. Don't you see, don't you see how incredibly fortunate their position is?" His voice churned out words. "Believe me, their situation is unfathomably different from mine. I can't simply walk away from everything. Surely you can see that. It would destroy you, destroy us. It might work for a few years, maybe one or two, but eventually life would catch up with us. Rebecca, please don't make this harder than it needs to be."

Rebecca set her head in her hands. "Could we not try staying together, getting through this dreadful time? Goodness knows you were there for me when I needed you. Don't you need the same from me?"

But he shook his head. "It's no place for you here."

"Oh, don't be so stubborn, Edward. I can live with you, support you."

"It's the last thing I want. You playing that role."

"What?" She was losing control of her voice.

"You'd become simply my wife. It would kill you, Rebecca. Forget about me."

She looked up at him, her throat constricting.

"If you think I could ever forget you," she said, "then you have never known me at all."

He didn't look at her. "It's best you go. I *want* you to go." He enunciated the words with great care. As if each one were measured.

Rebecca felt a bolt hit her, another blow at her chest. "You don't know if you meant any of it?"

"Rebecca. Enough."

Rebecca stood up, clasped and unclasped her hands. Paced across the veranda. "That night on the beach . . ." It seemed like another place now.

But still, he shook his head.

Rebecca let out a sob.

"Our lives are too different."

She nodded. So, appearances again. Just like her mother, just like his mother.

"You're taking the easy path," she murmured. "She won't make you happy."

He turned to her, his eyes with that searing, gasping pain that she felt.

And she waited. One last time.

"Please, go and do what you want to do. Live freely, Rebecca. I have no life to offer you now. It is over. I have nothing more to say."

And Rebecca stood there, she didn't know for how long. Cold realization washed over her. Her mind set itself, and in the end, when she spoke, her voice was hard.

"I simply want to love you," she said.

His entire body sagged.

She walked into her bedroom. Breathing was hard. Her eyes stung, but she moved around the room with the determination of a woman on a singular path. Her own path. That was what it was going to have to be. On her own. By herself. No mother, no family. No Edward. She choked down the emotion that welled up in her throat. All on her own.

She retrieved the envelope that contained all the savings she had. Meager, but it was something, from her job and the money that her uncle had given her toward her education. She had only spent one term's worth. And suddenly, as she flicked through her savings, an idea presented itself. It was the answer. It was the only one.

Silently, she packed some things in a knapsack, three drawings, a couple of changes of clothes, things that were light. Her tread was silent on the soft dark lawn as she made her way to the beach.

Moonlight radiated on the sea, glistening from some far-off place.

Rebecca rowed out to the island. The still water lapped against the oars. There was only one option. Only one thing to do. She would take things into her own hands. Carve out her own fate.

Rebecca pulled the boat ashore on the beach on the island, not caring that her espadrilles were soaked. And made her way along the path that wound toward the wild open sea, where she settled herself on her rock.

She picked up her sketching materials, placed them on her lap, and drew in great brushstrokes. Edward. She had fallen in love. Love had been fleeting, but then, so was life. And then she stopped, staring out at the inky sea. Perhaps she had it all wrong. Maybe love was not about holding on; maybe love was about letting go.

Her chest rose and fell as if in time with the sweep of the waves. She laid her drawings aside on the rock. There was only one way to do this.

She looked at the sketching materials that Edward had bought her at Haslemere.

Rebecca leaned down, scattering her drawing things across the rocks. Her pencil, her charcoal black pencil, bounced and slipped downward, tumbling like her heart, landing on a ledge, remaining there, glimmering in the moonlight. She let her sketching book go next, but the wind picked it up like a kite, and it dived and wheeled until resting almost down at the churning water's edge.

There. They would find them. That was all they needed for this to end.

And she eased herself off the rock, trudging back toward the causeway that linked the island to the town, wrapping her cardigan around her slender shoulders, her face down in the breeze.

Carmel-by-the-Sea, 1987

Rebecca set the glass of water she'd poured herself down on the table on her terrace and stared out at the inky sea. Memories that she'd pushed aside for decades, heaving them away and sinking them deep into quicksand, were coming hard and fast now. She could not stop them coming, she could not sleep, she could only ride with them until, like waves, they had all broken on the seashore, only to pull away from her again and bury themselves in the ocean, where she swore they would never surface again.

CHAPTER TWENTY-SEVEN

New York, 1987

Tess stood at the window in her office, looking out at the never-ending sea of movement that was Manhattan. She had to tell Edward she'd found Rebecca, despite the fact that she'd told Rebecca she wouldn't. There was simply no way Tess could keep this to herself. When the phone rang, she glowered at the distraction. Anything else seemed trivial now.

"Tess Miller," she said, running a hand through her hair.

"I'm sure you know why I'm calling."

Dread curled into her heart.

"How can you possibly justify—"

"Edward."

"How dare you." His voice was a growl.

Tess leaned her head in her hands. "Please."

"No. You couldn't resist delving into this in order to make a bloody buck. Your reasons are bogus, but you don't understand that. I don't think you ever will."

Tess's heart beat time like a metronome. She had to defend herself. Had to make him see sense. "Edward. It was not like that. I would never, ever have done what I did for publicity."

"You had no right to do any such thing without my consent. I was not convinced about you from our very first meeting. And now, I know that my sense was right. You are not the right editor for my book. You are clearly unable to separate your own need for material gain from the fact that you should be looking after your authors and their work. End of story. You had no right to go and disturb some woman in California. You will not be working for me anymore. Leon will tell you this, but I'm afraid that I wanted to have my say too."

Tess almost ran her teeth through her tender bottom lip.

"How you thought that contacting a famous artist on my behalf, without my permission, risking my reputation, my career, telling her my personal story without telling me a thing was even remotely acceptable as a professional is beyond me. Leon has had the decency to apologize on your behalf, and he's engaged James to edit my book."

"Edward!"

But then, he was gone. Just like that. He'd hung up.

The room spun. James? She couldn't hold back the laugh of cynicism that bit into her throat. He'd taken Edward.

She started toward her door. And collided with Leon.

"I want to talk, and now," he said.

Words, half-formed, danced on her lips. But she could only shake her head. Her hands gripped each other like steel. Leon sat down at her desk.

"Sit down, Tess," he said.

His blue eyes were a pair of glittering jewels. Tess held his gaze, chin up.

"Edward Russell has requested that James edit his book."

"It wasn't for publicity, Leon," she said, unable to form any other words. Her thoughts scattered like flotsam. But she sat as firm as a boulder. "I informed both you and Edward that I suspected the subject of his book was living, not dead. I felt I had a duty to everyone involved to find out, Leon. Rebecca could have made a terrible problem for the house and for Edward."

"You are an editor," he said, placing his glasses back onto his nose, looking at her over them, "with a project that I thought was going to push you into new depths. That was your job. I thought you were ready. Clearly, I made a mistake. Edward Russell could well sue the press if that artist reveals your visit, and you didn't tell me that he'd explicitly asked you not to see her."

Tess looked down at the floor. Did Edward know her at all, or Rebecca, for that matter?

"She won't say a thing," Tess said. "I'm sure of it."

Leon leaned forward. He enunciated his words with great care. "I want you to sign a waiver stating that you will not reveal any information about your dealings with Edward Russell or Rumer Banks to a soul. The legal team is preparing that document now. You are to tender your resignation this minute and leave the office immediately."

Tess gasped.

"Leon."

Her whole body shook. James. He'd been playing the long game. No wonder he wanted in on the dinner in Rome.

Leon stood up and straightened his bow tie. She sent him a silent plea. But he shook his head and walked away.

CHAPTER TWENTY-EIGHT

Victor Harbor, 1946

Rebecca stood alone on the main street of Victor Harbor. A couple of paper bags, remnants of someone's shopping expedition to Bell's General Store, fluttered up the road in the sea breeze. Two men lingered outside the Hotel Victor on the corner opposite the park at the end of the causeway, swaying with the effects of a night on the grog. Rebecca shuddered and gathered her arms around herself.

She clutched at her handbag, feeling instinctively for the money that was her lifeline now. It was a funny thing, that. The very notions that she and Edward had railed against—money and wealth, and everything that went along with it. But now she had to save herself. She had to work out how to survive. At least she had enough money to catch a bus from the little seaside village.

Rebecca made her way up the empty main street, passing Field's butcher, where the Russells' cook came to do her daily shopping, hurrying past a large boardinghouse called The Central and Bell's General Store before stopping at the small bus shelter where all buses left for goodness knew where. She sat on the cold green bench on the sidewalk.

At five o'clock in the morning, a bus heaved to a stop in front of her. Once the few passengers had alighted, Rebecca watched as the driver turned the painted wooden sign around while the refueling was done.

Perth.

Perth was good. The other side of the country, across the Nullarbor, one of the loneliest stretches of desert on earth. Rebecca placed her foot on the step of the bus, handed the few shillings' fare to the driver, and found a seat in the empty rows. As the bus heaved its way onto the road, she rested her head on the cold window, condensation running in droplets down her left cheek.

New York, 1987

Packing up the office took ten minutes. Tess stood and gazed around it one last time. She clutched the box that contained the sum of her things, held her head up, and moved out of the office toward the elevators.

Perth, 1946

Rebecca ran a sweaty hand across her forehead. The scarf that held her long hair away from her face was also damp with sweat. She reached for *The West Australian*, the newspaper that lay on the red Formica table in the lunch room at the laundry, not caring that her moist fingertips would become blackened with newspaper ink. She'd wash it off before she went back out to work. These newspapers afforded her the only link she had to the outside world, to the life she'd left behind. The women's shelter that had become her temporary lodging was akin to a nightmare zone. But even so, Rebecca was grateful that she had a job and a place to stay.

In this hot, searing city, making it through each day was the only thing that mattered. It was a blessing in some ways, because the ritual of survival forced her to drum everything else out of her mind. Rebecca flipped the pages of the well-thumbed paper as she had done each day since her arrival here in Perth. Her arms ached from the long hours at the ironing presses, smoothing men's shirts for the women who could afford to pay someone else to do that sort of work. When she was at the till, Rebecca smiled politely at the well-to-do wives, some of them not much older than herself, who were cosseted and loved by men. And pushed aside thoughts that she had done something wrong, while they, smug in their suburban lives, must have done everything right.

When Rebecca read the article on page six of the newspaper, something solid wedged in her throat. She stared at the picture of herself on the beach, just before things fell apart. She ran her hand over the image of her own face. She felt, suddenly, a wave of sympathy for that girl. The girl she had been. Even a couple of weeks later, Rebecca felt as if she were a different person. That old Rebecca was gone now. Perhaps she had disappeared into the sea after all—she may as well have. She read the short accompanying piece. So. The authorities decided she'd fallen from the rocks while sketching, just as she'd planned.

The funeral was yesterday because, after an extensive search, they had turned up nothing, no body was ever found. But the stretch of coast, the article went on, was infamous. Freak waves had claimed lives on the island before. The article went on to talk about safety, about the need to keep your distance from the edge of the rocks on such treacherous shores.

Rebecca raised her hands, checking that the scarf covered every piece of her long dark hair, her fingers running around its perimeter in a way that had become familiar, a comfort even. She tore out the article and tucked it into the pocket of her sack-like dress.

The following morning she stood in line at the docks. There was no time to be had. She had set herself up with a new name when she arrived at the shelter. Another woman resident knew what to do. But false name or not, she was recognizable now. A free passage was in her hand—organized by the same woman who made up false papers—in exchange for work to be carried out in the laundries on the ship.

She clutched the rucksack she had brought from the beach house, bulging with two shapeless printed dresses that the women's shelter had provided for her on her arrival in Perth. Among her other pathetic things. No pencils, no paper. Every penny had to count. In her handbag were her sacred false papers, her new name—Rumer Banks. The woman who'd organized it told her it was unusual, classy. Had eyed Rebecca and told her that she looked like a woman of class. Rebecca had turned away and told her to just get on with it. She didn't want discussions. Didn't want to get involved. Not with this woman.

Not with anyone.

That was it. A new life. A new way of living. Rebecca Swift was gone for good.

New York, 1987

Tess focused on the copy in front of her. Did not allow herself to be distracted by Caroline, sashaying around the office with a model in tow and a man pushing a rack of designer clothes in their wake. Caroline's hair hung in soft ringlets around her shoulders. On her left finger, her diamond engagement ring sparkled and her wedding ring sat snug beneath that. Caroline's stomach showed off a tiny baby bump.

"Tess, honey," she called across the open workspace. Tess looked across the chic, white room. People chatted on the phone, smart, creative types and editors. The place was abuzz with constant deadlines and activity and gossip. In the past month, Tess had been to more celebrity-filled parties than she'd ever attended in her life.

Now, she looked at the copy she was editing—an article on a rising supermodel. The girl was only sixteen and was doing the catwalks in Milan. Tess smoothed out her red dress and raised her eyes to her sister.

"That article on Alec Burgess. The interview?" Caroline called.

Tess nodded. No one else in the room cared or knew that she'd been his editor once.

"I've had to push on with it," she said. "Getting the new editor in for the interview? Is that okay with you?"

Tess shrugged. Sure, what did it matter? It was all in the line of business. Her mistake had been to become in some way personally attached to one of her authors, not to mention a colleague, and now she'd lost the sum of everything that was her life. And as for Edward and Rebecca, they'd gotten what they wanted too. Both of them. Rebecca was still, presumably, holed up in Carmel-by-the-Sea being Rumer.

Rebecca had lived such a life for decades, after all. Hiding away, doing what she had to do. And look at her. She'd been successful. More than successful. She'd become a phenomenon. There was no reason Tess couldn't carve out a wonderful career in magazines. She needn't work for Caroline for years. Tess had even thought about going to Paris. If she did well here in New York, who knew where that could lead her?

Paris could be the perfect idea.

"Thanks, Tess." Caroline sent her one of her most ravishing smiles. "Good for you. Moving right on. Thought I'd better ask."

Tess turned back to her work. A few moments later, her head shot up. She sat up, bristling.

"Tess." James strode into the new open-plan office wearing a visitor's pass around his neck. His hair was tousled and the expression on his face was grim. When he stopped at her desk, she saw the dark circles that ran beneath his eyes. "I managed to convince your sister to still run the article on Alec, but I had another motive. I have to talk to you. You haven't returned any of my calls."

She looked up at James, folded her arms. "If you're here to tell me about Alec's success, then please spare me. I have no desire to hear about it, James. And if you were calling to ask for tips on how to do my job, I suggest that you go figure it out yourself. You seem pretty good at doing that."

James leaned forward on her desk. "You've got it all wrong."

She let out a laugh. "Oh, spare me. I'm sorry, but I can't ease your conscience on top of everything else."

"No. Listen to me."

She looked up at him, her head tilted and her eyebrows raised in the most cynical manner she could conjure up.

"I took on Edward because they were going to give him to Martin Haymes."

Tess had to shake her head at the thought of Martin plodding along with Edward. The book would never be finished. Although Edward might get away with no deadlines . . .

"So you want me to thank you, James? You've done me a favor? Is that it?"

"I took Edward on so that I can work with you to put things right." He leaned closer.

Tess kept her arms around her body, tight.

But he didn't move an inch. "Tess. Rebecca can't afford her identity to be revealed because if it is, then her whole life becomes a sham—people have trusted that she's Rumer Banks. People in Australia trusted that Rebecca Swift was dead."

"I thought you said you had something new, James."

"Edward," James went on, tapping his finger on her desk, "believes in authenticity to the extent that he looks down upon any form of commercialism in his work. He's convinced that you'd go to any bizarre lengths to sell books."

Tess put her head in her hands. "Yes. So if you knew my real reasons, then why—"

James thumped down in the chair opposite her desk. "Exactly. That's the answer. You're the answer, Tess."

"Now you're making absolutely no sense."

"The reason you want this to work isn't commercial, is it, Tess?"

Tess looked up at him through the fingers that were laced over her face.

"Listen to me. You want Rebecca and Edward to get back together, don't you?" His voice was dark honey laced with spice. "It's nothing to do with commercialism. It's about love and that is the most real, authentic thing in this world, Tess. You might have ignored every call I've made to you in the last couple weeks, Tess, but you can't get away from the fact that you want that decades-old love story to end happily, and that has nothing to do with selling books."

Tess looked to the side. Away from him. She bit on her bottom lip.

"You don't want to work here, in this magazine. You need to get your job back. But just like Rebecca, you've run away. You're about to take on a half-life just like she did, aren't you? If you're not careful, you'll get to her age and regret not standing up for yourself. I know it's hard, but you need to convince Rebecca to come clean about her identity. We both know Edward's still in love with her. He fell for her the first time they met. He could never just turn off his feelings for her. It's not something we humans can do."

Tess looked across at him. Caught his eye. "You lost me my job. I trusted you with the fact I'd gone to see Rebecca. I misjudged you. And now you have the gall to show up in my office and tell me that love is some sort of balm to fix all this—that it's going to be easy to convince Rebecca to come clean about her past, that she should go and talk to Edward Russell about it, of all people?"

James spoke in a low, controlled voice. "Since the day I met you, I've been trying to make things right. I've been trying to . . . goddamn it." He stood up and took a few paces in a circle around her desk. "Tess!"

Tess took a furtive look around the room. Caught a couple of interested glances pointed in her direction. She glared at James and lowered her voice to a whisper. "James. If you think you can walk in here and tell me that you're helping me . . ." she hissed. "How dare you. Please, would you leave, and let me get on with my life? Because everything was just fine before you came along."

"Was it?" He kneeled down by the desk, whispering now. "Was it, Tess? Come on. You were hiding behind that career of yours. Trying to impress people and please your family in the best way you knew how because for some darned reason, you didn't think you were good enough being you."

"How dare you." Tess curled her fists until her nails bit into her palms.

People were watching. She let out a loud breath.

"James," she said. "Please go away and sort out your problem with Edward Russell and Rebecca Swift by yourself, and leave me alone. Because, in case you've forgotten, I've been fired."

He stood up. Straightened himself. "We both know that I never, ever would have hurt you. You have to promise me that you believe that.

Because I've fallen in love with you. You and I both know that. But right now, you're hiding again. Just like Rebecca. And if you want to live your life in the way she has, then I can't stop you. Good choice. Excellent decision. But I'll tell you this. I'm one hundred percent sure that I will never care about someone as much as I care about you.

"I've done everything I can to make things right. I know you were overlooked at Campbell and Black. And now, well, if you don't mind, I'll keep on trying to make things right. I'm leaving for Rome at eight o'clock tonight. I'm going to convince Edward to rehire you as his editor and get him to insist Leon give you your job back. I've kept all your authors on track for you, but I'm only willing to do so until you return. More to the point, Tess, I'm also going to try to convince Edward to see Rebecca. I want to finish what you started, and I'm going to begin exactly where you left off."

He had an audience.

Tess smiled at her new colleagues, a tight, forced smile like leather stretched over a shoe. This was a gossip magazine, for goodness' sakes!

James leaned closer, his voice soft. "I know what you really cared about. I can see that you wanted Edward and Rebecca to have another chance. I know that you understood their relationship was real. And I believe in what you were doing, Tess. If you want to come with me to Rome, then meet me at the airport. I'll wait until the very last moment for you. And I'll never, ever give up hope." His voice cracked on the last words.

Tess felt her breath shaking. She could not look him in the eye.

But slowly, ever so slowly, she shook her head. She'd trusted him too many times, allowed herself to be sweet-talked before. And look where she'd ended up. So she watched him leave, and she sat there, glaring at the copy in front of her.

"Wow, if you don't want him, I'll have him," one of the editors quipped.

A laugh resonated through the space.

"Okay, Tess?" Caroline asked.

Tess nodded, and turned the page of the article on her desk. Her face tingled with embarrassment. Slowly, the chatter in the workspace started up again.

Two hours later, finally, finally, when the clock had dragged itself to six o'clock, Tess made her way out of the office and ran to the nearest subway station as fast as she could.

"Flora," she said, almost dive-bombing her phone once she reached her studio. She gave Flora a rundown of James's visit and told her James was going to Rome. "Drink. Please? Now?"

"Right. Where are we meeting?" Flora was in action mode.

"Caffè Reggio," Tess breathed.

"I'm there," Flora said.

Tess changed her heels into a pair of ballet flats, ran a comb through her hair, and marched down to the café, pushing the door open and slumping into the nearest seat.

"Hey." Flora was there five minutes later.

Tess sighed. "Time to move on."

Flora stared at her and shook her red head. "What. Do you mean?"

Tess threw her hands in the air.

Nico appeared at the table.

She rubbed her aching shoulders as he stood there, tying his white apron around his waist. He looked at her. "What is it, lovely Tess?"

Tess put her head into her hands and leaned against the table. "I don't know," she said. "This is madness."

"Yes, you do," Flora said. "Go with him to Rome."

"Roma?" Nico's voice belted into the quiet. "Of course . . . that was the answer from the beginning."

"No!" Tess groaned.

"What's the alternative? Sitting here in your sister's shadow while she runs *Floodlight Magazine*, has a baby? Lives her life to the full while you slave away trying to be like her, while you desperately cast around for ways to impress your family? Although I guess it's what you've always done."

Tess's head ricocheted up.

"James is the first person who has interested you and challenged you for years," Flora went on.

Tess stared openly at Flora.

"Okay, you've thrown everything into your work. There's nothing wrong with that. You've had considerable success." Flora stretched her hand across the table.

"And lost it all due to James," Tess said, waving her friend's hand away. "You've completely forgotten the fact that he wrecked everything with Edward. My mistake was in trusting James. And you think I should do so again?"

"But he didn't contact Edward and set all of this in motion. Leon obviously rang him and assumed that Edward was okay with your seeing Rebecca. You took the reins in your own hands and went to Carmel-by-the-Sea when Edward begged you not to. You're making your own mess, Tess, honey. You've just got to stop. It's that simple. Fix it. You're in love with James, too, by the way, and you should tell him so. In case you hadn't noticed—he's in love with you too."

Tess stared at Flora. Nico's head swiveled from Tess to Flora and back. He sat down at the table. Tess felt a stone land in her heart.

"You have two choices." Flora's voice was strangely calm. "You either move forward, or you don't. You either follow your instincts, which are, and I know it, that you're in love with James, and you help work things out for Rebecca and Edward—or you sit on your own and risk never, ever feeling something so real again as long as you live. In short, you hide from your life, like Rebecca did. It's time for both of you to live. It's time for both of you to stop hiding from whatever the heck it is that scares you from taking a leap."

"Life is short, Tess," Nico added. "If you hide from your passions, they do have this habit, you see, of coming back and slapping you in the face."

"Which is what happened to Edward," Flora said. "I don't think Rebecca or Edward was happy without each other for one minute. But while Rebecca ran away, it was Edward who made a sacrifice, and that sacrifice was himself. Don't do the same thing. Because I can tell you, you have no reason to do so. No good reason at all. Be true to yourself, or what's the point?"

Tess looked at them both and let out a shuddering sigh. Pictured her life. Without James. On her own. Could she fall in love with someone else?

The answer was most probably not.

She placed her hands on the table, reaching out to her pair of friends. "Airport?"

Flora glanced up at Nico.

"I have my Fiat 500 parked outside," he said. "Come on, Tess. I will get you to Roma!"

Tess sat in the back of Nico's minute car, closing her eyes every time he nearly hit a truck. But he'd grown up in Rome. Clearly, road rules didn't matter. Once he'd pushed through the traffic, he stopped right outside JFK. Tess forced herself to stay focused. What she was doing was anybody's guess. She'd thrown together a few things in her suitcase. Flora had found her passport; Nico had been waiting outside her building. Once he'd wedged her suitcase in his tiny car, he'd taken off. Now they were here. There was no looking back.

"Now," he said. "You have enough time. Go and find him, sort it out."

Tess kissed him on his stubbled cheek.

She ran to the check-in counter of the airline, the one they had been to the last time. There was no sight of James.

She lined up at the counter. She would get a ticket for the eight o'clock flight and try to contact him once in Rome. Someone from Campbell and Black would know where he was staying.

But she jumped as a voice caught her from behind.

"Tess. Thank goodness."

She turned around, and he stood there. She took a step toward him, to find herself encircled in his arms.

CHAPTER TWENTY-NINE

Rome, 1987

As the taxi wound its way along the freeways that led into the ancient city, the driver changing lanes and tacks with alarming ferocity, Tess leaned into James. He dropped a kiss onto her forehead.

They left their suitcases at the lobby of the elegant hotel and made their way straight through the alleyways and the piazzas to Edward's apartment. James pressed the buzzer on the street outside the building. When the door was unlatched, he turned to Tess and ran his hand over her cheek.

"Ready?"

She nodded.

She looked upward as soon as she entered the cool interior of the building. Edward stood at the top of the winding staircase, dressed in a pair of camel-colored trousers and a blue-and-white striped shirt. His hair was combed neatly, and as Tess approached, she could smell the scent of his aftershave.

Tess stopped on the stairway when he saw her, hesitating at the glare that said everything.

"Tess," Edward growled. "Bloody cheek. Why are you here?"

"Edward," James said. "We all need to talk. I thought we could get coffee."

Edward looked down, ran a hand over his hair, and took in a breath. And looked back to Tess. She held his gaze. If he wouldn't agree to James's suggestion, she would talk to him right here. Finally, after what seemed an age, Edward sagged, his body looking older now than she'd ever noticed before.

A few minutes later they were in the dim interior of a café on Edward's street, sitting in a booth that was overlooked by a gilt mirror, a reminder of late nineteenth-century grandeur. There was a silence.

"Edward," Tess said. "If you will forgive me, I want to cut to the chase. It seems that while both you and Rebecca have done everything you could to let go of the past, the past won't let go of you." Tess leaned forward, lowered her voice. "Don't you want to see her again? Even once? I have found her, seen her, talked to her. You have both kept your love in your hearts for decades. The love that is between you is stronger than the choices you made when you were young."

Tess took in a breath.

James reached out a hand and covered her own with it.

Edward stared down at the round cookie on his plate. He traced his fingers around its edge, following the rough, handmade circle, his eyes running over it the entire time.

"I have to admit," Tess said, her voice barely above a whisper now. "Your story has changed me. I didn't believe, you see, in love, before I read your book. I didn't believe in its power. I had no idea how strong it could be. Can't you see how your story might help other people, people who are . . . stuck, like me? Like I was. After the war, you and Rebecca had the gift of being able to see what life should be in its purest form. After everything had been destroyed, you fought to hold on to the things that mattered, but also to reach out and start again with something new."

Edward slowly raised his head.

"You let Rebecca go because her dreams and her talent would have been destroyed were she forced to live with your family and all those strict rules that you and Vicky grew up with, that Sunday Reed escaped, that Edith accepted, and that were all your mother ever knew. But your love for Rebecca is stronger than any of that. It doesn't surprise me that as soon as Edith was gone, your love for Rebecca came back to find you. Because it's remained steadfast inside you throughout your entire life. Your love for her was just waiting for the right time to show up again. It stayed with you all these years. Please, would you let me go back to Carmel-by-the-Sea, talk to Rebecca again, see if I can convince her to see you? It's not too late. Not yet."

Edward gazed out the window, the expression on his face unreadable. Tess sat stock-still.

When he finally opened his mouth and spoke, there was nothing arrogant or angry in his tone.

"It was what the Heide group were all about," he said, his well-modulated voice ringing out into the room. "Getting to the heart of things. Those artists, those writers, they knew what mattered. We were young moderns, that's right, Tess. Class, money, race, color, background, none of these things make any difference when we die."

Tess resisted the impulse to reach out, to take the old man's hand.

"I guess I have been searching for that again. I thought I might find it in Rome," he said. "You know, I never settled with Edith. It was hopeless. But I would never have left her, could never have hurt her."

"I know that," Tess whispered.

"After my brother died, then my father, I had to look after my mother and Vicky. They had no education. Not like you. Not like today. I'm only grateful that Rebecca survived. Goodness, she didn't just survive. She thrived. No thanks to me." He let out a shuddering sigh.

Tess waited.

Edward reached down and brought out Rebecca's three sketches of the young moderns, of Max Harris, Joy Hester, and Edward. "Take these to her," he said, running his hands over the old drawings. "Tell her they are hers. And Tess . . ."

Tess took the small sketches, careful not to let her fingers run over the black brush and ink on the top one. The one of Edward.

She looked at him.

"Tell her I will always be hers, no matter what. Even if we are not together. I want her to be happy because I adore her so much. It's not . . . a selfish thing, my love for her. That was the point . . ."

"I know," Tess said. "It's the very best sort there is. You wanted what was best for her. You wanted her to be happy and you wanted her to be whole."

"Edward," James said, his voice soft and low, but causing Tess to startle a little. "Tess lost her job because you fired her."

Edward raised his hands in the air. "And yet you are still here, trying to help me with my life?" he asked. There was a silence for a moment. "In that case, I want you back editing my book. But only on one condition."

Tess looked at him.

"The only thing that matters is that the story is to remain true to itself."

Tess leaned forward in her seat and picked up her coffee spoon for a moment, the steel cool against her fingers.

"Well. We don't know the ending yet."

"I'm leaving that to you."

"Thank you!" Tess rolled her eyes.

James tightened his grip on her hand.

Tess shot a look at Edward, saw the old man's face break into a grin.

"Carmel-by-the-Sea, Tess?" James asked.

Tess turned to him and nodded. "Absolutely."

But she had a feeling that Rebecca might be a little harder to crack.

Edward tapped his fingers on the table. "Tess, I'm going to ring that boss of yours and have a wee chat. Nice chap. But a bit conventional, stuck in his ways, not open to our way of thinking, don't you feel?"

Tess laughed, and as she stood up, James stood right behind her and placed a hand in the small of her back.

"We'll be in touch, Edward," he said, shaking his hand as if this were the end of any professional business meeting.

James stood aside for Tess to leave first. And she made her way out of the café into the timeless Roman sunshine.

CHAPTER THIRTY

Carmel-by-the-Sea, 1987

The boldness that had overwhelmed Tess in Rome dissipated the closer they got to Rebecca's house.

"You know that simply turning up at her house is the only way to approach her," James said.

Tess smiled, liking that he was reading her thoughts. She drove the rental car out of Carmel-by-the-Sea onto the long road that ran along the sea's edge. They swept past rocky shores and beaches with tumbling surf, the vibrant colors clear in the daylight, unlike the time she'd come out here in the dark with Sunday.

She slowed the car as they rounded a bend that seemed a little familiar. And there it was. The white mailbox that had flashed in the sheen of Sunday's headlights last time. Rebecca's mailbox.

Rolling fields spread out on either side of the gravel track. What Tess hadn't noticed in the dark on her last visit was that the driveway was lined with Australian eucalyptus. She shot a glance across at James's handsome profile, unshaven after another night spent on a plane.

Tess pulled up in front of the modern house and climbed out of the car. She took in the front garden that Rebecca had planted. Fruit trees were arranged in rows. Beyond this, to the side of the house, was a vegetable garden, and a wild sort of flower garden stood just in view beyond.

It was a complete replica of the way Edward had described Sunday's garden at Heide. She took a few steps toward the wild garden. And stopped. There, on its edge, cut into the lawn, was a garden bed in the shape of a heart.

A heart garden.

She turned to James. "Sunday Reed planted exactly such a heart garden at Heide after Sidney Nolan left her in 1947, finally leaving her to her marriage with John after he realized she'd never leave John for him. Sunday, in her grief at the end of the affair with Sidney, poured all her love for him into a garden shaped in a heart, planted with chamomile and lavender. She tended it as a memorial to her love for him, and as a reminder that like life, a garden always renews itself. The earth may be emptied, the soil replenished and turned over every now and then, but eventually new plants always grow to replace the old ones."

It was so very Sunday. So very Rebecca—the real Rebecca Swift.

A smile passed across Tess's face. James stood beside her, an arm around her shoulders. She lingered a moment, taking in the perfect heart shape, the testament, Tess knew, to Rebecca's love for Edward, to two souls that should never be apart. Tess moved toward Rebecca's house and knocked on the front door. James was right behind her. Nothing, no response. She knocked again.

"Her car isn't here."

James had his hands in the pockets of his jeans. His blue shirt hung loose. "What next? It's your call."

She fixed her gaze on the spot where the car should have been. Only one person would know where she was. "We find her daughter, Sunday," she said.

James nodded. "Sounds sensible." He scratched his unshaven chin. "Tess, how the heck do we do that?"

An hour later, fueled by instant coffee and a hasty sandwich in one of the town's cafés while scouring the owner's phone book for Sunday Banks, Tess pulled up outside a green-painted wooden house in one of the town's tree-lined streets. Heat pounded down onto the sidewalk, blistering through the crevices that shimmered between the leaves.

"Ready?" Tess turned off the engine.

"Craziest thing I've ever done, Tess."

Tess grinned as she opened her car door. "Slight aberration for me, I must admit."

His head was tilted to one side. "Really, Tess? The tough business-woman, going on a chase across continents to bring two former lovers together? Who would have thought it?"

She tipped her sunglasses down on her nose and looked at him. "Watch it, Cooper."

"I'm watching, don't you worry." His voice was warm butterscotch and he leaned over to drop a kiss on her lips.

Tess averted her gaze to the sidewalk as James held open Sunday's picket gate. Neat mowed grass lined each side of the pathway that led up to the wooden house.

Tess took the steps up to the front door. She knocked, then stood and waited.

It was a little while before Sunday opened the door. "Tess?"

"Sunday . . . could James, this is my . . . friend, and I come in for a moment?"

Sunday nodded, but a myriad of other expressions passed across her face. Tess stepped into the house, hoping she at least looked more confident than she felt. Sunday offered them a seat in her bright kitchen. Tess told her, without faltering, what Edward wanted her to say to Rebecca.

Sunday picked up her car keys. "I know about Edward," she said. "But I'm the only person who does. I've always thought he let her go only because he knew her life with his family would be impossible."

Tess took in a breath. "It would have been awful for her. He knew that. He was protecting her. And he couldn't abandon his responsibilities no matter what his life philosophies were. He did the right thing. There's nothing wrong with that."

"Let's go. Let's go and talk to her," Sunday said. "I have no hopes that we'll convince her, though."

And yet, as Tess followed Sunday out to her car, Tess pictured Rebecca's heart garden, because it had given Tess hope.

When Sunday drove up Rebecca's long driveway, Tess chewed on her lip.

"But she's not here," Tess said.

"Just wait," Sunday murmured. "I know where she is." Sunday followed the driveway around the house until it became a rough track that dipped down a hill. The sea spread in front of them, a blue, endless curtain.

Tess saw Rebecca before Sunday said a thing. She was silhouetted, seated on a rock looking out to sea. She wore a wide-brimmed straw hat and a white dress. Sunday stopped the car.

Rebecca did not turn around as they approached. Didn't react to the sound of three car doors slamming. The only accompaniment to their footsteps crunching on the dry soil was the roar of the ocean and the whip of the wind.

Tess's gaze fell on the sketching things that were laid out next to Rebecca on the flat rock. Rebecca sat on a red-and-white checked rug—perhaps the cold, hard rock was not comfortable for her anymore. A car was parked ahead of Sunday's, and next to Rebecca there was a thermos and a coffee cup, along with a plate on which a slice of fruitcake sat. Sunday placed a foot on the line of boulders that edged the sea.

"Mom?"

Rebecca turned around slowly, the expression on her face as clear as a translucent lake. And the moment she caught Tess's gaze, she held it.

Tess reached into her bag and pulled out the sketches. The sketches Rebecca had done on the night that had changed her life.

Rebecca reached out, taking the sketches from Tess. The older woman's hands were speckled with age spots now. She held a hand up to her mouth as she slowly studied each one in turn.

After a while, Tess spoke. "Rebecca," she said. "He let you go because he knew how burdensome it would be for you to deal with all the responsibility that had been heaped upon him. After Robert's and his father's deaths, Edward had to take over. It would have stifled you. You could never have had your career while living in that world with all its rules. He set you free. But he loved you. And he always will. I'm sure he never stopped."

Rebecca remained focused on the sketching paper that she held against her knees. Her face was obscured by the wide picture hat. After an interminable while, she laid down the pictures and stared out to the sea.

"How is he?" she asked, finally, her voice low.

"Still in love with you," Tess said. "His writing is honest. He can't hide from the truth when he writes."

There was no point in leaving things unspoken. There had been more than enough of that.

Rebecca leaned back on her hands, stretching her legs out in front of her, and she didn't turn back from the sea.

"He loved you so much that he set you free. It was that sort of love," Tess said. "He wrote about you the very moment he could because he had to. The moment he was free to do so, he came home, he came home to you."

Tess felt now as if she were whispering some old sea song as the waves swept in and out from the shore. "He did everything that was expected of him for forty years, Rebecca. But now," Tess chose her words with great care, "it's time for him to go full circle, to come back to you, to where he belongs, to his real home. And he has done so. He has, Rebecca. And now, I can also see that he had great faith in your talent, that he knew you could thrive, but that you needed freedom of the spirit to do so."

Tess took a step closer to Rebecca. The sea was burnished with sunlight, shimmering on the surface of the water.

And then Rebecca did something that surprised even Tess. She reached out her hand to Tess, and Tess took it, and sat down with her, watching the sun fall toward the horizon.

The end of something.

CHAPTER
THIRTY-ONE

Haslemere, 1987, two months later

Richard gazed out at the vast gardens from the veranda at Haslemere, shading his eyes as the sun threw its last light over the old house. Sometimes he wondered if he had the word "idiot" blazed across his forehead. Most of the time, he knew that his love for the old station was irrational. The moment he and Phil had walked onto the property, he knew they had to have it. It was almost as if the place were calling out to them, to restore the old mansion, to live here, to try to run sheep on what was left of the once-fertile wool station.

Now the old wool sheds sat, cathedral-sized monuments filled with echoes of the hard work that characterized the pioneering spirit of those first Russell men. Countless cottages remained abandoned on the property, dense with weeds that clung to their old walls, their windows streaked with red dust and neglect. The colossal conservatory had collapsed in on itself, and a few scraggy peacocks were all that remained of the great Russell family's once-splendid stock.

Long days, backbreaking work; the painstaking replacement of leadlight panels in the conservatory bit by bit, all done by hand, according to the rules of preservation; meetings, endless meetings about heritage requirements; poring over nineteenth-century garden plans in an effort to be true to the illustrious past; searching for long-lost photos of the place; talking to neighbors, the council, the local townspeople—all of these things had replaced his life in merchant banking in Sydney.

But slowly, after four years of hard slog, the old house and garden had started coming back to life again, and their lives had turned from endless work to something that Richard now found rewarding. Hints of beauty had started to peek through the decay, rendering his and Phil's efforts worthwhile. The seedlings they'd tucked into the soil thrived now, replacing the remains of what had been extravagant gardens. They raised funds to restore things that could not be thrown away—the velvet curtains in the formal sitting room that had been laced through with pure gold silk. They engaged a local student who redesigned the wild rockery garden outside the old guest wing as part of a school project.

Every tree had been heritage listed, every room restored to its original colors, wallpapers matched, carpets replaced, bathrooms renovated according to heritage guidelines. Phil had even found an old painting that had been in the family for generations, of two children whose eyes seemed to follow you wherever you went. Now it hung where it always had, where it would remind any guest who visited that this place had something both eerie and beautiful about it.

The story of the land and the house was only the start. The family, those long-gone characters, was what loomed large in Philip's and Richard's heads. They became entranced with the tale of the pioneer who had walked three hundred sheep across Australia from New South Wales over the course of six months in 1841, who had built up the farm, to be followed by his son, who gentrified the entire estate.

And then, double tragedy, mired by the alcohol that wrecked so many lives after the wars. And a younger son who tried but was unable to fund the vast old station.

Guests, friends, swore that the place was haunted, swore that the old matriarch of the family, Celia Russell, wandered the hallways at night. One of the housekeepers swore that Celia had appeared in front of her and threatened to drop the old grandfather clock on her head while she was dusting, announcing that everything was wrong. A young girl was supposed to haunt the bedrooms, one of the many Russell daughters who'd been married off to some colonial family and always yearned for home.

But in spite of the lingering stories, and in spite of what Celia Russell might say, everything seemed just right to Richard. He and Phil had found a new lease on life in this old place.

Richard wound his way through the immaculate garden paths. The suit he'd put on for tonight felt strange since he was so used to getting about in the old dungarees that did duty for clothes these days. His smart suits hung mostly neglected in the main bedroom of the house. Apparently it had been a ballroom once, built for a state visit for the Prince of Wales. He moved past the fountain that played again, toward the peacock house that was filled with white doves and the descendants of those original proud, jewel-toned birds that the Russell family had once bred.

He went through his favorite green wooden door that was set into the old brick wall that surrounded the garden, made his way past another derelict cottage that once housed the master of dogs, its late nineteenth-century facades built in grand Tudor style.

Then, on toward the vast stable yard, the clock on the northern wall told the right time now. The stables were warm once again and horses poked their heads out of the immaculate stalls. The stable cat stretched out in the sun.

As he moved toward the old Clydesdale Pavilion in which he and Phillip hosted weddings, a smile passed across his features.

He stopped at the entrance, taking in the long tables that sat under the myriad fairy lights. Roses tumbled out of crystal vases that had once belonged to Haslemere—Philip was the one who adored antiques. He'd scoured the local area, offering to buy back pieces that had been sold at auction when Edward and Edith had to give up.

Richard stepped into the old pavilion, its soaring ceilings as high as any cathedral in Europe.

She stood there among his staff, who were setting everything up. And she turned to face him once he came in. She was gracious and elegant in her deep red dress. She held out her hands to him, moving toward him through the vast space.

Richard kissed her on the cheek.

"He is here, you know," Richard whispered. "He's getting changed in his old bedroom. Putting on a tux."

Richard noticed the way Rebecca's eyes darted to the vast double doors at the entrance to the pavilion. He didn't let go of her hands. Instead, he caught one of the waitstaff's attention. The man appeared with two glasses of champagne on a silver tray.

"Drink up," Richard murmured. "A little Dutch courage is what you need now."

Rebecca sensed something as she took her first sip of champagne. She would have felt him in a crowd of a thousand people. When Richard stepped away from her, like a curtain that parted in a theater, she found herself face-to-face with Edward.

Her awareness was only of him, not the milling waitstaff, not the first guests who were arriving to the fundraiser where she had pledged to auction off the entire collection of her early artwork, with the blessing of the descendants of the Heide group; the artwork she created at Victor Harbor and Heide in 1946 would raise money for the restoration of Haslemere. She moved toward him as if compelled by something that was other than this world, as if by some sort of magic that only existed between the two of them. Their little circle—or was it a heart?—in which the two of them were safe and together and complete.

And then she stopped.

Everyone in the pavilion was silent.

Edward took a step closer. "For all those years we weren't together, I was always with you, you know that," he said. "And we always knew," he went on, taking her in his arms—she felt his chin resting on the top of her head—"that it's the things we cannot see that matter in this world."

Rebecca reached up, her arms curling around him just as they always had, the same arms that belonged to that young girl on a beach in Melbourne. The same two hearts. Ending up in the right place—it was all that mattered in life.

New York, 1987, six months later

Tess surveyed her office. Everything was back in place. Her author list, thank goodness, had remained intact because of James. The proofs of Edward's book sat on her desk, ready to go off for printing. Rebecca's revelation—her decision to announce who she truly was to the public—had stunned the art world. The fact that she, as the most famous recluse in the country, had declared her true identity after a career that spanned over thirty years, while coming out with her explosive story, had propelled interest in Edward's book into the stratosphere. They had become a pair of sixty-something darlings across the country, not to mention instant celebrities back in Australia. They seemed to be handling it with aplomb. Edward's early poetry was being reprinted, and Rebecca's work had reached new records in auction sales.

The news that Edward was releasing the entire love story with such honesty had sent people into a frenzy. Tess had been approached by countless production companies eager to turn the book into a film.

Tess gathered her red coat. The streets in New York were dressed for Christmas. Lights and dazzle and color decorated Manhattan. She gazed out of her office window for a moment, before turning.

"Tess." James stood at her office door in a dark cashmere coat. "We should celebrate."

They had celebrated the huge presales success of Edward's book, *Secret Shores*, the night before. Dinner with the entire staff.

Tess looked at him.

"Come with me?"

Tess couldn't stop the fluttering that began in her heart.

"I want to take you somewhere," he whispered.

She could not stop the smile that formed on her lips.

He walked with her through the freezing, icy streets. He chatted and made her laugh, her breath curling out in frosty swirls. And then he stopped. Outside the Met.

A uniformed guard stood outside the building, but once he saw James, he unlocked the front door and let them in. And James, still holding her hand, followed the guard into the building, through the vast, empty lobby, into an elevator to the second floor, past the gift shop area where everything was locked up, to a single, solitary door.

"What are we doing?"

"It's a surprise."

The guard shook James's hand and disappeared into the distance.

James held the small door open.

"After you," he said.

She climbed the narrow staircase inside as it wound up through the building, passing all those iconic artworks. She stopped at the top of the icy cold stairwell. James reached forward, his gloved hand pushing the door open at the top.

Tess stepped out. And gasped. The rooftop of the Met, just opened, with the most spectacular and romantic view of Manhattan that anyone could imagine spread before them. The city's buildings sparkled against the inky night sky.

Tess turned back then to the man who had stood beside her through everything, joining her as her equal, in a relationship that Tess knew would be based on mutual respect. And now she knew that this life could indeed be filled with love and with kindness. They were the things that mattered. And she was never going to deny herself those things again—not for any reason.

James drew her toward him, and as he leaned down toward her, she reached up, their lips touching each other in exquisite unison, like a perfect, eternal song.

AUTHOR'S NOTE

This book, while a work of fiction, was inspired by several personal stories which led me to delve into the wider context of the modernist movement in Australian art. Sunday and John Reed, Max Harris, Joy Hester, Albert Tucker, and Sidney Nolan were key figures in the rise of modernism in Australia, but all other characters and the story in this novel are entirely from my own imagination.

ACKNOWLEDGMENTS

I am deeply grateful to my editor, Jodi Warshaw at Lake Union Publishing, for her support and enthusiasm for this novel and for my writing. Every writer needs someone who believes in them and I am incredibly fortunate to work with Jodi. I thank the team at Lake Union—Gabriella Dumpit, Michael Grenetz, and Devan Hanna. Thank you to Shasti O'Leary Soudant for her beautiful cover design that has captured Rebecca and, extraordinarily, the real Granite Island. Thanks to Tegan Tigani, my amazing structural editor, with whom it is a complete delight to work, to my copyeditor, Amanda Gibson, for her wonderful attention to detail, and to my proofreader, Ramona Gault.

I would like to acknowledge and thank Andrew Morphett of Anlaby Station for his hospitality, for his help with my research and for talking with me about some of the true stories that inspired this book. To the staff at Heide Museum of Modern Art—you do a wonderful job keeping the spirit of Sunday and John Reed alive, and the fact that Heide is one of the most popular art galleries in the country is testament to your efforts and your belief in their modernist vision.

Thank you to Sue Brockhoff at Harlequin Australia for your support of my work, to Nas Dean, and to the Historical Novelists' Society of Australasia, especially Elisabeth Storrs and Chris Foley. Huge thanks to my wonderful readers—in particular to Helen Sibritt, members of ARRA, and all those readers who contact me on Facebook and via email. You are the ones who bring these books to life.

Thanks to my friends and family, particularly to my children, Ben and Sophie, and to my sister, Jane.

This book is in memory of my mother, who was of the World War II generation and who had personal links with the people who inspired this book.

ABOUT THE AUTHOR

Photo © 2014 Alexandra Grimshaw

Ella Carey is the international bestselling author of *The House by the Lake*, *From a Paris Balcony*, and *Paris Time Capsule*. A Francophile who has long been fascinated by secret histories set in Europe's entrancing past, Ella has degrees in music, nineteenth-century women's fiction, and modern European history. She lives in Australia with her two children and two Italian greyhounds.